Need You Dead

ALSO BY PETER JAMES
FROM CLIPPER LARGE PRINT

Dead Man's Footsteps
Dead Simple
Denial
Looking Good Dead
Not Dead Enough
Faith
Dead Tomorrow
Dead Like You
Dead Man's Grip
Perfect People
Not Dead Yet
Dead Man's Time
Dead Letter Drop
Want You Dead
You Are Dead
A Twist of the Knife
Billionaire
Love You Dead

Need You Dead

Peter James

W F HOWES LTD

This large print edition published in 2017 by
W F Howes Ltd
Unit 5, St George's House, Rearsby Business Park,
Gaddesby Lane, Rearsby, Leicester LE7 4YH

1 3 5 7 9 10 8 6 4 2

First published in the United Kingdom in 2017
by Macmillan

A CIP catalogue record for this book is available
from the British Library

ISBN 978 1 51007 384 5

Typeset by Palimpsest Book Production Limited,
Falkirk, Stirlingshire

Printed and bound by
T J International in the UK
Printforce Nederland b.v. in the Netherlands
Ligare in Australia

TO CAROLE BLAKE

My absent close friend and mentor.
A brilliant star who left us far too soon.
You will always shine brightly in my sky.
RIP

CHAPTER 1

Thursday 14 April

At the first salon she worked in after qualifying as a hairdresser, Lorna had a client who was an anthropologist at Sussex University. He'd told her his theory, and it intrigued her. That early human beings communicated entirely by telepathy, and we only learned to speak so that we could lie.

Over the subsequent fifteen years she'd come to realize there really might be some truth in this. There's the side of us we show and the side we keep private, hidden. The truth. And the lies. That's how the world rolls.

She got that.

Boy, did she.

And right now she was hurting badly from a lie.

As she brushed the colour into Alison Kennedy's roots, she was thinking. Distracted. Not her usually chatty self. Thinking about Greg. Devastated by what she had discovered about her lover. She was desperate to finish Alison and get back to her laptop before her husband, Corin, came home in an hour's time.

Her six Labradoodle puppies that she had bred from their mother, Milly, yapped away in the conservatory adjoining the kitchen that doubled, these days, as her salon. She'd started working from home, much to Corin's annoyance, so that she could indulge in her passion of breeding these lovely creatures, and it brought in a decent extra bit of income – although Corin sneered at it. He sneered at pretty much everything she did these days, from the food she put in front of him to the clothes she wore. At least her dogs loved her. And, she had thought, so did Greg.

Client after client opened up to her, treating their time with her, whilst she did their hair, as being in a kind of psychiatrist's chair. They would tell her their most intimate relationship problems, and reveal even the secrets they kept from their partners. Alison was babbling away excitedly, telling her about her latest affair, this time with her personal trainer.

Was there anyone who didn't have a secret? Lorna sometimes wondered.

She had also just discovered, by chance from a client earlier today, sometime before Alison, something intensely painful. Finding out the truth about someone – in particular someone you love – can hurt like hell. A truth that a part of you really wishes you hadn't learned. A truth that can turn your entire world upside down. Because you can't unlearn something, can't wipe that discovery from your brain the way you can delete a file from your computer, however much you might want to.

After Alison Kennedy left, at a few minutes before 6 p.m., Lorna hurriedly opened her laptop on the kitchen table and stared once more at the loved-up couple in the photograph in front of her. Stared in numb disbelief, her eyes misted with tears of hurt and anger. Anger that was turning to fury.

CHAPTER 2

Thursday 14 April

You bastard. You lying bloody rat.

Lorna balled her fists, lunging at the air, imagining she was punching his smug face, his smug smile, his phony sincerity. Punching his bloody lights out.

Eighteen months into their affair, Lorna had suddenly, unhappily, found out the truth about him. Discovered that the man she was besotted with, and with whom she had been planning to spend the rest of her life, had been lying to her. Not just lying. Living a total second life with her. Everything he had told her about himself was a lie.

She was gutted. And angry at herself. What a bloody fool she had been, again.

She had trusted him totally. Believed his endless promises that he was just waiting for the right moment to tell his wife. He'd given Lorna one excuse after another for delaying: Belinda was ill; Belinda was close to a breakdown; Belinda's father was terminally ill and he had to support her through it until he died; Belinda's brother was in a coma following a motorcycle accident.

Poor sodding Belinda. And now Lorna had found out she wasn't even called Belinda.

'Greg' had recently come back from a holiday with 'Belinda' in the Maldives. The doctors had told him his wife needed a break to recover her mental health. Before he went, he'd promised Lorna that he was going to leave Belinda just as soon as he could after their return. They'd even been planning a date. His escape from 'Belinda'. Her escape from her bastard of a husband, Corin.

Yeah?

How stupid did 'Greg' think she was?

Until just a few days ago, Lorna had been feeling really happy and secure. Believing that the soulmate she thought she had finally found in life, who had for the past year and a half made the nightmare of her abusive marriage just about tolerable, would rescue her from her living hell.

Then her first client today, Kerrie Taberner, who she had squeezed in at the last minute, had come in looking more beautiful than ever, with a glorious tan from a holiday in the Maldives. She'd shown Lorna some of her pictures of the island of Kuramathi on her phone and there, totally by chance, was one of a couple she and her husband had met in a bar one night. A totally loved-up couple, Kerrie had said. She had wittered on about how nice it was to meet a couple who clearly really loved each other, when so many couples who'd been married a long time just seemed to end up bickering constantly.

The man in the photograph was, unmistakably, 'Greg'.

'Greg' and 'Belinda'. Arms round each other, laughing, looking into each other's eyes.

Except those weren't the names that they'd given to Kerrie. They'd given quite different names. Their real names.

What a bastard. What a stupid bastard. Didn't it occur to him that it might show up on Facebook or somewhere like that?

'Belinda'!

Belinda and Greg.

And what hurt most of all was that she had believed him. Trusted him.

Trusted 'Greg'.

He'd lied about his name. He wasn't bloody 'Greg' at all. And she wasn't 'Belinda'.

Once she had his real name it had only taken her moments on Google to find out who he really was.

But now she knew, in her confused, angry state, she wasn't sure whether she was glad to know the truth or not. Her dream was shattered. Her dream of a life with this man – this two-timing love-rat bastard. Everything he had told her was a lie. Everything they had done together was just a bloody lie.

She sat at the kitchen table of the house – the home – she had shared with Corin for the past seven years, and stared bleakly at the huge glass fish tank that took up almost an entire wall. Brightly coloured tropical fish swam or drifted through the water, some gulping bits of food from the surface. Corin was obsessed with them, knew all the breeds. Gobies, Darters, Guppies, Rainbow fish, Gars, and all the rest.

He doted on them. Several of them had mournful expressions, reminding her of her own life. Just as they were imprisoned in this tank, which was all of the world they would ever know, she was imprisoned here in this house in Hollingbury, on the outskirts of Brighton, with a man she despised, scared this might be all the world she would ever know. And now that seemed even more likely.

God, it had all been so different when she had met Corin. The handsome, dashing, charming computer sales manager, who'd swept her off her feet and taken her to St Lucia, where they'd spent wonderful, happy days, snorkelling, sunbathing, making love and eating. They'd married a few months later, and it was soon after then that it had all started to go south. Maybe she should have recognized the signs of a control freak when they'd been on that idyllic holiday; by the obsessive way he had laid out his clothing, applied his suntan lotion through measuring applicators and chided her for squeezing the toothpaste tube in the middle, instead of rolling it from the end. From the way he planned out every hour of every day, and had been unhappy when they'd gone off schedule, even by a few minutes. But she hadn't, because she'd been crazy for him. She had paid for that, increasingly, day by day, ever since.

The first time she had become pregnant with the child she so much wanted, she had lost the baby after Corin punched her in the stomach in a drunken rage. The second baby she'd lost when he had pushed her down the stairs in another rage. Afterwards he would cry, pleading forgiveness or try to make her think it had never happened, that she had imagined it. And each time she had, dumbly, forgiven him, because she felt trapped and could see no way out of the relationship. 'Gaslighting', her friend Roxy had told her was the expression for what Corin was doing to her.

Things had become so bad with him that she'd secretly started to record on her computer all the times he hit her, and her thoughts. Then she had met Greg in Sainsbury's in West Hove, when their trolleys had collided coming round the end of an aisle. It had been an instant attraction and they'd become lovers a week later.

They'd rented a tiny flat – their *love nest*, Greg had called it – on the seafront. They'd met there whenever they could, twice or even three times some weeks, and when his wife was away, flying for British Airways long-haul. They'd had the best sex of her life. It was like a drug they both craved. Driving home afterwards she sustained herself by thinking about the next time, and how to pass the days before they met again – and survive Corin's endless bullying.

It was a relationship founded totally and utterly on lust. Yet she had sensed something far, far deeper was going on between them. Then, one afternoon, lying in each other's arms, 'Greg' had said, almost apologetically, 'I'm in love with you.'

She'd felt closer than she ever had to any human being, and told him she was in love with him, too.

She'd read somewhere, once, that good sex is just one per cent of a relationship. Bad sex – the kind she'd been having for years with Corin – is ninety-nine per cent.

One per cent.

Great.

Do you have any idea how it feels to be just one per cent of someone you love's life? she thought.

I'll tell you.

It feels pretty shit.

Everything about this sodding bastard had been a total lie, she realized. Except for the orgasms. They were real enough. Hers and his.

Mr One Per Cent.

God, I'm a fool. She felt so much anger inside her. Anger that she had been so stupid. Such a fool to believe him. Anger that her entire dream had been shattered. Anger that her husband was such a loser.

She sat back down and stared at the photograph on her screen.

You know what I'm going to do, Mr One Per Cent? I'll tell you what I'm going to do.

I'm going to ruin your life.

CHAPTER 3

Saturday 16 April

At 11a.m., suffering the hangover from hell, Lorna sat at her kitchen table, drinking her third double espresso. At that moment, just when she thought her day could not get any worse, it suddenly did.

An email pinged into her inbox.

Dear Mrs Belling,

You have until the end of today to either give me ownership of your Mazda MX5 car or repay me the sum of £2,800 which you are pretending not to have received. I know all about you and your dirty little secret. Give me the car or pay me back or else.

You're probably wondering what 'or else' means, aren't you? Just keep wondering. I know about your lover, you slut. You know what you owe me. I know your husband's name. Do the right thing, because if you don't, I won't either.

CHAPTER 4

Saturday 16 April

Dear Mr Darling,

I don't understand what has happened, but I've just checked my PayPal account and there is still no money from you showing. As soon as I get notification it is there, the car is yours. I've sent PayPal an email, to see if it has somehow gone astray, and I'll let you know soonest. In the meantime, please be patient, I'm sure we'll get it sorted out very quickly. I can assure you, I'm a completely honest person.

Yours sincerely,

Lorna Belling

CHAPTER 5

Saturday 16 April

Oh right, Mrs Belling. If you call screwing someone behind your husband's back 'honest', then I'm a banana. SD.

CHAPTER 6

Monday 18 April

PC Juliet Solomon was thirty-two, and had been in Brighton and Hove Response for almost a decade; she still loved it, although she was hoping for promotion to sergeant soon. Her slender, petite frame belied a very tough character, her lack of height never a disadvantage in awkward confrontations.

A few minutes into her early shift, she sat at a desk, mug of tea beside her, typing up her report on an incident she had attended yesterday – a local café proprietor had called in that a man had run off without paying and with another customer's handbag. They'd spotted the suspect a short while later, from the proprietor's description, and chased him on foot before finally arresting him – and she was pleased to be able to return the handbag to its owner.

Juliet's stocky, shaven-headed and bespectacled work buddy for this shift, Matt Robinson, two years her junior, was a Special Constable – one of a number of unpaid volunteer police officers in the Sussex force. At this moment he was hunched over his mobile phone, talking to someone at the company he owned, Beacon Security.

Working 'Section', on alternating shifts, responding to emergencies, is the ultimate adrenaline rush for young police officers – and for some older ones who never tire of it. No officer on Response can predict what will happen in five minutes' time. The one certainty is that no one – apart from the occasional drunk or nutter – dials 999 to tell the police they are happy.

The team was housed in a long ground-floor space in Brighton police station. The recently refurbished room spanned the width of the building, with windows on one side giving a spectacular view to the south, down to the English Channel, and on the other side the car park and a drab office building beyond. Blocks of work stations were ranged along both sides, the cream-and-blue walls and charcoal carpet giving it a smart, modern appearance. It smelled a lot fresher than its predecessor, which had always had an ingrained reek of sweat, spilt coffee and years of microwaved meals and takeaways.

Most of the occupants were in uniform black tops, with shapeless black trousers and heavy-duty boots. A cluster of stab vests and yellow hi-vis jackets hung on pegs and police radios sat on several work surfaces, emitting incessant low-volume bursts of sound. The room was manned round the clock, the twenty-four hours divided into three shifts – earlies, lates, nights – and there was a briefing at the start of each shift to update the incoming officers on all ongoing police activities in the city, and potential situations.

Some crews went straight out on patrol in vehicles. Other officers, as Juliet Solomon was doing, remained at their desks, filling out forms and reports, transcribing statements from their notebooks, radios sitting just below their chins in their stab vest pockets, listening out for a Control Room request to attend a call, or sometimes a more mundane delivery mission.

Shortly after 7 a.m., Juliet's radio came alive.

'Charlie Romeo Zero Five, are you available to attend 73 Crestway Rise, off Hollingbury Road? Distressed call from a woman who says her husband has just pushed dog faeces into her face. He's threatening to kill her. She's locked herself in the toilet. Grade One. She's hung up, but I'm trying to call her back.'

All calls were graded. 'Grade One' meant immediate response. 'Two' meant get there within one hour. 'Three' was attend by appointment. 'Four' was no police attendance required and to be resolved over the phone.

Juliet turned to Matt. 'OK?'

'Rock 'n' roll,' the Special Constable replied. They grabbed hi-vis jackets from the rack at the far end, and the keys to a pool car, then hurried downstairs.

Less than two minutes later, with Juliet driving,

they pulled out of the car park in a marked Ford Mondeo estate, turned left and headed down the steep hill towards London Road. Matt leaned forward against his seat belt, punched the buttons for the blue lights and siren, then tapped the address into the satnav, whilst at the same time listening to further information from the call handler. The victim's name was Lorna Belling.

Juliet knew from her years of experience just how scary and dangerous a situation like this could be.

CHAPTER 7

Monday 18 April

On a Friday afternoon in September 1984, a quietly spoken man with an Irish accent checked into room 629 at The Grand hotel on Brighton's seafront. He signed the register under the name of Roy Walsh. Just one of the numerous late-season visitors to the seaside resort. Probably on business, the front-desk clerk had thought, judging from the dark suit he was wearing. She was wrong.

His real name was Patrick Magee and he was a field operative of the Irish Republican Army. In his luggage was a 20lb bomb made of Frangex – a brand of gelignite – wrapped in cling film to mask the smell of explosives from sniffer dogs. It was fitted with a long-delay timer made from video recorder components and a Memo Park Timer safety device.

Some time before checking out two days later on the morning of Sunday 16 September, he unscrewed a panel beneath the bathtub, activated the timer, placed the device inside the cavity and carefully replaced the panel. In little under a month's time, the annual Conservative Party Conference would be taking place in Brighton. From earlier intelligence-gathering, Magee knew that the British Prime Minister, Margaret Thatcher, would be staying in the room below this one.

Three weeks and five days later, on Friday 12 October at 2.54 a.m., the bomb exploded. Five people were killed, and over thirty were injured; several, including the wife of cabinet minister Norman Tebbit, were left permanently disabled.

The mid-section of the building collapsed into the basement, leaving a gaping hole in the hotel's facade. While her husband, Denis, slept, insomniac Margaret Thatcher was still awake at the time, working on her conference speech for the next day in her suite. The blast destroyed her bathroom but left her sitting room and bedroom unscathed. Both she and Denis were shaken but uninjured. She changed her clothes and they were led out through the wreckage, and driven first to Brighton's John Street police station and then to a room in the safety of a dormitory building for new recruits and informants at Malling House, the Sussex Police Headquarters in Lewes.

Later that morning the IRA issued a statement:

> Mrs Thatcher will now realise that Britain cannot occupy our country and torture our prisoners and shoot our people in their own

> streets and get away with it. Today we were unlucky, but remember we only have to be lucky once. You will have to be lucky always. Give Ireland peace and there will be no more war.

For many of the hundreds of police officers who either attended on the night or took part in the investigation, this incident, which came close to wiping out the government of its time, was the high point of their career. Roy Grace's father was one of those on duty that night who was sent urgently to the scene. He was then delegated to be part of the escort team taking the Prime Minister and her husband to a safe place.

Detective Superintendent Roy Grace had always had an open mind on the paranormal, dating back to a childhood experience. If pressed on religious views, he would describe himself as agnostic, but privately he believed that there was something out there. Not a biblical God on a cloud, but something, for sure. And he'd consulted mediums on a number of occasions in his quest to find out the truth about what had happened to his first wife, Sandy.

Coincidence was another thing that had always intrigued him, and sometimes put a smile on his face. His recent office move from the industrial estate in Hollingbury, which had housed Major Crime for the past fifteen years, to his current office, in the Police HQ at Malling House, had done just that: directly across the corridor from where he now sat was the very suite where his father, along with several fellow police officers, had brought Margaret and Denis Thatcher to safety on that terrible morning.

His new office, small, narrow and stark, had formerly been a bedroom in one of the dormitory buildings. The one window, behind him, was shielded with vertical silver blinds. It had the smallest sliver of a view, through a narrow gap between two other identical brick buildings, of the soft round hills of the South Downs in the distance.

To the left of his desk was an array of plug sockets and switches, left over from when it had still, until recently, been a bedroom. Facing his spartan desk was another, in mirror image, which replaced the small round conference table he'd had in his office at Sussex House. No doubt in time he would get used to these new quarters, but for the moment he found himself, almost ridiculously, missing the old building, with its inefficient heating and air-conditioning, and its absence of any canteen – and the occasional treat from Trudie's, the stall up the road selling delicious bacon rolls and fried-egg sandwiches.

The facilities here were certainly way better. In addition to an on-site canteen, there were dozens of delis and cafés nearby, and Tesco, Aldi and the more upmarket Waitrose supermarkets were only a ten-minute walk away.

One thing did make him smile. Something his

father had told him while he was only days from dying of cancer in Brighton's Martlets Hospice, which had looked after him so wonderfully well, right up to his last minutes. Jack Grace had been a big, burly man, the kind of cop you'd never want to mess with unless you were a drunken idiot. But in the final days, as the cancer had eaten away all those pounds of flesh, leaving him almost skeletal, his father had still retained his sense of humour and his sharp mind. He had told Roy the story of the hunt for those responsible for the IRA outrage, and the unintended problems that it had caused.

The police had gone back through six months of The Grand hotel register, calling up the phone numbers of all the guests to check on them. The first number his dad called had been answered by a woman. He'd asked her if she could verify that her husband had been staying at the hotel on that weekend. She'd replied, in shock, that her husband had told her he had been in Scotland on a fishing trip with his mates.

The vigilant enquiries by Sussex Police had eventually unearthed more than a dozen husbands and wives who had lied to their spouses about their whereabouts on that weekend, resulting in seven divorces. It led, ultimately, to a change in the way the police conducted future enquiries, to a more subtle line of approach.

But as he thought about that again now, he was reminded of his own past life. One lesson Roy Grace had learned in his twenty-odd years in

Sussex Police was that if you wanted to work in Homicide, you just had to accept the unpredictable nature of the job. Murders seldom happened at convenient times for the investigators. Time and again, whatever plans you had made, whether it was your wedding anniversary, or the birthday of a child or a loved one, or even a holiday planned months in advance, they might have to be shelved without notice.

The rate of relationship break-ups was high. His marriage to Sandy had been just such a casualty, when she had left him and gone missing for a decade. He was determined never to let that happen with Cleo, his second wife. And he was feeling all kinds of conflicting emotions.

Facing him was a bank of shelves on which were stacked the box files and policy documents relating to the cases he was working on. Trials of several murder suspects he had arrested during the past twelve months were impending, one of whom was Brighton's first serial killer in many years, Dr Edward Crisp. This workload, combined with his Senior Investigating Officer call-out responsibilities, was heavy.

But temporarily eclipsing that were the worries about the responsibilities now facing him following the death in Munich of Sandy. In particular, responsibility for her ten-year-old son, Bruno.

His son, as he had only recently discovered.

He'd agreed with Cleo that Bruno should come to live with the two of them and their baby son,

Noah. But he was worried by what kind of upbringing his former wife had given him – especially during the two or three years Sandy had been a heroin addict. He would find out soon enough. He had to fly to Munich later this week to deal with all the formalities and to meet with the boy, who was currently staying with a school friend, and bring him to England. At least, apparently, he spoke good English. How would he feel about being uprooted to another country? What were his likes and dislikes? His interests? God, just so much to think about, and very importantly right now, too, Sandy's funeral.

Initially he had thought it should be a quiet one in Munich, which she had made home for her and Bruno. Her maternal grandmother was from a small town in Bavaria, near Munich, and it was possible she had been seeing some of her family there, although he doubted it. People who deliberately disappeared knew the dangers of making contact with anyone from their former lives. But her parents, claiming to be too old to travel all the way to Munich, had pleaded for her to be brought back to England.

He had never got on well with Derek and Margot Balkwill at the best of times, and since Sandy's disappearance even less so. He was convinced they'd believed in their hearts for all these years that he had murdered their daughter and only child. It wasn't her parents who changed his mind, it was Cleo, suggesting that it might be comforting for Bruno to be able to visit his mother's grave easily, whenever he wanted to – if he wanted to.

All the time that he was making these arrangements, vitally important though they were, he could not risk taking his eye off the ball on the prosecution cases he was in charge of – not while he had his boss, ACC Cassian Pewe, on his back.

And just to complicate matters further, due to recruiting issues resulting in a shortage of detectives, Surrey and Sussex Major Crime Branch were dangerously short of manpower. Kevin Shapland, the detective deputizing for him as Acting Head of Major Crime, was away on annual leave, and Grace had agreed to stand in and cover his week as the on-call SIO.

Ordinarily, even with Shapland away, it wouldn't have been a problem as he could have shared some of his workload with his colleague and close friend, Detective Inspector Glenn Branson. But Glenn was also abroad on holiday with his fiancée, Siobhan Sheldrake, a journalist on the *Argus* newspaper, staying at her parents' villa near Malaga. Instead he asked another colleague, Guy Batchelor, currently a temporary Detective Inspector, to come and see him. Batchelor was an officer he had come to respect and trust enormously. Grace felt confident that between the two of them, they could cope with the workload for the couple of days it would take him in Germany – he hoped – to sort out the arrangements for his late former wife and his son.

He felt a lot less confident about bringing a child he had not known about until these past few weeks into his and Cleo's life.

But he had no option.

Did he?

Cleo understood. She said it would be fine. Somehow.

He wished he shared her optimism.

CHAPTER 8

Monday 18 April

Matt Robinson peered out of the window, through the heavy drizzle, looking at house numbers. They raced round a long crescent, past a shabby parade of shops – a newsagent, an off-licence, a community centre – and then up an incline. The whole street had a neglected, unloved feel about it. The houses, erected in the 1950s post-war building boom, were a mishmash of terraces, semis and the occasional, slightly grander-looking, detached one. But most of them were badly in need of a fresh coat of paint and hardly any of the small front gardens showed any sign of loving care.

'You know, this could be a lovely street,' he said. 'Why does it look so crap? Why doesn't anyone care for their garden?'

'Coz that's where they wipe their feet when they leave,' Juliet Solomon said, cynically.

It was an old police joke, when entering a shithole of a dwelling, that it was the kind of place where you wiped your feet on the way out. Except it wasn't a laughing matter. Too often they went into a dwelling where the carpet was covered in mouldy food cartons, dog faeces and vomit, with a baby crawling around – but inevitably a brand-new, massive TV screen on the wall.

'There! Seventy-three!'

He pointed at a house that was a definite cut above the others. A decent-sized three- or possibly four-bedroom detached structure, the front facade recently painted white, a shiny navy blue and rather classy front door, new-looking leaded-light windows that were over-ornate for the place, making him wonder if the owners had been the victim of a persuasive double-glazing salesman, and a neatly tended front garden with two beds of healthy-looking daffodils and rather grand stone balls on top of each of the two brick pillars. Parked on the drive between the pillars was an old model MX5 sports car, with gleaming red paintwork, a black hardtop and a hand-written sign in the rear window: FOR SALE, £3,500.

As Juliet brought the car to a halt, Matt informed the call handler they'd arrived. She replied that she had still not managed to re-establish contact with the caller.

They climbed out of the car, pulling on their hats, and hurried up the path to the front door. Matt had attended more domestics than he could remember. There would be at least one on every shift, and you never knew what to expect when you rang the doorbell. One time he'd been punched in the face by a gorilla of a man, and on another occasion the door had opened and a glass vase had hurtled past his head.

Juliet rang the bell, which triggered the yapping of several dogs. She pushed open the letterbox, peered through, then let it flap shut and stood back. Matt joined her, instinctively dropping one hand to the holster containing his Captor pepper spray.

The yapping increased. They heard a woman's voice shouting, 'Down! Back! Get back!'

Moments later the door opened a few inches, and an attractive-looking woman, elegantly dressed but with slightly dishevelled blonde hair, peered out at them, a bunch of shaggy puppies around her ankles. She looked nervous and her mascara had run down her tear-stained face. Her lower lip was split, with a trail of congealed blood below it. There was more congealed blood below her nostrils. She was clutching a mobile phone.

'Mrs Belling?' Juliet said gently. 'Mrs Lorna Belling?'

She nodded, as if unable to speak, then nodded again. Then in a trembling voice, barely above a whisper, she said, 'Thank you for coming. I'm sorry – sorry to have bothered you.'

'I'm PC Solomon and this is my colleague, SC Robinson. Is your husband inside?' Juliet asked.

She shook her head. 'No – I saw – heard him – leave for work about ten minutes ago.'

'Can we come in and have a chat?'

'Please,' the woman replied, weepily. 'Please. Let me just put the dogs in another room so they don't run out.'

She closed the front door, then a few moments later opened it again, and ushered them into a small, immaculately tidy hall, with white wall-to-wall carpeting on which were several urine stains, two of them looking fresh. The dogs, in another room, were all still yapping.

The officers followed her through into a small kitchen, with one wall taken up by a huge tank filled with tropical fish. On the table were laid out hairdressing tools and a number of bottles of shampoo, conditioners and sprays, along with a laptop. Through a sliding glass door they could see a large dog and a bunch of puppies in a small conservatory, and a beautiful garden beyond, with a hot-tub, wicker furniture and several ornaments.

The woman indicated for them to sit down and then pulled up a chair opposite the wooden table and laid her phone on the table's surface. 'Would you like some tea or coffee?' she asked.

'We're fine, thank you,' PC Solomon said. Suddenly there was a loud voice over her radio and she turned the volume down, then pulled out her notebook. 'Tell us what happened?'

The woman stood up, walked over to the worktop and tore off a sheet of kitchen towel, which she used to dab her eyes. As she sat back down she said, 'I'm breeding puppies – Labradoodles.'

'Awww,' Juliet Solomon said. 'I love those dogs, always wanted one!'

'They're adorable. But my husband hates them. He was just about to leave for work this morning when one of the puppies got out of the conservatory' – she pointed at the glass door – 'and pooed on the carpet. Corin picked up the poo in his hand and pushed it into my face. Then he punched me, several times, screaming that he was going to kill me, and take them to a dogs' home when he got back this evening. Then he hit me again. I ran upstairs and locked myself in the bathroom, and called – dialled – 999.'

'The Control Room told me that, according to our records, it's the third time this has happened in recent months – we want to try and help you to be safe.'

Lorna Belling nodded and wiped her eyes. 'I'm sorry,' she said. 'I know I'm being a nuisance. I'm just at my wits' end – I'm really scared of him.'

'You are not being a nuisance at all,' Juliet said.

Lorna's phone pinged with a text and, momentarily distracted, she peered at it to see who it was from.

'Where does your husband work?' Matt Robinson asked.

'A tech company, South Downs IT Solutions.' She looked at the text message again.

Juliet Solomon wrote the name of the company down. 'How does he get to work?' she asked

'By train. He's lost his licence – for drink-driving.'

'Is that why you're selling the car?'

'No, that's – well, was – my reason.' She pointed in the direction of the dogs. 'I need to get an estate car for that lot. But there's a bit of a story behind selling the car – some fraud involved.'

'Do we know about this?'

'Yes, your colleagues do know – but it's not connected to . . .' She opened out her hands in a gesture of despair.

Robinson stepped away and spoke into his radio.

'Who owns this house?' Juliet asked her.

Lorna pointed at her chest. 'Corin was made redundant not long after I met him. He moved in with me, then we got married.' She thought for a moment. 'Seven years ago. Since then we've remortgaged but I own the larger share.'

'Why don't you tell him to leave, Lorna?' Juliet asked her, gently.

'I'm planning to,' the woman said. 'But you know what it's like, there's never a right time.' She pointed at the huge tank. 'There's five thousand pounds' worth of tropical fish in here – he's the only one who knows how to clean and maintain it.'

The police officer peered at it for some moments. 'Have you thought about sushi?' she asked.

Lorna laughed, lightening up for the first time. 'I wish.'

'Would you like me to contact one of our DV caseworkers for you? They could help you,' Juliet said.

'DV?'

'Domestic Violence.'

After some moments she said, bleakly, 'Yes – please – thank you.'

Matt Robinson came back over and sat down. 'There's a car on its way to your husband's office. They'll arrest him as soon as he arrives.'

Lorna clapped a hand over her mouth. 'No,' she said. 'Please don't.'

'You can't live like this, Lorna,' Juliet said.

Lorna burst into a flood of tears. Then she looked at her watch.

'Oh God,' she said. 'My client's due – my first of the day. My eight o'clock.'

The two officers stood up. 'I'll call the case-workers, Lorna. Someone will be in touch, OK?'

Lorna nodded.

'And if your husband turns up back here, don't let him in, but call 999 immediately.'

As the two officers climbed back into their car, Juliet Solomon turned to her colleague. 'You know the saddest thing of all with domestic abuse, Matt? So many of the victims are terrified to leave and face an uncertain future alone. So they find excuses why they have to stay or why they won't kick their partner out.'

'Like cleaning the tropical fish?'

'Exactly.'

CHAPTER 9

Monday 18 April

Just over an hour later, as her client was leaving, Lorna's phone rang.

'Hello?' she answered.

'Lorna Belling?'

'Yes?'

'My name's Cassandra Montagnini, I'm a Domestic Violence caseworker. Is it safe to talk?'

'Yes, yes, it's fine. Thank you.' She glanced at her watch. Her next client wasn't due for half an hour. She had two more bookings this morning, then the prospect of another very interesting lunchtime!

Screw you, 'Greg'.

'So, how are you, Lorna?'

'I'm OK.'

'The officers told me about the incident at your home a little earlier this morning. Would you like some help from us? We can give you support to try to make you feel safer.'

'Yes, yes, I would, please.'

'OK – I wonder if we can just talk things through.'

'I have my next client coming in about half an hour – I'm a hairdresser.'

'Would you like me to call back later?'

'Now is fine.'

'OK, if your client comes we can continue later. Is that OK?'

'Yes, thank you.'

'How did your husband hurt you?'

'He punched me in the face and chest, and I think I may have a cracked rib. He usually hits me where it doesn't show. He also tried to push dog crap into my mouth and covered my face in it. Now I'm really terrified of him. He does this when he gets into a rage about something, which seems to be more and more of the time these days.'

'What are you frightened of, Lorna?'

'The police said they're arresting him. He'll be livid when he comes home. It'll be even worse.'

'OK, I'll talk to them. I've been told they're waiting for him to arrive at his office, where he'll be arrested. We will make sure that if and when he is released you are safe. OK?'

Lorna thanked her again.

'How are you feeling in yourself?'

'I'm just so depressed, I'd never hurt myself but I constantly feel like shit.'

'Have you considered moving out at all?'

Boy, had she considered that. For the past eighteen months of her living hell she'd been planning her new life with Greg. Just waiting for him to give her the word and she was out of here. Now, from what she had learned, that was not going to happen and she was back to square one. 'Yes,' she answered.

'Other than how you feel, are you healthy, Lorna?'

'I'd say so. I walk the dog or go to the gym most days.'

'Your husband has quite a history with the police. He's been arrested for attacking you twice previously, hasn't he?'

'Yes. But this is the first time I've spoken to your organization.'

There was a brief pause. Lorna heard the putter of typing on a keyboard.

'Do you and your husband have any other problems?'

'No, but money's tight. He had a very good job as a salesman with a tech firm, but when he got done for drink-driving and lost his licence, he lost his job. He got another job with this firm in Burgess Hill, but at much less money, so he's not contributing much.'

'How else does he treat you?'

'He's very controlling. He calls and texts me throughout the day, wanting to know what I'm doing, who I'm seeing, and why I'm not at home whenever I go out. It's driven me to getting a second phone he doesn't know about, so he can't track me all the time.'

Cassandra Montagini said, 'Lorna, from what

you have told me I think we need to get someone out to you to complete a proper risk assessment. Would you be comfortable with that, and, if you are deemed high risk, that I refer you to an Independent Domestic Violence Advisor?'

'Um – well, I – I don't know. Yes, I suppose I'd be fine with that,' she said, hesitantly. 'Actually, I'd be very grateful.'

'Perhaps we should consider moving you somewhere else, before your husband is released? How would you feel about that?'

'I – I – can't – I've got clients booked in to see me – I can't let them down. And we have all these tropical fish – I – he has – he has to look after them – I mean he – and I have – six tiny puppies.'

'Your safety is the most important thing at this stage, Lorna.'

'Yes, thank you, I appreciate that. But I can't leave – not at the moment. Not until the puppies are old enough in a few weeks – they've all been reserved. But I have to keep them until they can go to their new owners.'

'All right, what I'll do is have an advisor call you as soon as possible. Are you going to be in for a while?'

'I am, yes, until around lunchtime.'

As soon as the woman ended the call, Lorna read the text that had come in on her new private phone. Very few people had the number.

Instantly, her spirits lifted a little.

Only to be dashed again, moments later, by

another incoming email on her laptop from the current bane of her life, Mr Nasty.

> I'm not going to go away, so you had better reply, because you are going to have to speak to me again eventually. You've had your telephone company block my calls. But not only do I know where you really live, I know what's going on in your other place, your secret place, your nasty, dirty little secret place. Might be worth offering me a refund for that reason alone. I'm running out of patience, Mrs Belling.

CHAPTER 10

Wednesday 20 April

It had all been so naughty back then – so deliciously naughty! The clandestine meetings in their secret love nest, a tiny, shabbily furnished studio flat. Snatched hours whenever they could both get away, breathless with the excitement of seeing each other, and both feeling the terrible wrench each time they parted.

The flat was on the third floor of a dilapidated apartment block on Hove seafront, overlooking the King Alfred leisure complex. They didn't care that the lift never worked, that the entrance hall and stairwell smelled of damp, nor that the wiring was a fire hazard. All that mattered was they had somewhere to meet, with a double bed – albeit a bit rickety – a little fridge where they could keep wine chilled, and a bathroom where they could freshen up before returning home to their respective spouses. She'd made it look as homely as she could, with a couple of framed photographs of themselves, scented candles, and a sheepskin rug on the floor.

Lorna had found it and it was ideal for many reasons. It was an easy location for them both to get to, with plenty of parking in the side streets. The rent, which they shared, was cheap as chips, because the building was due to be refurbished as part of the redevelopment of this whole area, and the landlord, happy to accept cash monthly, didn't ask any questions. A big bonus was that nothing overlooked it. They were private.

Not, Lorna thought, that she and Greg would have been here for much longer. When they'd originally taken it, believing his promises, she'd figured it would be for a few months only until he left Belinda, and they'd find a proper home together. The months had dragged into a year, then a year and a half. But not any more, oh no. Soon Greg and this place, which once she had loved but now hated so much, would be history.

And that numpty with his vile emails and pathetic hint at blackmail – he'd be history soon, too.

As would Corin.

She had her own plans now, a decision she'd made over the past weekend after discovering the truth about Greg. She was going to visit her sister, Melanie, in Australia and look into the possibility of making a new life there. Mel was a year younger, but they had always been so close they could be twins. Recently divorced from a wealthy stockbroker, and living in a gorgeous beachfront house in Tamarama, Mel was having a ball. And imploring Lorna to come out and join her.

Well, she had made up her mind, and she was off. Going to start a new life. Without Corin's knowledge she had started putting up for sale, through eBay and Gumtree, everything she possessed of any value – jewellery, handbags, the Cartier watch she'd inherited from her mother. She'd originally advertised the car because she needed a more practical vehicle for the dogs. But now she wasn't going to need a replacement and the cash would be useful.

There had been a big hiccup on that particular sale, but hopefully it would soon be sorted.

The puppies were going to be fine, she'd already taken deposits for all of them, and over the next few weeks they would be gone to their new homes. Someone her best friend Roxy knew, whose dog had recently died, was keen to take the puppies' mother. Sorted. Nearly. Very nearly. Her excitement was growing by the day, helping her get over her anger towards Greg. Every few hours she would go online and google Sydney. Staring at the stunning views of Tamarama Beach and neighbouring Bronte, Bondi and Coogee. And at the Sydney waterfront. The blue ocean, the brilliant sunshine.

The sunshine that Corin, a total mood hoover, seemed to suck out of the sky. She couldn't remember the last time she'd noticed the sun shining when she had been with him. Greg had changed that, he had put the light back into her life. Until . . .

Until . . .

Standing in her dressing gown, preparing herself for her confrontation with the bastard, she stared out at the ominously dark sky and falling rain, feeling the draught through the window and listening to the constant rumble of traffic along Kingsway down below. Stared at the dreary, crumbling red-brick edifice of the King Alfred – the pool where she had learned to swim as a child. Then around at the tiny room. The worn carpet was pink – *old-lady pink*, as Greg had jokingly called it. The walls were knobbly Artex and the ceiling was the colour of nicotine. The sagging double bed had a fake-fur throw she'd bought when they first got the place; there was a two-seater sofa, an armchair with a busted spring and a tiny kitchenette with a breakfast table. Through louvre doors was a bathtub, also in old-lady pink, with a hand-shower with a rubber hose that you stuck over the taps, a matching washbasin and loo.

The wiring scared her. Every time she came in and turned on the light, sparks shot out of the switch. She used a three-pin plug in the bathroom – which Greg said was illegal – for her hairdryer. On a couple of occasions she'd mentioned the wiring to the landlord, but he had never got back to her.

Right now she could not wait to leave.

A Van Morrison CD was playing. *Days Like This*.

With a huge grin, she began to nod her head along to it. Balling her fists in the air, she suddenly sang out loud, 'Days like this! Yayyyyy!'

Then her phone – her private phone – pinged with a text.

> On my way! 29.272 mins to arrival! Crazy to see you! Get naked for me!

Shit, she thought. *Shit, shit, shit.* She looked at her watch. It was 5.25 p.m. An hour sooner than she had been expecting him at the very earliest. *Shit!*

She ran into the bathroom and stared in the mirror. Her hair looked like she'd been through a tornado, and her make-up could have been applied by Jackson Pollock. She turned on the taps, and whilst the bath was filling she peered into the rapidly misting-up mirror and started to sort out her face, glancing intermittently at her watch. She wanted to be ready for the bastard and looking her best for the confrontation.

She plugged in the dryer, carefully, holding it with two fingers. As she switched it on there was a fizz and crackle from the socket. The machine whirred into life and she directed the hot air at the misted-up mirror. Some minutes later, when the bath was full, she dropped her dressing gown, eased herself into the tub, and began soaping her body, thinking back dreamily over the past couple of hours.

In what seemed like an instant later, a good fifteen minutes before she expected him, Greg, in a sharp navy suit, striped shirt and a collegiate tie at half mast, was towering over her, holding in his hand a bunch of weary-looking flowers, which had *petrol station* written all over them.

'My baby! God, I've missed you!' He leaned down to kiss her on the lips, and as he did so, she turned her head away, offering him her cheek.

'Uh?' he said, standing back up with a frown.

'Fuck you,' she said.

'Hey, baby – what is it?'

'Had a nice time in the Maldives last month with poor, sick "Belinda" did you? Helped her recover her mental state?'

'It was shit,' he said. 'I've told you. I had a terrible time. We barely spoke a word to each other for the entire fortnight. I woke up every morning wishing it was you with me.'

'Oh yes?'

'I promise you, Lorna. Every single day I said to myself, "Another shitty day in paradise. Because I'm with the wrong woman."'

'Go and take a look at my laptop on the dining table, Greg. Do you really think I'm an idiot? Go on, take a look! I've left it on, and disabled the password, so you can sodding see for yourself.'

He backed out of the room. After some moments he came back in. 'Where did you get that from?'

'Does it matter, *Greg*? You had a terrible time, did you? Poor you. It doesn't look like you were having a terrible time – you and *Belinda* look quite cosy to me.'

'Baby, listen – please listen to me. I know what it must look like.'

'Do you? Do you really?'

'Yes.'

'No you don't, you have no idea.'

'Listen—'

'No,' she interrupted him. 'You listen to me for once. I've believed your bloody lies all this time. Now I know who you really are, you bastard. *Greg!* Ha! Did you really think I'd never find out? How stupid do you think I am?'

'Baby!'

'*Baby!*' she mimicked. 'Don't *baby* me. I'm not your *baby*. I'm not your *convenient little shag on the side*. Not any more.'

'Hey, I love you, baby.'

'No, you don't love me. You just love shagging me.'

'It's not like that at all, trust me. Please, baby.'

'I've trusted you for all this time, you lying creep. God, I feel a fool.'

'Lorna – Jesus – don't be like this.'

'Oh, how would you like me to be? Naked in bed, listening to more of your lies? For months you've been promising to get me away from my nightmare with Corin. For months you've told me one lie after another about poor, sick *Belinda*.'

'I haven't!'

'Oh yes you have. She's not even called Belinda. You've lied about your name, about who you really are, about what you do for a living. How many other girlfriends do you have all lined up, waiting for you? Are you doing the rounds of all your conquests? Is Wednesday Lorna's turn for a shag?'

'I love you, Lorna. I really do.'

She shook her head. 'No, if you really loved me you'd have told me the truth long ago. I trusted you. I believed you. I thought you were who you said you were, but you aren't, are you? Is there anything you've ever said to me that hasn't been a lie?'

He stared at her for a moment. 'Listen, let me explain—'

'No, you let me explain. Let me explain just how angry I am. I'm angry enough to destroy your life, you lying shit. One phone call is all it's going to take and your career will be fucked. Believe me. Then one more and it'll be your marriage. To poor sweet, sick *Belinda*.'

His face ashen, he said, 'No, Lorna. Please listen.'

She tapped her ears. 'I don't have room in here for any more of your shit, my head's full of it. Bursting. No more room. Sorry!'

'I really do love you.'

'I hate you.'

'Don't say that!'

'You have no idea how much I hate you. Just get out! Get out of here, get out of my life!'

'Look – I'll make it up to you. I promise.'

'You promise? You really think I'd believe any promise you gave me, *Greg*?'

'Just let me explain,' he said again.

She shook her head. 'No, let me explain. I just

have to dial one number on my phone and your career will be over. That's going to happen ten seconds after you get the fuck out of here, you creep.'

He shook his head vigorously. 'Lorna, baby, please give me the chance to explain everything.'

She picked up the bar of soap in her hand. 'See this, *Greg*? You're just like this bar of soap.' She closed her hand on it and the bar shot up in the air then fell with a splash into the bath. 'You're just as slippery.' She glared at him, her eyes demonic, almost glazed. 'But at least the soap makes me feel clean – you just make me feel dirty.'

'Lorna, please.'

'*Lorna, please*,' she mimicked. 'You know the worst thing of all, *Greg*? I'm actually going to get pleasure out of destroying you. Totally fucking up your career and then your marriage. I really am. Hello, *Belinda*! You don't know me, but I can describe your husband's cock – every inch of it, in fact. I could email you some photos of it, if you'd like, but I imagine you already know what it looks like. Though perhaps you've forgotten since it's so long ago you last had sex – so *Greg* tells me.'

'Lorna. Come on. Look – let's talk reason.'

'*Reason?* You sound just like my husband. *Let's talk reason*. Do you know what my husband did on Monday? He tried to put dog shit in my mouth. Almost every morning he picks a row about something. And almost every night. Some days I count myself lucky if he just shouts at me. Other days he hits me.' She pointed to a bruise by her right eye. 'This is what he did last night after he was released by the police, when he stalked me here and went ballistic. I live in hell and I've endured it because I believed your promises that you were going to take me away from all that, that we would have a life together. Your lies.' She began crying. 'Your sodding lies.'

He pulled a towel off the rack. 'Come on, darling, let's talk about this over a drink. I've brought some gorgeous Champagne. Pol Roger, your favourite.'

As he leaned down to put the towel round her shoulders she lashed out, punching him on the chest. 'Screw you.'

'Owwww!' He fell back against the washbasin.

'Screw you, you bastard!'

'Lorna! Calm down, this is insane.'

She stood up in the bath, punching him repeatedly.

He grabbed her tightly round the throat and she started spluttering.

'Are you going to strangle me?' she gasped, incredulously, still pummelling him.

He pushed her back, trying to hold her at arm's length, desperately trying to restrain her. 'Lorna! Stop it! Stop it, Jesus Christ! Calm down!'

She grabbed a bottle of shampoo, flipped up the lid and squeezed it hard, sending a jet of the soapy liquid into his face, momentarily blinding him.

'You crazy bitch!' His eyes stinging and in a red mist of rage, he lunged forward and grabbed her shoulders, pushing her away. She fell back into the tub, sending water slopping over the sides.

'You lying, cheating bastard. I'm going to destroy you. Oh, you think you're untouchable, don't you? I'm going to teach you a lesson you'll never forget!' She heaved herself up. 'I'm going to make that call now.'

'No!' he shouted in fury. 'Don't you fucking dare!' He slapped his hand against her forehead, forcing her back down into the tub again, pushing her head right under the water for a brief moment. Then released her.

As she raised her head she spluttered, looking bewildered, struggling to breathe for a moment. Then, her voice panicky, she yelled at him, 'You jerk! What are you going to do? Kill me?'

Wriggling and twisting, she tried to worm out of the bathtub. In total panic, he grabbed the hairdryer in his left hand and held it above her. 'Don't move or I will fucking kill you.'

Lorna made a desperate lunge to lever herself out of the bath. Wild with anger, he shoved her hard back down with his right hand. There was a crack, as loud as a gunshot, as the rear of her head struck the tiled wall. As she slumped down, he saw a split in the tile where the contact had been, and a smear of blood.

Shit. Oh shit. Oh shit.

The hairdryer suddenly whirred into life.

Everything became a blur. He tried to focus, but couldn't; all he could see was mist, red mist – blood-red mist. He ran, crashed into a wall, ran again, fell over a chair, had to get out, out, out, had to get out.

He found the door, opened it and lurched into the corridor, his eyes blurred, like looking through fogged negatives, fogged red negatives, stumbling down fire-escape stairs, crashing from wall to wall. Then out, through the side entrance he normally used onto Vallance Street, tugging on the baseball cap and dark glasses he always wore to hide his face when visiting Lorna. Outside. The roar of traffic on the seafront a short distance away. Cold, damp wind with a salty tang.

He walked. Walked. Turned right, away from the seafront. Walked. Saw traffic lights in the distance. He was on a main road. Get on a minor road, mustn't be seen. Had to think, somehow, had to calm down, had to think.

Had to.

Oh God, what had he done?

Go back in and say sorry. Beg forgiveness. Just like her husband did every time he beat her up. Sure, she would buy that, wouldn't she? In her current mood.

How badly had he hurt her just now?

He turned left, into a wide, quiet street, and walked quickly, head bowed, clenching and unclenching his fists in agitation. He was hurrying, he realized, running almost, a man on a mission without a mission, without actually having anywhere to go.

Got to go back inside. Apologize. Explain. Got to calm her down. Explain he'd had a shitty day at work. This wasn't him. He'd never hurt a woman in his life.

He loved her. Shit, he really did. She just had to be patient, give him time; that photograph wasn't how it really was, no matter how it looked to her. Really. It wasn't.

OK, so he hadn't been totally honest with her. But he could explain that photograph, if she would just calm down and listen. He could.

He smacked head-on into someone. Someone rock hard.

'Sorry, sorry,' he gasped, winded.

Then realized he had walked into a pay-and-display parking machine.

CHAPTER 11

Wednesday 20 April

No crowd was too small to swallow up Seymour Darling. He looked almost invisible even when standing or sitting on his own. A small, thin man, who bent like a reed in the wind whenever anger blew inside him, which was much of the time.

Small and insignificant enough to almost be concealed by his own shadow, to the outside world Darling cut a meek figure. Inside, he seethed.

He seethed at the world which gave him nothing and took from him all the time. Took, took, took. As if he was doomed to be forever paying off a fucking debt just for having been born. All the world conspired against him, and laughed at him. The other kids had laughed at him because of his name. *Darling, darling, darling!* they'd teased.

He seethed at his ex-employers, at arrogant Mr Tony Suter, CEO of Suter and Caldicott Garden Buildings, who had 'let him go' after ten years of loyal service. True, he had made a few miscalculations as their South East Region salesman. But they could have given him a second chance, and they chose not to.

Just like his previous employers had chosen not to.

And now he was being screwed by his current employer, who hadn't told him when he started that he would only get paid his commission when the client paid them. Bastards.

But right now his grievance was focused elsewhere. On that evil, scheming bitch Lorna Belling. It was his wife, Trish's, fiftieth birthday next week. For years, Trish had hankered after an MX5 sports car. He'd decided to use the remainder of his redundancy money to buy her one, even though they did not get on. He saw the car as a temporary way of making a peace offering, but more as an investment, something to sell for a profit after she died. On eBay he'd found the perfect model. Ten years old, bright red, the colour she'd wanted, just two owners, and low mileage – 45,000. Put on sale by a woman called Lorna Belling. She had a good sales record on eBay – clearly faked, he now realized.

They'd taken the car for a test drive. It was real, proper. She was asking £3,500. He'd offered £2,800 and she'd accepted. They'd shaken hands and he'd paid the money – money he could not really afford – by PayPal.

Then the bitch, Lorna Belling, had told him she had not received it.

She was lying. Fucking bitch, she had conned him.

She didn't know who she was messing with.

He stood in the shadows again, across the street from her love nest. Her dirty little secret love nest.

Her visitor had just come out.

She was up there on the third floor, alone.

That dirty little adulteress bitch needed a lesson. *Don't mess with Seymour Darling.* She was about to be sorry.

Very sorry.

CHAPTER 12

Wednesday 20 April

He was calming down now; an hour had passed, he realized, as he strode along the Hove seafront promenade by the Lawns, passing the beach huts, heading back towards the King Alfred leisure centre. A plan was forming. Apologize. He knew what he had to say to her, to convince her that he really was going to leave his wife for her.

He was sorry he'd lost his rag. He never normally lost it, ever. She knew that. All the sympathy he had shown her over these past lovely months. All those afternoons and early evenings when they had lain in bed, entwined, talking about that monster, Corin, and their future together.

Please, please don't let her have made that call. Please. Please don't. My career. God, my career.

He realized he needed to hurry back, to stop her.

They'd both been mad, totally out of character; she'd bloody started it. But surely they could work through this, sort it out? She had been angry, OK, he could understand. It wasn't the way it looked, really it wasn't. He'd explain to her, when they were both calmed down. Then everything would be how it always had been between them.

He loved her. He wanted a life with her. They were soulmates. So often he had told her that and she'd looked into his eyes and said the same back to him.

He reached the block of flats, let himself in the front door and climbed the stairs, not wanting to risk getting stuck in the lift. Lorna had once been stuck in it for three hours.

Back inside the flat, he closed the front door and called out, a tad apprehensively, 'Lorna? Darling?'

Silence.

The room was dim, with no lights on and no music playing.

He didn't like the silence.

Nor that he could not see her.

'Lorna?'

He pressed the light switch on the wall but nothing happened.

'Lorna!' he called out again, walking towards the bathroom. 'Lorna, darling?'

Had she left? Gone home?

Oh God, Lorna, please still be here.

Then, entering the dark bathroom, he smelled burnt plastic. Where on earth was she? *Shit.* He felt sick with fear. He went back into the living room and dialled her phone. Seconds later he jumped as he heard it vibrating right behind him.

His panic deepened.

She always had the phone with her, on silent. So they could talk whenever she could get away from Corin.

He switched on the torch app on his phone and went back into the bathroom, walking slowly. Slowly. Pointed the beam at the water.

Saw the cable.

And froze.

Lorna lay back in the tub, where he had left her. Beneath the surface of the water. Looking utterly, stunningly beautiful.

Utterly motionless.

The hairdryer in the bath with her.

No. Oh please, no.

His heart plunged down through his insides. He saw the cable, and the blackened plug socket.

Noticed again the acrid smell of burnt plastic.

He dived for the socket and yanked the plug out of it.

'Lorna!' he cried. 'Lorna! Lorna!'

Christ. Had he done that? Had it fallen in, during his earlier fury?

He tried, desperately, to replay exactly what had happened. No, surely not, it wasn't possible, was it? He hadn't done that?

Please, God, no!

He lifted her out of the bath and laid her on the sitting-room floor, kneeling on the carpet beside her. There was still some daylight outside, just enough to see in this part of the flat. 'Lorna? Lorna?'

He pressed his mouth to hers, frantically trying to recall everything he had learned about CPR in the last refresher course he had done, and began to alternate mouth-to-mouth breathing and chest compressions, a rhythmic thirty pumps, two breaths, thirty pumps, two breaths, thirty pumps, two breaths, his panic growing deeper by the second.

CHAPTER 13

Wednesday 20 April

Roy Grace's anxiety was growing deeper by the second. Tomorrow afternoon he was due to fly to Munich to meet Bruno. He knew very little about the boy. He had some information from the German lawyer and from Anette Lippert, the mother of Bruno's friend, Erik, with whom Bruno was currently staying. And he'd had a couple of stilted phone conversations with him, not really knowing what to say, after his attempts at Skyping with him had failed.

He didn't even know Bruno's birthday, at this moment, and he had only seen a few photographs, including one taken a couple of years ago in a park, with Sandy, that had been emailed to him by Anette. But fortunately Bruno spoke good English. In the photographs he was nice-looking, neatly dressed, but with a deep sadness in his expression that the smile he had put on for the camera could not hide.

All he really knew, from what Sandy had written in her suicide note to him, was that this child was the reason why she had disappeared all those years back, leaving Roy bewildered and distraught – and searching for her for the last decade.

He felt totally ill-equipped to take Bruno on. How was the small boy going to feel meeting his father for the first time? How would he feel about leaving Munich and coming to England? To live with an entirely new family?

Should he take him to attend the burial of his mother? He'd talked to a child psychologist friend of Cleo, who told him he should, that it would be important for him to have a sense of closure with his mother, and to have a place he could return to in future years to pay his respects.

There was another problem for him. Sandy had left no instructions on whether she wanted to be buried or cremated, as was often the practice in German wills. He remembered once, many years ago, they'd discussed it briefly out at dinner one night, when the subject of death had come up – the husband of an old friend of Sandy's had drowned in a sailing accident on holiday. He was pretty sure Sandy had said she didn't care, that when you were dead your spirit departed from your body, leaving it an empty shell. She didn't care what happened to her shell. Roy and her parents had decided that burial would provide somewhere more tangible for Bruno to visit than a name on a crematorium memorial wall or a plant in a Garden of Remembrance.

He was in his office, with his workload of Crown

Prosecution files in front of him. He was meant to be preparing for an important forum here in half an hour. Present would be DC Emma-Jane Boutwood and Emily Denyer – Emily Gaylor's new married name – to discuss the financial aspects of the forthcoming trial of 'black widow' Jodie Bentley. But he was unable to concentrate on anything other than what would happen in Munich tomorrow.

Now that he and Cleo were married and had a son of their own, Noah, life was good. Or had been until the events of the past few weeks, when Sandy had surfaced in a hospital in Munich after being hit by a taxi, and had then committed suicide, leaving him the note informing him they had a son, Bruno.

And, suddenly, his life was turned upside down.

A son he had never known about, but now had no option but to care for. Permanently.

He picked up his phone and dialled a police friend and colleague, recently promoted Superintendent Jason Tingley, who had a son, Stan, of a similar age to Bruno. He asked him a load of questions about what a boy of ten might be interested in. Tingley was helpful and gave a large amount of information and advice, but Roy ended the call feeling even more worried. So much had changed; the world for a child today was so very different from how it had been for him.

Apart from football, Stan Tingley's world was one Grace knew virtually nothing about, and it revolved around few of the things he was familiar with. Stan had a vocabulary of slang; Snapchat and Instagram were his social media platforms. He rarely watched conventional television, instead he used the screen to play FIFA and a shooting game on his PlayStation. And he had his own YouTube channel. Tingley offered for the two boys to meet, inviting Bruno to come over to their home. Maybe the boys would click and become friends, Grace hoped. Finding friends for Bruno and getting him into a school where he'd be happy were going to be priorities.

But there was another thing really worrying him. It was the cryptic warning Sandy had written in her suicide note to him, about Bruno. He'd been fretting about this for days.

> *So please, when I am gone, take care of our son, Bruno. He worries me; you'll see what I mean.*

Just what exactly had she meant by that?

CHAPTER 14

Wednesday 20 April

'Lorna! Lorna! Don't do this to me! Baby. Baby. Lorna.' He shook her, frantically. Then he looked at his watch. He was sweating heavily. Thirty minutes had passed. Lorna's eyes were open, her pretty but often sad blue eyes, staring sightlessly up, clouded. A startled expression in them.

He was shaking. No. Jesus, no. This could not be happening. It just could not. It had to be a dream, a bad dream, a nightmare.

He was trying desperately to think clearly. Must not panic.

'Baby,' he whispered. 'Come on, baby.'

He thought he saw a tiny flicker of movement. 'Baby?'

Had he imagined it?

'Lorna?' He shook her again, pressed his lips to hers and gave her more breaths, then chest compressions.

The doorbell rang.

He froze.

There was a rap on the door.

He held his breath.

He glanced at his watch. 7.35 p.m. Who the fuck was calling at this hour? No one came here, no one but them.

Another rap.

Whoever was out there would know someone was in. Who was it?

He heard the rustle of paper. Shit, was someone coming in?

Shaking, he turned and saw a note had been pushed under the door. Tiptoeing across, he knelt and picked it up. It was a standard, printed form letter from a firm of electricians.

> Dear Occupier,
>
> We are currently working in this building. At the request of the landlord, we called today to make an appointment to upgrade the wiring in your flat. Please call us on the number below to arrange a convenient time for this work to be carried out.
>
> Yours sincerely,
>
> Gordon Oliver

Now it had his fingerprints on it, he realized. Idiot. Shaking almost uncontrollably, he folded it and pushed it into his trouser pocket, then went back to Lorna and stared down at her naked body. Her beautiful figure; her full breasts.

Fear gripped him, clawing at his skin, tightening his scalp. He gave one final try, his lips against her cold lips, then more compressions.

Nothing.

He peered into her eyes. Nothing. Then he felt again, hoping against hope for her pulse. There was none.

Behind him, somewhere below the falling darkness beyond the window, was a sharp squeal of brakes and angry hooting. He heard the cry of a gull. His brain raced, uselessly, showering fragments of thoughts.

Think.

CSI!

He went over to the kitchenette and tugged on the yellow rubber gloves Lorna used for washing up. Then, returning to her, he placed one arm below her knees, the other behind her back, and lifted her up. She was heavy, shite. She seemed much heavier dead than when she was alive. He staggered forward into the bathroom, where the acrid stench of burnt plastic seemed even stronger now, and laid her, clumsily, back in the bathtub. Water spilled over the edge, onto his suit trousers and his shiny black boots. Her head flopped forward, and in a way he was glad about that, glad that her eyes were no longer looking up at him.

But it didn't look like an accident any more.

He repositioned her so that the back of her head was against the bloodstain on the tiles.

Could fingerprints be taken from a wet body? DNA?

With shaking hands he grabbed the sponge, soaped it, then washed her face, neck and every part of her body, trying to remove all his fingerprints, all traces of him.

'Oh God, I'm sorry, my darling Lorna.'

All the time thinking.

Thinking.

Where else in here might his fingerprints be? His DNA?

When he had finished with her body, he took a bottle of bleach from the kitchen and wiped all around the surfaces of the bath. He was about to wipe away the smear of blood on the cracked tile, then hesitated. Better to leave it. He didn't want to make it obvious someone had cleaned up.

He lifted the hairdryer out of the bath by its cord. Its air vents were blackened. Using a towel, he carefully and thoroughly wiped the casing to remove any fingerprints, curled the fingers of her right hand around the grip, then laid it back in the water, between her thighs.

To make it look like suicide or an accident. She electrocuted herself and in the shock her head flew backwards, striking the tiles. Yes.

He was in such turmoil, he was finding it hard to think clearly in any way. What had he touched since coming here? The front door to the flat, which he had pushed open. Her computer keypad, to wake it up to look at the photograph. Anything else?

Could his prints be found on her body?

Once more, with the sponge, he soaped the back of her knees and then her back, then wiped it all away. He wiped all around the washbasin, the loo handle, the seat.

What else?

Think. THINK.

He carefully rinsed out the sponge in the basin, looking around the tiny bathroom, then took a few paces back and stared at everything in the little flat. The place that had become the centre of his life. Where he had always looked forward so much to coming. To seeing the woman he truly loved.

He opened the fridge, where earlier he had put the bottle of Champagne, wiped it clean and replaced it. What else? What else?

There was a framed photograph of the two of them on the table, by the fruit bowl. One of them high up on Wolstonbury Hill, with miles of open Sussex countryside below them. He debated whether to simply remove the photograph, or take the whole thing. A frame with no photograph would look odd, wouldn't it – to a trained eye? Evidence of someone trying to hide something.

His raincoat lay folded on the armchair. He put the photo frame, with the photograph still in it, on top, intending to conceal it with the coat as he left. Back in his car he'd rip up the photo and dispose of it in a bin, then the frame in another. He was starting to think more clearly, suddenly. THINK. THINK. THINK.

It was still not completely dark outside. Bloody British summertime. Probably another half an hour before it would be fully dark. It was OK, his wife knew he was at work, he'd told her he would be home late.

He walked back into the bathroom. 'Darling, you just got it so wrong,' he said, quietly. 'You did. I really was planning to leave her. I told you white lies, but I really, truly did believe we would have a life together.'

Oh God. What have I done? he thought.

Suicide?

Could the police believe she had committed suicide with the hairdryer?

His eyelids crushed his tears as he looked around the bathroom, checking it once more. What had he touched? To his horror, he saw the hairdryer plug lying in the sink. Shit! He pushed the pins back into the blackened wall socket and carefully wiped it.

What had he forgotten? Stepping back out of the bathroom he looked around again. The little dining table and the two chairs, where they'd eaten so many meals together, half naked, in the afterglow of having made love. Deliveries mostly. Pizzas; Chinese; Thai. He looked at the armchair. The fridge and kitchenette. The bed. Any other pictures? He checked. Just the two faded old

Brighton prints, in their cheap frames, that had always been there as part of the flat's meagre furnishings. However, her phone was a problem, her laptop another.

Her phone was a cheap pay-as-you-go job. The phone that she had told him her husband didn't know about. Corin, she'd said, was insanely jealous and she was convinced he'd installed tracking software on her phone, somewhere. So when she came here to meet him, she left her iPhone at home, so it wouldn't show any movement from the house, and only ever brought this one.

He picked it off the table, and studied it for a moment. His heart was still hammering and his hands shaking. He looked through the list of dialled calls. They were all to his own private iPhone number. Then he looked at her received calls. They were all from withheld numbers. Glancing down at the times of them, all except two tallied with calls he had made to her. One of the exceptions was three days ago, on a day he had not seen her. Another was earlier today, just after 11 a.m. this morning. He wondered who that was, and knew he would never find out now. Probably her best friend, Roxy, who was the only person, so far as he believed, Lorna had ever told about their affair.

How much did Roxy know?

Next he went to her text messages, but there was nothing there. All of them were deleted, as he'd expected. She was terrified of her husband finding this phone. At least if he ever did, there would be nothing incriminating on it.

He pocketed the phone. It was unlikely anyone other than her best friend and himself would know about it. When he got to his car he'd remove the SIM card, drop it down a drain, and dump the phone in a bin.

Then he went back into the bathroom and stared at Lorna for some moments. 'I'm sorry,' he whispered. 'I'm just so sorry.'

Craving a cigarette, he stepped back into the living room, pulled a Silk Cut out and lit it. But it did nothing to calm him down. He smoked it down to the butt and crushed it out carefully in the one ashtray they had, a souvenir from Madeira that Lorna had brought along soon after they'd got this place. Putting spittle on it to ensure it was completely out, he dropped the butt into his pocket and looked at his watch again.

He had time, all the time he needed. Had to use it. Had to clear this place of any evidence he had ever been here. THINK. THINK. One good thing was they'd not had sex for nearly a month, because he'd been away on a course straight after getting back from holiday.

He'd read somewhere recently, in a newspaper, that forensics had discovered DNA could be found in bed bugs for up to forty days. It had been close to that amount of time since he had last been here, so he decided to take a chance and leave the bedding as it was, again not wanting it to look obvious the place had been forensically cleaned.

He continued to work through the flat, wiping the door handles, light switches, the CD player. Every glass in the kitchenette cabinet. The kettle, the Nespresso machine he'd bought Lorna as a present. The cups, mugs, spoons, knives, forks.

Thinking.

Thinking how to cover his tracks absolutely and completely. Thinking about what he needed to do. Slowly an idea was forming. He sat in the chair and lit another cigarette, thinking it through. Again, when he had smoked it down to the filter he stubbed it out and pocketed the butt.

He stood up and paced around. His idea could work. Would work.

It had to work.

But he needed total darkness for it.

Shit. A bit longer yet.

He looked at the news on his phone. Another terrorist atrocity in the Middle East. A harassed and distressed-looking surgeon in scrubs was talking to the camera. He switched it off. Sat back down. Stood up. Went back into the bathroom and stared at Lorna.

What had he done?

Calm down. Had to calm down. Had to think it all through. Then suddenly he flipped up the toilet lid and the seat, knelt and vomited violently. He stayed, staring into the spattered mess around the bowl. Remembered the words of some comedian, he couldn't remember who it was, who said it didn't matter what you had eaten, when you vomited you always threw up tomato skins and diced carrots. It had been funny then; it wasn't funny now.

Nothing was funny now.

Nothing would ever be funny again.

The stench of vomit made him gag and he threw up once more. Then again. Retching just bile now.

Several minutes passed before he felt steady enough to stand. He flushed the toilet, wiped away the remnants still stuck to the bowl and flushed again, then used the toilet cleaner to squirt around the rim.

When he had finished he rinsed his mouth out with cold water and, glancing once more at Lorna's motionless figure, backed out of the bathroom.

He remembered the chilled Champagne bottle, which he had bought from an off-licence on the way here, tempted to drink some to try to settle his nerves. But he daren't open it, daren't have alcohol on his breath in case he got stopped, driving. Then in his panic he couldn't remember if he'd wiped it – his prints would be all over it.

He peeled off the off-licence's price tag, which had a serial number on it, and put that in his pocket, wiped the bottle carefully and laid it back on a rack in the fridge. Then he sat down on the edge of one of the chairs at the little table and tried to think clearly. To think through the idea he'd had. Suicide might work. But he couldn't rely on that, could he?

He'd done his best to remove any trace of his ever having been in the flat, without making it look too obvious. But he needed to cover his tracks better – perhaps by throwing a red herring into the mix. Point the police to her husband? She'd blown out their planned Monday reunion because that piece of shit had attacked her again. Make the police think it was domestic violence?

Yes, that might work.

And he knew one thing from Lorna about Corin which gave him a chance of doing just that.

CHAPTER 15

Wednesday 20 April

As he continued to work his way around the little flat, wiping, wiping, the one thing he knew he had to do was to keep calm, keep thinking. Not miss anything. But, shit, that was hard. His brain felt like a library in an earthquake. All the shelves were vibrating, everything on them shaken loose. Cascading down.

THINK!

She wasn't dead when he had left, was she? How long had he been gone, outside, pacing around? An hour at least? More? Long enough for someone to have entered after he'd left and –

Kill her?

Her bastard husband?

He stared down, as if the words of Rudyard Kipling's 'If' were lying at his feet.

If you can keep your head when all about you
Are losing theirs and blaming it on you,
If you can trust yourself when all men doubt
you . . .

If you can make one heap of all your winnings
And risk it on one turn . . .
And lose, and start again . . .
And never breathe a word about your loss . . .

That was all he needed to do. Keep his head. Just stand. Wait. Oh yes. He knew all about that. Shit happened. If you weren't living on the edge you were taking up too much space. And if you did live on the edge you got the highs, but it was where the shit hit the hardest. So hard it stung.

You could wash the stuff off, wash the smell away. And if you were of a strong enough mindset, you could wash away the memory. *Life breaks all of us, but afterwards some are strong in the broken places.* He was trying to remember who had written that, or something like it. That's what he needed to be right now. Strong in the broken place. He would be. Oh yes.

His mind was jumping all over the place. Focus. Had to focus. Calculate.

Panic made people screw up. Had to get rid of panic. And then just carry on as normal.

There was no other option. Well, not strictly true. Of course there was one.

But.

The other option was unthinkable.

CHAPTER 16

Wednesday 20 April

Roy Grace looked guiltily at his watch and thought, grimly, how true that expression was about the road to hell being paved with good intentions. It was 8.30 p.m. Yet here he was once again, in his office long past when he should have gone home. Sipping cold coffee, fretting about a crucial piece of evidence and waiting for a call from a Crown Prosecution lawyer to discuss it.

He took a moment out to schedule a timed Tweet, a 'Happy Birthday' greeting to DC Jack Alexander, who would be twenty-six tomorrow, then focused back on his work.

In a couple of weeks he had to go to the Old Bailey, the Central Criminal Court in London, for a plea hearing regarding his most recent case, a female sociopath – in his view – called Jodie Bentley, who was currently on remand in London's Bronzefield Prison. He had strong evidence that she had murdered a lover and then her husband, but he was pretty certain her death toll went beyond that. He still had hours of paperwork to read through. The barrister she'd hired, Richard Charwell, was a man he'd come up against before. Charwell had once ridiculed him in court for taking a piece of evidence in a murder trial – a shoe – to a medium. Although Grace had got the better of him under cross-examination in the witness box, the mud had stuck – and the killer had very nearly walked.

A canny, smart and manipulative lawyer, Charwell knew how to play a jury better than anyone Grace had encountered in his entire career. He had to make absolutely sure their prosecution case was belt and braces. This barrister was a man who could limbo dance a client below the smallest gap in a cell door.

Although the evidence against Jodie Bentley was strong, and the sometimes tricky Crown Prosecution Service had agreed, quickly, to bring a murder charge against her, it wasn't watertight. There were plenty of holes for a smart barrister like Charwell to drive a coach and horses through. Grace knew this woman was guilty as hell. He was confident that taking the witness stand in front of a sensible jury, he could say enough to convince them beyond reasonable doubt. And yet he was painfully aware that a defence barrister's job was to sow that doubt. For them it was a game. For the police it was the difference between a killer being put behind bars, or being free to roam the streets and kill again.

But juries were unpredictable, and never more so than now, when there was a lot of anti-police and anti-establishment sentiment. Some of it had been fostered by politicians, and some by the police themselves, after a series of bungled high-profile prosecutions of celebrities. He had no way of knowing how Charwell would play things in a future trial. His one certainty was that his immediate boss, Assistant Chief Constable Cassian Pewe, would be watching like a hawk, ready to pounce on him for the way he had handled the case if it went badly, but of course taking the credit if it went well.

Grace was gloomily aware of not being a magician. He couldn't always make things happen the way he wanted them to. All he could do was his best. To try to lock up the killers who took people's lives. He despised murderers with all his heart and soul. A thief could pay back some or all of what they had taken. But a murderer could never undo what he – or she – had done. And murderers didn't just destroy the lives of the victims, they destroyed the lives of all their victims' loved ones, too. For ever.

In general, homicide detection rates in the UK were high. Year on year, around eighty-five per cent of killers were caught. That compared, he knew, to just fifty-five per cent in America. But he would never be complacent. There had been a room at the old CID HQ, in Sussex House, occupied by the cold case squad, who carried out continual reviews on unsolved murders.

For Roy Grace, 'unsolved' was a euphemism for failure. There were thirty unresolved murders in the counties of East and West Sussex. Thirty, that was, of which the police were aware. How many more people were murdered every year that the police never found out about, was something never far from his thoughts.

Homicide investigations were never closed. Not so long as there was anyone still alive who was connected to the victim. And in some cases, beyond even that.

When Roy Grace had first joined the Major Crime Branch, he had made a pledge to himself. He was going to raise that bar from eighty-five per cent of homicides solved to as close as possible to one hundred per cent.

In his view, every killer made one mistake. Somewhere.

You just had to find it.

CHAPTER 17

Wednesday 20 April

He could, of course, set fire to the flat. That was the surest way to destroy all forensic evidence, he thought. But he was mindful of the dangers of doing this. The whole decrepit building was a fire trap, and unlike modern apartment blocks a fire wouldn't be contained to a single flat. It could end up killing others in the building.

Not an option he wanted to consider.

Shortly before 9 p.m., after the longest three hours of his life, it was finally dark enough outside. He put on his coat, took one final, careful look around using his phone torch, slipped the laptop and the photograph frame in the crook of his arm, and picked up the bunch of flowers he had brought and the two bin bags containing the other items he was removing from the flat. The last things he dropped in were the rubber gloves he had been wearing, then he walked to the front door.

In all the time they'd been meeting here, he could only ever remember seeing another resident on two occasions. One was an elderly lady in a dressing gown, who had looked half batty and wondered if he had seen her cat. The other was a young Chinese couple, who had looked like students and were so wrapped up in each other he doubted they had even noticed him.

All the same, he opened the door carefully, again using his handkerchief, listening for any sound on the landing before stepping out.

His heart seemed to be thudding even more loudly now, a steady *boof . . . boof . . . boof*, and his ears were popping. Ignoring the lift, he hurried down the three flights of stairs, then again hesitated as he reached the ground floor of the building.

As he did so, his phone began to ring.

He stood still in the small, dimly lit entrance hall of the apartment block, in the growing darkness, and pulled out his phone to see who was calling. In front of him was the constant roar of passing traffic along Kingsway. But although he could hear ringing, his phone display was dark and blank.

Then he realized. It was Lorna's phone.

He tugged it out of his pocket and stared at the display. *No caller ID.*

For an instant, his reaction was to answer it. To find out who was calling, and why. Then he realized that would be too dangerous.

Was it Roxy?

Had to be. No one else had the number, did they?

He let it ring on.

Two more rings then it stopped.

He waited, rooted to the spot. Waiting for it to ping with a voicemail. But instead, after some moments, the message *Missed Call* appeared.

He continued to wait, in case it rang again, puzzled as he remembered something. Some while back, when Lorna had been in the bathroom, her phone had rung. She'd asked him to see if it was Roxy on the display and if so to tell her she would call her back. Studying the buttons on the unfamiliar Samsung pay-as-you-go phone, he accessed the address book. As he had guessed, it contained just one name and number: *Roxy*.

If it had been Roxy calling just now, why would she have withheld her identity? But if it had not been her, then who? A wrong number? A telesales call? Unlikely on a pay-as-you-go. Could it have been her husband?

He'd never met this bastard, but from all Lorna had said about him, he wouldn't put it past him to have found the phone by searching her things when she was asleep or out. He was in the computer technology world, and probably knew how to track her movements on this phone, too.

Putting the phone back in his pocket, his head bowed, coat collar turned up and the peak of his baseball cap pulled low, he slipped out of the side door onto Vallance Street, turned right and hurried down the short distance to Kingsway, where he turned right again, passed the front entrance to the apartment block, then turned right yet again into Hove Street and headed up the busy road, past a line of parked cars, to his own elderly BMW. Starting the engine, his brain was racing. He needed to get rid of the laptop, phone and SIM card, photograph and its frame and the bin bags. But not around here. When Lorna's body was found – perhaps as soon as tomorrow, if the electrician came – they might well do a search of all bins in the area.

He drove off, down to the seafront, and turned right, heading away from Hove towards Shoreham, passing Hove Lagoon to his left. He needed bins. A mile or so on, outside an old warehouse, he saw a builder's skip. He stopped and, after a careful look around for any CCTV cameras, dumped one bag into it.

He drove on, thinking of another suitable location. He saw the slip road down to the harbour coming up to his left. Ideal, it would be totally dark down there, he thought. He took it and turned left again at the bottom, then right into a deserted parking area surrounded by warehouses on the wharf.

Looking around him, again making sure there were no cameras, he took Lorna's laptop out of the car, carried it across to the edge of the quay and tossed it into the black water. Making a small splash, it vanished, the water closing over it.

For some moments he considered losing the mobile phone here, too. But maybe it would be smarter to separate them, just in case. Highly unlikely they'd ever be found by divers, but why take the risk?

Back in the car, he headed through a small industrial estate along one side of the harbour and tossed his butts out of the window. Then, pulling out onto the main road, he saw another skip a short way ahead in front of a derelict building and pulled over, putting two wheels on the pavement.

Before getting out of the car he opened the back of the photograph frame and took the picture of Lorna and himself out, and – he couldn't help himself – sat and looked at it for some moments in the glow of a street light from above. He felt a lump in his throat. He stared at her long, blonde hair, strands of it lifted by the breeze; her beautiful face; her terrific, sometimes impish, sometimes incredibly sexy smile. High up on Wolstonbury Hill, on that glorious clear summer day, it had seemed the entire world was stretched out before them.

She was wearing a white halter-neck top and blue jeans, and had one long brown arm slung round his neck, pulling him tight so that their cheeks were pressed together for the photograph. The countryside close by was vast and pretty much deserted; it was one place where they felt safe to go when they wanted to be outside on a summer's day.

Shit. Shit. Shit.

He carefully ripped the photo into shreds. When he had finished he looked around for any sign of CCTV cameras, but could not see any. Good. He opened the door, taking the second bin bag, waited for a lorry to rumble past then stepped out and walked towards the skip. A car came by and he waited for that to pass. Then another. Then a man on a bicycle. God, he felt so conspicuous, as if all the eyes of the world were on him.

He dropped the bag in, then sprinkled the strips of photograph around the skip and shoved the photo frame beneath a sofa cushion; then returned to his car and was about to drive off when he realized there was a gutter right by the car. Perfect. He removed the SIM card from the Samsung and dropped the card down through the grille. Then, *shit* – a close call – he remembered the note from the electrician in his pocket. He tore that up and dropped it through the grille, too. He drove off quickly, still shaking, his thoughts jumping all over the place. Trying to figure out where to go.

He turned right up into the network of streets of Southwick, then saw a bin a short way ahead, at the end of a small shopping parade. Across the road was a row of terraced houses. Many shops these days had CCTV cameras inside and out. Before getting out of the car he checked carefully, but could see only one, outside a trophy and engraving shop in the middle of the parade, but no sign of one down this end. And no sign of one on any of the houses. Nor of anyone peering out of a window.

He carefully wiped the phone and, holding it wrapped in his handkerchief, opened the car door and deliberately dropped it onto the road. As he climbed out he stamped on it, pressing down as hard as he could with his heel, then again, hearing the crack and crunch of the outer case breaking. He stamped on it several more times for good measure, scooped it up with the handkerchief, dropped it in the bin, and sat back in the car.

So far so good. He did a quick check. Laptop. Phone. SIM card. Photograph. Frame. Cigarette butts in pocket. The next step might be trickier.

Just as he was about to start the engine, his phone rang.

On the caller display he saw it was his wife. He took a deep breath and answered.

'Hi, darling.'

'Where are you?' she asked. 'I was expecting you hours ago.'

'I'm stuck at work, I told you I wouldn't be home until late.'

'I've got problems with the television in the kitchen again. Sky's not working. I can't get any of my programmes that I've recorded.'

'OK – well, I can't do much from here, can I? I'll take a look when I get home.'

A motorbike was approaching with a loud rasping exhaust. He clamped his hand over the receiver until it had passed.

'Look, I've got the remote in my hand. I press

"Sky" right? Straight after switching on the television?'

'Darling, I can't deal with it now.'

'Huh. Do you want me to leave you something for your dinner?'

'No – I'm – I'm OK, I'll grab something.'

'Are you all right? You sound very strange.'

'I'm fine. Look, I've got to go. I'll sort the Sky out—'

'Oh – hey – the picture's just come on! I'm all right! Got it!'

'Great,' he said. 'That's great.'

As he ended the call, he realized he was dripping with perspiration. All over. Almost as wet as if he had stepped out of a shower. God, what a mess. How on earth had he let this happen? He hardly ever lost his temper and he'd never hurt a woman before, ever. Just what had got into him? The enormity of what he had done was dawning more and more. The potential devastation to his own life. It wouldn't just be his career and marriage that would be finished. Imagine his daughter knowing her father was a murderer. A life sentence. Not just years in prison, but the knowledge that was going to haunt him always of what he had done.

Am I a killer?

He needed to think it all through carefully, one step at a time.

The first priority was to cover his tracks and he had begun that process. He had to get this right, every step. Every damned tiny step. And first and foremost he had to calm down, stop sweating, stop looking guilty. Not make a mistake.

He started the engine.

People talked about the fragility of life. How it could turn on a sixpence, that was the old expression. And, boy, had it turned today. He badly needed a Plan B.

The problem was, just a few hours ago he'd never even had a Plan A.

CHAPTER 18

Wednesday 20 April

As the BMW headed east along the Old Shoreham Road, the showers had stopped. With the cruise control set at 30 mph, he was taking no chances of being pinged by a speed camera or being clocked in a radar trap. A short distance along he turned left, threaded around the side of Hangleton and joined the A27, where he reset the cruise control to 70 mph.

He stayed on the dual carriageway to the Hollingbury turn-off at the northern extremity of the city. Then he drove round a long crescent, past a parade of shops – a newsagent, an off-licence, a community centre – and up a hill.

He knew were Lorna lived, he'd been there a few times in their early days, when they had first met. It was before they'd got the flat, and had risky lunchtime meetings here while her husband was at work, and on a couple of occasions in the evening, when Corin had been away on business. But that had been a while ago and he sometimes lost his bearings in this complex network of streets.

Each of the houses he passed had rubbish bins pushed out to the front, many of them bulging, their lids partially raised. Good. Very good. That meant, to his relief, that the bin men had not been today. Tomorrow probably. Perfect timing. Please.

Then he recognized exactly where he was. The house was to his right, set back from the road behind two brick pillars, each topped with a stone ball, giving it the pretentious grandeur of a miniature faux-stately home. It used to make him smile, it looked so ridiculous. Lorna told him the pillars embarrassed her but Corin had insisted on them.

Their bin had, dutifully, been put out.

Good girl! Or perhaps, *Good, diligent Corin!*

He drove a short distance on, pulled into a space between a plumber's van and an elderly Shogun, switched off the engine and killed the lights. He sat in silence for some moments, checking all around him. It was completely dark now, and there was no sign of anyone. He raised his hand and deactivated the dome light, pulled on a pair of gloves, then opened the door and climbed out.

His sodden shirt, under his coat, felt cold on his skin and he shivered as he looked around. Closed curtains. Flickers of televisions behind some. He strode quickly back towards Lorna's house and stopped when he reached the bin. Again he looked all around him, furtively, then he switched on the torch on his phone, opened up the lid of the stuffed bin and shone the light in. Thinking. Thinking. What would fool the police?

Sitting on the top was a copy of yesterday's *Sun* newspaper. Beneath was what appeared to be a tiny printed circuit board from the inside of an electronic device. Perfect. From out of his pocket he tugged an empty plastic bin bag he'd taken from the flat, shook it open and dropped in the newspaper and the circuit board.

Underneath that the bin was rammed with empty tins of dog food, cartons of fish food and oxygenating tablets. Chinese takeaway cartons. He rummaged through them and came across a set of hair curling tongs.

He glanced around again, checking the coast was still clear, then delved further. The stench was vile. Fish bones. Prawn shells. The rotting remnants of a chicken. An empty tin of Brasso. What else?

He found a scooped-out tin of tuna but ignored it. Then, nestling in what looked like vacuum cleaner fluff, near the bottom, he saw an empty cigarette pack, and dropped that in the bag. Rummaging further, he found an assortment of cigarette butts and two Carlsberg beer cans. They went in as well.

Continuing to look around vigilantly, he reached right down, checking all the items in the bin. But he decided he had enough now.

He walked swiftly back to his car, climbed in and drove away.

It was going to be fine, he thought. Fine. Everything was going to be fine.

It had to be. Nothing else was an option. It was

all going to fall into his lap. He'd get through this. Think; plan; one step at a time. Just keep calm. And right now, that's how he felt. Calm.

It would be fine.

Really.

He headed off to his next destination, continuing to watch his speed like a hawk. Killers often got caught by the most stupid mistakes. Panic clouded their brains. Red mist. He wasn't panicking any more. He was thinking clearly, perhaps more clearly than ever before in his life.

Maybe that was because he had more at stake than ever before.

But that was fine.

He knew how to handle this.

He really did. And, just possibly, Lady Luck might hitch a ride alongside with him.

CHAPTER 19

Wednesday 20 April

The sign on the green machine read: **BRIGHTON AND HOVE COUNCIL. PAY & DISPLAY PARKING. CONTROLLED PARKING 9 A.M. – 8 P.M. ALL DAYS.**

It was now 10.23 p.m. A heavy shower was coming down. Good. Another sign that Lady Luck was with him. And a further sign was that he still had his golf bag in the boot of his car, from his regular game on Sunday. He tugged out the old black umbrella with one broken spoke, the one that lived in the golf bag, and put that up.

Keeping the umbrella down low over his head, clutching the bin bag, he hurried from the side street where he had parked, headed down to the seafront, turned left and made his way along to the apartment block. He let himself in through the side entrance on Vallance Street, listened carefully for any of the other occupants, then closed the umbrella, sprinted up the three flights of stairs, unlocked the front door of the flat and stepped into the semi-darkness.

And stood still, listening. Shaking and sweating heavily again. What if—?

Don't be ridiculous. There's no way she has got out of that bathtub.

Even so, it took some moments before he dared step forward and switch on the torch again. Swallowing hard, he walked up to the bathroom door and stopped, scared to go inside. He inched forward, shuffling, then took a bold step and shone the beam straight at her. And froze.

She was staring back at him.

'Shit!'

He dropped the phone onto the linoleum floor and backed out of the room, colliding clumsily and painfully with the door. His heart was jumping all over the place.

Surely her eyes had been shut when he'd left her?

Calm down, calm down.

He knelt and picked up the phone and saw to his relief the screen wasn't broken, then pointed the beam back at her. She lay in the position he had left her. But had her eyes been open? He tried to remember, to think back.

They must have been open.

Must have been.

No way could she have opened them after—

No way.

He went back out into the living room. *Get a grip.* He went over to the table where the ashtray was. With trembling, gloved fingers, he opened the bin bag, then tipped the butts out into the ashtray. Lorna did not smoke, she had given up some years ago, but told him that Corin was a heavy smoker. He mashed each of the butts in turn into the ashtray, making it look as if they'd been stubbed out there. Then he realized there was no ash.

He lit a cigarette and smoked it hard and fast, tipping off the ash after each long drag. He stubbed it out and put it in his pocket. He lit another and smoked that too, and again put the stub in his pocket.

Next, he tipped the contents of the ashtray into a carrier bag he found in a kitchen drawer. Then, with his gloved hands, he pulled out the two beer cans and also placed them in the carrier bag.

Come on, think clearly! Focus!

He put the printed circuit board on the floor just under the bed, out of sight.

He peered back into the bathroom. Shone the beam across Lorna one more time. Then at the cable from the plug socket into the bath. Then at Lorna again.

How had this happened?

He perched on a chair, thinking again. Trying to wind the clock back.

Please could he wake up tomorrow and find this had all been just a terrible dream? He would give anything, anything in the world, for that to happen. But it wasn't going to happen. He was going to wake up tomorrow – if he could even sleep a wink tonight – and nothing was going to be changed.

Lorna would still be dead.

Murdered.

By her husband?

Or suicide?

The electrician would most probably discover her. And then?

Had he covered his tracks well enough? Enough to put Corin in the frame rather than himself?

Could he ever really get away with this? Or live with himself?

He shone the beam all around the bathroom again. Above him, very faintly, he could hear laughter. Some television show. He went back into the living room. What had he forgotten? Missed? What would a crime scene investigator find? A smart detective?

What damned trace?

It was on the wall, right in front of him. He couldn't believe it. Could not believe he had been so careless, so stupid. Where had he parked his damned brain?

They'd always had two photographs of themselves in here. One he had taken and disposed of, the framed one of them at Wolstonbury, which had been standing on the table. The other hung on the wall, a selfie Lorna had taken at the beauty spot near Eastbourne, Beachy Head. They stood close together, his arm round her, both grinning, with the English Channel behind them.

The thought flashed through his mind that Beachy Head was the country's most popular suicide destination. A sheer drop of over five hundred feet onto rocks. That was one option right at this moment. He could be there in half an hour.

Maybe that's what he should do. Just bloody end it.

As long as he had everything covered, so his wife and daughter would never have to endure the shame. The shame of knowing what he had done.

He pulled the photograph off the wall and tucked it inside his jacket. Reaching the door, he placed the carrier bag on the floor, as if it was waiting to be taken to the dustbin. Then he hurried downstairs.

As he stepped out of the entrance porch and onto the pavement, he kept his head down. Glancing quickly around, he couldn't see anyone.

But the man standing invisibly in his own shadow on the far side of the road could see him.

Not that he really cared now if anyone did see him. In an hour he could be dead.

All the same, as he headed towards his car, he emptied the cigarette butts from his pocket and tossed them onto the pavement. *I'm a naughty litter lout*, he thought.

But sod it.

One hour.

One hour and he might be out of here. Gone.

He'd be litter himself.

CHAPTER 20

Wednesday 20 April

The woods are lovely, dark and deep,
But I have promises to keep,
And miles to go before I sleep . . .

The words of a poem he had once read went round in his brain, like a needle stuck in a vinyl groove. He was trying to remember who wrote it, as he drove along the narrow, winding black ribbon of road leading up to Beachy Head. To his left, invisible now in the dark, was a vast open landscape of South Downs farmland, and to his right a short expanse of grass and then the sheer cliff edge, with sky beyond. And sea below.

The Seven Sisters. A series of cliffs rising sheer out of the English Channel. It was a long drop almost anywhere along it, but the highest point was Beachy Head. Certain death. Tried and tested. So long as you went off in the right place.

He'd never been good with heights, but they fascinated him. Often as a boy he'd lean over railings and peer down, wondering what the falling sensation would be like. Would you be liberated knowing that in moments, at the end of your fall, there would be nothing any more? No you. Gone.

Was it going to hurt, your very last moment?

He was wondering that now.

Wondering if it would hurt, and trying to think who had written that damned poem.

Strange, he thought, as his headlights picked up the movement of sheep over to his left, he had a few times in the past joked with friends about what each of them would do if given just twenty-four hours to live. Sex, food and booze always featured heavily in everyone's answer. But now that he had just minutes, he wasn't thinking about any of those things. He was trying to remember the name of a damned poet, and wondering if death would hurt.

Would it be instant? Or would he lie there on the rocks, his bones all smashed to pieces, but conscious for seconds, minutes, maybe hours, while his life ebbed away?

And still trying to think of the name of the poet.

It didn't matter. He felt calm. He couldn't remember ever feeling this calm in his life. All that had happened this evening had receded into a hazy past. His family had too. Everything seemed so very simple, as if he had taken some kind of a happy pill.

Who wrote that poem?

Not that it mattered; not that anything would

matter in a few minutes' time, ever again. Not to him.

The road signs flashed past. Five miles . . . Two miles . . . Then soon after he saw ahead of him the illuminated sign of the Beachy Head Hotel.

It might have been a hotel once, but these days the long, low building was just a pub and restaurant, serving drinks and food to visitors at this famous beauty spot, and the hikers walking the South Downs Way. But to his relief there weren't many hikers – or visitors – to this desolate, windy, rain-swept spot, twenty miles east of Brighton, at 11 p.m. on a Wednesday night in April. In fact, judging from the empty car park, there did not appear to be any at all.

He drove into a bay, careful to align his car between two white lines. Why, he wasn't sure. Probably because he had a naturally tidy mind, he thought. He didn't like the idea of his car being reported to the police tomorrow morning. *Badly parked, straddled two bays, selfish bastard.*

As he killed the engine the dashboard lights went off. He sat there in the darkness, feeling the elements rocking the car. Oblivion was just a few hundred windy, salty, rain-lashed yards away.

So easy.

The woods are lovely, dark and deep.

Who wrote it? Who? Come on, come on, I won't bite!

He was momentarily startled by headlights looming out of the darkness behind him. Then he heard the sound of a car passing at speed, and his calm returned.

I am doing the right thing.

There was no other realistic option.

I'm a murderer.

Are you?

No. Of course not.

Someone had gone in there, during the time I was out walking around. That was the killer. I could never have killed anyone, could I?

All kinds of memories tugged at him, but he ignored them. Just step over the edge in the right place – and he knew more or less where that was – and then . . .

Nothing.

The stuff that was there before existence began, would still be there after it ended.

The void would always win. It just played a waiting game, that was all.

He debated for some moments whether to phone his wife. Confess. Tell her what he was about to do – the decent thing.

But he couldn't face that.

He could send her a note. And say what? He pulled his phone out and began writing a text.

Darling, a situation has happened. I

He stopped. Deleted it. There wasn't anything he could think of that would make any sense. Instead, opening the car door, he climbed out.

Instantly he felt the force of the wind making it hard to stand still, and the rain, hard as shotgun pellets, against his face. Pressing the key fob, he locked the doors. Not that he would care whether the car was stolen or not.

Goodbye, cruel world.

Getting drenched – but who cared? – he walked up the steep incline, guided by the beam of light from his phone, then crossed the road. Over to his left some lights in the Beachy Head Hotel were on. Perhaps it was still open? He was tempted to walk over to the place, have a pint, maybe two, maybe three – and some whisky chasers. To give him courage.

Dutch courage, they called it, although he wasn't exactly sure why. Something from way back in history, during the Thirty Years War, when Dutch soldiers drank gin to calm their nerves and give them courage in battle.

Dutch courage would have been good now.

Instead he walked up a steep bank, and then strode across wet grass towards – total darkness.

The clifftop. The rocks and the black water at the bottom.

The wind seemed to increase in strength the nearer to the edge he walked.

As did the darkness.

Way in the distance he saw a tiny speck of light. A ship. Everyone on it as unaware of him as he was of them. They didn't know that earlier this evening he had murdered a woman. His lover.

Except he hadn't, had he?

Life could never be the same again.

But whatever, there was nothing he could do to change the fact that she was dead. Nothing he could do to bring Lorna Belling back to life.

Nothing.

He did not know when he had last prayed. Not since early childhood, when he used to pray for things he wanted for Christmas or his birthday. A radio-controlled aeroplane. A BMX bike.

Not really a great relationship to have with God, based on *want this, want that, won't pray again if I don't get . . .*

But then again, where was God in his hour of need?

Not here, for sure.

Life was much simpler for animals. He and his wife had had a German Shepherd dog called Romy, who had lived to twelve. Her back legs had eventually gone and she was a pitiful sight, dragging herself around the garden, desperately trying to still be her old self. The vet had told them that it had come to the point where it was cruel to keep her alive, because she was suffering so much. A few days later they'd agreed with him. He came to their house with a veterinary nurse, and gave Romy an injection to put her to sleep. Within moments the wonderful, bright, intelligent dog was dead. No longer suffering. Alive one second, gone the next.

Why not with humans too?

He was about to find out, he thought, as he approached the cliff edge, shining his phone torch beam down at the long, wet grass bent in the wind. Through the howl of the wind he could hear the sea, a long way below.

Moments later, a beam of light danced in front of him, crossing his.

Then he heard a bluff, friendly voice right behind him.

'Hello!'

He turned.

A middle-aged, bearded man in a sou'wester stood there, holding a powerful torch. 'Just checking you are OK, sir?'

'OK?'

'You are a bit near the edge. We've had a lot of erosion recently. It's not safe to get too close – some of the chalk is very unstable.'

'I see. Thanks for the warning.'

'Would you like to have a chat?'

'Chat?' he said, blankly.

'I'm with the Beachy Head Chaplaincy Service – my name's Bill, what's yours?'

'It's – Robert,' he said. 'Robert Frost.' Remembering the poet now.

'Is everything all right? Not a nice night to be out, and with these strong gusts of wind it can be even more dangerous than normal near the edge.'

'No, all's fine,' he said. 'Absolutely fine. I'm – I'm working on a poem – I thought I'd come here for some inspiration.'

'You're a poet?'

'I am, yes.'

'Robert Frost's your name?'

'That's right.'

'I'll keep a lookout for your work, Mr Frost.'

'Yes, good, thank you.'

'So, OK, you're absolutely sure everything is all right?'

'All good, thank you.'

Actually, it wasn't. It wasn't all good. He'd just realized he'd left on the passenger seat of the car the photograph of himself and Lorna – the second one that he'd noticed and taken down from the wall.

As he walked back towards it, he was aware of the Good Samaritan from the Chaplaincy following him at a distance.

He got back in, closed the door and switched on the ignition. His brain was such a jumble, a million thoughts all broken loose from their mountings. He had to stop somewhere, stop and think.

Think.

And find a bin and dump the photograph.

And then?

He didn't know.

Go back to Beachy Head? Just drive over a cliff somewhere nearby?

A song was playing on the radio. It had been playing the first time he and Lorna had made love and it had kind of become their song. Billy Joel's 'Uptown Girl'.

Shit.

So many memories. So many beautiful ones.

What a bloody mess I've made of everything.

He shivered, suddenly realizing he was freezing cold. It would be cold in the mortuary, too. Lorna would be lying in there tomorrow. And if they found him? Would they be in the same mortuary together?

He shivered again.

The car rocked in the wind.

Thinking. What? What? What was he going to do?

Throw himself out into that inky, cold darkness?

I don't have to.

I've covered my tracks.

I didn't do it.

CHAPTER 21

Thursday 21 April

Andreas Thomas, the German lawyer whom Sandy had appointed as her executor, spoke reasonably good English, but Roy Grace sometimes found him hard to understand on the phone, and the conversation was a lengthy one as he had to ask him to repeat himself frequently.

The documentation allowing Sandy's body to be repatriated to England had been completed, and a firm of funeral directors in Brighton had everything in hand. The funeral had been booked for the following Thursday at the vast Hove Cemetery, coincidentally where both of Sandy's grandparents were buried. His own had been cremated at what Roy thought was the much prettier Woodvale. He had still not yet decided which of the options he would choose for himself. Neither appealed that much. It was something he knew he should confront but – and he knew it was stupid – it felt that to make the choice was almost inviting his own death.

Many German wills did not include funeral

instructions because, Andreas Thomas explained, often they would not be discovered or read until many weeks after death. The lawyer agreed that burial would be the better option for Sandy.

The one grey area currently was Sandy's substantial estate. A short while before she had left Roy, Andreas Thomas informed him, she'd had a windfall inheritance from an aunt that she'd kept secret, instructing the funds to be sent to a numbered Swiss bank account, clearly in preparation for leaving Roy. It could even have been this inheritance that gave her the courage to leave him, the lawyer speculated. Sandy had left clear instructions that almost her entire estate be put in trust to pay for private education for Bruno, until the age of twenty-one, when he would receive the balance of the money. The estate was now worth four million euros.

In the weeks before her accident, Sandy had been anxious to establish this trust and to Roy's dismay had left instructions in her will for her parents to be appointed fellow trustees, along with the Munich lawyer.

Grace told the lawyer that he wasn't worried about the money. He would take responsibility for Bruno, and bring him back to live with himself, Cleo and Noah, in England, and would put him into a good school – the money to pay for it could be sorted out in due course. He wanted to make sure he was in the driving seat on this one, not Sandy's parents.

He arranged to meet Andreas Thomas at his office in Munich the following morning. As he ended the call, he was about to dial his travel agent when his work phone rang. It was the duty Ops-1, Inspector David Graham, known to everyone by his initials, DG, in the Comms department, which was housed in a modern block on the far side of the Police HQ campus from the Specialist Crime Command offices. A call from him was not going to be good news.

'Roy, I was told you're the on-call SIO – I thought you were off active duty for a while?'

'I am, DG, but I'm covering for Kevin Shapland this week. What's up?'

'We've got a suspicious death. Woman in a bathtub in a block of flats in Hove. It was called in by an electrician who had apparently gone to the premises to carry out some rewiring work. A Response Unit attended, along with an ambulance crew, who declared her dead – sounds like she had been dead for a while.'

'A while? Any idea how long? Days, weeks?'

'No, but some hours – perhaps overnight.'

'What about the cause of death?'

'It looks like she might have electrocuted herself, but the officers attending were not happy about an injury to the back of her skull, and blood on the bathroom tiles, and requested supervision. Their sergeant attended and agreed with them, declaring it a potential crime scene. A senior CSI was called in, along with the duty divisional DI.

There are a number of factors that make me think this looks like a job for Major Crime – can you attend and take command of the investigation, Roy?'

'Have they got scene guards?'

'Yes, in place.'

'Good. We'll need to inform the Coroner's Officer.'

'I've done that.'

'Good. OK, if you let me have the address and any other details I'll get there right away. What information do you have on the victim and what are the other factors you mentioned, DG?'

'Her name is Lorna Jane Belling. She's a domestic violence victim – white female, thirty-five, married and works from home, in Hollingbury, as a hair-dresser. But the location where she has been found is a flat on Hove seafront, Vallance Mansions, where she has a monthly tenancy. It's a run-down old block, with a landlord who's had a ton of complaints over the years from his tenants. Health and Safety did an inspection a couple of years ago and reported him.'

'So the landlord could be in the frame for a manslaughter charge?'

'Well, possibly, but here's one complicating factor. On Monday of this week a Response crew attended at this same woman's marital home, following a violent assault by her husband, Corin Belling – his third reported assault on her in a year. He was subsequently arrested and the IDVA were notified and made contact with her. Then he was released on bail the following evening, just short of thirty-six hours, because his wife refused to press charges. It sounds like this flat in Hove might be her secret bolthole.'

'Or love nest?'

'Possible.'

'Has the husband been informed?'

'Under the circumstances, not yet, sir.'

'Good, let's keep it that way for now. Do we know where he works?'

'A company called South Downs IT Solutions.'

Grace frowned. 'That name sounds familiar.'

'It should be, Roy! They used to be about three hundred yards from Sussex House – on that industrial estate – near the old *Argus* building.'

'Duh! Of course.'

'But they're in Burgess Hill now.'

Grace immediately called Temporary DI Guy Batchelor, who was in the new Detectives' Room, an open-plan area on the floor above, and asked him to come to his office right away.

Two minutes later Batchelor knocked on his door and entered. A burly, shaven-headed man, suited and booted conservatively, reeking as usual of cigarette smoke, he had a warm personality and the physique of a rugby player. In his previous office, Roy would have sat at the small, round conference table with him. Now all he could offer was the empty desk in front of his.

Grace brought him briefly up to speed and asked,

'How do you feel about attending as my deputy SIO, Guy? I'll come with you today, then I'll leave you in charge until I return. Are you comfortable with that?'

'Fine, boss,' Batchelor responded, nodding pensively.

'It's a big responsibility – if you'd rather, I could ask DCI Best, who's the on-call SIO from tomorrow.'

'No, I'd be very happy to do this.'

'If it does turn out to be a homicide this could be a great career break for you, Guy. I'd prefer to keep the job rather than hand it over to Nick Best, though if you find you need any urgent guidance you could speak to him – I'll let him know.'

'Thanks, boss, I'm very grateful. Sounds like we already have a possible suspect. Track record of abusing his wife. We might be able to wrap this up very quickly.'

'ABC, Guy,' Grace cautioned him with the police mantra. *Assume nothing. Believe no one. Check everything.*

'Ingrained on my soul!'

Grace grinned. He liked Batchelor a lot. He was a smart detective who he believed would go far in his career. Probably further than he himself had ambitions for. All the way to the top. He could see him being a chief constable one day. 'Good man,' he said.

'I won't let you down, boss.'

'That's why I've chosen you.'

CHAPTER 22

Thursday 21 April

As Grace drove the unmarked job car past the security gate of the Police HQ, out onto the residential street and up the hill, his right leg, where he had been hit with eleven shotgun pellets a few months ago, was still causing him discomfort. But he ignored it as he talked Batchelor through the initial procedures to follow, while the DI noted everything diligently on his pad for Operation Bantam, the random name generated by the Sussex Police computer system.

They drove through the Cuilfail tunnel under the cliffs on the edge of the county town of Lewes, and then onto the A27. Grace was feeling the same surge of adrenaline he always got when heading to a potential murder scene. The weeks of paperwork were necessary, but the real bang for him always had been and, he knew, always would be, leading a murder enquiry from the front. Excitement, mingled with both fascination and a little dread, too, at what he might be about to see. Coupled with the knowledge of the almost overwhelming burden of responsibility that came with it. All he could hope to achieve was justice for the victim, and some sort of closure for the victim's family. The victim's family was the most important of all. Until the offender was convicted and sentenced, the family could not start to move on.

He never forgot that.

This sounded potentially a simple case, with a prime suspect already on the radar. Eighty per cent of victims were killed by someone they knew, and with Lorna Belling's history of domestic abuse by her husband already well known to the police they had a good starting point. But, equally, he well knew from his years of experience that things were not always as they seemed.

'We need to check out the electrician's story, Guy. We also need the names of all the tenants in the building and background checks on them. And all the tradesmen who call regularly, and any other contractors working in the building, or who have recently worked there. We'll need a list of all her friends and relatives, and any work colleagues and clients.'

Batchelor continued to make notes. 'I should also have a check done on any known offenders against women who might recently have been released from prison, with links to Brighton and Hove.'

'Absolutely, Guy, good thinking.'

Fifteen minutes later, crossing the lights at the junction of Hove Street and Kingsway, and making a left along the seafront, he didn't need the satnav to find the building, just a short distance ahead. There were two marked police cars outside, a white CSI van and another car with a crest and the words HM CORONER on each door. An outer cordon of crime scene tape, attended by a uniformed PCSO scene guard, flapped in the wind outside the entrance to a shabby-looking, 1950s low-rise apartment building. So far, he was pleased to see, there were no reporters, although it would not be long, he knew, before they arrived. But he preferred to be fully informed before engaging with them.

Many detectives had an intense dislike – fuelled by mistrust – of the press, and of social media. But Grace took a different view. He believed the public had a right to know what was going on, and his years of experience had taught him that, if respectfully treated, the press could not only be a great ally to the police, but could be invaluable in helping encourage the public to come forward with information. He had been one of the first officers to embrace social media as an investigative tool and, like many of his colleagues in Sussex Police today, regularly used Twitter in particular.

He parked just ahead of the other police vehicles, and he and Batchelor climbed out, opened the boot and grabbed their forensic suits from their go-bags. They walked up to the outer cordon scene guard, signed the log and ducked under the tape.

As they did so, Grace heard the familiar voice

of Roy Apps, the Duty Inspector. He walked towards him, his face the only part of him visible in his full protective clothing.

'Good to see you, Roy.'

'You, too,' he replied. 'Someone told me you're retiring?'

'Yes, next year.'

'Sorry to hear that, I'll miss you.'

Apps gave him a wan smile. 'It will be strange.'

'Going back to your old career?'

'Well, something involving the countryside. Not sure what yet.'

'You'll be a big loss to the force.'

'Us old buggers have to make way for new blood, eh?'

Grace wasn't so sure about that. When he had joined, the rule was that you retired on full pension after thirty years. To a nineteen-year-old that had seemed a lifetime away. But now turned forty, he was glad the retirement age had been extended. The force lost many talented people in their late forties. Officers who had enormous experience – and so much money invested in them. He had a lot of respect for Apps, who had originally been a gamekeeper before joining the police. He was one of the best uniform inspectors he'd ever known, an immensely able man.

'Sure you're not going to miss it, Roy?'

'I'll miss the camaraderie, but not the politics. Too much of that, these days. Know what I'm looking forward to most of all?'

'No – what?'

'It's being able to go into a pub and say what I really think, without having to worry that one of my bosses gets to hear about it, or the local paper printing a piece saying, *Brighton police inspector says young offenders would be better off with a slapping from their local bobby.*'

Grace smiled. 'Yup, I have to say I can't disagree with you. So what do we have?'

'Doesn't look good,' Apps replied.

The two detectives broke the seals and wormed their way into their blue paper forensic suits. They pulled on their overshoes, hats and masks, then snapped on their gloves.

It is normal at a crime scene in a public space to have an outer and inner cordon for protection – especially somewhere like this apartment block, where residents had to be permitted to enter and leave their homes. The inner cordon would prevent access to the actual flat itself.

Ignoring the ancient lift, Apps led them up three flights of stairs. As they emerged on the landing they saw the inner cordon, with another PCSO scene guard outside. They signed her log too, and as Apps stepped aside, Grace turned to Batchelor. 'Remember the first rule, Guy, *clear the ground under your feet.* OK?'

The DI nodded. 'And Locard's Principle.'

Locard, a Frenchman born in 1877, was regarded by many as the pioneer of forensic science. His principle was that every contact leaves a trace:

> Wherever he steps, whatever he touches, whatever he leaves, even unconsciously, will serve as a silent witness against him. Not only his fingerprints or his footprints, but his hair, the fibres from his clothes, the glass he breaks, the tool mark he leaves, the paint he scratches, the blood or semen he deposits or collects . . . Physical evidence cannot be wrong, it cannot perjure itself, it cannot be wholly absent. Only human failure to find it, study and understand it, can diminish its value.

'And one other thing,' Grace reminded him. 'Always think the unthinkable.'

'Yes, boss!'

Grace pushed open the door and, followed by Batchelor, entered the living area of a small studio flat, with a window overlooking the seafront and the King Alfred complex. It felt chilly, and there was a smell of manky carpet and burnt plastic, but also a faint smell of disinfectant and bleach.

'See that, boss?' Batchelor pointed at a knotted carrier bag on the floor by the door. 'I wonder what's in there – might be of interest.'

Grace nodded. 'Make sure the forensic team pick that up.'

The room was furnished with a small sofa, an armchair and a cheap-looking kitchen table, on which lay a dirty ashtray; two wooden chairs were drawn up to it; there was a double bed with a fur throw; two Brighton prints hung on the walls, one of the old Brighton chain pier, which from his limited knowledge of Brighton's history was destroyed in a storm in 1896, and the other depicting the Old Steine from around the same era. To the right of this print he noticed a rectangle, very slightly darker than the rest of the cream Artex wall, with a picture hook in the middle.

Had another picture been removed recently, he wondered? He pointed it out to Batchelor, who made a note on his pad.

The two detectives entered the bathroom. Grace tensed as he went in first. If he had been asked to count the number of dead bodies he had encountered in his nearly twenty-two years in the police force, he would not have been able to give a figure. Nor would he have been able to describe his reactions to each one of them. But there was one thing that every murder victim had in common, and that was just how utterly motionless they were.

With a living human, even one comatose, there was constant movement. But a dead person was like a waxwork figure. Sometimes he had to really focus his mind to remember this had been, just a short while ago, a living human being. And someone's loved one.

He glanced at Batchelor's pale face, and realized that although the DI had been involved in many murder enquiries and seen many bodies, they always had an effect. Especially ones like this, with their sightless eyes open.

'You OK?' he asked, gently.

Batchelor nodded. 'Fine, boss, I'm good.'

Grace studied Lorna Belling's body carefully. She was lying in the tub, with water up to her midriff, her head lying back against the tiles. The hairdryer cable ran from the blackened plug socket down into the water. There were bloodstains on the cracked tile behind her. She must have hit the wall with some force – pushed? Thrown back by the force of the electric shock? Slipped in the bath?

She had an almost classically beautiful English-rose face, shoulder-length fair hair tinted with highlights, and a toned figure, but with a number of bruise marks on her upper torso and above her right eye. There were pale lines round her neck, which had darkened from the blood that had drained down from her head, and tiny clusters of red dots, each the size of a pinhead, were present on her forehead and cheeks. He peered into her eyes and could see more of them there. Clear signs of strangulation.

God, what kind of a bastard of a husband could have been this violent? The answer, he knew, was far too many. Domestic abuse always angered him. Regardless of the sex of the abuser.

Cleo had given him a ton of books to read relating to her Open University degree course in philosophy, and he had been dutifully working through them ever since they had first started dating, aware of just how much knowledge he lacked from his own education. Some of the stuff he had found impenetrable, but he had learned a lot from others. The words of one writer, the American poet and philosopher Henry Thoreau, had stuck in his mind: 'lives of quiet desperation'.

He looked at the bruises on Lorna's body. Had that been her tragic life? One of quiet desperation? Had this little place been her escape?

He pointed out the marks on her neck to Batchelor. 'What do you think, Guy? Any hypothesis?'

'Well, boss, I'd say from what we know of the husband, he might have murdered her and then tried to make it look like suicide. But I don't think we can rule out anything at this stage, even suicide.'

Grace nodded. 'She could have been attacked by her husband. Or by someone else. Or suicide. Until we find her phone, laptop or other electronic devices we won't know for sure she didn't write or send a note.' He stepped back out into the main room and looked at the ashtray. 'Was she a smoker?'

Then he was interrupted by his phone ringing. 'Roy Grace?'

Instantly his heart sank as he heard the voice of the most pedantic of all the Home Office pathologists on-call to Sussex Police. Frazer Theobald.

'Hello, Roy. I'm just finishing off a job in Woking, then I'll be heading down. Should be with you in about two hours.'

The most pedantic, but the most thorough, Grace acknowledged with grudging respect as he ended the call. 'I'll be leaving you to it shortly, Guy. OK?'

'Absolutely, boss.'

'Thanks, I appreciate it.'

'I'll take care of everything. You won't need to worry.'

'Check out the Murder Manual when you get back to the office, OK? It has everything you need as an SIO.'

'I will.'

They stepped out of the flat, not wanting to disturb the crime scene more than they needed, and were met moments later by Crime Scene Investigator Alex Call, who had just arrived. Grace introduced Batchelor, explaining his role. Then he instructed the CSI to lay down a forensic grid, and to ascertain if there were any fast-track opportunities for forensic retrieval of evidence. He and Batchelor would wait out here whilst Call did his first cursory sweep.

Grace looked at his watch, working back from the time he needed to be at the airport. Lorna's husband needed to be informed, and he wanted to break the news himself to the man. How he reacted could be vitally significant. But he needed to remain here at the crime scene with Guy, waiting for Alex Call's initial assessment, in case there was something blindingly obvious he had overlooked, which Call's trained eye spotted and could lead them to a swift resolution.

They stood on the landing chatting to the scene guard, then the Crime Scene Manager who arrived with James Gartrell, a CSI photographer, who would video the scene.

Ten minutes later Call came back out, closing the door behind him. 'Right,' he said. 'I've done a quick sweep; there are a number of things of interest. Firstly it looks as if some attempt has been made to clean the flat up. I've found cigarette butts and beer cans in the plastic bag left by the door. In fast time I've developed marks on two of the cans, which I've already sent off electronically to the fingerprint bureau. I've also swabbed the victim's body.'

'Good work, Alex. What about a mobile phone or laptop?' Grace asked.

'Not that I've come across so far.'

Grace frowned.

'Could have been taken by her killer,' Batchelor said.

'A botched burglary, do you think, Guy?'

'Possible.'

At that moment there was a ping, and the CSI pulled his tablet from his pocket and stared at the screen. 'We have a match!' he said. 'From the prints on the cans.'

'Oh?' Grace replied.

Call looked at both detectives. 'Corin Douglas Belling. That gives us a starting point.'

CHAPTER 23

Thursday 21 April

If they made an arrest within hours of the murder being reported, it would not only reflect well on him, Grace thought, as he left the building. It would take any pressure off him having to explain his sudden absence for a few days.

If.

If they had the right person.

Corin Belling had violently assaulted his wife three times in the past year – at least, three times that the police were aware of, having been called by his wife. In all probability it was many times more than that, unreported. Such was the normal pattern. Abusers would assault their partners, then apologize and beg for forgiveness. Over and over. The average was, incredibly, forty assaults before the partner would contact the police. And still after then the assaults would continue. Until one day they went that bit too far.

There was a ton of questions he needed answering. The first was Lorna's reason for having this flat.

Did the husband know about it? Or rather, when had he found out about it? Was Lorna a secret smoker? If not, who had been using the ashtray? Corin? DNA might provide the answer if they could find any on the cigarette ends.

In the meantime they had the print match on the beer cans. Lorna's husband, Corin.

Corin had been released from custody after his arrest earlier in the week for assaulting his wife.

Lorna had been renting the flat for over eighteen months – secretly, Grace presumed. Paying cash. Why? And why no phone? Or computer?

The obvious explanation was to give her a bolthole to escape from her husband when he became violent. Maybe she left her computer at home. Maybe also she left her phone. If the husband was a control freak there were any number of ways these days he could track her through her phone.

Another possibility that he'd already considered was a secret trysting place with a lover.

It was unlikely for her husband and her to have a place close to the seafront as a kind of weekend holiday home. But if that was the case, why would it have been in her name and why was she paying in cash, giving the landlord no other address?

He razored away that last explanation, leaving just the first two options.

The husband's prints, clearly recent, on the cans of beer put him at the scene where she had been found dead.

Had he discovered her bolthole and gone there

to confront her? Then turned violent? He looked at his watch. Time was running out on him. He wanted to break the news himself to the man, and see from his face and body language how he reacted.

Grace decided to go to the man's workplace and talk to him. He was aware of the forensic considerations of going straight from a crime scene to a suspect, but in this case he judged there would be no cross-contamination issues.

Needing a collaborating officer for the questioning and potential arrest, he thought for some moments about who from his team was available, then called DS Exton, gave him the address and asked him to head straight there and meet him outside.

CHAPTER 24

Thursday 21 April

Burgess Hill is a small but sprawling town a few miles to the north of Brighton, and Roy Grace always got lost there so, before setting off, he programmed the address into the Mondeo's satnav.

Twenty minutes later, driving up Station Road, he was lost again as the satnav sent him on a detour back to the roundabout he had just crossed, and then down a dead end. Cursing, he turned round, pulled over, and entered the address into the Maps app on his personal iPhone, which he often found was more reliable. It showed his destination to be over a mile from where he currently was. 'Great!' he said aloud, annoyed.

A couple of minutes later he made a sharp left into the shopping precinct of Church Road, passed a large Specsavers shop on his left and turned right into yet another one-way system taking him out of the town. He drove through a network of streets, then finally, some minutes later, he passed a swanky Porsche dealership and, a short distance on, another sports car dealership displaying the name BAYROSS SUPERCARS, then entered a complex of modern, high-tech-designed industrial units. Almost at the far end, he saw to his right a two-storey building bearing the sign SOUTH DOWNS IT SOLUTIONS.

There was a black Ferrari, a grey Bentley Continental and a row of other high-end motors ranked outside, with an assortment of less exotic vehicles occupying most of the rest of the car-parking area. One vehicle he recognized, in a visitors' parking space, was similar to his own, a silver unmarked Mondeo. He pulled alongside it, gave a wave of his hand to DS Exton who was seated inside it, on his phone, and climbed out.

Exton was one of the longest-standing members of his team and Grace liked him a lot. Tall, and normally neatly turned-out, he was a polite, incisive and highly observant detective, who missed little and was very popular with his colleagues. He was the kind of man, Grace always felt, you'd want to have covering your back in a tight corner.

Moments later, accompanied by Exton, he strode towards the main door and entered a smart reception area. There were sofas to his right and left, and a glamorous-looking young woman sitting behind a curved glass reception module, on the phone.

As they walked up to her she ended the call and gave them a smile.

'We'd like to have a word with Corin Belling, who I believe works here.'

'Yes he does – do you gentlemen have an appointment?'

Grace showed her his warrant card. 'Detective Superintendent Grace and Detective Sergeant Exton from Surrey and Sussex Major Crime Team.'

She looked at it carefully, then said, 'Oh, right, one moment please.' She handed them each a visitors' pass form to fill in.

As Grace filled in his details and car registration he heard her on the phone. 'David, there's a Detective Superintendent Grace to see Corin. Right, thank you.'

She took the forms back, tore them off and folded each into a plastic holder with a lapel clip which she handed to them. 'If you take a seat, someone will be along to take you to him.'

Grace sat down on a bright-green sofa, glancing at a neat display of computing magazines on a table in front of him, mentally comparing the neat, ordered feel of this place to the shabbiness of most police reception areas. Then he shot a glance at Exton. The lean detective was looking slightly scruffy today, he thought, surprised at his turnout. His charcoal suit could have done with a pressing, his cream shirt had several vertical creases in the collar and he had several days' growth of stubble. Going for the modern look, he wondered? But Exton wasn't the type – he was conservative, tidy, orderly.

As Grace was still pondering his uncharacteristic turnout, a long-haired man in his early thirties, in a black suit over a black T-shirt, cool glasses and trainers strode up towards them with a hand outstretched. 'Hello, can I help you? I'm David Silverson, CEO.'

Grace stood up. 'Thank you.' He repeated his and Exton's names and ranks.

'Is something wrong? Something I could help you with? Presume you know we're working with your Cybercrime team at the moment,' Silverson said.

'I didn't – but they're good people.'

'Terrific. We're helping them out on a series of frauds on older people in Sussex.'

'This is a separate issue,' Grace replied. 'We'd like to have a word with an employee of yours, Corin Belling.'

Silverson looked uncomfortable. 'Is this to do with the issue he had earlier this week?'

'I'm afraid I can't say. Was he at work yesterday?'

'He was working from home yesterday – we have a flexible policy here. Would you like me to give you a private conference room?'

Grace thought for a moment, then decided he'd like to surprise the man and not give him a chance to think. 'No, actually, we'd like to see him in situ in his office.'

'Sure – come with me, I'll take you up.'

The detectives followed the CEO up a flight of stairs, into a huge, partly open-plan office with several small offices off it. Around forty people, Grace estimated, all in their twenties and thirties, were seated at desks, almost all concentrating hard on their screens.

'That's him over there,' Silverson said, pointing to a small glass-walled office at the far end. He led them down towards it. Inside was a sullen-looking, lanky man in his late thirties, with a mane of fair hair that fell across his forehead and a sly face with thin lips, who was swigging from a can of Coke. His suit jacket was slung over the back of his chair and his shirt collar was unbuttoned, his tie slack.

'Corin, there are two police officers to see you,' the CEO said, and ushered them in.

Grace entered first, followed by Exton, who closed the door.

'It's Mr Belling, is that correct?'

'What of it?'

'I'm Detective Superintendent Grace and this is my colleague Detective Sergeant Exton. I'm afraid I've got some bad news about your wife.'

The man's eyes flashed up, warily, at them. 'Is this about the argument the other night? I'm not going to prison, I'm not going to be locked up over this or lose my job over that bitch.'

Without warning he swung his arms across the desk, sending the Coke can flying, spewing out its contents, pushed his chair back, barged past the two detectives, flung open the door and ran out.

Grace, followed by Exton, gave chase. Belling

disappeared through a door marked FIRE EXIT. They reached it a few seconds later. Grace heard steps below him and ran down. As he did he heard a clang, followed by the wail of a fire siren. Moments later, reaching the ground floor, he saw a heavy fire door swing shut. He pushed it open and saw Corin Belling sprinting across the car park. He ran after him, shouting over his shoulder to Exton to radio for backup.

Belling glanced behind him, clocked him, then increased his pace even more. Grace increased his, wishing he wasn't wearing a sodding suit and boots. He followed the man out onto the road that threaded through the industrial estate, past several industrial units, gaining on the bastard. Gaining on him with every step. Every few moments Belling threw a backwards glance.

I'm going to sodding get you.

Grace hadn't chased a suspect since his accident, but he was reasonably fit from his regular jogging. Except his right leg was starting to hurt. He put it out of his mind – he didn't care, the pain didn't matter. Nothing mattered except getting this creep with his floppy hair and thin lips and penchant for beating up, strangling and murdering his wife.

He was gaining.

Gaining.

Past the Bayross Supercars forecourt and on. They were reaching the Porsche dealership.

Ran on past it.

Closer.

Closer.

Approaching the main road. Traffic was coming down it in both directions.

Belling threw another glance and stared right into the whites of Grace's eyes.

Just a yard between them now.

Half a yard!

In his days of playing rugby, Roy Grace had been on the wing because he was fast. As president of the police rugby team, he had stood on the touch-lines of numerous games. He still knew what to do and how and when to do it.

Now!

He launched himself shoulders first at the man's waist, arms round his midriff, then pulled him into his body, squeezing hard and twisting his upper body. He continued pulling and pushing until Belling began to fall, with himself crashing down on top of him.

Before the man had time to react, Grace grabbed his right arm and pulled it up behind his back in a half nelson.

'Get the fuck off me!' the man screamed.

'Corin Douglas Belling, I'm arresting you on suspicion of murder. You do not have to say anything, but it may harm your defence if you do not mention when questioned something you later rely on in court. Anything you do say may be given in evidence.'

'Murder? What the fuck are you talking about?'

'Your wife's dead, and we believe you may have

killed her,' Grace said, pulling out his handcuffs with his free hand.

Like a serpent, Corin Belling twisted, breaking free of Grace's grip, and a fist slammed, agonizingly, into the detective's face, momentarily stunning him.

CHAPTER 25

Thursday 21 April

Guy Batchelor continued his assessment of the crime scene, reminded all the time of Roy Grace's words.

Assume nothing. Believe no one. Check everything.

Clear the ground under your feet.

Every contact leaves a trace.

Think the unthinkable.

The unthinkable.

A beautiful woman lay dead in a bathtub just a few feet away. From the marks round her neck it seemed someone had tried to strangle her. A hair-dryer in the tub.

Think the unthinkable.

Had the husband killed her? Too obvious.

How had the hairdryer ended up in the bath?

Think the unthinkable.

If not the husband, who? Could she have hated someone so much she'd made it look as if someone had tried to strangle her, then committed suicide?

Unthinkable?

The fury of a woman scorned?

A history of being abused by her husband, dead in a secret bolthole. Had Belling done it or, perhaps, had he been fitted up?

CHAPTER 26

Thursday 21 April

Roy Grace saw, through his haze of pain, the bastard running away. Belling was a hundred yards ahead of him, maybe more. He clambered, shakily, to his feet. His nose was hurting. Busted? That would be the third time in his career. But right now that wasn't important. One thing and one thing only mattered. That fucker, Corin Belling.

Glancing round, he saw Exton lumbering towards him, speaking urgently on his phone. He broke into a loping trot, then stepped it up into a sprint. His eyes were watering. He was going to catch that wife-beating shit.

Going to catch him.

That bully boy.

Murderer.

He increased his pace. Faster. Faster. His right leg felt as if it was on fire, but he ignored the pain, running on through it. They were beside a main road now, heading towards a roundabout. There was a wide grass verge on either side. Corin Belling ran straight across it, onto the island, right in front of a motorcycle which had to swerve to avoid him, then on again, across to the far side, passing a sign that read **BRIGHTON A23.**

On along the road.

Grace took the same route, racing across in front of a lorry with blaring horn. His chest was hurting. His nose was agony. His leg was throbbing.

He blanked it all.

He was going to get the bastard. Going to get him. Going to see him in court.

Corin sodding Belling, you are breathing your last gulps of air as a free man for the next twenty years. Enjoy them, savour them, you miserable little wife-abusing murderous shit.

He was gaining on him.

Could see the man's shirt stuck to his back with perspiration.

Perspiring from fear.

The pain in his right leg was fading. So was the pain in his chest. His speed was increasing.

Increasing.

The gap between them closing.

Fifty yards.

Thirty yards.

Twenty yards.

Corin Belling shot a glance over his shoulder.

Ten yards.

Five yards.

Another glance over his shoulder. His expression utter defiance. He turned sharp right, and raced back across the road, right across the path of a lorry bearing down on him.

The lorry blocked any view of the yellow Lamborghini that was overtaking it.

It was being driven by a potential customer of Bayross Supercars, the salesman encouraging him, as he said later in court, 'To give it some wellie!'

The client was giving it wellie all right. The car was doing, so the officer from the Collision Investigation Unit established later, 85 mph at the time of impact. In a 40-mph zone.

CHAPTER 27

Thursday 21 April

Grace stopped in his tracks, staring in disbelief. He heard the scream of tyres. Saw Belling cartwheeling up over the bonnet of the car, smashing into the windscreen, then hurtling thirty feet, maybe higher, into the air, clothes shedding from him, two long, broken sticks each flying off in different directions.

Vehicles swerved, brakes squealing.

There was a thud, like a sack of potatoes dropped from a great height.

Then a moment of utter silence.

For an instant it was as if someone had pressed a freeze-frame button on a video.

Momentarily numb with shock, Grace looked at the scene in front of him, trying to absorb it.

The blue sky. The wide, well-kept road. The surface so black it might recently have been painted. Cars, a grey van, a man in Lycra on a bicycle, all stopped, many at strange angles as if some unseen hand was playing with a giant set of Dinky Toys and hadn't quite figured out where to put all the vehicles.

Then he saw a young man run to the middle of the road, towards the half-naked, crumpled heap, from where a long, dark stain of blood was spreading. He saw the man stop, turn away and throw up. Grace's head was spinning.

A woman was screaming. Standing, holding on to the door of her purple Honda Jazz, shaking, screeching like a banshee.

Two men were climbing out of the Lamborghini, which had a dented bonnet and cracked windscreen. The front of the roof was buckled.

Pulling himself together, Grace's professional training kicked in. He took out his phone, requested an ambulance and to be put through to the Ops-1 Inspector, informing him what had happened and requesting urgent police backup. Then, with the woman standing by the Honda still screeching, a piercing, terrible sound, he ran towards Belling.

And as he reached the body he had to swallow hard to avoid throwing up himself. He was looking down at a partially clad, legless torso. The head was split open, brain and blood leaking out. One leg, still covered by part of the grey suit trousers he had been wearing, was on the grass verge to his right; the other, bare, severed just above the knee, lay on the other side of the road, close to the cyclist.

A big, thuggish bloke of around thirty, in an anorak and baggy jeans, was walking towards the body, calmly filming with his phone.

In fury, Grace pulled out his warrant card. 'Police! Put that away and step back!'

God, he felt sick. How long would it take for the first backup car to get here?

What a bloody mess.

The thug, as if in defiance, was now filming one of the severed legs.

Grace stepped up to him, grabbed the phone and said, 'The taking of pictures is inappropriate.'

'Hey! Hey!' the man shouted. 'You can't take that!'

'I just did. You'll get it back when we're finished at the scene with the photos wiped. You're not Jake Gyllenhaal in *Nightcrawler*.'

Leaving the man open-mouthed, Grace turned away, pulled an evidence bag out of his pocket, slipped the phone in and sealed it. At least, he thought, grimly, this made leaving Guy Batchelor in charge of the crime scene less important. Their prime suspect was dead. The fact that he'd bolted said volumes. Innocent men didn't run away from the police. But a bully like Corin Belling might well have done – because bullies were often cowards.

Looking all around him again at this strange – almost surreal – scene, he realized just how far out of his comfort zone – and depth – he was.

The driver, a young, ashen-faced guy, wearing expensive-looking casual clothes and sporting a large gold medallion and several flashy rings, came slowly towards him, as if sleepwalking, followed by a man in his thirties in a smart suit. 'Police? Are you police?' the first man said.

'Yes.'

'I – I – oh God – he just came out in front of me. I – didn't have a chance.'

'No,' Grace corrected him. 'I saw it. It wasn't you who didn't have a chance, it was him. OK? What's your name?'

'Stavros. Stavros Karrass.'

'OK, Stavros Karrass, I'm arresting you on suspicion of causing death by dangerous driving. You do not have to say anything, but it may harm your defence if you do not mention when questioned something you later rely on in court. Anything you do say may be given in evidence. Now stay here with me.' He turned to the older man standing behind.

'Who are you?'

'I was the passenger – I'm Chris Bayross, the owner of Bayross Supercars.'

'OK, go and stand by the car and wait there until I come back to you. Don't get in the vehicle, and don't touch anything on it, understand?'

'Yes, sir.'

The driver, shaking badly, asked, 'Can – can – can I call my girlfriend – she's waiting – you know – in the dealership. She chose the car – she liked the colour, you see.'

'No phone calls, you've been arrested.'

Phone her, Grace thought, bitterly. *Tell her you like it, tell her it goes like a bat out of hell. Tell her it's a real head-turner.*

CHAPTER 28

Thursday 21 April

A whole mix of thoughts was tumbling through Roy Grace's spinning mind as Exton ran up to join him.

'Shit, Roy,' he said.

Grace pointed at the Lamborghini's driver, standing beside him. 'I've arrested this man – stay with him until backup arrives.'

He was thinking fast. He needed to protect the scene, that was the first and most important thing. He needed to get names and addresses of witnesses before they left. To his relief he heard the wail of the first siren, rapidly getting louder and closer. Then an engine started. A young woman in a grey and white Mini was about to drive away.

He sprinted over and stood in front of her car, his hands raised. She lowered her window, looking in complete shock. 'I – I've got to go, I'm late for a doctor's appointment.'

'I need your name and address, please.'

'I didn't really see anything.'

'Your name and address!' he said, abruptly. She immediately turned off the engine, startled.

Out of the corner of his eye he saw a liveried police BMW estate pull up. 'Stay here,' he commanded the woman, then ran over to the traffic car as the two Road Policing Unit officers climbed out.

He briefed them on what had happened and left them to secure the scene. One of the officers, PC David Puddle, whom he knew, told him he had blood running from his nose, and he wiped it away, gratefully. More sirens were now approaching. He ran back to the Mini and told the driver he was sorry, but she wasn't going anywhere for some time yet.

Puddle and his colleague, PC Simon Rogan, were hauling ROAD CLOSED signs out of the BMW's tailgate.

Twenty minutes later, with Belling's body and each leg covered with a small tent, an ambulance and more police cars had arrived, one belonging to the on-call RPU inspector, James Biggs, who took over command as the SIO. Officers were busily taking names and addresses of all witnesses.

Finally, satisfied the scene was now under control, Roy Grace gave Biggs a quick summary of what had happened, including the fact that he had arrested the driver of the Lamborghini, and told him he would be in touch later to give him a detailed statement. Then, with Exton, who had been relieved by a traffic officer, he walked back towards South Downs IT Solutions. He was going to have a lot of explaining to do, hours of bureaucracy ahead to satisfy the Independent Police Complaints Commission, who would automatically investigate. He was already thinking about the questions he'd be asked. Did you need to give chase? Did you shout any warnings? Could you see you were chasing him in a dangerous location? Did you need to chase him at all?

But that was for the future.

For now he had declined the offer of a PIM – a Post-Incident Manager – and had made arrangements to give an initial account about the circumstances of the arrest, chase and fatal accident. On his return from Germany he would present himself to give his detailed account. All officers were required to do this in any situation where death or serious injury followed police contact – known as a DSI. But that was the least of his worries at this moment.

Shaken to the core, he was having to make an effort to keep his focus. Why had Belling run? He'd said something about an argument – but he would have to deal with all of this later. His big worry at this moment was Munich. He was booked on an evening flight. Bruno was all packed and ready to come to England. Cleo had decorated the spare room for his arrival. Coming to England to live. Coming to England to bury his mother.

And for him to bury his former wife.

His own emotions were all over the place right

now. Somehow he was going to have to deal with all this and still go.

He had to go.

And meet a ten-year-old boy, for the first time, who was the son he had never known he had. He was more nervous about that than anything. Wondering how the little boy would be, what they would talk about. His son. A virtual stranger.

He called Puddle and Rogan to check they had everything they needed and left them to it.

He climbed into the car, planning to drive back to Police HQ where he had parked his Alfa earlier, with his packed suitcase in the boot, and then head up to the airport. But his hand was shaking so much he struggled to get the key into the ignition.

The general public assume police officers are immune to horror. But that wasn't his experience. Several officers he knew who had attended the recent Shoreham air disaster, when a vintage Hawker Hunter plane had crashed killing eleven people on the ground, had suffered severe post-traumatic stress disorder. Officers often needed counselling after attending cot deaths, or horrific murders, or traffic collisions. Anything.

How could you prepare any human being for what they might feel looking at a battered torso lying on a road?

He remembered the words of the Head of the Ambulance Service at a recent fund-raising dinner he'd attended with Cleo, in aid of the Sussex Police

Charitable Trust. '*Wearing a uniform does not protect you from trauma.*'

He'd be fine, he knew – somehow. He wouldn't need counselling. But he sure as hell was going to need a very stiff drink later, on the plane – or before he boarded. He was going to stay tonight at the home of the Munich Landeskriminalamt detective, Marcel Kullen, and one of the many things he liked about the guy and his wife was the copious quantities of alcohol they enjoyed when Kullen was off duty. He was sure going to need dosing up tonight, to get over the shock of what he had just seen – and all that awaited him tomorrow. Meeting with Sandy's lawyer, then meeting his son for the first time and flying back to England with him tomorrow evening for the start of his completely new, and alien, life – and his mother's funeral next week.

As he headed up the A23 he took a few deep breaths to calm himself down, before dialling Cassian Pewe's number on his hands-free. *Retaliate first* was one of his maxims. The ACC would have a field day over Belling's death if he heard about it second-hand. To his slight relief the phone was answered by Pewe's assistant, Allison Lawes. He gave her the details of what had happened and asked her to inform her boss that he would be out of the country for the following twenty-four hours.

Next he phoned Batchelor, who was still at Lorna Belling's rented flat.

The Home Office pathologist, Dr Theobald, had

arrived, Batchelor informed him, and was carrying out his initial, painstaking examination of the scene.

'I'm not sure whether what I have to say is good or bad news for you on Operation Bantam, Guy,' Grace said, and brought him up to speed.

'God, Roy, I'm sorry. But to be honest, I don't think anyone's going to miss that vile creep.'

'I'm with you on that one, Guy. But let's hold off celebrating until we get the DNA and post-mortem results.'

'I'll put the Champagne on ice, so it's ready.'

'I like your style!'

'Thanks, boss – and hey – I'm sorry you had to witness it, but it sounds like karma to me.'

'One thing Belling said to me was about an argument – can you find out what he meant by that?'

'I just heard from an NPT officer – apparently the bastard threw all the little puppies Lorna was breeding out into the street when he came home yesterday evening. A neighbour managed to rescue them before any were run over – they've been taken along with their mum to an animal welfare centre called Raystede for the moment until we establish if they're all spoken for or need to have new homes found for them – and the mother.'

'Good to know there are still some decent people in the world, Guy.'

'And it looks like one low-life has removed himself from the gene pool.'

'It does indeed. But let's wait for Frazer's confirmation before cracking the bottle, OK?'

'Yes, O Wise One!'

At least no smart-arsed lawyer was going to be getting Corin Belling off this one, Grace thought. He'd had that happen to him too often over the years. Equally, convictions had to be safe. If you locked up the wrong person on a murder charge, that meant the real killer was still at large – and might kill again.

Grace ended the call with a thin smile.

CHAPTER 29

Thursday 21 April

The Akashic Records. He'd been thinking about them since last night, amid all the other stuff that was going on inside his head. The Akashic Records were meant to be like a 24/7 video recording of every thought you had, every emotion that you felt and deed that you did during your time on earth. When you died you had to sit in a room with a representative of Big Goddy and talk through every moment of your life – and explain.

He hadn't been inside a church to pray since he was a child and had been dragged along to Assemblies by his Plymouth Brethren parents, who believed literally in every word of the Bible. The reward for their religious devotion was to be wiped out in their car by a tired French lorry driver who'd come off the Dieppe–Newhaven Channel ferry and had driven on the wrong side of the A26 a few miles north of the port, forgetting he was no longer in France.

His uncle and aunt, also members of the Brethren,

had told him they were such good people that God had recalled them early. They were lucky.

Of course! How lucky was that? What could be luckier than for the front bumper of a fully-laden eighteen-wheeler, weighing thirty-six tons, to come crashing through your Ford Escort's front windscreen and punch both your heads out through the rear window and fifty yards up the road?

He should have been in the car that day, en route to a prayer group. But God had given him mumps, so he was home in bed.

Mr Lucky.

Maybe he'd get lucky with those Akashic Records, too.

Awfully sorry, we had a technical glitch, your tapes got wiped. You've arrived here *tabula rasa*. We don't know your whereabouts on the afternoon and evening of Wednesday, 20th April. Are you OK with that? Have we missed anything significant?

Just like his parents, he had to hope luck ran in the family. Cling to that thought.

He was clinging to it tightly.

The one thing that worried him – slightly – was how easy he had found it to lie. To now believe completely in his innocence.

He needed to talk to someone, to explain. Someone who would understand, tell him it was OK, that under the circumstances he had done the right thing. Done what anyone would have done.

Perhaps he should talk to a shrink. But were they bound by the Hippocratic oath these days or had that changed? It used to be that if you fessed-up to a shrink, they had to keep it a secret. But did that still apply, or were they now obliged to report it? He was pretty sure the latter.

Maybe a priest would be better? The secrets of the confessional?

CHAPTER 30

Friday 22 April

Shite. Roy Grace's head was pounding. For some moments he could not figure out where on earth he was. The hideously bright green digits of a clock radio, inches from his face, read 4.53 a.m. A child was crying. Noah?

It didn't sound like Noah.

His mouth was parched and his head felt like someone had spent several hours poking red-hot wires through his skull.

Slowly it came back to him. He was in the guest room of Marcel Kullen's house, somewhere in the Munich suburbs. Just how much had they drunk last night?

The child cried again.

The Kullens had three young children; the youngest was two years old. He had originally intended to stay in a hotel but Marcel would not hear of it, and in truth, arriving at the airport a total bag of nerves about what awaited him in the morning, and still having flashbacks to the horrendous accident earlier in the day, he had been grateful for his hospitality. He liked Kullen and his pretty wife, Liese, and their small house had a cosy, welcoming feel. But, boy, did they pour drinks down his throat. Weissbier, followed by a local white wine, then a stonkingly powerful Italian red. Then a clear schnapps, followed by another. Then possibly a third. He'd gulped everything down, grateful for the calming effect of the booze, and the feeling of confidence it gave him about the next day.

But now, as he rummaged through his overnight bag, desperately hoping he had some paracetamol in there, somewhere, he wondered just what it was about the human brain which told you that if you had just one more digestif late at night, you'd feel a lot better in the morning than if you didn't have it?

To his relief he found the small blue packet. Just two tablets left. He popped them out of the blister pack and downed them with an entire glass of water, then climbed back into bed and double-checked the time on his phone. And saw a text message from Cleo.

> Miss you. Love you. Hope it's all going OK.
> Sleep tight my darling. XXXX

Shit. It had been sent at 10.30. Was that UK or German time – and how come he hadn't seen it? He wondered whether to reply but decided against, not wanting the ping to wake her. An hour ahead here, it was only coming up to 4 a.m. in England. He'd call her at 7 a.m., her time, hoping he'd catch her before she left for work.

Switching off the light, he lay back on the soft pillow, beneath the heavy duvet, and closed his eyes, hoping the pills would kick in quickly. Outside he heard the first tweets of the dawn chorus. A big day today. Massive. Meeting his son and taking him to England. To his new home, new life.

And it sounded like he had a major charm offensive ahead. Bruno was currently staying with his best friend, Erik Lippert. Yesterday evening, when he had landed in Munich, Grace had spoken on the phone to the friend's mother, Anette, about today's arrangements. She'd warned him that Bruno was, understandably, very distressed by his mother's death, and not at all happy at the prospect of being taken away from his homeland.

Just how great was it going to be today to meet his son with a hangover, breath stinking of alcohol, and a developing bruise, thanks to Corin Belling, on one cheek?

He wished he'd thought to bring his jogging kit, so he could have gone for a run and got the booze out of his system and cleared his head. He lay tossing and turning, desperate for another hour or so of sleep, but just felt increasingly wide awake, watching the minutes tick away. Then the crying began again.

Finally, at 5.30, he switched the light back on, got out of bed, dressed, pulled on his coat, and let himself out of the house in the dark, chilly dawn air. Across the road a small BMW started up, the reversing lights came on and it backed out into the street. He breathed in the smell of the exhaust as the driver accelerated away, the engine making a harsh rasp, then began to walk, after logging his bearings.

It was strange, he thought, as he crossed a road and carried on past the dark, curtained windows of houses. For many years – well over a decade now – Sandy had often dominated his waking thoughts, and, at least once a week, his dreams. For a long time he had felt he could never move forward in life until he knew what had happened to her. Now he did know the truth – or at least some of it – and it didn't make him feel any better.

In some ways, quite the reverse.

A road-sweeping truck was coming towards him, brushes swirling. He walked on past it, then made a right turn into a small park. His thoughts switched for some moments to the crime scene he had left in the Hove seafront flat. Lorna Belling dead in the bathtub. Then the sight of Corin Belling's body cartwheeling past the yellow Lamborghini.

Case closed?

Why would Belling have done a runner when he and Exton had gone to his office to see him, then punched him in the face and run off again, if he wasn't guilty? Surely not because there'd been an incident and he had thrown her tiny puppies out into the street – something that made Roy Grace, who loved dogs, really angry.

Equally, he knew he always had to keep personal prejudices out of any investigation. If you summarily believed someone was guilty, you were in danger of obstructing the search for the truth. This would be a good case for Guy to cut his teeth on.

A woman in a tracksuit jogged past him, murmuring *guten morgen*. She was out of earshot by the time he replied, his focus switched back to the day ahead – and beyond.

He wished now that he'd encouraged Cleo to come with him to Germany. But she had been resolute in her view that he needed to have some time with his son on their own. The little boy already had a huge amount to contend with. Being uprooted would have a massive impact on him in ways they could not even guess. They were going to have to take it very gently, one step at a time.

He and Cleo had spent many hours during recent evenings googling about introducing a step-child into a family with a baby. One issue was what Bruno might call her, and she him. Son? Stepson? They had decided it was best to wait to see what Bruno was most comfortable with. She didn't mind whether she would be known by him as 'mum' or Cleo – or something totally different. Whatever the case, it wasn't going to be an easy transition for any of them. They couldn't expect to meet one day and all be best friends the next.

It was going to take time and a lot of effort – which he and Cleo were completely prepared for.

What could he say at the funeral in England next week that would be meaningful? How many people would be attending? Sandy's parents, an aunt and uncle and four cousins. She had never been one for friends in England. She had just one girlfriend, Chantal Rickards, and they'd never been that close. Chantal had genuinely been as surprised as he was by her sudden disappearance nearly eleven years ago. She'd told Chantal that it was hard at times being married to a cop who was married to his work, but she said she had accepted that.

A few of his friends and colleagues would attend, among them Glenn for sure, and Norman said he wanted to come. And his old friend Dick Pope, also a detective, and his wife, Leslie. He and Sandy had been good friends with them – and had been due to go out for dinner with them to celebrate his thirtieth birthday on the night that she'd disappeared. They had been good to him in those terrible months immediately after, inviting him over for meals and providing lots of support. But when Dick had later transferred to the Met they'd moved closer to London, and he barely saw them any more. He was glad they were coming.

He was less glad about Sandy's parents, who were making things awkward. He'd learned long ago not to take the fact that they didn't like him personally – so far as he could see, they didn't actually like anyone, not even each other. Her mother looked permanently angry and her fantasist father, Derek, spent his time immersed in the world of model Second World War aircraft, telling anyone who would listen how his father had flown seventy-five missions in the legendary Dambusters squadron. In fact, his father had never even been up in the air during the war – sure, he was stationed at 617 Squadron at Lossiemouth in Scotland, but he was an aircraft fitter and never left the ground.

But now, decades later, Derek Balkwill had finally managed to drop a bombshell himself. He and his wife had decided they wanted a Catholic funeral for Sandy because, they informed him, they had brought her up Catholic. It was news to him.

When he and Sandy had married it had been an Anglican service and neither of her parents had made any comment then. Subsequently Sandy had pretty much rejected all religion, and had once told Roy that if she died before him, she would want a Humanist funeral. He'd told Derek and Margot Balkwill this at a tense meeting at their house last week, after breaking the news to them over the phone. He'd been there for nearly an hour before being offered anything to drink – a miserably weak cup of tea that tasted like it was the bag's third or fourth outing. Margot was the kind of woman so mean he could imagine her hanging used teabags out to dry.

'It's the boy you have to think of,' she had said, coldly and a bit oddly. 'This funeral is not about our daughter – we lost her years ago. We all know what our daughter wanted, which was to turn her back on us all. Now it's about our grandson. We need to nurture his spiritual wellbeing. Bring him up in the sight of our Lord.'

Eventually they reached an uncomfortable compromise. It would be a religious service but an Anglican one – and Grace would approach the senior police chaplain to see if he would be willing to conduct it, which he had done. The Reverend Smale had asked Roy if he or anyone would be giving a eulogy. It was something he had been thinking about and had not yet come to any conclusion. What could he say – just talk about the Sandy he had known? But then how would Bruno feel, to have a total stranger suddenly talking about how wonderful his mother had been?

He tried to put himself in Bruno's shoes. How would he have felt in this situation? But he didn't know. He really didn't. And he hadn't long to figure it out.

CHAPTER 31

Friday 22 April

Dr Frazer Theobald was trying to figure it out. In the grey grimness of the tiled postmortem room at Brighton and Hove City Mortuary, and the sense of studious concentration around the dead woman, Guy Batchelor, who had barely slept all night, was trying to lighten his mood by recalling an observation someone made, years back, in classic police gallows humour, describing the hollowed-out torsos of bodies.

Canoes.

Right now, Lorna Belling's torso, opened all the way down, her sternum removed, along with all her internal organs, did indeed look, with a small stretch of warped imagination, like a canoe.

Coroner's Officer Michelle Websdale, the CSI video photographer James Gartrell, as well as Cleo and her assistant, Darren, all stood in attendance, whilst the Home Office pathologist proceeded at his normal pedestrian pace through his examination and dissection of each of her internal organs, pausing frequently to dictate notes into a recorder he kept on a shelf on the far side of the room.

Something else made the DI smirk, more gallows humour. The knowledge that husband and wife were both in Sussex mortuaries right now. Victim and offender. Corin Belling was in one of the fridges in Haywards Heath mortuary. His post-mortem would be done by Theobald after he completed this one.

A family affair!

He stepped out of the room, not wanting anyone to see the grin on his face, walked through to the tiny office and switched on the kettle to make himself a cup of coffee. But, actually, after his sombre time in the tiny flat while Theobald carried out his inch-by-inch examination of Lorna's body, and now this long, slow process, he was starting to feel elated. What a golden opportunity had fallen into his lap. His very first murder as a deputy SIO, and every chance it could be wrapped up in the next twenty-four hours, giving him the kudos, thanks to Roy having to be away.

The fingerprints on the beer cans already put Corin Belling at the scene. The DNA results on the cigarette butts in the flat should be back imminently, and hopefully they would add further confirmation of Belling, a chain-smoker, being there.

He unscrewed the lid of the coffee jar and spooned two heaped teaspoons into the mug, then poured in the milk – something his Swedish wife, Lena, had taught him. It stopped the boiling water from scorching the grounds, and made it taste more like percolated coffee.

Just as he picked up the kettle, his phone rang. It was Roy Grace.

'Boss!' he said. 'How's it going in Munich?'

'Just about to go and meet my son,' he replied. 'What's the latest?'

'Theobald is hard at work, we should be finished sometime before the start of the next ice age.'

'DNA on those butts back yet?'

'No, I'm about to chase the lab.'

'Anything else?'

'No, boss, we're good. Just wondering if we need to hold a press briefing, but at the moment it looks such an open-and-shut case I don't know if there's any point. Shall I wait until you come back?'

'Unless there are any unexpected developments, yes.'

'OK – and – er – boss – I'm sorry for what happened yesterday afternoon – you know – sorry for you – but I really think that Corin Belling running, then giving you a smack in the face, says it all. He's just a piece of shit – sorry – let me rephrase that – he's now several pieces of shit!'

Roy Grace laughed. 'Let's hope when they start putting him back together they don't find a bit left over – like I always used to do as a kid putting together model aircraft.'

'I'll make sure of it.'

Grace smiled.

'Good luck today, Roy. Tough call.'

There was a long silence. Then a very distant and faint, 'Yes.'

Batchelor ended the call and poured the water into his coffee, stirred it and noticed how much his hand was shaking. He hadn't had any breakfast, he remembered. He'd climbed out of bed feeling totally shattered, made himself a double Nespresso, then showered, shaved, dressed and driven straight here. He removed the lid of the biscuit tin, munched a couple of shortbread biscuits, and then carried his mug through to the postmortem room.

As he entered, he felt a change in the atmosphere. The short and stocky pathologist was staring at him with his beady, nut-brown eyes, the only feature of his face currently visible.

'Detective Inspector Batchelor,' he said, holding up a glass vial with an air almost of triumph. 'I have found something that may be significant.'

CHAPTER 32

Friday 22 April

Guy Batchelor stared at Frazer Theobald. 'What?'

'The presence of semen.'

'So she's a sailor?'

Theobald looked at Guy Batchelor strangely. Humour had never been a part of the pathologist's canon of talents. Most people, when thinking about it, realized they had never even seen Dr Frazer Theobald smile. 'Sailor?' he quizzed.

'Sorry, just a bad joke. Semen. *Sea men.*'

The pathologist continued to stare at him, without getting it. 'I'm afraid you've lost me.'

Batchelor noticed the creases around Gartrell's and Websdale's eyes. They were both grinning.

'It's OK. What can you tell us about it – are you able to say how recently she had intercourse before she died?'

Theobald lowered his mask, revealing almost in full his Groucho Marx moustache. With his diminutive frame, all he needed was a large cigar to complete the look, Batchelor thought, struggling to keep that thought to himself.

'Without laboratory examination, I can't tell you how fresh it is, but I would estimate that sexual intercourse had occurred within the last forty-eight hours. From the briefing you gave me, I understood this unfortunate lady was renting the flat she was found in as some kind of a bolthole – to get away from her abusive husband. I would hardly consider the presence of semen to be a surprise. You told me earlier that her husband's fingerprints were found in this apartment, indicating his knowledge of it. It is reasonable to assume that he had sex with her, consensually or otherwise. Unless of course she was having an affair. DNA will establish this one way or another.'

'I'll get it fast-tracked,' Batchelor said.

Theobald carried on, while the DI made notes on his pad, intending to update Roy Grace in a short while and ask him how he wanted him to handle the investigation from here.

Something bothered him a lot about the semen. Sure, to the Home Office pathologist the presence of it in the woman's vagina, given the circumstance of her relationship with her abusive, dominating husband, was entirely plausible. But not to Guy Batchelor.

It told him a very different story.

Had she met a lover there? Had sex with him? The DNA result, which could be back in twenty-four hours, with luck, might provide an answer.

If it came back with a match to the husband, and his DNA was found on the beer cans which had been sent to the lab following the fingerprint identification, then it would be case closed.

But if not?

He hoped so much it would turn out to be the husband. To have solved this before Roy Grace had even returned from Germany would make him look very good.

But a feeling he could not explain told him that this wasn't the whole picture.

CHAPTER 33

Friday 22 April

Nothing, in all his life, had prepared Roy Grace for this moment. He'd dealt with horrific crime scenes, including a father who had murdered his baby son, a beautiful young woman murdered for a snuff movie, and a decent young doctor's charred remains found on a golf course.

Little shocked him any more.

Little scared him.

But right now, just before midday, as Marcel Kullen pulled up his white VW Sirocco outside the Lipperts' elegant modern villa in the Gräfelfing district of west Munich, he was shaking. Before leaving England he had debated what to wear. Both Cleo and his style guru, Glenn Branson, had texted him advising him to go casual. Glenn had urged him to look cool, adding with his usual dry humour that he didn't want his son's first impression of him to be a dull old fart – he'd find that out soon enough . . .

So, with Kullen wishing him luck, he removed

the chewing gum from his mouth, climbed out of the car dressed in leather jacket over a black T-shirt, jeans and boots, and shut the door behind him. As he walked up to the house he realized he was still shaking, aware Bruno's eyes might already be on him, watching from behind one of the windows. It felt like a blender had been switched on inside his stomach. But at least his pounding head was calming down.

Something his friend had said last night resonated, repeating over and over. *Remember this, Roy, your last shirt has no pockets.*

He couldn't get that damned expression out of his head.

We come into this world with nothing, and we don't need pockets when we leave it, because we take nothing away with us; nothing to put in our pockets, Marcel Kullen had explained. *Whatever we have is left behind for others.*

Sandy was gone, and had left him Bruno.

What the hell was he going to say to him when he went through that door – the home of Bruno's best friend, Erik, where Bruno had been staying since his mother, Sandy, had been run over by a taxi and lay comatose in hospital. Before hanging herself in her room soon after she had begun, seemingly, to recover.

And charging him in her suicide letter with their son's care.

Glancing over his shoulder, he saw Marcel Kullen smiling at him. He gave him a cursory nod.

Could anyone possibly have any idea what was going through his mind right now?

As he rang the bell he found himself, irrationally, hoping – praying – that no one would be in.

The door opened.

CHAPTER 34

Friday 22 April

A casually dressed red-haired woman in her thirties stood there with a welcoming smile. 'Roy?'

He held out his hand. 'Anette?'

She nodded, and stared at him intently. 'Wow, your son is so like you!'

'Really?'

'Incredible!'

He noticed a rucksack and two large suitcases in the hallway behind her.

'Would you like some coffee? Or perhaps as an Englishman you'd prefer some tea?'

'OK. Coffee would be good, thank you.'

'Would your friend like to come in?'

'No, thank you, he's happy to wait. I think it would be best if I'm on my own.'

'Yes, I think so. You met with Andreas Thomas?'

'Yes, I've just come from his office.'

'I think he's a good lawyer.'

'I liked him – he seems very sensible and practical.'

'Good.' Then she looked hard at him again and smiled. 'You really are just so alike!'

A lanky, serious-looking man, dressed in a sweat-shirt and jogging bottoms, appeared in the hall.

'This is my husband, Ingo,' she said.

The two men shook hands.

'It's good to meet you,' her husband said, also in excellent English with a pronounced American accent.

'I'm very grateful to you both – and your son – for taking care of Bruno.'

'It has not been a problem, I think our Erik has enjoyed having his company. He is going to miss him,' Ingo said, a tad stiffly. 'So are you ready to meet your son?'

He smiled, nervously. 'Absolutely!'

They led him through into a large, bright modern kitchen, with a view out onto a sizeable, well-kept garden, mostly laid to lawn, and woods beyond. Two goalposts, complete with nets, were positioned on part of the lawn.

'Is Erik keen on football?' Grace asked.

'Crazy about it!' his father replied.

'What team does he support?'

'Bayern, of course! But also he likes in your country Manchester United.'

'Oh?'

Ingo shrugged. 'Bruno, also, he likes football.'

'I'll have to get him to switch his allegiance to Brighton – the Seagulls!'

'He's been talking about them.'

'Good.' Then he hesitated. 'So, how is he?'

He caught the fleeting glance between the German couple, before Ingo responded. 'Oh, he's doing well, you know. It's difficult, yes?'

'Incredibly, I would imagine.'

There was an uncomfortable silence.

'But he's a strong boy,' Anette added, with a reassurance in her voice that was not matched by her expression.

And in that moment, picking up on their unease, he thought, but did not say, *They can't wait for him to be gone.*

Anette called out, up the stairs, 'Bruno! Your father is here!' Then she walked over to the coffee machine and began filling it with water.

Ingo ushered Grace to the island unit in the middle of the kitchen and both men sat up on bar stools.

'You and your wife speak very good English,' Grace said, politely, then instantly wished he had used this time to ask him something about Bruno.

'We were for three years in New York.'

'Ah, right. Great city.'

'Oh sure.'

'So, can you give me any advice about Bruno – from what you know of him?'

He noticed the evasive look in the man's eyes. 'Advice? Well – you know – Anette and I—'

Then he fell silent. Grace saw that he was looking past him, and turned.

An extremely good-looking, slim, small boy

stood in the entrance to the room. Still. As if he had appeared like a ghost.

And Roy Grace's heart stopped.

The boy was dressed in a checked shirt, tight chinos and a canvas jacket. His hair was gelled and neatly brushed, and his expression was intensely serious.

Christ. It could have been his father standing there. A miniature – bonsai – version of his dad, Jack Grace.

He slid off the stool, then walked towards him. It felt as if he was walking in slow motion. Aware of the eyes of both Lipperts on him.

The boy's face was blank, registering absolutely no emotion. As if he was on sentry duty.

As he reached the boy, he was uncertain for a moment whether to hug Bruno or more formally shake his hand. He stopped in front of him and smiled.

He hadn't known what to expect, he realized. The kid to run towards him screaming, 'Papa, Papa, Papa,' with delight? A handshake?

Then the boy held out his hand, and Roy's heart began to melt.

'Bruno,' Roy said, shaking the small, warm hand. 'Hello. I'm your father.'

There was a long, awkward moment as the two of them stood there, father and son. Total strangers, but with one immensely strong link. He continued to hold the boy's hand, afraid to let it go, to break this tiny bond between them.

'Hello, Papa,' the boy said quietly, with a slight American accent.

'It's great to meet you, Bruno. Listen, I'm so sorry about everything – I wish we could be meeting in a different situation. How are you feeling about coming to England?' He let go of the boy's hand and it dropped to his side.

Bruno looked down at the floor with a forlorn expression, as if he was close to tears.

There had been few occasions in his life when Roy Grace had been lost for words. This was one of them. As he stared back at the sad-looking youngster he struggled, very hard, to think of something more to say.

It felt like an eternity before the right thing occurred to him. 'I'm told you like football – what team do you support?'

The boy's reply was a barely audible whisper. 'Bayern.'

'I like football, too.'

Bruno said nothing for some moments, then he asked, very politely, 'Do you support Bayern, too?'

'I think they're brilliant,' Roy said with a smile. 'I watch them a lot in the Champions League, but my home team is Brighton, the Seagulls.'

His son nodded, then said, 'They have a good season so far.'

'That's right, they've had a run of bad luck just recently, but should make the play-offs.'

Again the boy nodded. Then he asked, with a

sudden flash of excitement in his eyes, 'Will you take me to a football match?'

'Sure, of course. You'd like that?'

He shrugged. 'If they are any good.'

Grace smiled, happy to have a channel of communication with him, and feeling a burst of optimism. It was going to work out fine, it really was.

He hoped.

CHAPTER 35

Friday 22 April

As the postmortem continued, with Dr Frazer Theobald moving at his customary slow – at times glacially slow – pace, Guy Batchelor stepped away several times into the tiny office, to make calls. He was trying to find a relative of Lorna Belling who could make the formal identification of her body, as well as assembling his enquiry team, but it wasn't proving easy. She had a sister who was in Australia, whom he had managed to contact, but it would be at least two days before she arrived in England. And Lorna's parents, who were on a cruise, had been contacted, but could not get back here until sometime after the weekend.

He appointed a crime scene manager, an office manager, a POLSA – police search advisor – a HOLMES team, an analyst, and the small group of detectives Roy Grace had requested, all but two of whom were available. The first briefing would be at 6 p.m. this evening.

He had already organized an outside enquiry

team, and set their parameters. They were to speak to the landlord and the letting agent, if there was one; to all Lorna Belling's neighbours in the building; to check any CCTV footage they could find in the immediate surrounding areas to see if they could place the husband around the flat; to try to make contact with her friends; and to contact her dead husband's work colleagues to see if he'd disclosed anything to them. A search of the Bellings' home was currently under way, and any computers or phones found there would be taken to Digital Forensics – formerly known as the High Tech Crime Unit – to be interrogated. Batchelor also instructed them to make sure they found the appointments book for Lorna's hairdressing clients.

Determined to make a good impression in his first SIO role, he logged on to the Murder Manual, ticking through every rigid step of a murder enquiry, dutifully and laboriously writing his decisions down in his pale-blue Policy Book. It was the document with which all SIOs covered their backs – details of every decision you made, and the reasons. If an investigation ever went south and you were called to account, you had it right there, in black and white. And in this modern age of accountability in the police force, where you walked constantly on eggshells, it seemed at times, sadly, that covering your back had become almost more important than solving the crime.

He felt pleased that this one was falling into place. If the lab could follow up the fingerprints on the beer cans with DNA matches from around the tops of the cans and maybe on the cigarette butts – and add to that the husband's DNA from the semen in Lorna Belling's vagina – it would be strong evidence. Overwhelming.

Case closed.

Then his phone rang. It was Cassian Pewe. And he was surprised at what the Assistant Chief Constable was telling him. Equally, there was no way he could refuse.

'Yes, sir,' he said, bemused, as he ended the call. 'Of course we'll look after him, sir. It will be a pleasure.'

CHAPTER 36

Friday 22 April

As Marcel Kullen drove him and Bruno from the Lipperts' house, Grace heard the ping of an incoming text and glanced at his phone. It was a message from Guy Batchelor:

> Hi Roy, tried calling but it goes to voice-mail. Pls call me urgently.

He apologized to Kullen, and to Bruno on the rear seat, who appeared absorbed in something on his phone, and called Batchelor immediately. He answered on the first ring. 'Boss, sorry to bother you at such a tough time.'

'It's no problem – what's up?'

'We have a new member of our team foisted on us by Pewe – one of these Direct Entry guys.'

'What?'

The Home Secretary had introduced a controversial new scheme under which people from civilian life – the community at large – could bypass all the usual training and career ladder process of the police force, and instead of starting as probationers, then becoming constables, then moving on through the ranks, were able to come straight into the police at inspector level and higher.

Grace understood that there were advantages to having people with business experience coming into the force, but the value they could bring, in his view, was in management roles – not operational ones.

'The ACC has dumped a civilian bean-counter on us, in the role of detective inspector.'

'What do you know about him?'

'Get this. He was previously a sales manager at a pharmaceutical company and you're going to love his name. Donald Dull.'

'You're kidding. Sounds like a real Mickey Mouse detective!'

'Very good, boss. He pronounces it *Dool.*'

'Have you met him?'

'I've got that treat coming up shortly. He's going to be just the kind of person I'd be happy to know was behind me, protecting my back as I crash through the door of an armed suspect.'

'OK, I can't do much right now. Just put him in a role where he's not any danger to any of the team – or himself. I'll do what I can when I get back.'

'What's the police motto?' Batchelor said. 'To serve and protect? I thought we were meant to protect the public, not count their sodding beans!'

CHAPTER 37

Friday 22 April

Like everyone in Major Crime, Guy Batchelor was still getting used to his new surroundings. For all the inadequacies of their old HQ in Hollingbury, at least there had been parking in and around the place. Here most of the team had to leave their private cars a good fifteen to twenty minutes' walk away from the entrance, angering the local residents by taking their parking spaces, to the point where cars were being vandalized. Officers heading home, exhausted after a long shift, were finding they had flat tyres, or worse, keyed paintwork.

One of the perks for Batchelor of his current role was that he was permitted to use an HQ car park.

At a quarter to six in the evening he settled into one of the twenty red chairs arranged around the long, light-coloured table in the narrow conference room on the first floor. The cream walls were bare, apart from a large flat-screen monitor and a round white clock. On one end of the table sat a Polycom telephone conferencing device that looked a bit like a three-legged drone. It had a round, brushed-metal head on a stalk that, voice-activated, would swivel disconcertingly like a robot towards whoever might be speaking.

He'd set up four whiteboards. On one, headed OPERATION BANTAM, were crime-scene photographs of the victim; on the next were postmortem photographs; on the third was an association chart for Lorna Belling, to which was also pinned a police mugshot of her husband, Corin; and on the fourth a street map of the area around her flat, with the building ringed in red.

He suddenly noticed one of his team had stuck on the door the name of the operation, together with an image from the old film *Chicken Run*. It brought a smile to his face.

In front of him, Guy had placed a mug of coffee, his Policy Book and the notes for the briefing printed out by Roy Grace's secretary. He ran through them, feeling apprehensive at managing his first ever murder briefing as an SIO, yet confident they were already close to a conclusion. Supremely confident, actually, thanks to the information that had just come in.

Ten minutes later his team was assembled around the table. There were the trusty regulars that Grace favoured, DS Norman Potting, DS Jon Exton, DC Jack Alexander, as well as DC Kevin Hall, the temporary replacement for Tanja Cale who was away on holiday, David Watkinson, the Office Manager, Georgie English, the Crime Scene

Manager, Sergeant Lorna Dennison-Wilkins, the POLSA, and Annalise Vineer, the HOLMES indexer. In addition there were two new detective constables, Velvet Wilde, a slim, attractive woman in her late twenties, with close-cropped blonde hair and a distinct Belfast accent, who had recently moved from uniform to CID, and Arnie Crown, a short, wiry American of thirty-six, who had been seconded to Major Crime from the FBI as part of an exchange.

In addition they were also lumbered with the Direct Entry detective inspector, Donald Dull. He looked fittingly named, a quiet, mild-tempered man in his late thirties, in a slightly old-fashioned suit. With his porcine figure he looked like he would have struggled with the 'beep' test – the fitness test that officers had to pass every year. But maybe Direct Entries were exempt from this, Guy wondered – especially if they were Cassian Pewe's pet. Peering into a tablet in front of him, over the top of a pair of half-frames, Dull exuded all the charisma of a back-room accountant. Batchelor sensed he was going to be trouble.

'This is the first briefing of Operation Bantam, the investigation into the death of Lorna Jane Belling,' Batchelor read from his notes, and went on to outline the circumstances surrounding her death, and the initial findings of the pathologist. 'After an assault, causing a head trauma, and a possible attempt at strangulation, resulting in severe bruising round her neck and sufficient oxygen starvation to cause petechial haemorrhages, death appears to have been caused either by electrocution from a hairdryer dropped into the bathtub where she was partially immersed or by head trauma. We are not ruling out suicide at this stage.'

Norman Potting raised a hand, and Batchelor acknowledged him. 'Yes, Norman?'

Potting's hair was short, after having his head shaven for a recent undercover operation. Everyone thought this style suited him, and looked a lot better than his usual limp comb-over. It also knocked a good decade off his fifty-five years. Wearing a smart blue suit he'd been given for the same operation and new glasses, he was looking almost cool. His rural West Country accent was the only remnant of his former persona. 'Guv, is it established it was the same offender who strangled her and put the hairdryer into the bath?'

'Good question, Norman. No, not at this stage. On the balance of probability it would seem likely, but there were no prints found on the hairdryer nor round her neck, so we can't be certain.'

'Unless this lady had a lot of enemies,' Jon Exton said, with his usual serious intensity, 'it would be a bit of a stretch to think that one person strangled her and left her for dead, and another person entered the flat and finished her off.'

'I have some further evidence that has just come in this afternoon,' Batchelor said. 'As I mentioned to a number of you earlier, we have a prime suspect, her husband, Corin. There is already considerable evidence linking him to the crime. During the past year Lorna has called the police to report instances of domestic abuse by him. The most recent was on Monday of this week, when she complained he had tried to push dog crap into her mouth. He was angered by the mess the litter of puppies she had bred was making. He was arrested, but she refused to press charges, out of fear I understand, and he was released on Tuesday evening, a day before we believe she was killed.'

'What a bastard,' Potting said.

'His fingerprints were found on a couple of empty beer cans at a flat she had rented in Hove – possibly as a bolthole to get away from the husband.' Batchelor pointed at the red-circled area on the street map. 'There were also a number of cigarette butts of the Silk Cut brand he is known to have smoked found at this same address – we've established from the victim's sister that she was a non-smoker. We had these butts and the beer cans sent for fast-track DNA testing and the results have just come back in. His DNA has been found present in saliva around the tops of two cans, as well as on two cigarette butts. During the post-mortem, Theobald found semen in her vagina, indicating she had intercourse sometime shortly before her death.'

'Could it have been after, boss?' Kevin Hall asked in his friendly but blunt voice.

'A bit of necrophilia?' Potting butted in. 'Dead good sex, eh?'

He looked around, but no one laughed, or even grinned.

'Thanks, Norman,' Batchelor said, sharply, then replied to Hall. 'It's a possibility – we'll know more when it has been analysed. At this stage my hypothesis is that once released from custody, the husband went to the flat and killed her. We're hoping that the DNA from the semen will add strength to this theory. If it is him, there will need to be a review and of course the Independent Police Complaints Commission will become involved, looking into the circumstances of his release. It's just unfortunate that the husband will never be brought to trial – I think all of you know the circumstances of his death? Detective Superintendent Grace and DS Exton went to his office to talk to him, and he did a runner, which is a fairly good indicator of his guilt.'

'A good defence brief would get him off, guv,' Potting said.

'Oh?'

'He'd just say he was legless at the time.'

Even Batchelor found himself grinning at this. As the SIO, perhaps he should have considered coming down on him like a ton of bricks. But he knew the old detective was still in a fragile state following the death of his fiancée, Detective Sergeant Bella Moy. And, dammit, when he'd first joined Major Crime, gallows humour had been everyone's way of coping.

DI Dull raised a hand. 'Guy, I don't want to be the party pooper—'

'But you're going to be, right?' Batchelor retorted, interested to see what this new addition to the team had to say.

'Well, I hope not. I'm just bothered by this *bolt-hole* idea.' Dull tapped a key on his tablet. 'From what we already know, Lorna Belling had been renting this flat for some time. I've done a spreadsheet on rents in the area.' He began to pass round copies. 'The rent she has been paying is relatively low for the area, because of the condition of the place, but even so, how could she have afforded it, working from home as a hairdresser? I've done another spreadsheet on the charges made by home hairdressers – compared to those in salons.'

'Huh!' interjected David Watkinson. 'You should see my wife's hairdressing bill. The bloke she goes to could afford to rent Buckingham Palace!'

'Not as much as our young DC here spends on his barnet!' Norman Potting said, ruffling Jack Alexander's hair, much to his irritation.

'Well,' Dull said. 'That's not exactly my point. If she rented a bolthole to escape from her husband, she'd have done a runner there a long time ago. I think we might be making a dangerous assumption here.'

'OK, Donald, so what do you think?' Batchelor said.

'Maybe it's not a bolthole but a secret love nest, boss. A year and a half on, something's gone wrong. They had a lovers' tiff that turned violent?'

Batchelor nodded. 'It's a possibility, but don't

dismiss the DNA evidence from the beer cans and cigarette butts. We need to find out if any neighbours heard arguing or a fight. I will make it one of our lines of enquiry.'

The Crime Scene Manager, Georgie English, raised her arm. 'Sir, I've a number of concerns about what we haven't been able to find. The first is any laptop belonging to Lorna. We found a Mac charger plugged into a wall in the kitchen of the home she shared with her husband. We know he was a PC user – from the laptop that was recovered from his office. Also, we found her mobile phone on the kitchen table in the house. Isn't it a bit strange for anyone to leave home without their phone these days? Unless of course they've forgotten it?'

'Good thinking, Georgie,' Batchelor said. 'That would explain why there was no mobile phone at the flat.'

'But not the computer, right?' Arnie Crown said.

'If we work on the hypothesis that the husband murdered her,' Batchelor said, 'perhaps he took the computer because he was worried it might contain something incriminating him. Maybe she had been keeping a log of his abuse? Does he have anywhere he might have hidden it? The other possibility is he dumped it somewhere. The phone has been sent to Digital Forensics – let's see what their analysis and interrogation of it brings.'

She nodded, satisfied, and then continued to give the team an overview of the forensic search of the flat to date. 'There is some evidence to suggest many of the surfaces have been wiped clean, possibly with a disinfectant; there are a number of marks that we have developed for fingerprint assessment; we have taken multiple swabs and we have seized a number of items that will be subject to further forensic examination. I hope we will have finished our work there in the next twenty-four hours.'

Batchelor jotted a reminder in his Investigator's Notebook to update his Policy File after the briefing, then continued. 'If we recap, we have a known abusive relationship; we have fingerprint and DNA evidence putting Lorna's husband, Corin, at her flat; we have the fact that he did a runner when approached by Detective Superintendent Grace; we have the fact that he assaulted Roy when apprehended, and ran on. If we get a positive result back from the lab on the DNA from the semen in Lorna's vagina, confirming it's her husband – then things wouldn't be looking too good for him.'

'I'd say they're not looking too good for him right now,' Arnie Crown said. 'He's in a mortuary fridge minus his legs, with his head cracked open like a coconut.'

'Yep,' Jack Alexander said. 'If you think you're having a bad day, you know what? His is probably worse.'

CHAPTER 38

Friday 22 April

Roy Grace, accompanying Bruno, limped across the short-term airport car park. It was just gone 8 p.m. His right leg was in agony after his cramped seat on the flight. Despite his coaxing, the boy had eaten nothing during the journey, although he had at least drunk a small Coke on the plane. Bruno had his rucksack on his back and Grace carried his son's two suitcases as well as his own overnight bag. They had with them all his worldly belongings, except for his drum kit, which had been sent on by road and should arrive early next week.

So far nearly all his efforts to engage Bruno in conversation had failed. He seemed very distressed and had spent almost the entire journey concentrating on a game on his phone. Grace had asked him about school, about what sports other than football he liked, what were his favourite foods, what he liked to watch on television, what computer games he liked to play.

To every question the only responses had been short and distracted.

As they approached his black Alfa, and he pressed the key fob, unlocking it and making its tail lights flash, he saw a sudden flicker of interest in Bruno's face.

'Do you like cars?' Grace asked, hoping the idea of a ride to his new home in a sports car might cheer the boy up.

'My mother had a Porsche Cayman Carrera. Its top speed was two hundred and ninety-two kilometres per hour. How fast does this go?'

'Fast, but not that fast.'

'How fast?'

'I'm not sure of its top speed. We're restricted in England to seventy miles per hour – that's about one hundred and twelve kilometres.'

'In Germany we have no speed limits on the autobahns.'

'Yup, I know.' Roy Grace opened the boot and hefted the cases in. 'Fun, eh?'

'*Ja*.'

Bruno walked round to the driver's door and opened it.

'You going to drive?' Grace asked him.

'Your wheel's on the wrong side,' Bruno said.

'That's the side we drive on here.'

'Why do you drive on the wrong side?'

'Well, about a quarter of the world drives on this side – on the left.'

'Why do they do that? What happens if they meet on a bridge between two countries? One driving on the right and one on the left? There could be a big accident!'

'I don't think there are any places where they drive on opposite sides where they could just go over a bridge, Bruno.'

'But it's so stupid. Why doesn't everyone drive on the same side as we do?'

'It goes back a long time in history – to the days before cars when there were just horses. Most people are right-handed, so people rode on the left and had their swords on the right so that they could draw them and fight off any highway robbers.'

'Are we going to be attacked by highway robbers now?'

'Hopefully not!' Grace grinned. 'If we are, I'll rely on you to protect us. OK?'

'*Ja*, sure!' Bruno grinned back.

He opened the passenger door for his son. Bruno climbed in. Grace reached across to help him with the seat belt and Bruno brushed away his hand, dismissively. 'I know how to put on a seat belt. So why does not everyone drive on the left in every country?'

'I think it has something to do with the Americans – from the days of the stage coach drivers.'

'So they didn't have highway robbers in America?'

He smiled. 'Maybe not.'

Bruno pulled out his iPhone and began tapping

the keypad. Grace saw he was on Snapchat. He made a note in his mind to get him a British phone, or at least a UK SIM card.

'When will my drums arrive?' Bruno asked, suddenly.

'They're on their way – they'll be with us in a few days,' Grace said. 'I'm sure we can make space for them in your new room.'

Anette Lippert had previously told Roy about Bruno's passion for drums, and he and Cleo had been worried about what they were going to do to accommodate a full acoustic drum kit – and the effect the noise might have on them, let alone little Noah. But then Anette had reassured him that soft pads and earphones made the noise minimal.

He remembered she had also mentioned the memory box that Bruno had started making with mementoes of his mother.

'You have your memory box with you, Bruno?'

'Yes,' he said, quietly.

'Do you have a favourite photograph you'd like us to get framed to have in your room?'

'Maybe.'

They drove out through the ticket barrier in silence. Grace thought about the phone update Guy Batchelor had given him as soon as they had landed. Everything seemed to be stacking up nicely against Corin Belling. The case could be closed by early next week. Apart from the hours of questioning that lay ahead for him about Belling's death. But he was confident he could answer, satisfactorily, any of the criticism he knew would be levelled at him. Especially if the DNA on the semen came back positive.

He turned his focus back to his newly found son, who was now on Instagram on his phone. 'Have you ever lived in the countryside, Bruno?'

He shook his head.

'We have a dog called Humphrey, he's a little bit mad. Do you like dogs?'

'Erik had a dog, a schnauzer. It was called Adini.'

'Schnauzers are lovely. They're one of Cleo's favourite dogs.'

'He doesn't have it any more,' he said, flatly.

Grace glanced at him. 'I'm sorry. How old was it?'

'Two years.'

'Two? What happened?'

'It disappeared.'

'Ran off?'

'It disappeared.'

'That's sad. Was he very upset?'

'Very. The Lipperts looked for her everywhere. They posted on Twitter and Facebook.'

'But never found her again?'

'No.'

'How long ago was that?'

He shrugged. 'A few weeks.'

'Maybe she'll turn up.'

'No, I don't think she will turn up.'

'I'm very sorry.'

'She bit me.'

'The schnauzer bit you?'

'On my hand. I don't think she was such a nice dog.'

'You'll like Humphrey, he's crazy and loves everyone. We also have twelve chickens.'

'Why?'

'We like to have our own eggs.'

'Can't you buy eggs in England?'

Grace grinned. 'Yes, in lots of places. But we like to eat our own eggs, we know what the hens have been fed on, and that there aren't any chemicals in the eggs.'

Bruno fell silent for several minutes. Then, suddenly, he asked, 'Why did my mother do it? Why did she die? Why did she?'

Grace thought carefully, as he drove, before answering. 'I don't know, Bruno, that's the honest truth. There is so much I don't know about your mother and your life with her. But I did love her very much and I do know that she loved you very deeply.'

'Do you think she was ashamed of me?'

'Hey!' He put a hand on his son's shoulder, but felt him stiffen beneath the touch. He put it back on the steering wheel. 'Don't ever think that.'

'What should I think?'

The rush-hour traffic had thinned out, and the motorway was quiet. They'd be home in around an hour. He'd known, all along, before flying to Germany, from everything that Anette Lippert had told him, that it was not going to be easy for this boy to adapt to an entirely new life. But he felt that they had started to bond.

How did he reply? What had Sandy told him about her past? What did Bruno, who was clearly highly perceptive, know about his mother? Had she ever told him the truth about why she had disappeared when she knew she was pregnant? Become for a short while a Scientologist? Then joined another sect and bigamously married its wealthy leader? Divorced him before he later died in a car accident? Then became a heroin addict? Got cleaned up and went into therapy? Hit by a taxi crossing a Munich street, leaving her crippled and permanently disfigured?

What a disastrous waste of a life Sandy had led since leaving him. Just what did Bruno know, what would he be prepared to talk about – and how much had her erratic existence affected him? Maybe he would know all of it in the fullness of time, but not now. Glancing at him, he said, 'Right now, Bruno, I don't have answers. What I can promise you is that my wife, Cleo, and I will love and take care of you, and do everything we can for you. Cleo is not a replacement for your mother and never can be, but we will love you every bit as much as we love Noah. Noah's too young at the moment to understand what has happened, but I'm sure you will be an amazing big brother and role model to him as he grows older.'

Bruno did not respond.

'Oh, and Cleo loves fast cars – she has an Audi TT.'

'Will I have any friends?'

'The son of a friend of mine – his name is Stan Tingley – is looking forward to meeting you. He's a really nice boy. And when you go to school there'll be loads of other kids your age. I'm sure you'll be making a lot of friends, very quickly.'

'Can Erik come and stay?'

'We can invite Erik over to stay once you are settled in. Absolutely.'

'What football team does Stan – support?'

'Crystal Palace.'

'I think Crystal Palace do not like the Brighton Albion team, the Seagulls.'

'You know your football teams!'

'Kayla the Eagle is the Crystal Palace symbol. The eagle is on my country's flag. It is our national emblem of Germany.'

'OK, so, what does that mean to you?'

He shrugged. 'Nothing. It is not my country any more.'

Grace took that as a positive.

CHAPTER 39

Saturday 23 April

Guy Batchelor had an early-morning coffee and cigarette outside, then went in, out of the chilly wind, to his temporary SIO office on the ground floor, and sat down with his back to the window thinking hard about the day ahead on Operation Bantam. He read through the notes he had taken during yesterday evening's briefing, and also what he had written in his Policy Book, so he could bring Roy Grace, who was due in shortly, up to speed. His phone rang, interrupting his thoughts.

No caller ID showed on the display.

'Guy Batchelor,' he answered.

It was Julian Raven from Digital Forensics. 'Sir,' he said. 'Regarding Operation Bantam, we've come up with some information on the deceased Lorna Belling's iPhone we were asked to look at. It was passcode protected, but we've managed to get into it.'

'Bloody hell, how?' He was mindful of recent press publicity where the FBI in the US had failed with court orders to get Apple to unlock seized phones.

'It had fingerprint security activated. We have Surrey and Sussex Forensics to thank. They took it to the mortuary – they've developed some fancy new technology to use the finger of a deceased to work on the button.'

'Brilliant!'

'Yep, pretty impressive. So, in the week before Lorna died there were forty-seven calls from one number. And fifteen messages, many of them abusive.'

'Really – what do the messages say?' Batchelor said, his hopes rising again.

'They appear to relate to an MX5 sports car advertised for sale on eBay by Lorna Belling. The bidder had offered £2,800 which she accepted. He made payment via PayPal, but she then appears to have denied receiving the money. He had been accusing her in his messages of stealing his money.'

'Go on.'

'He's been threatening her with dire consequences if she doesn't either give him the car or his money back. He's particularly angry because he wanted this car for a surprise for his wife's birthday – he's explained that in his messages. We've done a triangulation survey and cell-site analysis with his mobile phone service provider, O2, which puts him in the vicinity of the deceased's flat, Vallance Mansions, on several separate occasions. The most recent was last night.'

Batchelor felt a buzz of excitement. 'What do we know?'

'His name is Seymour Darling. He's logged as having made a complaint to Sussex Police on Saturday, 16th April, about a fraud. The complaint is being investigated by DC Hilary Bennison from the Economic Crime Unit. I've spoken to her and it seems Darling might be the victim of an online scam that's currently pretty widespread.'

'What kind of scam, Julian?'

'It's one of a number, where people get sent an email with payment instructions. It looks like the sender's address but there is a subtle change. The moment the money's paid over, it's gone.'

Batchelor thought hard. '*Seymour Darling?* Why's that name ringing a bell?'

'He's got three previous convictions, the first in 1997 for shoplifting, for which he got a fine and community service order. The next was 2003 for demanding money with menace – for which he got two years suspended. The third was in 2005 for GBH, when he permanently blinded a woman in one eye in an assault in a pub – for which he got four years. I have his address; 29 Hangleton Rise.'

'Well, he sounds quite the charmer. Let me have his number and any details you've got – and I'll also get a full background check on him.'

As he ended the call, Roy Grace came into his office. Seeing the big grin on the Acting SIO's face, the Detective Superintendent said, 'What's up?'

Batchelor told him.

Grace pulled up a chair at the empty desk opposite him and sat down, absorbing the information. 'Interesting form,' he said.

'Very.'

Grace entered Seymour Darling's name on the computer and studied the man's criminal record for some moments. 'Hmmm,' he said. 'Darling seems to be a man who likes getting into disputes. BHIMS have been involved with him twice – once sorting out a boundary dispute with a neighbour, and another time some issue with a dog.'

'BHIMS?' Batchelor queried.

'It stands for Brighton and Hove Independent Mediation Service.' Then switching subjects, he asked, 'When are we expecting the semen DNA results from the lab, Guy?'

'They only went off yesterday afternoon, so probably sometime tomorrow, with luck, boss.'

Grace nodded, thinking. Rape was often an escalation from minor crimes. And it was often more about anger and power over a woman than sexual gratification. A classic scenario for a rapist was a burglar foiled by the owner of a property he had entered, deciding that next time if it was a female he would incapacitate and rape her, almost to show her who was boss. Darling's criminal history showed just such a scale of progressive escalation.

'How was Germany? How did it go?'

'Do you know that old Chinese curse? *May you live in interesting times.*'

'It went badly?'

Grace shrugged. 'You've got a daughter, right?'

'Anna, yes, great kid.'

'In part because she's lucky enough to have great parents.'

The DI smiled. 'I like to think that's part of it. But it's not everything.'

'But we know, don't we, Guy, the percentage of offenders who come from broken homes, single-parent families, alcoholic or drug-using families, abusers, you name it. It doesn't always start that way, but nine times out of ten you can show me a man – or a woman – in a prison cell and I'll show you the train crash of a family that brought them up.'

'Is he screwed up, your kid – what's his name again?'

'Bruno. I don't know. He's complex, that's for sure, but I think he's OK. He's a bright boy, with a lot of curiosity about things. Hell, you'd have to be a bit screwed up with all the shit his mother's put him through. I think he's fragile; he's obviously spent a lot of time on his own, and seen his mother having to deal with a lot of issues, including drugs. On top of all that he's now been taken away from his homeland and friends. We'll try to give him all the love and attention we can, and we're going to have a chat with an expert in the child psychology field to see what's best. I'm sure he'll be fine once he's settled.' He shrugged and peered again at the computer screen.

Batchelor leaned forward a little. 'If you don't mind my saying it, you look whacked. Do you want to take the weekend off? I can handle everything.'

'Thanks, Guy, but I think it's better for me to be here for a while. To give Cleo a little time this morning alone with Bruno to try to bond with him.'

'So what's he actually like?'

Grace shrugged. 'What would any of us be like, being told our mother had committed suicide, and that our father, whom we had never met, was going to come and take us to a foreign country where we didn't know a soul?'

'Tough call.'

'Yep. You've said it. Tough call. One of our priorities is to get him some friends. Jason Tingley's kindly taking him to a Crystal Palace game this afternoon, with his son, Stan.'

'Is that wise? Getting him to fraternize with the opposition on his first day?'

Grace grinned. Since Brighton and Hove Albion's biggest rival was Crystal Palace, this had long been a friendly bone of contention between Grace and Tingley.

'If it helps him make a friend here, then what the hell. Anyhow, enough about me, let's focus. We need to talk to Seymour Darling, PDQ.'

'Want to take a ride with me over to his house?'

Grace thought for a moment. His plan had been to spend a few hours catching up on all the emails that would have come in for him during the past day and a half that he had been away in Germany. But this development excited him. One thing that he had missed as he had risen through the ranks was what all officers who got promoted away from frontline duties and became increasingly desk-bound missed. And that was the adrenaline rush of action.

'Good suggestion,' he said.

CHAPTER 40

Saturday 23 April

Roy Grace had a fondness for the sprawling, hilly mass of the Hangleton estate, to the northwest of the city. It was where he and Sandy had been the happiest, the first five years of their married life, in a tiny flat, with a view out across the rooftops on the far side of the street towards the hilly pastureland of the South Downs.

The village of Hangleton was recorded in the Domesday Book of 1086. Its small, beautiful Norman church, St Helen's, is one of the oldest surviving buildings in the whole city of Brighton and Hove. And its close neighbour, medieval Hangleton Manor, is the oldest secular building in the city. But not much else in Hangleton is historic. Most of it was developed in the first half of the twentieth century and subsumed into the city at the same time.

Grace sat in the passenger seat of the unmarked car, as Guy Batchelor drove. He felt the same emotions he always did when in this area. So many memories.

They swept down a hill, made a right, up a steep incline, then a sharp right again into a crescent-shaped close. Batchelor slowed to a crawl as they peered out at the house numbers. Grace pointed to the right. 'Twenty-nine over there.'

Moments later Batchelor halted the car outside a squat little house, with a large bay window, that looked only a few years old. A small, dog-wee-yellow-coloured hatchback was parked on the driveway.

The two detectives climbed out of the car and walked up to the front door. Batchelor rang the bell, which set off loud barking from inside.

Moments later the front door opened a fraction, accompanied by more deep barking, and a coarse female voice shouting out, 'Shut the fuck up, Shane!'

The door opened wider, and they saw a tiny woman, with a mass of tangled black, wiry hair and almost absurdly large black-rimmed glasses, dressed in a brown velour tracksuit. She was stooping down, struggling to restrain a massive Rhodesian Ridgeback by its collar. Behind her was a small, dingy hallway. The place smelled of damp dog.

Batchelor held up his warrant card. 'Detective Inspector Batchelor and Detective Superintendent Grace, Surrey and Sussex Major Crime Branch. We'd like to have a word with Mr Seymour Darling. Is he in?'

'Not, if I have anything to do with it, for much longer.'

'Are you Mrs Darling?' Batchelor asked.

'So what if I am?' She turned back to the dog and yelled, 'Fuck you! Shut the fuck up, Shane! OK? Shut the fuck up!' Then she turned back to the two detectives. 'He's not in, he's gone to the football.' Then she turned back to the dog. 'I'm fucking warning you!'

'May we confirm your name, please, madam?'

'You know it, don't you, you just said it.'

'And your first name?'

'It's Trish. Trish Darling. And I don't want any funny comments about it, had enough of them.'

'What time are you expecting your husband home, Mrs Darling?' Grace asked.

'I don't know and I don't care.'

'Beautiful dog,' Batchelor said.

'Yeah? You want him? Take him, he's yours! Seymour can't handle him, I can't handle him, he's a fucking nightmare. And my husband goes to the footy, leaves me to walk him. I can't walk him, I ain't got the strength.'

Batchelor handed her a card. 'We'd like to have a word with your husband. Could you call me – or ask him to call me – when he gets home?'

She took the card in her hand, dubiously, without glancing at it, as if she had been handed a leaflet by a street peddler. 'I'll be the one having a word with him when he gets home.' Then, darkly, she added, '*If* he gets home.'

Picking up on this, Batchelor pressed her. 'Does he sometimes not return home?'

Staring back at them, as if realizing, albeit late in the day, that they might actually be allies, she replied, 'Lately he's become very strange. I don't know what's got into him. If you want to know the truth.'

'We very much want to know the truth,' Grace replied. 'What can you tell us?'

'I think he's having an affair.' As the dog barked again she yanked hard on his collar. 'That's what I think.' Then as she leaned closer, Grace smelled alcohol on her breath and saw the blaze of anger in her eyes. 'Whoever she is, she's welcome to him. Good luck to her. She clearly sees something in him I don't – and you want to know something? It can't be the size of his weeny, that's for sure.' She raised her free hand in the air and made a curling motion with her index finger.

CHAPTER 41

Saturday 23 April

'I think I'd have an affair, too, if I was married to that witch,' Roy Grace said as they climbed back into the car.

'Or shag the dog, which is prettier,' Batchelor said.

'You're a happily married man, Guy, right?'

'Yes.' Batchelor gave him an odd look.

'How much would you spend on a birthday present for your wife?'

'I dunno. I usually buy Lena a few things, you know – one big present, a piece of jewellery or something, and some smaller bits and pieces. A hundred quid, maybe a bit more. Hundred and fifty. Why?'

'Me too – that's sort of what I would spend. Maybe a bit more if it was a significant birthday. Seymour Darling bought a car – or thought he had – as a surprise for his wife. Two thousand eight hundred pounds – seems a lot, don't you think? Especially when you look at their very modest house – and the state of their relationship.'

'Are you saying it's dodgy money? Is he drug dealing?'

'How about *guilt* money?'

'Guilt money?'

'A man who's been unfaithful will often buy an expensive present for his wife, out of guilt.'

Batchelor gave him a strange look. 'I trust you're not talking from experience, boss? Tut tut tut, and you a newlywed!'

Grace smiled. 'Thanks for your faith in my integrity!'

The DI raised a placatory hand, also grinning. 'No offence meant.'

'None taken. Affairs have never been my thing – unlike, it seems, my late ex-wife.'

'She had affairs? Sandy? You're serious?'

'She was kind enough to tell me in her suicide note. Not information I particularly wanted or needed to know.'

'Shit, I'm sorry.'

Grace shrugged. 'Maybe I was more of a rubbish husband than I ever realized.'

Batchelor was silent for some moments, then he said, 'Don't ever think that. If that's what she did, then she was the one in the wrong.'

'You're lucky – I don't know you two well, but it seems to me that you and Lena are very solid. She's a lovely lady.'

'She is, I'm very lucky.'

'You are. I've been a reluctant confidant to quite a few officers over the years, who've told me about their tangled love lives. That's how I know about the gifts.'

'I see where you're coming from with Darling.'

Grace nodded. 'Wracked with guilt over his affair, perhaps he decided to buy his wife her dream car, to compensate. He paid the money over – money he could barely afford – and either Lorna Belling stole it, tucking him up, or as seems more likely to be the case, he's been the victim of online fraud. Either way, he's angry at her, blames her, wants his money back. So he calls her forty-seven times and makes ten visits to her flat. What does that sound like to you?'

'Someone's anger escalating to danger point.'

'Precisely. The report you have on the cell site puts Darling outside Lorna Belling's flat on ten separate occasions in the past week, as well as on the night of her death. The most recent was last night – two days after her death. We know that killers have a habit of returning to their crime scene and observing.'

'Yes.'

'One hypothesis I have is that he went into the flat, had a confrontation with her, raped and killed her. If there's a DNA match with him and the semen found in her that would be pretty strong evidence.'

'I like your hypothesis, boss.'

'So, Plan B?'

'Plan B?'

Grace explained it to him.

As soon as he had finished, the DI punched a series of numbers into his phone before going hands-free. Moments later, as they drove away, it was answered.

'Julian Raven, Digital Forensics.'

'Julian, it's Guy Batchelor. That phone number you gave me earlier, for Seymour Darling?'

'Yes, sir?'

'I need the current triangulation on it. Can you get on to your O2 phone company contacts and find its current whereabouts?'

'I'll do what I can, sir. It may take a while, because it's the weekend.'

'Fine. Call me when you have it.'

'Yes, sir.'

CHAPTER 42

Saturday 23 April

A few hours later, shortly before 7 p.m., Roy Grace sat in the passenger seat, as Guy Batchelor drove down Hove Street towards the seafront. They stopped at the red traffic lights, Batchelor indicating left. When the lights went green he turned, past the front of Vallance Mansions. Across the road from them was a cyclist heading west, a jogger heading east, towards Brighton, and a small man standing still in the shadows close to a street light.

'That might be him,' Batchelor said, making another left into Vallance Gardens, an upmarket street of elegant red-brick Victorian villas and one white art deco house. They looked for anyone else standing still, but saw only a man striding along with a small dog on a lead. At the top, Batchelor made a left, taking them back to Hove Street, and another left back down to the traffic lights at the seafront junction.

The man they had both clocked previously,

diagonally across Kingsway, was still standing motionless, barely visible.

Then Grace hit the dial button on his phone, calling the number he had entered earlier.

Both detectives, holding their breath, watched the man suddenly bring the phone to his ear.

'Seymour Darling?' Grace asked.

'Who is this?'

He ended the call, slipped out of the car and, dodging through Kingsway traffic, crossed the road, trying to look unobtrusive. As he reached the pavement on the far side he saw the man, still holding his phone to his ear.

Grace walked towards him, trying to look casual, like any Hove resident out for an evening stroll. He saw the man hold up his phone, looking at the display.

Showing his warrant card, Roy Grace said, 'Seymour Darling?'

The man grunted. 'No.'

'What's your name?'

'Freddie Man.'

'Freddie Man? OK, what's your date of birth?'

'Er – erm – it's – March 2nd – 1966.'

'So, Freddie Man, what's your star sign?'

'Star sign?'

'Yes, what's your star sign?'

'What's it to you?'

'I'm curious – I'm interested in people's star signs.'

For a moment he looked bewildered, then he said, 'It – it's Taurus – I think.'

'You *think*?'

Early on, when Grace had been a probationer on the beat, at the start of his career, and frequently had to stop suspicious people on the streets, he had memorized all the star sign dates. Everyone knew their star sign. It was always a reliable, quick test to find out if someone was lying to him by giving a false identity and date of birth.

'Really, Freddie? March 2nd would make you a Pisces. I don't think you're Freddie Man, at all, are you?'

'What of it?'

'Are you Seymour Darling, of 29 Hangleton Rise?'

'What if I am? Who the fuck are you?'

'Detective Superintendent Roy Grace, Surrey and Sussex Major Crime Team. I'm arresting you on suspicion of murdering Lorna Jane Belling. You do not have to say anything, but it may harm your defence if you do not mention when questioned something you later rely on in court. Anything you do say may be given in evidence.'

Seconds later Guy Batchelor joined them, proffering a pair of handcuffs.

'Yeah?' Seymour Darling said. 'Well tell this to the court. Tell the fucking bitch's heirs to give me my money back.'

CHAPTER 43

Saturday 23 April

Saturday night, Grace had learned many years back, was not a good time to book someone into custody. But as the arresting officer, he had to stay with his suspect throughout the whole procedure, to avoid the possibility further down the line, when the case came to court, of a smart defence brief picking holes in the chain of evidence.

On every Thursday, Friday and Saturday night a massive police presence, Operation Marble, did its best to prevent central Brighton from becoming a war zone of drink- and drug-fuelled fights. He was lucky to have arrested Darling relatively early in the evening, and he'd had to wait for little over ninety minutes before the man was processed and banged up. A couple of hours later and he could well have been there, waiting his turn among the drunks, until dawn.

As he headed home, just after 10 p.m., having conducted with Batchelor a brief interview of Darling, during which he had gone no-comment on them, he was thinking hard. The clock was ticking. Thirty-six hours was the maximum time the police could keep a suspect in custody without applying to the magistrates' court for an extension to detention.

Darling had made numerous threats to Lorna Belling. He was standing outside her flat the night of her murder, and on a number of occasions prior to then. The police had cast-iron grounds to arrest him. The man had a grievance over the money he had paid for her car and, as was usual, requested an on-call legal aid solicitor. By giving him a chance to talk to the lawyer and having had an overnight breather, hopefully the facts would be clearer in the morning. And with luck sometime tomorrow they'd get the DNA results from the semen back from the lab.

In his mind he ran through the possible scenarios, creating other hypotheses. Darling had raped her but had not murdered her. Darling had not raped her but had murdered her. Or Darling was an innocent – if angry – bystander.

What about Lorna Belling? The victim of domestic abuse. With a cheap rental apartment. Had her husband known about it for some time, or just discovered it? What bit of equipment had the printed circuit board with his fingerprints on come from and why was it lying there, seemingly discarded?

So many questions, so many things that didn't add up.

Did Lorna have this place just to escape from

her husband, or was there another reason? A shag pad for her and a boyfriend? Her sister in Australia had confirmed she had hopes of moving out there. Was she trying to earn enough money to give her sufficient cash to flee? Could hairdressing have been her cover, and she made her real money from her activities in the flat?

Was she dealing drugs or stolen property from there?

So often in his experience it was the obvious answer that was the correct one. However obscure it might seem at first. But equally he knew he could not always rely on that.

Right now one possibility was that Seymour Darling was Lorna Belling's killer. DNA would establish if it was his semen inside Lorna. If it was, that would be strong evidence.

And if not?

That would not necessarily mean he hadn't killed her. But it could mean that someone else had. He needed some fast-time intelligence on the woman if the DNA failed to produce a match with Darling.

Was Darling too obvious a suspect? Because the husband was still in the frame. It would be interesting to see what examination of his electronic devices revealed.

He couldn't explain why, but all his instincts, backed by his experience, were telling him there was something more than the obvious going on here. Ordinarily he would have delegated the interviewing of a suspect like Darling to two trained cognitive suspect interviewers from his team. But he didn't want to do that. Instead he decided that he and Batchelor, who were both also trained interviewers, should do it themselves.

Grace called the DI and told him to meet him in his office at 7 a.m.

Ten minutes later he pulled up outside the country cottage on the edge of the village of Henfield, which now truly felt like home, and walked up to the front door. As he opened it, an appetizing smell of cooking greeted him, and he heard the sound of the television. Canned laughter, then an indignant female voice. More laughter. Moments later, Humphrey rushed up to him, barking.

'Hey, boy!'

Cleo appeared from the kitchen, in jeans, a loose jumper and battered slippers, looking all-in. He put his arms round her and kissed her.

'Missed you,' he said.

'Missed you, too. How was your day? You're limping badly. How's your leg?'

'Hurting a lot. But, hey, we could have a result!'

'Really?' She suddenly looked genuinely excited. 'Talk me through it over a glass of wine!'

'Over three glasses, I think. Maybe four! And I'm craving a fag. So, how's Bruno?'

'Yes, OK, I think. Actually, he seems a nice boy. I can see a lot of you in him – particularly when he smiles. I took him for a walk with Humphrey and let him feed the hens some scraps. We had a nice chat – I think we're going to get on.'

'What did you talk about?'

'He asked if his friend Erik could come and stay with us some time. I told him of course, he'd be very welcome.'

'He asked me the same thing.' Grace smiled.

'We talked about what he likes to eat – for breakfast, lunch, supper. About his school in Munich – and about going to St Christopher's school in Hove. The former Chief Constable's wife, Judith, teaches there. I've already had a word with her and she'll make sure Bruno is well looked after when he starts.'

He frowned. 'If they accept him. Didn't you say they have strict criteria?'

'They're going to give him some assessment tests on Monday in verbal and non-verbal reasoning – and they've said they'll make an allowance for him being bilingual – but that can also be an asset.'

'What happens if they don't accept him?' Grace asked.

'Plan B,' Cleo said.

'Which is?'

She smiled. 'I haven't figured that one out yet. There are other private schools in the area. I'm told that the Lancing Prep in the Droveway is a good one. I'm sure it will be fine, darling, we'll just have to see what happens. Bruno's a bright boy. From everything Judith Martinson has told me, I can't see there's going to be a problem.'

They walked through into the kitchen. 'So what

other interests, apart from his drums, does he have? Have you found out?' Grace asked.

'He told me he likes to swim. Listen, there's that really nice country club down the road that has an indoor pool. It also has a spa with a sauna. Didn't your physio tell you that regular saunas would be good for your leg?'

He nodded.

'What about joining this club – it's called Wickwoods.'

'Darling, we've got enough expense with this house. I'm not sure we can afford the membership fees of a country club.'

'They do a really reasonable weekday membership rate. And I thought you were getting something towards medical expenses for your leg from the police?'

'Well, I might be, yes.'

'I had a word with the manager and he's offered us the full family membership with one month's free trial. What do we have to lose? It would be great for Bruno to do his swimming. And it might help your leg. I could ask Mum and Dad to help us with the fee if you can't get any money from the police fund.'

He liked Cleo's parents but was reluctant to take any charity from them. 'What are the rates? Let's take a look at them.'

'I've got them here.' They sat down at the small oak kitchen table. The television was still blaring in the living room. Cleo poured him a large glass of Australian Chardonnay, then put an ashtray, a pack of cigarettes and a lighter on the windowsill in front of him.

He took a large gulp, leaned over and opened the window, then lit a cigarette and sucked in the sweet smoke, gratefully. For some moments it made him feel dizzy. It was the first cigarette he had smoked in over a week, he realized. He talked Cleo briefly through the events of the evening.

'What a little shit,' she said. 'Seymour Darling sounds horrible. Even his name! Yech, creepy!'

'You should have met his wife. She was a charmer.'

She pinched a drag of his cigarette. 'Yup, well, as my mum always says, there's someone out there for everyone.'

He smiled. 'So where are the kids?'

'It's going to take a while to get used to the *plural.*' She sipped some wine and hunched her shoulders. 'Noah's asleep, he's been fine all day – really taking an interest in his play mat thing – and finishing *The Times* crossword.'

Roy grinned. 'Maybe I should let him read my investigator's notes on Operation Bantam. He might solve it for us! And Bruno – where's he?'

'In his room, gaming – the last time I looked in.'

'What kind of game?'

'Football. He's playing it on his television with Erik in Germany.'

'So how was it with Jason and Stan at the football game today – how did he get on with Stan?'

'He was a bit subdued when he came home – I think he was shattered, to be honest. But it sounds like it was OK. Jason said he'd have a word with Stan about inviting him over to play. And as soon as he gets settled in at school, I'm sure he'll make more friends.'

'Has he had supper?'

'I made him spaghetti bolognese, because that's what the Lipperts told you he liked. But he only had a few mouthfuls before excusing himself, very politely, and going up to his room. Probably because he was exhausted.'

'I'm not surprised.' Grace smoked some more of the cigarette. 'It's hard to imagine what this is like for him. This kid's been brought up as a single-parent child, by a wonky mother who spent part of his childhood a junkie. She commits suicide, and the next thing is a father he'd never been told about pitches up, takes him away from his home, from everything he knows, and dumps him in the middle of nowhere, in rural England, with a bunch of strangers. How would that feel if it was you?'

She pinched another drag of his cigarette. Exhaling the smoke, she replied, 'Like I'd won the bloody lottery!'

'Maybe he doesn't see it quite that way.'

Noah began to cry. Cleo shot an irritated glance upstairs. Then she picked up her wine glass. 'That was a frivolous answer I gave you, I'm sorry. But, honestly? I don't know.'

'Something I read in one of those books on

philosophy you gave me – I can't remember the title – kind of makes sense here.'

She looked at him, quizzically.

'It was one of the American Indian tribes. *Before you judge any man first walk ten moons in his shoes.*'

She seemed about to say something, then fell silent.

'What?' Roy Grace asked.

She remained silent.

'What, darling?'

She shook her head then drank some wine. 'I want to help Bruno, make him happy. I guess I don't know where to begin.'

'Do you think I should go up and say a quick hi to him, and see how he is?'

'I think that would be nice.'

His phone rang.

'Roy Grace,' he answered. Then with dismay he heard the voice of his boss, Pewe.

'Roy?' Pewe said. 'Are you back from Germany? Sounds like it from your ringtone.'

'I am, sir.'

'Why has no one given me an update on Operation Bantam?'

Grace held his temper. 'As you're off this weekend, I thought the good news could wait.'

'*Good* news?'

'We have a suspect in custody.'

For a brief, sweet moment which he relished, Roy Grace knew that he had rendered the ACC, albeit momentarily, lost for a snide reply.

CHAPTER 44

Sunday 24 April

Roy Grace and Guy Batchelor met in HQ at 7 a.m. on Sunday to plan their interview strategy. Grace had worked so many week-ends during his career that it never felt odd for him to be suited and booted on a Saturday or Sunday. His right leg was giving him grief, and he knew he needed to organize some massages and time in a steam room. Cleo's idea about joining Wickwoods was a good one, but he had no time right now.

Seated in his office, cradling a mug of coffee, Grace yawned, feeling tired. He discussed with Batchelor the order of the questions they would put to Darling, their tactic being to try to get him to say as much as possible, before they revealed what they knew. He often thought suspect inter-views were like games of poker, at times. The cards you held in your hand and the way you bluffed could be the key to winning.

This was assuming the creep didn't continue going no-comment on them, as he had done last night. Hopefully he'd have been talked out of that by his solicitor, if he had nothing to hide. It was of course everyone's right under questioning, but that was a big waste of time and most briefs knew that it did not look good to a jury when endless 'no-comment' replies from the accused were read out in court.

Grace looked at his watch. 'Probably too early to call the lab, especially on a Sunday. Let's try them in an hour. If we can get a DNA match to Darling with the semen that would be very helpful.'

'But equally I guess, boss, if it isn't a match, that doesn't necessarily mean he *didn't* murder Lorna.'

'I agree. Let's see what we can get out of him now – it might make the DNA irrelevant one way or another.'

At 8.30 a.m., with a light drizzle falling, they headed into Brighton in one car, so they could continue talking. The custody block, where they had booked Darling in last night, was located right behind Sussex House, the building on the edge of the Hollingbury industrial estate which had been Roy Grace's second home for the best part of a decade.

He wondered what had happened to Duncan on the front desk, who was also a runner like himself. It was strange to think it was now empty and would soon be demolished. 'Bugger!' he said, suddenly.

Batchelor looked at him. 'What, boss?'

'I'm craving a coffee. Was just thinking about grabbing a couple from Asda for us, but I forgot it'll be shut.' He glanced at his watch. 'Doesn't open until ten on Sundays.'

'Yup.'

'You OK, Guy?'

'OK?'

'You're very quiet.'

'I'm fine, boss, thanks. Had one of those nights where I couldn't get to sleep – brain whirring.'

'I get plenty of those sleepless nights, particularly when my leg's playing up. Hate them.'

Batchelor braked and turned in, pulling up in front of the massive green-painted steel gate. He wound down his window and pressed his card against the wall-mounted reader. Moments later the gate began to slide open. They drove through and up the short, steep incline to the rear of the custody block itself, with the row of green garage doors which prisoners under arrest were driven through, and then escorted straight into a small bare room, furnished with nothing except a hard bench and a notice pinned to the wall telling them the procedure they were about to undergo.

To be stripped of all possessions, searched and then put into a cell, the door banged shut deliberately hard and loudly on you, is a humiliating process. It takes only a few hours for any suspect to start feeling institutionalized.

Both detectives were hoping that after his night on the hard, narrow bed in the bare room, Darling might be more cooperative this morning.

CHAPTER 45

Sunday 24 April

Seymour Darling and his solicitor were already seated at the metal table in the sparsely furnished, windowless interview room. Darling seemed even smaller than the night before, as if these few hours in a cell had shrunk him further. The fifty-three-year-old's own clothes had been removed for forensic purposes, and he was now dressed in faded police issue clothing that seemed a size too big for him. His narrow face, with its swarthy complexion, dark eyes too close together and slicked hair, combined with the shabby clothes, gave him the furtive, somewhat sleazy look of a street drugs peddler.

His solicitor sat beside him. An alert-looking woman in her early forties, with a mop of ginger curls, she wore a chalk-striped trouser suit over a white blouse, and fashionable glasses. A bottle of mineral water sat on the table in front of her, beside her large leather-bound notebook.

After cursory greetings, Grace and Batchelor sat down facing them, Grace positioning himself directly opposite Darling so he could watch his eye movements and body language. The fragrance the solicitor wore barely masked the rank odour in the room, which he realized must be coming from Darling. It smelled as if the man had slept and sweated into his clothes all night – which he probably had.

Both of Darling's hands were flat on the table, as if he was trying to look calm, but his fingers gave him away. All of the nails were bitten to the quick, and on several there were raw marks on the surrounding flesh where they had been gnawed away very recently. Had he lain awake most of the night in his cell, tearing away at his nails, worried?

Would he be so worried if he was innocent?

Grace could have murdered a coffee, but had to put that out of his mind now. Maybe he'd get one in the staffroom when they took a break. He activated the video recorder, and the police officers identified themselves for the benefit of the tape. Then he gestured in turn to the suspect, then the solicitor. 'Could you please state your names for the recording?'

For a while he was unsure whether the man would speak or not. The suspect just stared at him, sullenly. Then he said, 'Seymour Rodney Darling.' Moments later the woman said, 'Doris Ishack, of Lawson Lewis Blakers, solicitor for Mr Darling.'

Grace continued. 'I'm confirming the time as being 9.02 a.m., Sunday, April 24th.' He looked hard at the suspect. 'I'd like to remind you,

Mr Darling, that you are still under caution. However, I will repeat the caution.'

Darling looked at his solicitor, who nodded to him. Then she said to the two detectives, 'I've had the chance to speak to my client, and he is prepared to answer *some* of your questions.'

'Good,' Grace said.

'Thank you,' Batchelor added.

'Mr Darling, what is your current occupation?' Grace asked, focused intently on the man's eyes. After some moments they moved to the right.

'I work for a fencing contractor – pricing up fencing.'

'How long have you been there?'

Again the eyes momentarily flicked right. 'Just over two years.'

That confirmed to Grace which way his eyes would move when he was telling the truth. They were likely to move to the opposite side – the left, to the *construct* side of his brain – if he was lying. As Grace knew, it wasn't infallible, but eye movements, combined with general body language, would be a good indicator. He next addressed the solicitor. 'We have already disclosed to you, Ms Ishack, that your client has recently become known to the deceased, and it appears there has been a dispute of some kind between your client and the deceased.'

'I may have been in dispute but I didn't kill her,' Darling said, flatly. His eyes remained dead ahead, but now he folded his arms, which was a defensive, challenging position.

'How long had you been in contact with Lorna Belling?' Guy Batchelor asked him.

'A couple of weeks.'

'How did you get to know her?' he continued. 'What were the circumstances, and what was the nature of your relationship?'

'Relationship? What are you insinuating? I met her about a bloody car she advertised on eBay. An MX5. I wanted to buy it as a birthday present for my wife.'

'Did you have a nice bonus from work – or make a big sale?' Grace quizzed.

'Is this relevant?' the solicitor asked.

'Yes,' Grace said. 'It seems a rather unusual and expensive present.'

'Yeah, well I had some redundancy money from my previous job, and it's actually a very special birthday,' Darling said.

'A milestone?' Grace asked, jotting down a note.

'You could say that. This will be her last birthday, she has terminal cancer. Four to six months is the prognosis. She's always loved those little Mazda sports cars. I thought, you know, summer's coming, her last summer, she can put the roof down.'

'I'm sorry,' Grace said. Batchelor nodded his sympathy, too. Then after a short pause he asked, 'Can you give us details of exactly what communications you had with Mrs Belling?'

'I'd been looking around for a car on all the sites, you know? Autotrader, Gumtree, eBay – she particularly wanted that red colour. I saw the one Mrs Belling had up on eBay, and I arranged to go and see it.'

'And you went?' Grace asked.

'Yes.'

'When was that?'

His eye movements revealed to Grace he was telling the truth. 'About a fortnight ago.'

'Where did the meeting take place?' he asked.

'In the street outside her home.'

The two detectives shot a glance at each other. 'What was the address?' Batchelor asked.

'A block of flats. Vallance Mansions. Right opposite the King Alfred leisure centre.'

Grace wrote on his pad: *1. Did not know before. 2. Been in contact. 3. Met. 4. Why there?*

'Can you tell us what happened at the meeting?' Batchelor asked.

'Yes. I thought she seemed a straightforward woman. The car looked nice – better than she had described it, in fact. Maybe I should have twigged then.'

'Twigged?' Batchelor asked.

'That I was being set up for a con.'

Grace gestured with his hands. 'Just continue with what happened, for a moment, please.'

'We took the car for a short test drive. I liked it a lot, but I couldn't afford more than £2,800 – I'd been offered a loan, but it was at extortionate rates. She'd advertised it for £3,500 but no one pays the asking price, do they?'

Neither detective commented.

'So I told her £2,800 was my best offer, she said she was in a hurry to sell and would take it. We agreed I'd make payment on eBay through PayPal – that was what she wanted – I would have been happy to give her folding, but she wanted it through PayPal. I understand why now. I should have smelled a rat then.' He gave a bitter laugh.

'Smelled a rat?' Batchelor asked.

Belling glanced at his solicitor, who gave him a nod of encouragement. 'I don't know if you've ever bought a second-hand car, detective, perhaps your police salaries are so high you don't need to?'

'I wish,' Batchelor said.

Darling and his solicitor both gave fleeting smiles. 'Yeah, well in all my past experience, vendors negotiate. I offered what I thought was a ridiculously low price, expecting her to come back with a counter – perhaps three-two. But she didn't. She just said, fine, she'd accept £2,800. I asked her how quickly we could complete the transaction – I wanted to get the car valeted, and then put it outside our house, with a ribbon around it and some flowers in the boot, so my wife would be blown away on her birthday. She said I could take the car away just as soon as she received payment and she sent me her PayPal details. So that's what I did, the following day. I told her the payment had gone through, then the bitch told me she'd not received any money. She was lying.'

His body language was consistent with someone telling the truth, Grace thought.

'What happened then?' he asked.

'We'd agreed I would collect the car last Saturday morning. I had made payment in full through eBay's checkout page into her PayPal account on the Thursday – the one she had given me. The money should have been there instantly, but she denied all knowledge of receiving it, the bloody thieving bitch.'

'The Economic Crime Unit think you may have been a victim of online fraud,' Grace said. 'Did you consider that?'

'Yes. Yes, I checked, of course, right away, with PayPal. They told me there was no such account, the details she had given me were not for a PayPal account.'

Batchelor frowned. 'What account were they for?'

'I still haven't found out. She was a bloody scam artist. Instead of arresting me and locking me up, perhaps you'd like to go and recover my sodding money for me, so I can do something nice for my dying wife?'

Still watching him closely, Grace asked, 'Would you like to tell us your feelings about Lorna Belling?'

Doris Ishack raised a warning hand and leaned over to her client. Belling nodded, then answered, once more his eyes moving left, first. 'I've just told you, she was a con artist.'

'What makes you feel it's her who was the con artist and that you've both not been a victim of cybercrime fraud?' Grace went on.

'How would you feel if you were in my position, detective? You've just paid out more money than you can afford, and you find out you've been screwed. Go on, how would that make you feel?'

Privately, Grace considered that perhaps Darling knew he had been conned but had thought he might bully or frighten Lorna Belling into handing over the car – given the man's track record of violence. But he would leave that one for the prosecution counsel, if it came to court.

'Angry enough to kill that person?' Grace tested.

'That's a leading question, Detective Superintendent,' the solicitor interjected.

The two detectives sat whilst Darling and Ishack conferred in whispers. Then, with an irritatingly smug expression, Darling said, 'No comment.'

Grace leaned forward and pressed a button on the recording control in front of him. 'Interview suspended at 9.20 a.m.'

CHAPTER 46

Sunday 24 April

Grace, followed by Batchelor, stepped out of the interview room, closing the door behind them.

'What do you think, boss?' Batchelor asked in the corridor.

'We know there's been a spate of frauds around PayPal recently,' Grace replied. 'Mick Richards at the Economic Crimes Unit briefed me on it yesterday. Mainly Romanians involved. They bring homeless people over here, give them a chunk of change, get them to open bank accounts then send them home with a nice lump sum. They track eBay and Gumtree transactions, spot a transaction such as this one with Lorna Belling's car, upload malware and give the purchaser a fake PayPal account number. The purchaser – in this case Mr Darling – pays the money in and, whoosh, it's gone. Washed through an account and immediately transferred abroad. All his body language says he's telling the truth about the purchase. He's a victim of cybercrime fraud, in my view.'

'Where does that leave us?'

'With one very angry man.'

'Angry enough to kill her? Judging from his past form?'

'Let's go back in and see what we can find out.'

They entered the interview room again and sat back down.

Pressing the record button on the control unit, Roy Grace said, 'Interview with Seymour Rodney Darling recommenced at 9.25 a.m.' He turned to the suspect and reminded him he was still under caution, then continued. 'Mr Darling, can you tell us where you were on the afternoon and evening of Wednesday, April 20th?'

Darling's eyes went to his left. That indicated to Grace the man was constructing a lie. 'I was working that day. In the afternoon I went to measure up for a fencing quote for a customer in Hurstpierpoint.'

'Can you let me have the customer's name and address?'

Hesitantly. 'Yes. Stuart Dwyer – at West Point Lodge, Church Lane.'

'Mr Dwyer could verify that?' Grace asked.

Hesitantly again. 'Yes.'

'And after that?'

'I went home. The wife and I had a row.' He shrugged, seeing the intent stares of the two detectives. 'The medications she's on make her very edgy. I went out, took the dog for a long walk.'

'Where?'

'Up on the Downs.'

'Did anyone see you – could anyone verify that, Mr Darling?' Batchelor asked.

'I didn't see anyone.'

'What time did you leave the house and return?' Grace watched his face intently.

'I left about five – I got back around nine p.m.'

'A four-hour walk?'

'I often go for long walks.'

Grace noticed how uncomfortable he looked. 'Do you and your wife row frequently?'

'We rowed all the time before her diagnosis. I've been trying to be understanding since. But—' He fell silent.

'But?' Batchelor prompted.

Darling looked each of them in the eye, in turn. 'Just because someone has terminal cancer, it doesn't mean they're any less of a fucking bitch than they were before.'

Doris Ishack gave him a cautioning stare, then turned to the detectives. 'You need to understand my client is under a lot of stress at the moment.'

'I imagine Lorna Belling found being murdered quite stressful, too,' Grace retorted. He looked at Darling. 'I am very sorry to hear about your wife's circumstances.'

'Is that right?' Darling said, bitterly. 'Do you have any idea what it feels like to know you are going to lose your wife?'

'I can only try to imagine.'

'Then try a bit sodding harder.'

Ignoring this last outburst, Grace said, 'I'd like you to think back to Wednesday night very hard. Are you absolutely sure you went straight home after your walk on the Downs?'

'Yes.'

'What was the route you took on this walk?'

'Is this relevant?' the solicitor asked.

'It is.' Grace looked at Darling.

'From where we live, it's a few minutes to the tracks of the old railway line that used to run from Aldrington Halt up to the Dyke. I took the dog there – it's a safe place to let him off the lead.'

'I used to live in Hangleton some years ago,' Grace said. 'I know that route. You walk through beautiful countryside, with great views on a fine day to the south, of Brighton and Hove and Shoreham.'

Darling nodded agreement.

'To get up to the Dyke and back would take about ninety minutes, from memory, although I may be a little rusty. It was some years ago,' Grace went on, ignoring Batchelor, who was giving him a strange look.

'If you went straight up and back down, yes,' Darling said.

'But of course it would be longer if you carried on and went down into the village of Poynings, to the Royal Oak pub there, or even further to the village of Fulking and the Shepherd and Dog pub. Would that be correct?'

'Yes,' Darling said. 'That's exactly what I did. I went down into Fulking.'

'Did you stop anywhere?'

'Yes, actually, I had a pint at the Shepherd and Dog.'

'Did you talk to anyone in the pub? Is there someone who would remember you were there?'

'I had Shane, the dog, with me, couldn't take him inside. So no, I didn't talk to anyone. Got my pint and went straight back outside.'

'Did you ask for a bowl of water for your dog?'

'There was a bowl outside.'

Watching his eyes intently, Grace asked, 'Would the person who served your pint remember you?'

'Possibly.'

'What beer did you order?'

A moment of hesitation. 'Harvey's.'

'Do you remember the person behind the bar who served you?'

'It was very busy in there – I don't – don't really recall.'

Grace made another note. 'How did you pay for your drink?'

'Cash, I think.'

'You *think*?'

'Yes, yes it was cash.'

'So you took your pint of Harvey's outside, sat down with Shane, you drank your pint, and then you walked home. That accounts for those four hours?'

'Yes.'

'Are you certain you've not forgotten anything, Mr Darling?'

'I'm certain.'

'Thank you,' Grace said.

'You've heard my client's account,' the solicitor said. 'Unless you have anything further to add, I'm requesting that you release him immediately. He has a very sick wife to take care of and it is inhuman, given his domestic circumstances, to prevent him from going home to her any longer.'

'I do have some further things to add,' Grace said. 'I am mindful of your client's domestic circumstances, but my priorities lie at this moment with the victim of the brutal murder I'm investigating.' He turned to Darling. 'So after your walk you went home, arriving at around 9 p.m., you said. Is that correct?'

'Correct.'

'What happened when you came home?'

Darling shrugged. 'I had some supper, then watched television – well – I had it watching television.'

'What did you eat?'

'Really, Detective Superintendent!' the solicitor said.

'Some leftovers in the fridge.'

'What exactly?' Grace asked, ignoring the solicitor.

Darling thought for some moments. 'Lasagne – I microwaved it. Had it with a bit of salad that was in the fridge.'

'What kind of lasagne? Meat? Fish? Vegetarian?'

'Really, Detective Superintendent, is this important?' the solicitor said.

'It could be.' He looked quizzically at his suspect.

'Vegetarian. My wife's on a special vegetarian-only diet for her cancer.'

'What about the dog – Shane – did he eat?'

'He only eats once a day, in the morning. It's meant to be better for them.'

'So you ate your vegetarian lasagne and salad in front of the television?'

'Yes.'

'What did you watch?'

'I don't remember.'

'How would you describe your memory, Mr Darling?'

'Describe it? What do you mean?'

'Do you have a good memory in general?'

Darling hesitated for some moments, his eyes flicking between the two detectives, as if aware they were trying to catch him out. 'Normal,' he said. 'Pretty average, I'd say.'

'Are you sure?' Grace pressed.

'Yes.'

'I'm not sure I agree. I don't think you have a very good memory at all, Mr Darling.'

'Why do you say that?'

'Well, when we arrested you, you couldn't remember your own name, or date of birth, or star sign. You don't remember who served you a pint last Wednesday. You were hesitant about how you had paid. You don't remember what you watched on television that evening. Is there anything else about that evening that you don't remember?'

Darling shrugged. 'No, nothing.'

'You arrived back home from your four-hour dog walk, ate microwaved lasagne and salad from the fridge whilst watching television? Is that correct?'

'Yes.'

'What did you do after that?'

He hesitated, then said, 'I went to bed.'

'And your wife?'

'This is very personal,' the solicitor interrupted.

'It is actually relevant,' Grace replied, sternly.

Ishack turned to her client. 'You don't need to reply.'

'I'm fine,' he told her, then turned to Grace and Batchelor. 'She was asleep in bed, as she is every night from around 9 p.m.'

'You didn't go out after your supper?' Grace asked. 'You didn't take your dog out for a final night-time walk?'

'No, I never do. I just let him out in the back garden to do his business.'

'Thank you,' Grace said, courteously. Then he leaned forward and pressed the pause button on the recording control and said, 'The time is 9.45 a.m. Interview with Seymour Rodney Darling suspended.'

Addressing the solicitor, Grace then said, 'DI Batchelor and I are going to step out for a short break. I'd strongly advise you to ask your client to think further about his actions and whereabouts on the afternoon and night of last Wednesday.'

The two detectives went out.

CHAPTER 47

Sunday 24 April

'I need a snout,' Guy Batchelor said as they entered the corridor, closing the interview suite door behind them.

'I'll come out with you,' Grace said.

They let themselves out into the courtyard and stood outside the grim facade of the building. A marked police car, with two uniformed officers in the front and a thin, miserable-looking man in the back, drove past and entered one of the receiving bays. Just one of the dozens of people who would be arrested every day and brought up here to Custody for processing, Grace thought. Burglars, muggers, drunk drivers, drug dealers, abusive partners, shoplifters. Many of the city's low-lifes were frequent flyers here. And mostly their childhoods would have a similar dysfunctional pattern. Followed by their first arrests – for petty thieving, joy riding, street running for drug peddlers – and their first time banged up in a young offenders' institute. Welcome to the criminal justice system, where a life of crime beckoned.

A dry, blustery wind blew and spring seemed a long way off. Batchelor pulled out his cigarette pack and offered one to Grace. He shook his head. 'Thanks – too early for me – but I'll enjoy yours passively!' He yawned again, then smelled the sudden waft of smoke as his colleague sparked up.

'What do you think, Roy?'

'It's going our way, Darling's walked straight, slap-bang into it, the lying little scrote. Let's see what he has to say for himself in a few minutes.' He grinned.

Batchelor nodded.

'The time is 9.57 a.m. Interview with Seymour Rodney Darling recommenced.' Grace once more repeated the caution. Both Darling and his solicitor seemed confident, almost cockily so, presumably bolstered by the chat they'd had whilst he and Guy had been out of the room. They wouldn't be quite so smug in a few minutes, Grace thought.

He made a deliberate play of looking down at his notebook before he looked back at the suspect. 'Mr Darling, do you possess a mobile phone?'

'Yes.'

'Could you let me have the number?'

Darling gave it to him and he wrote it down. Then he asked, 'Have you at any time during the past week lost your phone?'

Darling was silent for a moment. 'No.'

'Where do you keep it?'

The solicitor looked anxious, having an inkling where this might be going, but said nothing.

'With me,' Darling replied.

'All the time?'

'Yeah. All the time, like most people.'

'Are there any occasions when you don't have it with you?'

'No. Not intentionally. I've left it behind at home, on occasions.'

'Did you leave it at home on Wednesday, April 20th?'

'No.'

'Are you certain?'

Hesitant. 'Yes.'

'You seem unsure.'

'I had it with me.'

Roy Grace produced a sheet of paper on which was printed a street map, with a small red circle drawn on it. He handed it to Darling. 'I'd like you to take a look at this.'

The suspect and his lawyer both studied it.

'Do you recognize it?' Grace asked Darling.

'It's a street map.'

'It is. Are you familiar with this area?'

'Should I be?' He sounded sullen.

'Well, it does look as if you've spent a bit of time there recently. Which supplier do you use for your mobile phone, Mr Darling?' Grace asked.

'O2.'

'The map I've handed you is a street map of the area of Hove immediately around Lorna Belling's flat at Vallance Mansions. Do you see that red circle?'

'Yes.'

'Do you know the location where it is drawn?'

'It's the area around Vallance Mansions.'

'Correct. We obtained this map from the phone company. It's a triangulation report on your phone number. You told us a short while ago that on the afternoon of Wednesday, April 20th, you were measuring up the grounds of a property in Hurstpierpoint, and afterwards that evening you were walking your dog up on the Downs. Is that correct?'

'Yes.'

'According to O2, your phone, which you said you had with you all the time, was in the vicinity of Vallance Mansions from 1 p.m. until 10 p.m. on that day. Can you explain that?'

Darling stared at him, then at Guy Batchelor, and suddenly seemed to shrink even further.

'I'd like to speak to my client in private,' Doris Ishack said.

'A little work on jogging his memory, perhaps?' Grace said, unable to resist. It was met with stony stares.

'Interview suspended at 10.07 a.m.,' Grace announced for the benefit of the recording device.

CHAPTER 48

Sunday 24 April

Roy Grace went outside with the DI so that Guy could have another cigarette. A former heavy smoker himself, some years back, Grace understood you'd never get the best out of anyone whilst they were craving a cigarette. There were patches of blue in the sky. Maybe later he'd get a chance to go home and kick a football around with Bruno. But for now Operation Bantam was his priority.

'Give Darling time to sweat a bit, Guy?' he suggested. 'Let him start wondering what else we know about him.'

'Yes, I like it. How long have we got before we have to release him – or apply for an extension?'

Grace looked at his watch, and did a mental calculation. He was interrupted in mid-thought by his phone ringing.

'Roy Grace,' he answered. It was Georgie English, the Crime Scene Manager. 'Sir,' she said. 'I've just had the report from CSI Chris Gargan, on the semen that was found in the body of the victim.'

It had been sent to LGC Forensics for analysis – one of the labs to which Surrey and Sussex Police sent evidence for DNA testing. She began to list out for him the details of the lab's findings. All the differences in the DNA of the semen found inside Lorna Belling, when compared to her husband's DNA. Georgie English reeled off jargon: *restriction enzymes*, *nitrocellulose*, *radiolabelled probe microbes hybridizing to DNA fragments*, *polymerase chain reaction*, *alleles*.

It was like an impenetrable foreign language. He didn't need this much information. English could have cut the crap and simply said, *You're screwed!*

Or rather, *Lorna Belling had been.*

By someone not her husband.

Shit, shit, shit.

'Shit,' he repeated, and then said, 'Is Chris Gargan sure, Georgie?'

Dumb question, he knew. Of course the lab were sure. The lab knew the importance of 100 per cent accuracy. It was what they had built their business on, police forces being able to rely on their reports in court. Belt and braces. No smart-arsed brief was ever going to pick a hole in their findings.

There was no match to anyone on the DNA database, she informed him with clear regret in her voice.

With Seymour Darling's past criminal history, his DNA would have been on file. Although that still did not exclude him as a suspect. But it weakened the case against him.

He thanked her and ended the call, then relayed the essence to his colleague.

Batchelor took a final drag on his cigarette and crushed the butt in the wall-mounted receptacle, then they went back inside, both officers thinking hard and going through the ramifications.

'So Lorna Belling had had sex with someone the day she was murdered. That doesn't necessarily mean her husband didn't kill her, does it, boss?'

'It could have given him even more of a motive. Had he found out she was having an affair, which had been the trigger?'

Batchelor nodded. 'Yup, that has currency.'

'But what this information does do is blow this case wide open. It's suddenly become a lot more complex. Whose sperm was it? What was her relationship to this person? Could this person, rather than her husband, be her killer? There's a lot more work to be done,' Grace said.

'Meantime, what do we do about Seymour Darling?'

'We have to release him on bail.'

'I still have a feeling it's him.'

'He's a lying little scrote, for sure,' Grace said. 'But we don't have enough evidence to charge him. Not yet. Keeping him in custody any longer would just be a distraction for us.'

Batchelor looked pensive for some moments, then nodded, reluctantly. 'You're right, boss.'

Grace looked at his watch. There was now a mountain of work to be done on this case, but he was mindful of his responsibility to Bruno, too. He was also aware it was three days since the murder had been discovered and they were going to have to hold a full press conference. 'Guy, let's hold a planning meeting at midday. Ask someone from Media Relations to come along so we can prepare a press release and briefing for first thing tomorrow. Do you know who's on call?'

'Oliver Lacey, boss, I already checked.'

'Good, he's smart. Let's think about the message we need to get out.'

'We need witnesses who were in the vicinity of Vallance Mansions on Wednesday night,' Batchelor suggested.

'Yes. Anything else?'

'Anyone who knew the couple? Clients of the deceased?'

'Yes. But most, if not all, would be on the mobile from her home, which Digital Forensics have,' Grace said.

'Anything else, boss?'

'Any householders in the area who had CCTV cameras pointing at the street in front of their property? But that should be covered by the outside enquiry team.'

'It should be.'

'What are we missing that we could appeal to the public for?'

Batchelor shrugged. 'I dunno. Vehicles in the area?'

'Yes, vehicles in the area. Unfamiliar ones. If

she's been having an affair, it might have been going on for a while. Her lover might well have arrived in a car. Someone, a vigilant member from the local Neighbourhood Watch scheme perhaps, may have spotted a car they did not recognize parking for a couple of hours and then leaving.'

'Good point.'

'Make sure the Crimestoppers number is included on any images.'

'It will be, boss.'

'This is a good exercise for you, Guy.'

'Oh yes?' He shook another cigarette out of the pack.

'This is a good case for you to cut your teeth on. To see the complexities of a homicide investigation. This is turning into what I call a real *Gucci* job.'

'Gucci?' Batchelor looked down at his shoes. He was wearing a pair of black Gucci loafers he'd bought in a designer outlet sale on a recent shopping expedition with his wife.

Grace smiled. 'Nice shoes. Wasn't meant to be personal. *Gucci*'s what I call a proper investigation, rather than just low-life on low-life. We've got a real puzzle on our hands here, Guy. Your big chance to shine as my deputy.'

'I'll rise to it, boss!'

'I know you will. You're smart. As SIO I'll be watching every step you take.'

'You sure you don't want to take it over, now you're back?'

'You're doing well, Guy.'

'I appreciate your faith.'

'I'm sure you won't let me down,' Grace replied.

Confidence smiled back. 'I think we should have one final interview with Darling before we release him,' Batchelor said. 'Now he's had time to think.'

'Oh?' Grace quizzed.

'Something that's just occurred to me.'

CHAPTER 49

Sunday 24 April

'Interview with Seymour Darling, by Detective Superintendent Roy Grace and DI Guy Batchelor, in the presence of his solicitor, Doris Ishack, of Lawson Lewis Blakers, recommenced at 10.35 a.m.,' Grace said, and re-cautioned the suspect.

'Do you have anything to say about being in the vicinity of Mrs Lorna Belling's flat, in Vallance Mansions, Hove, on the afternoon and evening of last Wednesday, April 20th, the day she died, Mr Darling?' Guy Batchelor asked.

'Actually, yes, quite a lot.'

Batchelor gestured with his hand for him to proceed.

'I think the bitch was having an affair.'

Batchelor shot a glance at Grace, who looked poker-faced.

'What makes you say that?'

'I saw him.'

Batchelor and Grace exchanged a glance. 'Saw who?' Batchelor asked.

'He stood in the porch and rang the bell. Minutes later I saw them in the window, all wrapped up in each other's arms. Snogging.'

'The same man who was in the porch?'

'I couldn't swear.'

'So he could have been visiting someone else in the block? There are over fifty flats. What makes you so sure it was Lorna Belling he was visiting?'

'Because—' He hesitated. 'He had the same build.'

'That's all? The same build? As who?'

Darling hesitated again. 'Yes. I – he kind of looked smooth.'

'In what way did he look *smooth*?'

'He reminded me a bit of James Bond.'

'James Bond? Which James Bond? Daniel Craig? Pierce Brosnan? Roger Moore? Sean Connery? One of the others?'

'I – it was sort of the way he carried himself.'

'So while you stood outside her flat, seething with anger, James Bond was inside, busy murdering her?' Batchelor pressed.

'I don't know what he was doing.'

'Was this the first time you saw him? According to the phone records, you stood outside Lorna's flat most of Monday, April 18th, and most of Tuesday, April 19th. Did you see James Bond on either of those days, too? Or are you going to deny you were there then?'

Darling squirmed, visibly. 'I was there, yes.'

'Shouldn't you have been at work? Quiet week, was it?'

'I had jobs measuring garden fencing in that area.'

'Is that right?' Batchelor asked. 'Your employer would be able to confirm it, if I called them, would they?'

Darling reddened, suddenly looking panic-stricken. 'Look – please – I was outside, watching her flat. I was angry. I was waiting for her to come out and I was going to confront her. I did see him – this *Bond* character – on Monday afternoon. About 2 p.m.'

'Was he abseiling up her wall?'

'No, he had a bottle – I think – it looked like a bottle in a carrier bag – and he looked nervous. He went to the porch and then went in. I saw them up in her window a few minutes later.'

'You saw him twice in broad daylight,' Batchelor said. 'But you can't tell us what he looks like? Are you sure he exists? He's not some figment of your imagination?'

Darling shook his head. 'He was looking around, nervously, like. You know? Like he didn't want anyone to see him. Like a man – having an affair.'

'Are you talking from experience?'

'I don't think that is an appropriate question,' the solicitor interrupted.

'I'm sorry, but I think it is,' the DI said. 'I'd like your client to tell us more about why he thinks James Bond – if he exists – was having an affair with Lorna Belling and was in her flat on the day she died.'

Doris Ishack leaned across and conferred with her client in whispers for a moment. Darling nodded, then turned back to the detectives.

'No comment,' he said.

'Mr Darling, would you recognize this – er – *James Bond* if you saw him again?'

'I – I might.'

'You saw this man outside Lorna Belling's apartment building twice, in broad daylight, less than one hundred yards across the road from where you were standing, and you claim to have seen him in her window twice, but you are not sure you could identify him if you saw him again. Are you really sure he is real?'

'He drives a matt-black Porsche.'

'Oh? In the books, from memory, James Bond drives an elephant-breath-grey Bentley. In most of the films he drives an Aston Martin. But your James Bond drives a Porsche?'

'I notice cars. It's just coming back to me. I saw the same Porsche – a 911 Carrera 4S – driving around slowly, like it was looking for a parking space, on the Monday afternoon, and again on Wednesday.'

'You can identify cars, but not their drivers?'

'It had darkened windows.'

'Did you get its registration number?'

'No, why should I have done?' Darling gave him a pointed look. 'I'm not a sodding detective.'

'Fair play,' Batchelor conceded. 'I don't suppose you'd remember whether it was a normal or a personalized plate?'

'You *don't suppose* right.'

There was silence for several moments. The solicitor broke it. 'If you have no more questions for my client, I'd be grateful if you would release him immediately.'

The two detectives stepped out of the room for a few minutes. When they returned, Guy Batchelor said to Doris Ishack, 'We are not happy with a number of the answers your client has given us. We will release him on police bail whilst we continue with our enquiries.'

He turned to Darling. 'Your solicitor will explain the full conditions. But, basically, during the period you are on police bail you are to live at the residential address you have given us. You are to surrender your passport to the police so you cannot leave the UK, and you will report weekly to a police station at a time and place we agree with you. If you do not adhere to these conditions you can be re-arrested and may be kept in custody. Is that clear?'

'Clear as mud,' Darling said.

At that moment Batchelor's phone, which he had switched to silent, began vibrating. Stepping away from the table, he answered it.

It was Julian Raven, from Digital Forensics. 'Guy,' he said. 'We've been working on Lorna Belling's phone and there's something that might be of interest to you.'

'Yes, what, Julian?'

Raven told him.

Batchelor made some notes on his pad, thanked him and hung up, with a beat of excitement. He turned and signalled to Roy Grace and the pair walked to the door. As they reached it, Darling called out, 'Hey, Mister Detectives – thanks a lot, for nothing.'

CHAPTER 50

Sunday 24 April

'Tell me?' Grace asked Batchelor as they left the custody suite building and headed over to his parked car.

'Julian Raven says Lorna Belling had been in regular contact with one particular phone number a few days before her death. She had disguised the name on her phone contacts list.'

'Do we have a name?'

'Better than that!' Batchelor said with a grin. 'We have a plot on his movements.'

Twenty minutes later, back in his office, Grace removed his dark-blue suit jacket and hung it on a hook behind the door, then slipped behind his desk, with his back to the window. Batchelor sat down in front of him.

'Might this be the *James Bond* that our friend, Darling, was referring to?' Grace pondered.

'His name's Kipp Brown, he's an IFA with his own very successful business in Brighton. Kipp Brown Financial Services. He has ads all over the place in the *Argus*, *Latest Homes* and on Juice radio

– always featuring himself with his catchphrase, "*Trust Kipp!*"'

'Does he have any form?'

'No.'

As Grace wrote the name down on a pad, Batchelor glanced out of the window behind the DS. He could see a man with a clipboard looking up towards the roof of the building.

'According to Raven,' Batchelor continued, 'triangulation on Brown's mobile phone puts him in the vicinity of Vallance Mansions on two occasions in the past week. The first was for a two-hour period, 2 p.m to 4 p.m. on Monday, April 18th, and the second – here's the interesting bit – between 1.45 p.m. and 3.55 p.m. on Wednesday, April 20th.'

'Bloody hell! That tallies with what Darling told us.'

'Seems like we might have another suspect, boss.'

Grace was pensive for some moments. His private phone pinged with an incoming text and he was momentarily distracted by it. The text was from Cleo and there was an accompanying photograph. It showed Bruno in bed, with Humphrey curled up on the duvet, on his stomach.

> Looks like Humphrey has a new best friend! XXX

He smiled, raised an apologetic hand to Batchelor then texted back.

How great is that???? Love it!! Love you.
XXXX

Then he focused back on the information he'd just received, thinking hard. On his desk was a copy of Friday's *Argus* newspaper. The seventh page was dominated by a dramatic photograph of the scene where Corin Belling had been run over. Halted cars and blue and white police tape. The headline read:

HUSBAND KILLED BY CAR HOURS AFTER WIFE FOUND DEAD

From the story accompanying it, Guy Batchelor appeared to have handled the press release skilfully, giving enough to satisfy the reporters, but nothing for them to sensationalize. Just bald facts. Lorna Belling had been found dead in her rented apartment on Thursday morning. She and her husband had a history of domestic violence and the city support service, RISE, had been in the process of intervening. Corin Belling had run from his office when police officers (Grace appreciated the anonymity Batchelor had afforded him) had gone to interview him, and, attempting to flee, had run into the path of oncoming traffic. The incident had been referred to the IPCC.

He held the paper up. 'You did a good job, Guy. Let's hope it goes just as well in tomorrow's briefing with the press.'

'Protecting our backsides, boss. I did my best.

Let's hope the buggers at the IPCC don't make it too hard for you.'

'Yep, Cassian Pewe won't need much encouragement to take a pop at me. But hey, let's focus. Kipp Brown. Could he be Lorna Belling's anonymous sperm donor?'

Batchelor smiled. 'Shall we go and talk to him?' He looked at his watch. 'Screw up his Sunday for him?'

Grace looked at his watch, also. It was too late to try to catch someone having a Sunday morning lie-in, and he was mindful of the potential damage that it could do to Brown's life. He reminded Batchelor of the aftermath of the IRA bombing of The Grand, and the distress it had caused. Then he added, 'We need to get Kipp Brown checked out. He has his own, very successful business, he isn't going anywhere. Let's find out all we can about him today, then talk to him tomorrow – perhaps on his way into his office – or at his office.'

'We need to get his DNA. What do you suggest?'

'The smart way would be to arrest him tomorrow. We've got more than enough to do that. He's on the phone with her and then goes to her flat hours before she was found dead. We've enough to arrest him – or am I missing something?'

'No, boss, you're smack on the button!'

'If we get a DNA match to the semen, then we're cooking with gas.'

'I've a good feeling about this one, boss.'

'Keep that feeling, but assume nothing.'

CHAPTER 51

Sunday 24 April

'The time is 4.30 p.m., Sunday, April 24th, this is the fifth briefing of Operation Bantam,' Guy Batchelor said. Roy Grace, seated beside him in the conference room, was happy to let him continue in his deputy SIO role.

Batchelor brought the team up to speed on the developments of the day, regarding the interview with Seymour Darling, the results on the semen taken from Lorna Belling, and the new information that had come to light that she appeared to have had a lot of contact with a man they believed to be Kipp Brown. So far, he said, Brown did not appear on their radar, and had no history or form.

DI Dull, hunched over his tablet, raised a hand. 'Guy?'

'Go ahead, Donald,' he said.

Dull had a slow, monotone voice. As he spoke, Roy Grace wondered, privately, if he wouldn't be better employed providing sleep therapy to insomniacs. After thirty seconds he was ready to nod off.

'You can see from my spreadsheet,' Dull droned, pointing at a whiteboard to which a series of graphs were pinned, with highlights in orange, green and purple, 'I've put all the details about Kipp Brown that the search engines would provide. You'll appreciate the time constraints, so there may be omissions. I've made a matrix of his life on a spreadsheet – taking into account background, schooling, business and social interests, history of relationships. Then I've compared them to known data on six convicted criminals in related fields, as I thought it might give us some helpful insights.'

Grace stared at the man, listening intently and a tad impatiently. Dull seemed to be assuming the role of amateur psychological profiler. But fair play if he came up with something of interest.

Dull turned to another whiteboard, which had seven different graph plots on it. Six of them converged on several points. The seventh, in a thicker, black line, was well clear of the rest.

'The six different coloured lines that you can see here,' Dull said, standing up and pointing with a red dot from a laser pen, 'represent six individual convicted murderers. I've created spreadsheets on each of them, drawing on socio-economic backgrounds, offending histories, age and a number of other significant factors. The wider black line is a plot of Kipp Brown, from what I've been able to ascertain about him from a trawl through search engines and his LinkedIn profile. As you can see, his journey is completely different.'

Grace, a tad baffled, frowned. 'And your conclusion is what, exactly, Donald?'

'Well, sir, he doesn't fit any of these profiles of a murderer.'

'So we can safely ignore him?' Grace was trying hard to mask his scepticism.

'No, I wouldn't say that exactly, sir.'

'OK, what would you say?'

'Well,' he replied, ponderously, 'Kipp Brown is a person who could well slip under our net if we were to run a profiling matrix.'

Just what planet did Cassian Pewe find this guy on, Grace wondered, still unsure what the hell he was talking about. But, mindful that with Pewe's unpredictable machinations Donald Dull could end up being his boss in the near future, he kept his calm. 'So if I understand correctly, Donald, Kipp Brown is a potential suspect, albeit from left field?'

'You could interpret the data that way, sir, yes. But I wouldn't rely on it.'

'So is there something in your findings we can rely on?'

Norman Potting raised a hand. 'Yes, chief, getting a good mortgage deal from this man!'

He paused for a moment to look around but no one reacted.

'*Trust Kipp!*' Potting continued. 'He says it, so it must be true.'

'Thank you, Norman,' Grace said. 'If there's one thing I've learned over the years it's when someone tells you that you can trust them, it usually means you can't.'

'So,' Batchelor said, 'at this moment we have three possible suspects: Corin Belling; Seymour Darling; and now Kipp Brown. To recap on the evidence to date: we have fingerprint and DNA confirmation that Lorna's late husband, Corin, who had a history of abuse against her, was in the flat at some point prior to her death. We also know that he released six tiny puppies she had been rearing out onto the street, just to get at her. That's a pretty good indicator of the state of his mind.'

He looked around the room, then continued. 'We have Seymour Darling, extremely aggrieved about being screwed trying to purchase her car. He blames her, but might well be a victim of cyber fraud. And now we have in the frame Kipp Brown, a successful Brighton businessman – and a married man. What is his contact with our victim? And we still cannot rule out suicide, given the distressing history of her marital relationship.'

Jon Exton raised a hand, addressing Batchelor. 'What has this character, Brown, had to say, Guy?'

Grace had been looking at Exton carefully, several times, during this meeting. As he had noticed last week, the normally neatly dressed detective's hair was untidy, he was unshaven, and his complexion was sallow. He would have another quiet word with him later, he decided, concerned for him.

'We haven't talked to him yet, Jon. I'm intending to talk to him tomorrow.'

Batchelor then ran through the lines of enquiry to date. The most important at this time were the outside enquiry teams; they were interviewing everyone who lived in Vallance Mansions, as well as the tradesmen visiting the apartment building; checking for CCTV in the surrounding area, and talking to all the neighbours; checking vehicle movements with the nearest ANPR – Automatic Numberplate Recognition devices – to the area immediately around Vallance Mansions; and finding and interviewing all Lorna Belling's friends, relatives, clients and associates, and continuing to build the association chart for her – which was pinned up on the fourth whiteboard. He would hold a full press conference in the morning, at which he would appeal to the *Argus* and the local media in particular to put out a request to the public for any sightings of anyone unfamiliar in the vicinity of Vallance Mansions on the afternoon and evening of Wednesday, April 20th.

Fifty minutes later the meeting was terminated. Guy Batchelor told them the next briefing would be tomorrow morning.

He went back to his office, sat down at his desk, pulled up the information he had on Kipp Brown, which included the distinctive personalized registration number of his Porsche, then put in a request for an ANPR plot on the movements of this car during the past week.

Ten minutes later he had the information. Every weekday, the car left Brown's residence in Dyke Road Avenue, Hove, headed to Kemp Town, then turned back on itself, heading west across the city towards where the offices of Kipp Brown Financial Services were located. He frowned. Why did Brown dogleg across the city to get to work? Did he drop someone off en route?'

He looked back at the information Donald Dull had come up with on Brown, and then the penny dropped.

CHAPTER 52

Sunday 24 April

Twenty minutes after the briefing ended, there was a knock on Roy Grace's office door. He was looking forward to an evening at home with Cleo and the kids. 'Come in!'

Jon Exton entered, wearing a suit that seemed to be hanging off him. He was looking apprehensive.

How much weight had he lost, Grace wondered? Exton, a bright DS, was well overdue for promotion. But something was wrong. What?

'Have a seat, Jon.' Grace indicated the chair in front of his desk.

'Thanks, boss,' he said, perching awkwardly on the edge of it. 'You said you wanted to see me?'

'I just wanted to know if you are OK, Jon?'

'Me?' He looked surprised. 'Yes, yes I am. Absolutely.'

'You know you can come and talk to me in confidence if there's anything on your mind.'

'Thanks, but I'm fine.'

'Maybe it's your Sunday look?'

'Sunday look?'

'You haven't shaved and your hair's a mess. You're normally Mr Dapper. And you've lost weight. I noticed the change in your appearance a couple of days ago, but you now look worse. I'm just concerned about you.'

'Ah, you see, I'm training for the Beachy Head Marathon.'

'OK – respect!'

'I'm doing it in aid of the Martlets Hospice. Perhaps I could get you to sponsor me – I've got a Just Giving page.'

'Of course, good cause. Ping me the link.' He looked at him carefully again. 'You're sure there's nothing wrong? Nothing you want to talk about to a sympathetic ear and get off your chest?'

'No, absolutely nothing.'

'OK.' Grace smiled. 'See you tomorrow.'

Watching him leave, he remained unconvinced. There was definitely something very wrong. He picked up the phone and called Batchelor.

'Guy, I'm concerned about Jon Exton. I'd like you to keep a close eye on him. See if he'll open up to you.'

'Yes, of course. What's the problem?'

'He's not his normal self – I'm worried about his health. There must be something going on in his life that's not right. I don't know if he's having a mid-life crisis or something.'

'Leave it with me, boss, I'll see what I can find out.'

Grace thanked him then left for home.

CHAPTER 53

Sunday 24 April

Roy Grace loved this time of year, as the evenings became progressively lighter, regardless of what the weather was doing. Shortly before after 7 p.m. as he headed along Henfield High Street, which was becoming more and more familiar to him, he felt a new mood of optimism. Finally he was truly free of the shadow Sandy had cast across his life. He felt no bitterness or anger – just sadness for how she had ended up. That beautiful, intelligent and fun woman he had married, whose life had spiralled out of control; ending up a total wreck, both physically and mentally, in a Munich hospital, unable to see any kind of future.

But he could not help wondering. Perhaps Sandy would still be alive now if he had . . .

If he had what?

Not been married to his job more than to her?

If a few weeks ago he had walked out on everything he had and promised Sandy to start a new life with her?

Never.

He was in a good place, a happy place. He loved his wife deeply, he loved his baby son and he felt an overwhelming responsibility towards his newly found son, Bruno, who in time he hoped to love too. The more he thought about Sandy's strange message, the less concerned he was. Like all human beings, Sandy had always had her dark side – and perhaps it was that coming through in her final message to him? Just wanting to plant a little seed, so that she would go to her grave knowing she had denied her former husband the chance to be totally free of concerns. Her Parthian shot?

Whatever. So far Bruno seemed nice, if understandably a little withdrawn. Hopefully by taking a lot of interest in him and including him in everything, as well as him making friends when he started at school tomorrow, that would change. Grace lowered the window of Cleo's Audi TT and felt surprisingly warm air on his face. Summer was definitely coming, a welcome relief from a winter that had seemed almost unremittingly dark in so many ways. The car clock at the bottom of the RPM dial was still showing an hour back, but he did not know how to change it.

He turned left at the bakery, then halted, waiting for the lights to change at temporary roadworks that seemed to have been there forever. He had a quick fiddle with the controls to see if he could advance the clock, then gave up as the lights changed to green.

He drove along the lane, passing a modern housing estate, crossed a mini roundabout, then the Cat and Canary pub to his right, followed by open farmland. A short distance on he turned right and wound along a narrow rural lane, passing several substantial properties. Then he turned right onto their long, rutted driveway, driving slowly, mindful of the car's low ground clearance.

His heart skipped a beat as he crested a slight ridge and the house came into view. Although they had been here for a few months it still gave him a thrill to see the small, rectangular cottage that was now their home. A former farm cottage, the building itself wasn't pretty in any conventional sense, a mishmash of different shaped and sized windows, a porch that looked like it had been stuck on as an afterthought and a steeply pitched tiled roof. But the walls were clad with wisteria which was starting to come to life, masking some of the bland red brick, and some of the shrubs and flowers in the front – and the young cherry tree – were beginning to come into early bloom.

He pulled up behind his beloved Alfa, which Cleo had commandeered today because it had a rear seat where she had fixed Noah's car seat, in case she had wanted to take both boys for a drive. Neither of them had wanted to get rid of the cars they both liked so much in favour of something more practical, although with the arrival of Bruno, he wondered how long they would be able to cope with the Alfa's cramped rear seats and the even more cramped ones in the Audi. Also, they'd been lucky there had been no snow this winter – neither car would have made it up or down the drive easily. It was a problem they would have to address before the onset of next winter.

But right now he had more important things on his mind.

He opened the front door and Humphrey greeted him by rolling onto his back. He gave him a few moments of attention, kneeling and stroking his belly. 'Hey, boy! Hey, boy!' he said.

Cleo appeared in the hallway behind the dog, in jeans, trainers and a black pullover, with a big smile on her face. But he noted her slightly stooped posture.

'Darling, you're home much earlier than you thought, that's brilliant.'

'Managed to get away,' he said, hugging her gently. 'How's your back?'

'A bit rubbish.'

Cleo had suffered back pain since Noah had been born, but it had got a lot worse recently after she and a colleague at the mortuary had had to manhandle a thirty-eight-stone female corpse.

'When are you seeing the chiropractor again?'

'Well, I've got a firm she recommended, called Posturite, coming to the office tomorrow – they're going to do some kind of workplace assessment, to see whether an orthopaedic chair might help.'

'Good.'

Humphrey barked again, ran off and came

back with a squeaky toy, a rubber duck, in his mouth.

'Brought me a present? Thank you, Humphrey.' He leaned down to take it, but as he gripped the duck, Humphrey held on tightly, pulling back.

'Tug of war?' He shook it, and Humphrey shook his head, determinedly, making playful growling sounds.

'OK, boy, you win!' He let go and the dog, comically, shot back, stumbling, and almost fell over backwards. Turning to Cleo, he asked, 'So, how's everything else?'

'Well,' she said, smiling, 'it's been interesting.'

'Oh? What have you been up to?'

'Bruno and I went for a walk this morning – I took Noah in his pushchair. We went quite a way down the lane, and Bruno insisted on pushing Noah much of the way – he's quite the gentleman, you know.'

'Must have got that from his father!' Grace grinned.

'Then we passed a house – a very pretty place – and there was a guy outside who was cleaning his Porsche. Bruno went straight up to him and they had a ten-minute conversation – mostly about Porsche brakes, can you believe? The guy was charming – his wife came out and chatted to us, too. Nice people, they'd love us to come over for a drink sometime. Great to meet some neighbours.'

'Yes – do they have any kids – anyone Bruno's age?'

'Three kids but they're all much older. But the guy offered to take Bruno for a drive in his Porsche sometime, and Bruno's eyes really lit up.'

'Wow, great! So was Bruno chatty with you?'

'Not really. I tried to talk to him, but he wasn't that responsive today – he seemed subdued. Only really seemed to come alive when he saw that Porsche. Then we came home and had some lunch.'

'What did you have?'

'I cooked him some chicken, which he seemed to like – there's a bit left for supper. I've got some German recipes off the internet. I'm going to ask him if he fancies cooking any with me, like it says we should on the step-parenting forums.'

'Good thinking. Did you get up to anything else?'

'I thought he might like to get to know the area a bit and we could take a drive around, but he told me he'd agreed to play an online game with Erik. Then – this is interesting – when I was working on my uni stuff, Bruno was up in his room and Noah started crying. I left it for a few minutes, then, when I went up to calm him down, he'd stopped by the time I got to the top of the stairs. When I went into his room Bruno was standing by his cot, spinning his mobile and blowing raspberries – and Noah was giggling. Isn't that amazing?'

'It is. That's really good.'

'Maybe he's never really had a proper family life before. But it was lovely to see him with his little half-brother. He really looked quite besotted with him.'

'It's a good sign. Terrific.'

'One thing that I do know, Roy, is that we're going to have to do something about the bathroom now we're a bigger family – or if we can afford it, build the extension we've been thinking about with an additional one. It's been a bit of a nightmare this weekend with everyone trying to get ready at the same time.' She lowered her voice. 'Bruno seems to spend an awfully long time in the bathroom – especially for a boy. He's obviously meticulous but it's not great when I'm trying to get ready and sort Noah out as well.'

'Perhaps we could have an en suite fitted and leave the existing one for the kids and guests?' he suggested. 'Or one upstairs for Bruno – there is space up in the loft.'

'I've already been in contact with a bathroom company called Starling Row – the Porsche guy down the lane recommended them earlier – they're a small Sussex firm apparently – I've arranged for them to come and do a site visit next week, to give us some options.'

'Good thinking,' he said.

'So how was your day?'

'Interesting – to put it mildly. But the positive is that Guy Batchelor is handling his new role well, which is giving me a bit more time to get on with all the pre-trial paperwork I have to deal with.'

'Good, darling. I didn't think you'd be home

until much later so I told Bruno I'd take him to Wickwoods for a swim. Do you want to come with us? Maybe you could try the sauna and see if it helps your leg.'

'Sure, good idea. I'm sure Noah would love it too.'

She nodded. 'Oh, there's one other thing – that American band you like – Blitzen Trapper?'

'Yes?'

'I read in the *Argus* they're doing a gig in a pub on Queens Road, Brighton, next Sunday evening. Do you think you might be able to avoid working then?'

They were his current favourite band. 'Is the Pope Catholic?' he retorted.

'Is Luxembourg small?'

He hugged her again. 'Yes! How do we get tickets?'

'I've already booked them – online. And I've booked Kaitlynn.'

Kaitlynn Defelice was their nanny – a Californian currently living over here, who they both liked a lot, and even more importantly, trusted. The only issue, for Roy Grace, was a silver ring through her right nostril. But she had such a warm, engaging personality that he dismissed any problem he had over that, putting it down to a youth culture he was too old to understand.

'I knew there was a reason why I loved you,' he said.

'Only one?'

CHAPTER 54

Sunday 24 April

Half an hour later, Roy Grace in the fancy Gresham Blake swimming trunks with guns on them that Cleo had given him for his last birthday, and a towel slung round his neck, was perched on a lounger beside the large indoor pool at Wickwoods, watching Cleo and Bruno doing lengths. Noah was asleep beside him in his pushchair, breathing steadily, seemingly unfussed by the activity around.

They had the place to themselves. Cleo, in a turquoise swimming cap, was doing a steady backstroke, while Bruno, wearing goggles, did a powerful crawl, ripping past her as if his life depended on it. He reached the end and did a fancy flip turn, then raced past her in the opposite direction. He would ask Bruno sometime to teach him how to do those turns, which he had never got the hang of.

After ten minutes, Cleo climbed back out of the pool. 'Darling, I'm done,' she said. 'Go to the sauna, I'll sit with Noah.'

'OK, thanks. Oh – I meant to ask you, how do you change the clock on your Audi? Do you know how to put it forward an hour?'

She shook her head. 'Dunno! I just leave it – for six months every year it tells the right time!'

Grinning at her logic, he headed towards the sauna, pulled open the door and entered the blast of heat.

Laying out his towel, he sat down on it, grabbed the wooden ladle, spooned up some water and tipped it onto the electric brazier. Instantly there was a burst of steam and the temperature rose. He repeated the action, then leaned back, soaking up the heat, breaking into a sweat within moments.

His mind returned to work. To Operation Bantam. And to the caseload of trials looming up. Brighton's first serial killer in some years, the vile Dr Crisp, the man who had shot him – the reason why he was in this sauna now, to try to relieve the pain. Jodie Bentley, the black widow, whom he knew for sure had been targeting and murdering a whole series of rich elderly men – but he could not be certain, from the evidence he had so far, of getting a conviction. He had a lot of work to do on this case. And with both of these he had the shadow of ACC Cassian Pewe hanging over him.

And now he had Lorna Belling's suspicious death. Suicide was still a possibility, given her history with domestic violence. But there was an increasing list of suspects. Her dead psycho husband, Corin. Creepy Seymour Darling, the pissed-off and very dubious character who had been buying her car. Her newest acquaintance, Kipp Brown, whose involvement was yet to be determined.

He thought about Corin Belling. Certainly he had a history of escalating violence against her. She had lived dangerously, renting a flat – as a bolthole, or as a secret trysting place with her lovers? But letting the puppies out onto the street – that sounded like a message to her – something he wanted her to see, another nasty way of getting at her. If he had killed her, what would have been the point in doing that?

Gail Sanders, a counsellor he had spoken to earlier at RISE, told him that in her view, Lorna Belling had been playing with fire, apparently renting a place in secret. Discovering it could well have been enough to tip her husband over the edge. Corin Belling at this point had to be their strongest suspect, although pathetic and nasty Seymour Darling ticked a lot of boxes. They would know more about Kipp Brown when he was questioned.

Grace was glad that Glenn Branson would be back at work tomorrow. He was missing his mate, and he needed his help with the trial cases.

How well did any of us know anyone? He thought about Jon Exton. The DS had not convinced him when they had spoken earlier that all was OK. He was certain there was something troubling him, and he needed to get to the bottom of it. Then he returned to his thoughts to the case.

Was he missing something? The obvious that was staring him in the face?

Shit, it was getting hot in here. He had always been slightly claustrophobic, and this tiny sauna, with the misted-up window in the wooden door in front of him, and the searing heat, making it harder and harder to breathe, was getting to him.

He stood up, pushed the door. It did not move. Shit. He pushed harder and it still did not move. The heat felt like it was searing his skin and his lungs, and he felt panicky. He pushed even harder, and suddenly the door swung open, a cooling blast of air greeting him. Stepping out with relief, he pushed it shut behind him. He'd tell the receptionist the door needed looking at – someone less strong could easily get stuck in there.

There was a small, square plunge pool ahead of him, with a warning sign advising that people with a heart condition should consult their doctor before using it.

Holding his breath, he jumped into it.

Hooooooollllllllyyyy shit!

He was shivering as his head bobbed to the surface.

It felt like he had jumped into a vat of acid.

But he hung on in there. The cold biting away at him, until he couldn't stand it any longer. He hauled himself out and hurried back into the retreat of the sauna cabin, pulling the wooden door shut behind him again, but not quite so tightly this time.

As he sat back down on his now hot towel, he suddenly realized that his right leg wasn't aching any more.

Result!

He ladled more water onto the brazier, and lay back, eyes shut, as the steam exploded all around him. Within minutes it became unbearable.

But he stuck it out.

This is doing me good. Doing me good. This is doing me good. Doing me good.

Until he couldn't take it any longer.

He pushed the door, and to his surprise, even though he'd not shut it so hard, again it did not budge. He charged it with his shoulder, bursting through it, hurried through the changing room and jumped into the deep end of the pool.

Like a fish in its element, Bruno did a flip turn right beside him, and powered away towards the far end.

Grace swallowed a mouthful of lightly chlorinated water, spluttered and coughed. By the time he had gained enough equilibrium to start swimming, Bruno had turned again and shot past him. But he barely noticed, he was so deep in thought.

Every killer had a motive.

Corin Belling was a seriously twisted individual.

Seymour Darling had a sick wife. He believed Lorna Belling had screwed him out of the money he had paid for her car. Was that really enough of a motive to kill her?

Kipp Brown was the wild card. What might his motive have been?

Suicide? That was another possibility. But Lorna Belling had no history of suicide attempts.

Just what was he missing here, in all this mix?

Something.

All his instincts were telling him he was missing something.

The obvious.

It might be staring him in the face, but he couldn't see it.

He thought back, as he often did when stuck, to the words of Arthur Conan Doyle – through the mouth of Sherlock Holmes: 'When you have eliminated the impossible, whatever remains, however improbable, must be the truth.'

The truth; Grace made a mental note. Then another: *the improbable.*

Bruno once more flip-turned past him, with an expression of grim determination, and powered away towards the far end of the pool. As if he was racing ahead of an unseen demon.

Lorna Belling. What demon killed you? One of the men in your life, or your own private, internal demon?

CHAPTER 55

Monday 25 April

The electric wrought-iron gates slid open. When there was just enough of a space to squeeze through, Kipp Brown, impatiently revving the engine of his matt-black 911, tugged the paddle and the car moved forward towards the clogged morning rush-hour traffic on Dyke Road Avenue.

There was a gap between a white van and a shitty little Hyundai. The moment the Hyundai driver saw the nose of the Porsche, he moved to close the gap.

'Tosser!' Brown said, and pulled straight out, turning sharply left, causing the Hyundai to brake. The angry man at the wheel gave him a long blast of the horn. Some people hated Porsches but they didn't want a collision with one and the hike in their insurance forever after.

'Dad!' his wuss of a son, Mungo, admonished.

As the Hyundai driver hooted again, angrily, Brown raised two fingers, making them clearly visible through the rear windscreen.

'What?' Brown challenged.

'That was dangerous, we could have had an accident.'

He tousled his son's dark-brown hair. Mungo shrank away from him.

'You know what, old chap? Life's dangerous. None of us get out alive.'

'Yeah, well, we could have been killed just then.'

'By a shit-heap doing ten miles an hour? I don't think so.'

'You're a crazy driver.'

'Fine, you'd rather walk to school? Be my guest – want me to pull over?'

'Jeez!'

'*Jeez?* What's with *Jeez*? You're not in America, you're in England. That what they teach you at Brighton College?'

'You know what, Dad, you're an idiot.'

'Oh yes?'

'Yes. You're making me late for school, again.'

'We'd be even later if I hadn't pulled out like that.'

Ignoring him, Mungo peered down at his phone, tapping the keys furiously. His father glanced down and saw he was on Snapchat. He saw the words 'road rage', accompanied by a scowling emoji. Then his own phone rang. It was his PA.

'Yes, Claire?' he answered on the hands-free.

'When will you be in?' she asked.

'When Brighton and Hove council stop digging up every sodding road in the city at the same time!

Tomorrow. Or maybe the day after at the rate we're moving. What's up?'

'I've just had Jay Allan on the phone. He says he's been offered a mortgage rate of .75 per cent below ours fixed for five years from another IFA.'

'From who?'

'Well, he was reluctant to say but I managed to get it out of him. Skerritts.'

'Bloody Skerritts! That's the third time in the past week they've undercut us.'

'He wants to know if we can better it.'

'Remind me of the value of the property?'

'2.5 million.'

'Tell him to piss off.' He hung up.

His son looked up at him reproachfully.

'What?' he said, staring daggers at him.

Mungo shrugged and tapped on his phone again.

Thirty minutes later, and twenty minutes late for the start of school, Kipp Brown on the phone again, negotiating another mortgage deal, pulled up outside the grand, neo-Gothic front entrance of the school. His son shook his head at him, grabbed his rucksack from the rear seat and ran off through the archway.

Moments later, as he pulled away, shouting down the phone at a total twat at the North and Western Mercantile Bank, and pulling out a pack of cigarettes – his son didn't like him smoking, nor did his other two kids, nor his wife, but he sure needed one now – Brown saw the blue flashing lights of a police car in his mirror. He pulled over to the kerb to let the car pass, but instead it slowed, pulling in behind him, flashing its headlights twice at him and giving him a *whup-whup* on its siren.

He halted the car, terminating the call abruptly in mid-sentence, then slid down his window as a uniformed traffic officer approached from the BMW, straightening his cap.

'I was on hands-free,' he said as the officer, a fair-haired man in his late thirties, knelt to peer in, moving his face close to his own, too close, sniffing his breath.

'And I haven't been drinking – I don't drive my son to school drunk. Anything else I can do for you gentlemen?'

'Is this your vehicle, sir?' the officer said, politely.

'No, it belongs to Bart Simpson – I'm his chauffeur. He's in the back.' He gave the officer a grin.

'I see.' The unsmiling officer stood up, walked round to the front of the car, then spoke into his radio. He returned to the driver's door. 'Where have you come from, sir?'

'What is this? I'm really late for work.'

'Where have you come from this morning, sir?'

'Home.'

'And where is that?'

'Dyke Road Avenue.'

'Can you give me your address?'

'Wingate House, Dyke Road Avenue.'

'And where are you heading, sir?'

'To work.'

'And where would that be, sir?'

'My office, Kipp Brown Associates, Church Road, Hove. And I'm late – thanks to all the insane roadworks going on.'

The officer stood up and stepped away a few paces, speaking into his radio again.

Moments later he heard the wail of another siren. An unmarked silver Mondeo estate, blue lights flashing, pulled up in front of him, then reversed, coming so close he thought the car was going to ram him. Two men in suits climbed out. They walked up to the driver's side of the Porsche and showed Brown their warrant cards.

'Detective Inspector Batchelor and Detective Sergeant Exton,' the older man said. 'Would you mind stepping out of your vehicle and having a chat with us in our car, sir?'

'What is this? I'm already late for work and I have a very busy day ahead in my office.'

'Sir,' Batchelor said firmly. 'We can either have a chat in our car now, which shouldn't take more than a few minutes, or we will have to ask you to accompany us to Brighton police station.'

'Am I under arrest or something?'

'No, sir, but if we have to arrest you, we will.'

'Would somebody mind telling me just what this is about?'

'We will do, if you step out, sir.'

Reluctantly, and angrily, Kipp Brown switched off the engine, climbed out then pressed the key fob to lock the doors, pointedly. 'It's a yellow line

– I assume you're not going to ticket me for parking here?'

'No, sir, we won't.'

Accompanied by the two detectives, he walked to the Ford and climbed into the back seat. Batchelor and Exton sat in the front, closed the doors and turned to face him.

'Mr Brown,' Batchelor said. 'This may seem like an intrusion, but we have a very delicate situation here and we didn't want to embarrass you, or cause you any problems by visiting you at your home yesterday, or your office today. So we thought this would be the best place to have a talk.'

Brown raised his hands in the air. 'What do you need? An ISA? A new mortgage? Some advice on your police pension scheme?'

'Police pension scheme? That's another story,' DS Exton said, bitterly. 'Best not go there.'

'I hear you guys got stuffed by the Tory government. Theresa May? She's on a par with the Antichrist with you guys, right?'

Neither of them spoke, but he could see from their expressions he had hit a nerve. 'I can sort you out on that, if you give me the chance.'

Ignoring the comment, Guy Batchelor asked, 'Could you tell us, Mr Brown, where you were last week on the afternoon and evening of Wednesday, April 20th?'

He held up the cigarette pack. 'Mind if I smoke?'

'I'm afraid it's not permitted in this car, sir,' Batchelor said.

'Great.'

'Could you tell us, Mr Brown, where you were last week on the afternoon and evening of Wednesday, April 20th?' the detective repeated.

'What does that have to do with anything?' he replied.

'I'd be grateful if you would answer the question, sir,' Batchelor said, deadpan, watching him carefully.

The Independent Financial Advisor looked uncomfortable. 'Yes – I – er – I was at work – until late, then I went home. I worked in my office at home for a while, then I had supper with my wife on a tray in front of the television.' He began to look more relaxed. 'We watched an episode of *Homeland*. We've been watching it forever. How does anyone ever get to the end of all these long series? You know, they take over – we haven't watched anything else for weeks.'

'You didn't leave your office at any time during the day?' Batchelor asked.

Brown shook his head. 'No.'

'Are you sure about that?'

'I'd love to have the luxury of taking time out. But no way.'

'So,' Batchelor continued. 'You spent the entire day in your office, and then went home – at what time approximately?'

'I left – I don't know – about a quarter to seven.'

'And your office staff – they could verify that you'd not left the office all afternoon?'

Brown hesitated. 'Yes.'

'Does the name Lorna Belling mean anything to you?'

Brown's eyes shot all over the place. 'No. Lorna *who*?'

'Belling.'

He shook his head.

'You didn't visit her at her apartment in Vallance Mansions, on the afternoon of April 20th?'

'Absolutely not.'

The two detectives exchanged a glance. Then Guy Batchelor said, 'Mr Brown, I'm afraid in that case I'm going to have to ask you to accompany us to the police station for an interview.'

'No way. I've got a very busy morning, as I've told you.'

'So you are not going to come voluntarily, sir?'

'What part of *no way* don't you understand, officer?'

Again the two detectives exchanged a glance. Then Batchelor said, 'In which case, sir, you leave us with no option. Kipp Brown I am arresting you on suspicion of the murder of Lorna Belling. You do not have to say anything, but it may harm your defence if you do not mention when questioned something you later rely on in court. Anything you do say may be given in evidence.'

'What? You said I wasn't under arrest! You bloody lied!'

'No, sir,' the DI said. 'You're the one who's just lied.'

CHAPTER 56

Monday 25 April

Misdirection! The first principle of a close magician. Direct your victim's focus onto your left hand, while you do what you need to do with your right hand. Or have a fox chase a chicken across the room while you pick your mark's pocket.

We're all gullible, all easily suckered. The conman succeeds by offering something for nothing. Double your money . . . Treble it . . . Roll up, roll up! Three-card Monte! Find the lady! A tenner a go – easy money. Suckers! Marks!

He knew he just had to keep calm, keep remembering that the police are not superhuman. Not infallible. They could be misdirected, too, just like anyone else. Oh sure, he knew there were smart ones like Roy Grace.

You are smart, Detective Superintendent, but beware. You might just be too smart for your own good. You should cut a little slack.

Otherwise there won't be any slack in that noose round your neck.

Not that I want to kill you. But then again, I didn't want to kill Lorna Belling. Never intended to. Not sure I actually did. But hey, whatever. Get too much closer and I'll need you dead.

Shit happens, eh?

He stared in the bathroom mirror at his face. A killer's face.

This past week I seem to have aged ten years. I'm starting to think like a killer. Hey! I really might be a killer! There are all kinds of mitigating circumstances but let's not risk that route. Juries are too unreliable, judges too mercurial. We're into survival, self-preservation, Darwinian rules apply now. Survival of the fittest. Just remember, life's a game. Keep hold of that. I have to win. Coming second is not an option. Coming second means going to prison. Banged up, locked away. Forgotten.

Like I always say, no one remembers who came second.

CHAPTER 57

Monday 25 April

Roy Grace sat in the tiny observation room, watching on the screen the live video feed of Kipp Brown being interviewed by Guy Batchelor and Jon Exton. He was accompanied by his solicitor, Allan Israel, a smart criminal lawyer who had a practice opposite Brighton's law courts and was a regular thorn in the side of Sussex police.

Brown's face was familiar to him from his regular adverts in the media, although he looked a little older, and a lot less charming than he appeared on camera. In his mid-forties, now dressed in a crumpled police-issue tracksuit and old trainers, he had a hard, scowling face beneath immaculate, shiny black hair. He sat very upright, alert, as if he was the inquisitor, not the two detectives, looking around him with an air of contempt.

As Batchelor completed the interview formalities he looked at the IFA. 'Mr Brown, are you aware that having been arrested, we are now empowered to search both your home and your workplace and seize anything that we deem appropriate to the investigation?'

'You've already taken my phone and laptop.'

'We are aware of your very respected position in this city,' Batchelor continued. 'I am hoping that if you are cooperative now, we may be able to avoid any embarrassment for you.'

'Embarrassment? You just discoed my car outside Brighton College!'

'Discoed?' Batchelor frowned, looking at Exton, who was also frowning.

'I'm a Kiwi. Grew up in New Zealand. That's what we say when the police stop a car – all the flashing lights. Disco. Gettit?'

'Ah.'

Exton grinned and nodded.

'Mr Brown,' Batchelor said. 'If you had told us the truth when we were talking to you before, we could have avoided all this.'

'I told you the truth.'

Looking at his notes, Batchelor continued. 'I asked you if you had left your office at any time during the afternoon of Wednesday, April 20th last week, and you said you had not. Is that correct?'

'Correct.'

'I also asked you if the name *Lorna Belling* meant anything to you, and you said it did not. Is that correct?'

'Yes.' Brown shot a glance at his lawyer, who was busy making notes, then again checked his own notes.

'I further asked you if you had visited Lorna Belling at her apartment in Vallance Mansions, Hove, on the afternoon of that day – Wednesday, April 20th – and you replied, "Absolutely not." Is that correct?'

'Yes.'

'You are sure, Mr Brown?'

'Yes.'

Batchelor made a note, then nodded at his colleague, DS Exton.

'Mr Brown, can you tell us about your relationship with Lorna Belling?'

Brown stiffened and looked at his solicitor.

Allan Israel intervened. 'What relevance does this have? This is very intrusive into my client's personal life.'

'It's very relevant,' Batchelor said.

Brown looked embarrassed. Then he shrugged. 'Yes, I don't deny it. She's an ex-girlfriend of mine – from some years back. My wife and I are going through a bad period – since our third child was born she's gone off sex. Like most of the wives of my golfing pals who've had kids. OK?'

'When we talked to you earlier today,' Exton said, 'you denied knowing her. Your full phone records put you in the vicinity of Vallance Mansions, where she had an apartment, on three occasions in the past week. The first was early afternoon Friday, April 15th. The second was for a two-hour period, 2 p.m. to 4 p.m. on Monday, April 18th, and the third – here's the interesting bit – between 1.45 p.m.

and 3.55 p.m. on Wednesday, April 20th. Can you explain that? Can you tell us who you were visiting?'

Brown turned to his solicitor and whispered to him. After nodding several times, Allan Israel requested five minutes alone with his client.

Batchelor went outside for a smoke, head bowed against the pelting rain, while Jon Exton sheltered in the doorway, discussing tactics with him. Roy Grace joined them moments later.

'What do you think, Roy?' Batchelor asked.

'Early doors, but so far from what he's saying and from his body language, I'm seeing a serial adulterer, but I don't feel I'm looking at a killer.'

Grace's phone rang. He switched it to silent and let it ring on.

'We're going to need his DNA sample sent for fast-track analysis, sir,' DS Exton said. 'It might be different if we get a match with Brown.'

'Actually, Jon, I don't think that would take us any further.'

'Why's that, sir?'

'Because we think Brown and Lorna Belling were shagging,' Grace said.

His phone vibrated. He looked down at the screen and saw he had a voicemail message.

'I disagree that it won't take us further, boss,' Batchelor interjected. 'We don't know what happened between Lorna and Brown – maybe she was blackmailing him. Threatening to expose him.

A married man, in a vulnerable position. You've seen all his adverts around the place. *Trust Kipp.* How much damage would it do to his reputation if she'd gone public in some way? Put it out on Twitter or Facebook, for instance?'

'Do you really think that with her violent husband she would have dared do that?'

'People don't always act rationally, boss.'

Grace nodded, pensively. 'That's for sure.'

'Interview with Kipp Brown, in the presence of his solicitor, Allan Israel, resumed at 11.17 a.m.,' Batchelor said for the benefit of the recording. Turning to Brown, he asked, 'Is there anything you would like to tell us?'

Visibly blanching, Brown said, 'OK, look, I didn't tell you the truth, because – well – hell – I didn't want this to get back to my wife. I – I did go and see her a few times, yes. We had sex. But that was all, I didn't kill her. I mean – you know – I really liked her. Hadn't seen her for years and by sheer chance we bumped into each other in a pub – the Friday before last. She was upset and I gave her a shoulder to cry on. You know how it is. And we'd been in regular contact since.'

'You didn't kill her?' Batchelor retorted. 'Why did you say that, Mr Brown?'

'I read in the *Argus* that she was found dead the next day. You guys bloody scared me. I didn't kill her, it wasn't me. I'm not a bloody murderer.'

'We've established that you have lied to us – why

should we believe you didn't kill her?' Batchelor pressed.

'I liked her! Jesus! I thought she was lovely, always have. She told me about her shit life with her husband who abused her. He's the guy you should be looking at, not me for God's sake.'

'Can you give me one good reason why we should believe you, after establishing you've lied to us?'

'You just *have* to believe me.' He looked at his solicitor. Israel, busy making notes, did not react.

'We *have* to believe you?' Batchelor said. 'We should believe a liar, should we? How do we know anything you tell us is the truth?'

There was a long silence. 'I did not hurt Lorna,' he said, lamely.

'Did something happen between you and her last Wednesday that made you angry?'

'Not at all. We had a nice time – OK – we made love, then I left – I had to get back to work. We arranged to meet again on Friday. Then – then I read in the paper – the *Argus* – that she had been found dead.'

'You didn't think to contact us when you read that?' Batchelor asked.

'No. Maybe I should have done – but – I thought if I came forward, the news would get out – and my wife would hear about it. It's one of the downsides of being well-known.'

There was a long silence. 'Is there anything else you would like to tell us?'

'No – I – to be honest, I knew very little about her life now, apart from what she told me. As I said, I really liked her. I thought she was very attractive, smart, funny. A nice lady. She was . . .' He shrugged.

'She was what, Mr Brown?'

'Vulnerable, I guess. She was someone I felt I wanted to get to know all over again.'

'So not someone you needed to kill?'

He threw his arms in the air. 'That's ridiculous! Why would I want to kill her? I actually thought—' He ran his hand over the back of his head. 'I actually thought this was someone I might have a future with. I know it might sound unconvincing to you guys – but it's the truth.'

'How did you contact Lorna?' Batchelor asked.

'She gave me her numbers – you'll find them on my phone.'

After a few moments, Allan Israel said, 'Gentlemen, if you have no further questions for my client, I would ask you to release him. He is, as you know, a highly respected member of the local business community, and he is not going to do a disappearing act on you. He will be available for further questioning whenever you require.'

Batchelor and Exton left the room to parlay with Roy Grace. They returned a few minutes later and informed Kipp Brown that he was being released on bail.

'My client would like the laptop and mobile

phone that you seized from his car returned to him immediately,' the solicitor said.

'They'll be returned to your client when we have finished examining them,' Batchelor replied.

'This is outrageous!' Brown glared at them. 'I need them for my business.'

'I'm sorry about that, sir, and I appreciate the inconvenience. As soon as the Digital Forensics team have made copies of their entire contents they will be returned to you.'

'How long will that be?'

Batchelor decided not to inflame him further by telling him that the team were currently running on a six-month backlog. He would put in a request to have them fast-tracked. 'As soon as possible,' he said.

'This is not acceptable,' Allan Israel retorted. 'These are the tools of my client's trade. I hope you understand that Sussex Police will be held accountable for any financial loss my client suffers?'

'We understand,' Batchelor replied. 'We will return these items to him as soon as possible.'

'So where's my Porsche?' Brown demanded.

'It's being forensically examined, sir,' Exton said.

'How long's that going to take?' He glared again at both detectives.

'All being well, a couple of days, and then it will be returned to you.'

Turning to his client, Allan Israel said, 'I'll give you a lift to your office.'

'My car had bloody well better not be damaged or I'll be suing you.'

Guy Batchelor really hoped it was. Not that he was malicious or anything. He just didn't like the man.

CHAPTER 58

Monday 25 April

Back in his office, Roy Grace listened to the voicemail that had come in earlier. It was an apologetic-sounding message from a DS in Professional Standards, following up on a request from the Independent Police Complaints Commission to investigate the death of Corin Belling.

He was about to return the call when there was a rap on the door, and as usual without waiting for his reply, Glenn Branson sauntered in.

'Hey, mate, heard you've been making a right pig's ear of everything in my absence!'

'Very funny. Good holiday?'

'Brilliant! Stayed at Siobhan's parents' villa near La Cala – it was fabulous.'

'So the romance is flourishing? Siobhan hasn't seen through you?'

Branson frowned. 'What?'

'Nah, she couldn't have done, could she?'

'What do you mean? *Couldn't* have done?'

'Coz you're too thick-skinned!'

'Thanks, I don't know why I bothered to come back.'

'Because you missed me?' Grace ventured.

'Yeah, a whole seven days with no one insulting me started to get on my nerves. So, what's up?'

'Where do you want me to begin?'

'At the beginning – that might be a good place.'

'You know what? A couple of days ago I actually thought I was missing you. Now—'

'Now you know you can't function without me, yeah?'

'Dream on.'

Branson perched on Roy's desk. 'So, start with Bruno, give me the full download.'

Grace filled him in, briefly, on meeting him in Germany, and bringing him home, Bruno going to the football with Jason Tingley and his son, the way he had seemingly taken to Noah, and swimming last night.

'No lingo problems?'

'He's pretty much completely bilingual.'

'And he starts at St Christopher's today?'

'He's having his assessment.'

'If he gets accepted, that's going to cost you!'

Grace shook his head. 'Sandy had a stash of money – from a rich old auntie who died. There's a trust fund set up for Bruno.'

'Great Dr Hook song that – about a rich old uncle who died.' He cocked his head in response to Grace's blank expression. 'Yeah, he's a bit young for your generation. He didn't come on the scene until the late 1960s.'

'I'm not even going to dignify that with a reply.'

'So, work,' Branson said. 'Lorna Belling – you're leaving Guy in charge?'

'He's doing a good job so far, but I'm keeping a close eye on it.'

'Helped by you killing the chief suspect?'

'Very funny. I tell you, this is a very strange one. Are we in the midst of a domestic abuse epidemic or something?'

'What do you mean?'

'There are three suspects in Lorna Belling's murder – and we're not ruling out the possibility of suicide, either. Two of them have a history with the police for violence against women.'

'Seriously?'

'Her husband was arrested after shoving dog shit in her mouth a couple of days before she died – and he had previous for similar offences. The next suspect, a little toerag called Seymour Darling, turns out to have form for violence against women. And now we have Mr Respectable, Kipp Brown, one of the city's biggest charitable benefactors, who has become the latest suspect.'

'Kipp Brown? You mean that *Trust Kipp* guy?'

'Exactly.'

'What's your gut feeling?'

'I don't have one on this yet, I have a totally open mind.'

'Want me to get involved?'

'No, we've got enough people on it. What I need from you right now is a lot of help on the Tooth, Crisp and Bentley cases.' He tapped the three manila folders on the small desk. All three were bound with white tape, one marked OPERATION VIOLIN, another, OPERATION HAYWAIN, and the third, OPERATION SPIDER. 'Evidence on Tooth, Op Violin, and on Crisp, Op Haywain, is pretty strong. With Tooth, we have our suspect on life support in hospital, with the medics unable to predict the outcome, so all we can do is wait. I'm less confident about Jodie Bentley, Operation Spider.'

'What are your worries about her?'

'I've got a case conference in chambers coming. We've key evidence from four principal expert witnesses. Dr James West from Liverpool University; the herpetologist Mark O'Shea; the Home Office pathologist Dr Colin Duncton, and our forensic podiatrist, Haydn Kelly. We are very reliant on Kelly's evidence for identifying her in several key locations – I think you should start by going through the evidence dossier, pulling out everything we are planning to use that he's given us, and see if you can book him for a day to come down and go through it all with you.'

'Are you worried about his evidence, boss?'

Grace shook his head. 'No, he's rock solid and has never let us down. He was brilliant on Operation Icon, the Gaia Lafayette case, and everything we've used him on. Just make sure we've got every box ticked on Op Spider. He'll be wanting to cooperate – another conviction helped by his evidence will be good for his career.'

'I'll call him right away.'

'So – wedding bells ringing soon with you and Siobhan? Should I phone Moss Bros and book my suit?'

Branson suddenly looked coy. 'Yeah, actually, maybe. There's something I was going to ask you – well – at the appropriate moment.'

'Oh?'

'Is this appropriate?'

'You tell me?'

With a big smile, Branson banged his fist on the Detective Superintendent's desk. 'There you bloody go again!'

'Go again?'

'Yeah – you always used to drive me mad, and now you're doing it again.'

'Doing what?'

'Replying to everything I ask you with a question.'

'What have you asked me?'

'You're doing it again.'

'I'm sorry, mate, you've lost me. Wind your neck in!'

Branson raised one finger in the air, then a second, followed by a third, counting out loud. 'One . . . two . . . three . . .'

Grace grinned.

The DI took a deep breath. 'What I want to ask you is – Roy – would you be my best man?'

'Blimey, you're really scraping the barrel. Couldn't you find someone you actually like?'

'Screw you!'

'I'd be massively honoured. Thank you. Seriously.'

'So long as you promise not to trash me in your speech, yeah?'

Grace looked him hard in the face. 'You look so damned happy – I'm thrilled for you, matey, I really am! You two are really good together. So when's the big day?'

'We've not set it yet. We're thinking this autumn.'

'Well don't leave it too long – I'm getting the impression you think I'm so old I might not last many more months.'

'Just keep taking the tablets.'

There was a knock on the door.

'Come in,' Grace called out.

It was Guy Batchelor, looking pleased, waving a sheet of paper in the air.

CHAPTER 59

Monday 25 April

'What do you think, should we pull Brown back in?' Batchelor said.

Roy Grace looked at the printout that had been passed on by Surrey and Sussex Forensics. It was the fingerprint report on identifying marks found in the flat giving a match with the fingerprints of Kipp Brown.

'The problem is, Guy, as we've said before, this is not telling us anything new. Kipp Brown already admitted in the interview that he'd been in the flat, and had sex with Lorna Belling on the afternoon of April 20th. This report just confirms he was there. How would it help us to recall him now?'

Batchelor looked awkward, standing, nodding thoughtfully. 'Yes, I guess you're right, chief. I just got overexcited by this result.'

'Look, Guy, you need to remember, if you are building a case against a suspect in this kind of investigation, we work closely with the Crown Prosecution Service. They'll appoint a lawyer to work with us. They can be the bane of our lives but ultimately, however obscure at times it may seem to any of us, they are on our side. I've been in court too often in my career with an absolute slam-dunk of a case, only to see a villain walk free thanks to a smart defence brief, or a bonkers jury. That's what we have to arm ourselves against here, OK?'

'I'm suitably chastened, boss!' Batchelor said, and bowed his head.

'Don't be, you're doing a good job, Guy.'

'Say that when we have the bastard who killed Lorna behind bars.'

Grace grimaced, but said nothing. Privately, he wasn't sure that was going to happen any time soon. Neither Brown nor Darling's body language had signalled they were killers. He still harboured the feeling that the killer was in a mortuary fridge, short of his legs. But to be sure, he needed Batchelor to eliminate Seymour Darling and Kipp Brown – as well as any other possible suspects who hadn't yet shown up on their radar.

His phone vibrated. It was ACC Pewe.

'Good morning, sir,' Grace said. He disliked this man so much, it stung him every time he had to say the deferential word *sir*.

Dispensing of any pleasantries, Pewe cut straight to the chase. 'Roy, you are aware, are you not, of the budget cuts to Sussex Police?'

'Very aware – *sir*.' The current government's dislike of the police – and savage budget cuts – were something every officer was only too well aware of. The feeling that they had been let down by the Conservatives – normally a pro-police party – was palpable.

'In which case, can you justify the cost of keeping a 24/7 guard on someone on life support who is, according to the doctors, in a persistent vegetative state?'

'Yes, sir, I can.'

'I'm all ears,' Pewe said.

'This man is a professional killer – a hitman – who we are pretty certain murdered two people in the UK last year, one in Sussex, and nearly murdered a third, a young boy. We believe he came back here to carry out another killing, possibly more. We can't take the risk of him escaping.'

'For God's sake, Roy, the man has a Glasgow Coma score of three!'

The Glasgow Coma Scale is a way of assessing a patient's response and awareness. A score of three means the patient does not open their eyes, does not respond verbally and does not move when stimulated to do so.

'Tooth did have a score of three when first admitted, sir,' Grace replied. 'But he has improved since then. He has now been re-assessed to a seven bordering eight.'

'Seven bordering eight?'

'Yes, sir. That means he opens his eyes in response to stimulus, makes incomprehensible sounds and demonstrates abnormal flexion to painful stimuli.'

'What's his prognosis?'

'No one really knows, sir. He suffered severely venomous snake and spider bites, and the medical staff have no experience of someone bitten by a combination of these creatures. He's been seen by a leading specialist brought down from St Thomas's in London, who had never dealt with such a combination of poisons before. The venom from each species, apparently, inflicts different long-term metabolic damage. At this stage we have no idea whether he will pull through, but he's clearly hellishly tough.'

'The cost of the guard on him is simply not justifiable, with his condition. It's not a good use of resources.'

'He's escaped from us twice before, sir. This is an extraordinarily resourceful man. I don't think we can take the chance.'

'We can't afford to keep a 24/7 police guard on him, Roy. It's an unnecessary drain on resources. I've spoken to the consultant in charge of him at the hospital who agrees that in no way is Tooth a flight risk. Or indeed any kind of a risk to anyone.'

'What do you suggest, *sir*? Would you like my wife and I to invite him to come and stay with us for the weekend, perhaps?'

'There's no need to be flippant.'

'No flippancy intended, *sir*. I'm trying to be realistic. This is a man who jumped into Shoreham Harbour last year, whom we presumed was drowned. He also previously disappeared from hospital after being admitted unconscious and seriously injured from a collision with a cyclist. We now have him back, and whilst he is currently incapacitated, we would have one hell of a job explaining to the media if he escaped from hospital – however improbable that might be.'

'You just have no idea about operational intelligence diversity, do you, Roy?'

Puzzled, Grace said, 'I'm sorry, sir, you've lost me on that one.'

'I lose you on everything,' Pewe snorted and hung up.

'Have a nice day, *sir*,' Grace said into the dead receiver. Then as he turned back to Batchelor there was a rap on the door, and without waiting for any answer, Norman Potting came barrelling in.

'Chief! Sorry to interrupt.' He looked at both of his senior officers with glee in his face. 'I thought you ought to know right away – we have a major development on Operation Bantam.'

'Yes?' Grace said.

'We have a new suspect!'

CHAPTER 60

Monday 25 April

Potting perched himself on the empty chair beside Guy Batchelor, and looking at each of his three fellow detectives in turn said, 'I've just found another *best friend* of Lorna Belling's, a lady called Kate Harmond – and been to see her.'

'How did you find her, Norman?' Batchelor asked.

Looking rather pleased with himself, he said, 'Facebook. I went to Lorna Belling's page and looked at the people she liked and had messaged. There seemed almost a bit of code going on between these two ladies, so I figured they were more than just plain Facebook pals. I was right. She's the manager of a boutique in the Lanes. Wasn't too much of a hardship seeing her – cor – she's a belter!'

'Did you say we have a new suspect or that you have a new date, Norman?' Grace asked a tad impatiently.

'Sorry, guv.' Looking contrite, he pulled out his

notebook, opened it and read for a moment. 'According to Kate Harmond, Lorna had been having an affair for some while.'

Grace frowned. 'With whom?'

'Is it Kipp Brown?' queried Batchelor.

'No, someone called Greg,' Potting replied.

'Do we have his last name?'

Potting shook his head. 'No, she said she never told her his last name. She said his wife was called Belinda, but she was always very circumspect with her about him.'

'How come her other *best friend*, Roxy Goldstein, didn't give us all this information?' Batchelor asked.

'Perhaps she didn't know. Kate Harmond told me, in confidence, that Lorna had covered for her some years back when she'd had an affair – so she was reciprocating now.'

'Greg and Belinda?' Batchelor said. 'She's her best friend and she never told her his full name? Isn't that odd? What about his profession – what did he do for a living?'

'Sounds like he lied for England, chief,' Potting replied. 'Kate Harmond had a very tearful phone call from Lorna on Friday morning, April 15th, the week before she died. This man – Greg – seems to have been stringing her along that he would leave his wife, and that Lorna and he would have a life together. According to Kate, this was what kept Lorna going – sustained her – through her very abusive marriage. But he'd given her one excuse after another for not leaving his wife.'

Potting turned the page. 'She said Lorna had apparently found out the truth by chance. This Greg told her he was taking his wife away on a holiday to help her get over the trauma of her father's death and was going to break the news on their return that he was leaving her. A hairdressing client who was by chance on the same island in the Maldives had met them – Lorna Belling saw a photograph of them all looking very loved-up. Lorna did some checking on his real identity and found out this *Belinda's* father is still alive and well, that Greg had totally lied about his profession, and – one other thing that really floored her, that he had never told her – he had a daughter. He'd always told Lorna he and his wife weren't able to have children, and that when they got together, finally, they would start a family.'

'Shit,' Glenn Branson said. 'What a complete bastard.'

'So he was just stringing her along all this time?' Batchelor said. 'For a bit of sex on the side?'

'That's what it looks like,' Potting agreed.

'Right, we need to look at her appointments diary, which I believe has been recovered from her home, and as a priority action, trace all her clients. They may have something to add.'

'I'm on that, Guy,' Potting said. 'There's a bit of a problem – it seems to have been mislaid. It's not in the exhibits cupboard.'

'You need to find it quickly, Norman, and get on it.'

'Yes, guv.'

'So what was it this Greg told Lorna he did for a living, Norman?' Batchelor asked.

'Kate Harmond was a bit vague on that – she said he'd told Lorna he was in financial services.'

'That's interesting,' Batchelor observed. 'Just like our friend Kipp Brown.'

Then Grace asked, 'So what does he actually do, Norman?'

'Well, this is the thing. Kate was away on a week's buying trip in Italy when she had that call. She'd arranged to meet Lorna for lunch last Thursday, April 21st – the day she was found dead – and Lorna had promised she'd tell her all the details then. And here's the most significant bit – she said that Lorna was livid with this man and was going to expose him to his family and work and ruin his life. She didn't actually tell Kate what his job was. Kate said she told her not to act impulsively, to wait until they'd met up and talked it through – she was concerned for her about the consequences of blowing it all open and her husband finding out. Apparently Lorna replied that she didn't care. Her sister lives in Sydney, Australia, recently divorced from a wealthy guy with a big settlement and a fancy house, and she was planning to up-sticks and join her out there.'

The four of them were silent for some moments. 'Nice work, Norman,' Guy Batchelor said.

'So what we don't know is' – Glenn Branson was looking pensively up at the ceiling, as if thinking out loud – 'did Lorna Belling lose the plot with him on or before the day she was killed?'

'*Greg* is in financial services. Could it be Kipp Brown using a pseudonym?' Grace posited.

'It sounds like it could well be, chief,' Batchelor said.

'We need to find out urgently the real identities of *Greg* and *Belinda*,' Grace said. 'Are there any clues on Lorna's social media pages?'

'Nothing on Facebook about either of them,' Potting said. 'Lorna has a Twitter account, but she only has seven followers, all in hair products.'

'There's a problem with that, boss,' Batchelor said. 'We still haven't found her computer.'

'What about phone calls to him? She must have made calls or sent texts to him?'

'They've gone back two months on the phone that was in her house,' Potting said. 'In addition to Kate Harmond and Roxy Goldstein, Lorna Belling made calls to her husband, to the police, to a few takeaway places – a Thai, a pizza place and an Indian. To a couple of car dealers, and to the man we already have as a suspect, Seymour Darling. You'd have thought if she was having an affair there would be dozens of calls or texts, or both, to her lover. But nothing. That would indicate she had a second phone.'

'We know she had a second phone, from Kipp Brown's interview, and we have the number,'

Grace said. 'It's a burner – a pay-as-you-go – make a note that we need to get the records. Perhaps whoever killed her took both that phone and the computer and ditched them. It sounds possible that she confronted this Greg after catching him out, perhaps threatening to expose him, and he killed her to stop her from telling anyone, then took both that phone and her computer.'

'It's a good hypothesis, boss,' Glenn Branson said.

'Which puts this mysterious Greg as our prime suspect, do you think?' Guy Batchelor asked.

'It does, but I'm not ruling out anybody at this stage. We just don't know what happened between that call she had with her friend in Italy on the Friday and Wednesday afternoon or evening.' Grace thought for a moment. 'Greg and Belinda. Have we talked to any other friends of Lorna Belling?'

'We're working through her clients that we know about,' Potting said. 'After the *Argus* report some of them came forward, including a lady called Sandra Zandler who was due to see her early Thursday morning at Lorna's home address. There was no reply when she got there and she was devastated, because she was flying off early in the afternoon on a special fiftieth birthday trip, with her husband, to Venice. We asked if she knew any of Lorna Belling's other clients, but she didn't. I'm afraid without the appointments book it's very slow progress. We've definitely not spoken to everyone yet. DCs Jack Alexander and Velvet Wilde are on it – and our American friend, NotMuch.'

Grace looked at him. 'I'm sorry – who did you say, Norman?'

'Arnie Crown. NotMuch.'

'NotMuch?'

Potting nodded. 'Yes, he's very short – you know, chief. Not much cop.'

Branson and Grace both grinned. 'Very good, Norman. So you're planning to ruin any possible friendship we might have with the FBI?'

'Actually, chief, he told me that was his nickname in the States.'

Grace looked at his watch. 'OK.' He turned to Potting. 'You've done a great job, Norman. I'll leave you and Guy to get on with everything. Make sure you get hold of Lorna's appointment book.'

As the two detectives left his office, closing the door behind them, Grace said to Branson, 'So what do you think?'

'Four suspects, each with a rock solid motive. Her husband, Seymour Darling, Kipp Brown and now this *Greg*. And suicide still in the frame.' Then seeing the Detective Superintendent's quizzical look, he said, 'What?'

Grace smiled.

'Am I missing something?'

Grace shook his head. 'Not you specifically. All of us, including me. We're all missing something.'

'Oh yes – what is it?'

'I don't know. I haven't bloody figured it out. It's just a gut feeling – something's not right.'

'Not right?'

He was interrupted by his private phone ringing. It was Cleo.

Apologizing to Branson, he answered. 'Hi!'

'Can you talk?' she asked.

'I'm in a meeting. Anything urgent? How did it go at the school?'

'They've accepted him! Bruno can start right away – I'm just sorting out his uniform now.'

'That's brilliant news – is he pleased?'

'I'm not sure.'

'Listen, I'll call you back as soon as I can.'

'Love you!'

Sheepishly, looking at Branson, he murmured, 'Me too.'

As he ended the call, Branson asked, 'What's not right, Roy? What are we missing?'

Grace shoved the bundle of SIO files on Operation Bantam across to him. 'Can you take a look through it for me with fresh eyes and see if you can find out?'

'OK, sure. Want me to read it here or take it to my desk?'

'Take it to your desk, bell me when you've finished.'

Branson looked at the thickness of the file. 'In about three weeks?'

'Try three hours.'

CHAPTER 61

Monday 25 April

As the DI closed the door behind him, Grace sat and called Cleo back, but her phone went to voicemail. He left a message then sat quietly, thinking, ignoring the steady ping of incoming emails.

Few things in this imperfect world could ever be made perfect, or be made wholly right. But he knew in his heart that he always tried his damnedest. It had destroyed his first marriage to Sandy, and he hoped desperately it would never do the same for his second, to Cleo. But he knew equally from this career he had chosen, that however much he loved his family, there were always going to be times when, hard as it was on his private life, his work had to take priority.

Only occasionally, during rare moments of down-time when he had the opportunity to reflect, would he wonder whether, if he had known when he had chosen to work in Major Crime just what it would mean to his home life, might he have chosen a different career altogether – or at least a different area of policing? And always he came to the same answer. No, never. There was nothing in the world he would prefer to be doing. This job had almost chosen him – perhaps, he wondered sometimes, he had the same certainty about it as priests who had a calling. It felt like his destiny, and the principal reason he existed.

And this despite the knowledge that whilst the scales of justice hung from the statue on the roof of the Old Bailey, the Central Criminal Court, the crime and the punishment rarely balanced – especially when it came to murder. Sooner or later most murderers would be freed on licence. Killers might walk out of jail; but murder victims would never walk out of their final resting place.

In those moments of doubt, he would recall what he had learned at police college all those years back, when he had been training to be a detective. The FBI moral code on murder investigation, written by its first director, J. Edgar Hoover: 'No greater honour will ever be bestowed on an officer, nor a more profound duty imposed on him, than when he or she is entrusted with the investigation of the death of a fellow human being.'

There was something else, incredibly wise, that Hoover had also once said, that Roy Grace agreed with: 'The cure for crime is not the electric chair but the high chair.'

It wasn't only the impact on his family life that got to him at times, it was all the bureaucracy that the police were saddled with these days. Sure, public accountability was important – police officers were, after all, public servants. But the extent to which they had to justify every action could be wearing. The current Independent Police Complaints Commission investigation into the death of Corin Belling would take hours, if not days, of his time and quite possibly lead to a hearing which, if it went the wrong way, could result in him being disciplined – or worse.

But for now he put that aside, focusing back on Lorna Belling. He wanted Guy Batchelor to remain as deputy SIO, but at the end of the day the ultimate responsibility rested with him, and if there was a screw-up, Cassian Pewe would be giving him short shrift for delegating to an inexperienced officer.

Thinking hard, he opened his notebook and picked up a pen from his desk. Four suspects. Plus a potential suicide as an alternative explanation. Corin Belling was a plausible suspect. As well as Seymour Darling – *Mr Angry*? Possible but unlikely – although clearly an irrational man, he could not be ruled out. Kipp Brown? An old flame who wanted more? What would he have had to gain by killing her? Lorna's silence perhaps? OK, for a man in his position in society that could indeed be a motive. There were plenty of social studies that showed being a psychopath was one good qualification for succeeding in business. Kipp Brown displayed signs of psychopathy, for sure.

Suicide after discovering the bitter truth about

the man who had promised her a future? Possible, too.

And now the new suspect, Greg. Mr Mystery Man. He needed to be found urgently and eliminated. Or not.

When you have eliminated the impossible . . .

He leaned forward and tapped his keyboard, calling up the Murder Investigation Manual. Then waited and waited. God, the sodding computer system could be so slow at times. It was a common frustration he shared with every member of Sussex Police – and with every officer he had ever met from any other force around the country. Just how ridiculously slow at times the computers could be. Another example of police bureaucracy – by the time decisions were made on a new system – often taking years – it was already archaic. And by the time it was installed and everyone had got their heads round it, systems had moved on a decade. And, of course, there was no budget to upgrade.

The Manual finally appeared and he navigated the index, clicking on MURDER INVESTIGATION MODEL.

Despite all his experience, Roy Grace was always aware of the dangers of being complacent. There were times when he felt the need to check and tick every box in order. Both to ensure he did not miss anything, but also to cover his back with Pewe.

First up on the list was *Identify Suspects.* He checked his entries in his Investigators' Notebook, reading down the list; the reasons for each potential suspect, and the possibility of suicide.

Next came *Intelligence Opportunities*, which included house-to-house, CCTV and ANPR.

He updated the entries relating to the beer cans and cigarette butts, as well as Lorna's phone, her possibly missing laptop, and the circuit board found in the flat.

Postmortem Forensics. The interim report from Theobald gave the cause of death as being: 1A. *Head trauma.* 1B. *Electrocution.* He also made a note that he was awaiting DNA results.

Crime Scene Assessment. He refreshed the details, noting the apparent missing picture on the wall.

Witness Search. He wrote a summary of Seymour Darling's interview, and the further deployment of an outside enquiry team to do a house-to-house.

Victim Enquiries. He wrote a summary of Norman Potting's interviews with Lorna's friends.

Possible Motives. That filled two pages.

Media. He wrote down the appeals for information in the press release that had been put out to the *Argus* newspaper, the local television station, Latest TV, as well as Radio Sussex, Juice and the weekly *Brighton & Hove Independent.*

The final item was *Other Significant Critical Actions.* He checked through the details of his attempt to interview and his pursuit of Corin Belling, the arrests and the interviews under caution of Seymour Darling and Kipp Brown, and the latest information about the new suspect, known only as Greg.

When he'd finished he called Batchelor. 'Guy, I need you to speak to Seymour Darling, purely as a witness, with his solicitor present, and show him the recording of Kipp Brown. Ask him if this is the James Bond character he claims he saw outside Lorna Belling's rented flat.'

'Leave it with me, boss.'

'Let me know right away.'

'Absolutely.'

When he ended the call, Grace called the DI in Professional Standards for an update on the IPCC investigation, but he wasn't overly worried. Only one thing would make a man like Belling run away from a police officer wanting to question him – and that was guilt.

CHAPTER 62

Monday 25 April

He'd heard it said that you cross a personal Rubicon when you kill. And now he understood that. Murder was the one act for which there was no possible restitution. He preferred to think of it as an *act* rather than a *crime*. He wasn't a criminal and he still was not sure that Lorna Belling's death was as a result of his *act*.

Not completely sure.

Maybe he never would be. But the one thing he was sure of was that no one was ever going to get him over her death.

Detective Superintendent Roy Grace, you're a smart man and you have a smart team behind you. Honestly, if I ever had the misfortune to have a loved one murdered, you are the detective I would want to have heading the enquiry. Well, let's put this into perspective. Ordinarily I would.

Really, and I'm not just saying this out of bullshit. It's true.

Because you are so smart.

And this is the problem I have with you.

I can't go down over this, it's just not an option. If it ends up in a choice of you or me, I'm afraid it would have to be you.

I know you'll think I've probably lost the plot and you'd be right. Everything's broken loose inside my head, the fixings have all sheared, the stuff – my thoughts – are all over the place and I'm having a hard time holding them together.

But please take one thing with you – and it is this: My respect for you. You're good! Shit. You are really good! But get too close and you'll be a goner, just like sweet Lorna. And that thought makes me sad.

Really, very sad.

In another life you and I could have been just fine.

But it doesn't look like it's working out that way.

So sad.

CHAPTER 63

Monday 25 April

Juliet Solomon and Matt Robinson, partnered again on B Section, were an hour and a half into their eight-hour shift on lates. It was just gone 7.30 p.m. After catching up on paperwork whilst waiting around at Brighton's John Street police station for a shout – a call-out to an incident – they decided to take a car and go out *hunting*, as Matt called it. Cruising around, being the visible police that the Police and Crime Commissioner Nicola Roigard, and the public, wanted.

Juliet Solomon drove, heading down towards the seafront. They crossed the roundabout in front of the Palace Pier and headed along Kingsway. As they drove they were watching the streets and the occupants of cars, looking for the usual suspects – local drug dealers, criminals who had absconded from prison or failed to meet bail or probation terms, drink drivers, someone on their mobile phone whilst driving.

It was a foul night, with rain pelting down. 'PC

Rain', the police jokingly called it. The streets were almost deserted. Not many people ventured out on a wet Monday night. But the overcast sky wasn't completely dark yet.

'I like this time of year,' Juliet said. 'After the clocks have gone forward and it's suddenly lighter much longer in the evenings. Spring on its way. It always cheers me up.'

Peering at the road ahead through the wipers, then at the deserted pavements on both sides, Matt Robinson retorted, 'Spring? You must have good vision!'

'Ha ha.'

As they approached The Grand and Metropole hotels she nodded at the tower coming up on their left, which rose 160 metres into the sky. A mirrored doughnut-shaped glass pod – the viewing platform – was slowly rising, like a vertical cable car. Its construction had caused much local controversy.

'What do you think now it's finished? You didn't like it when it first started going up, did you?' asked Juliet.

'Yeah, actually I really like it now. It's pretty cool – took Steph and the boys on it a couple of weeks ago – awesome view! How about you?'

'I'm getting more used to it. I love the underneath of the pod, all mirrored – very UFO!' she conceded. 'I guess we now have to wait for the first jumper.'

'You're a right cynic!' he said. 'Or should I say pessimist.'

'You know the definition of a pessimist?'

'I think I'm about to. What is it?'

'An optimist with experience.'

He shook his head, grinning. 'I think it's sealed – no one could get up there to jump.'

'Sure they could, there's an inspection ladder up the inside – metal rungs.'

Matt Robinson shuddered. 'I don't have a head for heights.'

'I'm fine with them, my dad was a builder – I was always scaling ladders with him and crawling over rooftops when I was a kid.'

'Bloody hell – hadn't he heard of health and safety?'

'Clearly not, he fell to his death when I was eighteen, off one of the roofs at the Pavilion.'

'Wow, I'm sorry, that's so sad.'

They drove on along the seafront, but there was barely a soul around, and the traffic was light. They stopped a van with a tail light that was out, and Robinson hurried through the rain to the cab to advise the driver. Then as he got back in the car, and began wiping his glasses, a Grade One call came in. A man reported acting suspiciously outside an electrical goods depot on the Lewes Road.

Pleased at having some action, he leaned forward and switched on the blue lights and siren as his colleague accelerated forward, racing past two vehicles, and tapped in the address on the satnav. Then, as they turned right into Grand Avenue, they were told to stand down as two other response cars were now at the scene and the suspect was being spoken to.

They turned the car round, deciding to head back into central Brighton and cruise around there. As they drove they passed the time by discussing their favourite – and least favourite – kinds of incidents. He loathed minor road traffic collisions, he told his work buddy, when both sides were arguing hammer and tongs with each other and you could get no sense out of anyone. She replied that what she disliked most of all were domestics – fights between couples. Not many officers enjoyed intervening in those – too often a chair would come flying at you as you went in through the door, or one or other of the parties would turn on you.

Juliet said she liked blue-light runs most of all – the money-can't-buy adrenaline rush that was better than any fairground ride, in her view. Matt said he enjoyed getting in a roll-around in a pub fight.

As they turned left up Preston Street, a road lined with restaurants on both sides, and a regular hotspot of trouble later in the week, a swarthy man in a bomber jacket suddenly jumped into the road in front of them, flagging them down urgently.

Juliet Solomon halted the car, and Robinson lowered his window. Before he could say anything, the man, very agitated, pointed at a Ferrari parked just behind him.

'Look! Those fuckers in that shitbox Prius just reversed into me – and they're saying I drove into them!'

Robinson turned to Solomon with a quizzical expression. 'Want it?'

'It's all yours,' she replied.

Pulling on his cap, Robinson opened his door and climbed out into the rain, which was coming down even harder now. Although not tall, his hefty frame gave him the aura of a nightclub bouncer, and he had a particular glare for confronting troublemakers that he had honed to perfection over the years – and it generally worked.

Two men climbed out of the small saloon parked just up the hill from the Ferrari. One was tall, wearing a beanie, most of his face and hands covered in tattoos, the other short and mean-looking, whom Robinson recognized. A local scrote, with a barbed-wire tattoo round his neck, who had a long record of mostly petty crime – and jail.

'All right,' Robinson said calmly. 'Who are the drivers of both cars?'

The swarthy man and the scrote each said they were.

Robinson could have sworn that through the windscreen, in the dry warm interior of the Ford Mondeo, he could see his colleague grinning.

He raised two fingers at her behind his back.

CHAPTER 64

Monday 25 April

The Sussex Police Force Control Room is housed in a futuristic-looking red-brick structure on the headquarters campus. Inside is a large, open-plan area, covering two floors, with rows of computer terminals, many of their screens showing multiple images – some small-scale street maps, others live images from the Sussex Police's 850 CCTV cameras located around the county.

To the casual observer, with its atmosphere of quiet, purposeful concentration, it could be the offices of any number of different organizations – perhaps an insurance company, an online retailer, or a financial institution. But it is actually the nerve centre of policing the county, the hub where every emergency call to the force is received and responded to.

Evie Leigh looked at her watch and yawned. Two minutes to eight. Another four hours to go till the end of her twelve-hour shift. She looked at the clock up on the wall, as if expecting – willing – the hands to have jumped forward to hours later. But it said the same as her watch. 7.58 p.m.

Slow time. That police expression had a whole new meaning at the moment. What a dull day – quieter than she could ever remember. Not that anyone in here – or in the police in general – would ever dare say the Q word, as 'quiet' was known. It was an instant jinx. But she really felt like shouting it out now, just to liven things up.

She wasn't going to need to.

Evie loved her job as an emergency controller, because you literally never knew what was going to happen in ten seconds' time – a bank robbery, a serious accident, someone threatening to jump off a building, a pub brawl, someone breaking into a house – and normally the days shot by, often seeming too short when she was really busy and the adrenaline was pumping.

But today, she thought, you could be forgiven for thinking Sussex Police had done their job zealously and eliminated crime in the county. Sure, Mondays were never the liveliest of nights, particularly a wet one, but even so!

Fifty people worked down on this level and a further thirty on the upper level; most of them were civilians, a good third of whom were retired police officers who had returned to work, despite their pension pots, either because they needed the money or because they missed the job. The civilians here, like herself, were identifiable by their royal blue polo shirts with the words POLICE

SUPPORT STAFF embroidered in white on their sleeves, as opposed to the black shirts worn by the serving police officers.

They were presided over around the clock by a rota of Ops-1 Inspectors. The current duty Ops-1 was Kim Sherwood. In her early fifties, with a youthful face topped with short, fair hair, she was a year away from retirement – and dreading it. Kim loved every second of this job which carried huge responsibilities. Between the hours of 2 a.m. and 7 a.m. the Ops-1 Inspector was the most senior officer on duty in the whole of Sussex Police.

Her work station was a screened-off command centre with a battery of monitors. One, a touch-screen, operated as her eyes and ears on this whole department. Above her desk was a screen on which she could view the images from any of the county's CCTV cameras. With the toggle lever on her desk, Kim Sherwood could rotate and zoom over half of them directly.

At the rows of desks in front of her, and to either side, as well as on the split-level floor above, sat the radio operators and the controllers, each wearing a headset. The latter's role was to assess all emergency calls, grade them in terms of level of urgency and dispatch police officers – either in vehicles or on foot – to respond, to liaise with them until they were on the scene, and where possible follow progress on the monitors.

On an average day here they would get between 1,500 to 2,500 calls. Many of them were not emergencies at all – someone locked out of their flat, or a cat gone missing, or someone's lawn-mower stolen from their garden shed. And some were downright ridiculous, such as one she'd had yesterday from a drunk, saying he'd had too much in a pub and didn't think he should drive so he'd like the police to send a car over to give him a lift home.

Calls like that were a menace because they could block and delay a real emergency where every second counted – and those were the ones Evie liked best, the real heart-thumping, against-the-clock emergencies. So far, she'd not had one all day. Looking at the wall clock yet again, she realized the boredom was making her hungry. She was trying to diet, but one of her colleagues was going round collecting orders for a curry run to a balti house. The thought of eating her cold tuna salad whilst the room filled with the aroma of Indian spices, and everyone around her was munching on a poppadum, was too much, and her resolve crumbled. She added her name to the list, and as usual ordered far too much – an onion bhaji, chicken korma, garlic naan, two poppadums and basmati rice.

Then her phone warbled.

'Sussex Police, emergency, how can I help?' she answered, and immediately looked at the number and approximate location that showed on the screen. A mobile phone in the Hangleton area.

She could barely hear a response, a tiny voice,

just a whisper. She wondered for an instant if it was a child playing around with a phone – that happened often.

'Hello, caller, can you speak up please, I can't hear you.'

The terror in the woman's voice that came back chilled her bones. It was only very slightly louder, still whispering as if fearful of being heard, but now Evie could just about make out what she was saying.

'Help me, please God, help me, help me, he's coming up the stairs – he's got an axe – he's going to kill me.'

CHAPTER 65

Monday 25 April

'What do you mean you can't see any mark? There's a fucking great dent, officer!' The swarthy man in the leather jacket pointed at the front spoiler of his Ferrari.

Matt Robinson crouched down on the wet road, beneath the glare of a street light, and switched on his torch. Rain was spotting his glasses and running down the back of his neck. He shone the beam on the silver paintwork but was struggling to see anything beyond a tiny mark, no more than a centimetre long. 'I really can't see anything more than that scratch.'

'Do you have any idea how much paintwork on a Ferrari costs to repair? Fucking thousands, I'm telling you.'

'A bit of T-Cut would get rid of that.'

'*T-Cut?* What do you think this is – some old banger? This is a Ferrari LaFerrari, OK? It's a £350,000 car – and you're telling me to put fucking *T-Cut* on it?'

'With all due respect, sir, cars do get bumped when they're parked on streets – it's a fact of life.'

'Oh, right, what are you telling me? That you don't know how to make the streets of Brighton safe? That you police are not doing your job properly, right?' He jerked a finger at the driver of the Prius. 'That fucking moron shouldn't be on the roads, he's probably drunk – are you going to breathalyse him?'

It was then that Robinson smelled the faint whiff of alcohol on the man's breath. A voice came over his radio, but the din of the rain made it hard to hear what the Control Room was saying. 'Have *you* been drinking, sir?'

'Oh, that's great that is, how fucking great is that?'

'Would you mind answering my question, sir.' Matt Robinson stood up, to his full height, and suddenly saw the man's demeanour change.

'No – well – just one, a half, that's all.'

'I'm going to require you to take a breath test, sir.'

'What? You can't be serious. Some moron reverses into my parked car and now you're picking on me?'

'I'm not *picking* on anyone, sir, I will be requiring the other gentleman to take a breath test too.'

Suddenly Robinson heard his colleague calling out, urgently. He turned.

Juliet Solomon had the window down and was calling out to him. 'Matt, we're needed, a Grade One – someone's being attacked with an axe.'

'Looks like it's your lucky night,' Robinson said to the Ferrari owner. 'We've got to go.'

The man glared at him. 'My lucky night? Someone crashes into my car and that makes it my lucky night?'

'Sometimes the Lord works in mysterious ways,' Robinson replied, climbing back into the Mondeo. Before he had even shut the door the car accelerated hard away, up the hill, blue lights flashing and siren wailing.

'Well fuck you, officer!' the man yelled after it. Then, turning round to speak to the Prius driver, he couldn't believe his eyes. The car had gone, glided silently off. It was turning left at the lights, onto the seafront. 'Hey! Hey! Hey, you fuckers!' He sprinted down towards it, but the lights changed to green, and it was gone.

Robinson leaned forward, tapping the address Solomon gave him into the satnav. 'What details do we have?' Then he tugged out his handkerchief to wipe his glasses again.

'A domestic, but it sounds a bad one, husband's threatening her with an axe.'

'A lumberjack, is he?'

She grinned, then concentrated fiercely again on her driving. 'Left or right at the top, do you think?' she asked.

The satnav hadn't yet started. He thought for a moment, slivers of blue light flaring off the shop and restaurant windows on either side of them, working out the quickest route. 'Left.'

At that moment the satnav arrow confirmed this.

'We're getting all our favourites tonight,' he grumbled, as she turned through the red light and accelerated hard along Western Road. 'First a minor RTC and now a domestic.'

They heard the voice of the Control Room despatcher. 'Charlie Romeo Zero Five?'

'Charlie Romeo Zero Five,' Robinson replied.

'I have an update for you on the situation at 29 Hangleton Rise. The woman has barricaded herself in an upstairs room and her husband is trying to break down the door.'

CHAPTER 66

Monday 25 April

In the Force Control Room the semblance of calm continued. Everyone else was unaware of the drama that was unfolding for Evie Leigh and the Ops-1 Inspector, Kim Sherwood, who was now alerted and listening in.

Through her headphones Evie heard the woman's screams and dull thuds, each blow sounding louder, like a sledgehammer pounding against wood. The screams getting louder too, deeper and deeper terror. Then she was whimpering. Somewhere in the background a dog was barking furiously.

All her training kicking in, Evie kept calm, trying to give reassurance to the trapped woman, whose name she had managed to get from her. 'Trish,' she said. 'Just stay on the line. The police are on their way to you, they're only minutes away, you'll be OK.'

'I can see the blade of the axe! No! No! Oh, God help me. Help me, someone, please help me, please help me!'

'Trish,' Evie said, urgently but still calmly. 'Is there any way out of the room – can you get out of the window?'

'It's double – double-glazed – sealed units – only a tiny – tiny bit at the top – to stop burglars—'

Evie could hear another thud. A terrible scream – she could feel the woman's utter terror. Then the sound of splintering wood. At the bottom of the street map displayed on her screen she saw the call sign of the response car that had been allocated, Charlie Romeo Zero Five. As she continued watching, calculating the ETA, the pink symbol of the car moved a block nearer, then another, in rapid succession, as it then began heading west along the Old Shoreham Road. Good, she thought, they were sensibly bypassing the risk of getting delayed by the level crossing on Boundary Road if they'd gone that route. But they were still a crucial three minutes away.

Then she heard an even louder crashing sound, and now a truly heart-wrenching scream from the woman.

At her desk, the Ops-1 Inspector had to make a fast decision. Was this a firearms response, a uniform response but with armed tactical relocation, or a divisional response with local supervision to command. Kim Sherwood decided on the first option and noted her decision on the CAD. Out of courtesy she immediately asked for permission to talk through to the two officers in the response car attending.

'Charlie Romeo Zero Five this is Ops-1.'

Moments later she heard a male voice, 'Charlie Romeo Zero Five.'

'Charlie Romeo Zero Five, how far from the scene are you?'

'Ops-1, our ETA is three minutes.'

'The situation is critical. We understand a woman, Trish Darling, is locked in an upstairs room with her husband, who has a previous record of violence, attempting to break down the door. We believe she may be in a potentially life-threatening situation. Clear?'

'Yes, yes.'

'Use whatever force you need to get inside the house – put the door in or go through a window – and I'm granting you Taser authority. There's a marker on the house. The husband has a criminal record for violence against women, and there is an aggressive dog in the house. We believe the husband is at present armed with an axe. I have declared this a spontaneous firearms incident and I have more response units en route as well as a dog handler, but if you get to the scene first don't wait, go straight in and be careful.'

'Yes, yes, ma'am.'

Inside the car, Matt Robinson shot a glance at his colleague, who had been listening on her radio.

Juliet Solomon grimaced, and for a moment both of them were silent. Some call handlers could be overdramatic, and you'd arrive in a posse of cars, lights blazing and sirens wailing, to find it was nothing more than a baby screaming, or some violent scene on a television set turned up too loud, that had been reported by an overzealous neighbour as a person being attacked. But this job felt real.

Close to driving faster than she was truly comfortable with in these conditions, the PC pushed the speed up even more, both of them keeping their eyes peeled in the poor visibility, scanning the road ahead for someone not paying attention – or just plain bloody-minded – who might pull out in front of them, or an idiot cyclist with no lights or reflective clothing.

Robinson glanced at the satnav screen. 'Two minutes,' he said.

The voice of Ops-1 came through the radio again. 'Charlie Romeo Zero Five?'

'Charlie Romeo Zero Five,' Robinson answered.

'It sounds like the offender has broken through the door and is now in the room with the woman. How close are you?'

'Less than two minutes, ma'am.'

Robinson knew that just two seconds could be a long time in a fight. Someone could do a lot of damage in two seconds, let alone two minutes. He looked at the road ahead, then the speedometer, then the road again, thinking, trying to visualize Hangleton Rise. He knew the street, but not well. Small two-storey houses, post-war, a mix of terraces, semis and some detached. A couple of low-rise council blocks along there but mostly it was privately owned residential, with one short parade of shops.

Then Ops-1 came through on the radio again. 'Charlie Romeo Zero Five?'

'Charlie Romeo Zero Five,' he replied.

'Charlie Romeo Zero Five, I have a street plan and a Google Earth view of 29 Hangleton Rise. It's a detached property with easy access round to the side and rear. There'll be a second response unit with you within three minutes and a further following, as well as firearms who are six minutes away. All understood?'

'Yes, yes.'

Despite his years of experience as a Special, he had butterflies in his stomach. They'd be gone the moment he was out of the car, he knew, and all his training kicked in.

They made a right turn, into Hangleton Rise.

He reached across and unclipped his seat belt, as Solomon unclipped the safety strap on her Taser holster.

CHAPTER 67

Monday 25 April

Above the piercing screaming of the petrified woman, and the much fainter sound of an approaching siren, Evie Leigh could hear shouting through her headset, an ugly, angry male voice.

'You bitch, what you doing with that in your hand? Phoning the police – you think they'll help? You're better-off phoning a friend – or asking the audience, eh? Ask the audience, go on, ask them. Three questions – yeah? *Is my husband going to kill me? Is my husband going to kill me? Is my husband going to kill me?*'

On her screen, Evie saw the pink symbol of the car halt at the address; it was accompanied by the message she was always relieved to see. *Officers at scene.*

Usually that would be the end of her involvement, but not right now. No stranger to terror, she had been on the receiving end of calls from people in the middle of the night who had just heard breaking glass downstairs in their home; from a woman locked in the boot of a stolen car; from a mother whose baby had vanished from its pushchair outside a shop in a busy high street.

But nothing in all her experience was as heart-wrenching as this. She could feel the woman's utter fear and, despite remaining steady herself, trying to calm the woman down and get her to think of any possible options, in her heart she wanted to dash from the Control Room to the woman's home and do something, herself, to protect her from this bastard.

There were two other important reasons for keeping the line open. The recording would provide good evidence for anything that happened subsequently, including rebutting any allegation of excessive force by the police, and it would provide intelligence for other officers attending, as initially Charlie Romeo Zero Five would be too busy to provide much of an update.

There was a scream so piercing it sent shivers spiking through her.

Then again.

'Pleeeeeeeaaaasssssssssseeeeeeee no, no, no, no!'

Then a terrible thud, followed by a scream of agony. Then another. Another.

Another.

A groan.

Another.

'Trish?' Evie asked, her own voice quavering. She was shaking. 'Trish? Trish? Can you hear me, Trish? Trish?'

* * *

Matt Robinson had his door open before the car had come to a halt. He jumped out, with the wheels still rolling, his boots slipping on the wet pavement, the momentum unbalancing him and almost hurling him to the ground.

He ran round to the rear of the car, grabbed the yellow battering ram from the boot, then joined by his colleague, sprinted up the short path to the blue front door. In the distance he could hear the sound of an approaching siren, but it was some way off. He shot a glance at Juliet Solomon and she nodded, as if in confirmation. Without hesitating, he swung the heavy ram at the door, throwing all his considerable weight behind it, and stumbled over the sill as the door burst open, ripping away part of the frame with it.

As they entered the hallway, both shouting loudly, 'POLICE! POLICE! THIS IS THE POLICE!' they were confronted by a large, hostile brown dog, standing waist-height to Robinson and growling at them from what looked like the doorway to the kitchen.

Focused on the stairs, Robinson turned away from the dog, avoiding eye contact with it, but braced with the ram in case it came at him, and noticed his colleague taking out her pepper spray. He hoped the animal would stay where it was, not wanting to hurt it, and sprinted up the stairs, shouting out again, 'POLICE! POLICE!' Then, 'Mrs Darling? Mrs Darling?'

At the top was a short landing, and as Juliet

Solomon reached her colleague, the dog was standing at the bottom of the stairs barking at them excitedly, as if having decided this was now some great game everyone was playing. Neither police officer had to look far. Directly in front of them was a white door – or the remains of one. Its centre had been kicked or hacked out, making enough of a hole for a grown person to climb through. On the other side of it they could see a figure standing. A small, thin man in his early fifties, wearing a baggy knitted jumper and grey flannel trousers.

He was just standing, motionless, holding a wood axe, both hands gripping the handle, the way he might hold a barbell. There was blood on the blade and no expression on his face, none at all.

The floor and the walls around him that the two officers could see from the doorway were spattered with blood.

'Drop your weapon!' Juliet Solomon shouted, as Matt Robinson made an 'ambulance urgent' call on his radio.

There was no response from the man. He just stared blankly ahead, as if in a trance.

Outside a siren was coming closer.

'Drop the axe!' Solomon repeated, more loudly, and took a step closer to the door.

'Are you Mr Darling?' Matt Robinson shouted. 'Where's Mrs Darling?'

Again there was no response.

The dog was barking furiously again now.

There was the sound of voices and the clump of boots downstairs. Robinson heard Ops-1's voice on his radio, informing him that armed response officers were at the scene.

'I'll give you one more warning,' Solomon shouted, increasingly concerned. 'Put down your weapon!'

Very calmly and quietly, looking down at the blood-soaked floor, Seymour Darling said, 'She didn't give me any option, I had to do it. I needed to do it, actually. Sometimes in life you just have to do things. It is what it is.'

CHAPTER 68

Monday 25 April

Roy Grace heard gunshots as he stood outside the door. Several single shots in succession, then the rapid fire of an automatic weapon. He knocked on the door. There was no response. He knocked louder.

'*Ja?*'

He entered Bruno's small but cosy attic bedroom. The walls were painted red, with small white shelves artistically arranged around, all done by Cleo. On the walls were posters of a couple of Manchester United footballers, and another of a female rock singer Roy did not recognize. On one of the shelves was a white Star Wars stormtrooper with a clock in its stomach. Next to it sat a teddy bear wearing a Man U scarf. On another shelf was a row of Harry Potter and Anthony Horowitz books in German, and on another a Sonos player. Above it, a gangly stuffed toy monkey hung from its tail.

His son was lying back on his bed, with the bed linen also in the Man U strip. He was dressed in a red and white T-shirt, blue jeans and cream socks, holding a gaming controller in his hand. On the wall-mounted television screen in front of him a shadowy figure was darting through 3D alleyways in what looked like a Middle Eastern city. Bruno was aiming the sights of an AK47 at it, and as the figure jumped briefly into sight, he fired another burst, the bullets kicking up dust from the walls and ground. He glanced briefly at Roy, with a look of annoyance.

'How are you doing?' Grace asked.

Concentrating fiercely, waiting for his enemy to make his next move, Bruno said, 'Erik is winning. He has thirty-two kills, I only have seventeen.'

'It's ten o'clock, maybe you should think about going to bed – you have your first day at school tomorrow.'

Ignoring him, Bruno fired another burst and this time bullets ripped through the figure, blood spurting from his back. It jumped in the air and then fell forward. At the bottom of the screen the digits *18* appeared, next to *33*.

'No!' the boy shouted. 'No, this is not fair! Erik just got another one!'

'Bruno,' Grace said, more insistently. He wasn't really comfortable with his son playing these violent shooting games, but Bruno had been playing them at the Lipperts' house, and clearly for some time, and now was not the moment to try to change that. It was something for another day.

Still focused on the screen, Bruno said, 'It is

eleven o'clock in Germany and Erik is not having to go to bed.'

'You have your first day at school tomorrow.'

'So?'

'So maybe you should think about getting some sleep.'

'Erik has school, too.'

Unsure for a moment how to respond, he asked, 'So what time do Erik's parents allow him to go to bed?'

Two more shadowy figures appeared out of a doorway. One turned, pointed a machine pistol and began firing at them, while the other zigzagged along the alley.

Suddenly the screen froze. The words GOT YOU! GAME OVER! appeared.

Bruno threw the console down onto his lap in anger. 'Look what happened – you see – you distracted me. Now Erik has won again.'

'Does he often win?' Grace asked with a grin.

'He's good, he always beats me,' he said, sulkily.

'I think we can beat him!'

'How?'

'I was a firearms-trained police officer, Bruno. I know about gunfight tactics – would you like me to teach you sometime? There are techniques to shooting someone – and avoiding being shot yourself – in exactly the same situation as the game you are playing.'

He saw the glint of curiosity in his son's eyes. 'Can you teach me now?'

'Not now, but perhaps after your mother's funeral.'

'Then I'll beat Erik?'

'I guarantee it. I'll teach you to shoot like a policeman – and even more importantly, how to avoid getting shot.'

Bruno thought for some moments. Then he nodded, brightening a little. 'OK.'

'Then you and I will destroy Erik!'

For almost the first time since he had met him, his son grinned. Then he heard Cleo's voice calling out from downstairs.

'Roy – phone for you!'

'Later in the week, OK?' he said to his son.

'*Ja*, OK.'

Wondering who was calling, and strongly suspecting that at this hour of the evening it wasn't going to be great news, he went downstairs and picked up the phone. 'Roy Grace,' he answered.

He was right.

Some years ago, on a police management course, he had read a book called *The Peter Principle*. It was subtitled, *Why Things Always Go Wrong*. The central tenet of the book was that in many organizations sooner or later everyone gets promoted to the level of their incompetence. The man at the other end of the phone right now was testament to that.

Andy 'Panicking' Anakin, Duty Inspector of Brighton and Hove. It seemed to Roy Grace – and other officers he knew – that Anakin was unable to treat any situation calmly, and he sure wasn't calm now. The man sounded on the verge of a heart attack.

'Roy – oh shit, we have a situation.'

'Tell me?' Grace said, picking up the wine glass he had left on the living room coffee table, and taking a sip. He wasn't on call this week, so he was perfectly at liberty to have a drink, but he'd been careful tonight, as he had to work, and had drunk just a half-glass of a delicious white Burgundy that Cleo had bought at a bargain price from their favourite wine merchant in the city, Butler's Wine Cellar.

'I understand that you are interested in a character called Seymour Darling, in connection with your current murder investigation?'

'Correct, Andy, I am. Why?'

He told him, chapter and verse, his voice becoming increasingly hysterical with every detail.

'Seymour Darling's done this?'

'That's why I'm calling you – I thought you might want to pick this one up as you already have this charmer on your radar. Sounds like it was a domestic that escalated. He has past form – but not on this scale. What do you think – do you want this?'

Grace's brain was racing. He was thinking about all the evidence already stacked against Seymour Darling.

'Sure, Andy, it makes sense for me to take it on. I'll assign my deputy SIO, DI Guy Batchelor, to pick this one up. I want to keep this all within the same team.'

'Good, well, that's what I thought, Roy.'

'No flies on you, are there, Andy?'

'Only dead ones, Roy,' he said wryly.

As soon as he had all the details and ended the call, Roy Grace dialled Guy Batchelor.

CHAPTER 69

Monday 25 April

'Oh Jesus!'

In his twelve years of being a police officer, six of them as a detective in Major Crime, Jon Exton had never experienced a crime scene like this one. Standing alongside Guy Batchelor, both of them gowned up in protective paper-suits, gloves and shoes, he was staring, trance-like, at the severed head of Trish Darling. It was lying in a pool of dark crimson blood, on the cream shagpile carpet, framed by her straggly greying hair and still wearing glasses. He couldn't get the thought out of his head that she looked like one of those Halloween masks you saw in joke shop windows.

Except this was no joke.

One of her severed hands lay in a smaller pool of blood close by. The other lay on the other side of the room, together with segments of both her feet. Her torso had been split open down her midriff; there were blood spatters on every wall, on the carpet, on the bedspread, on the curtains and on the ceiling.

He turned away, struggling not to throw up.

'Hold it in, Jon,' Batchelor said. 'Not all over our crime scene!'

Close to fainting, Exton clung to the DI as if he were a life raft, in a desperate attempt to stay vertical. 'Sorry – sorry,' he slurred.

'It's OK, mate, happens to us all at times,' Batchelor sympathized. 'Don't worry about it.'

The sight, along with the coppery smell of the dead woman's blood, was making Guy Batchelor queasy, too. In the room with them were two Crime Scene Investigators, similarly clad to themselves, and the CSI photographer, busy recording everything on video.

Batchelor looked at his watch. It was just coming up to midnight. He yawned. 'You're not married, are you, Jon? Girlfriend, right?'

'Dawn.'

'Lovely lady – you brought her to the CID dinner last year – she's an Aussie?'

'Yep!'

'Could you imagine chopping her up into bits like this?'

Exton shook his head.

'Me neither – Lena. I mean, like – bloody hell, you've got to be more than a bit pissed off with your wife to do this.'

'That's probably the understatement of the year, Guy.'

Batchelor remembered meeting Darling's wife on Saturday. A total bitch. But no one deserved this. 'OK, the mortuary team will be here shortly, so there's not much else we can do. Some shut-eye?'

'Sounds like a plan.' Exton looked down at the severed head again, as if drawn to it by a magnet. The woman's eyes stared right back at him, sending shivers through him. It was as if she was saying, 'Do something!'

Involuntarily, and almost imperceptibly, he nodded at her. *We will,* he mouthed silently.

CHAPTER 70

Tuesday 26 April

At 8.30 a.m. the following morning, Guy Batchelor read from his prepared notes to the assembled team in the packed conference room. There were two new whiteboards alongside the four that had been up for some days, displaying crime-scene photographs of Lorna Belling's death and postmortem, her association chart, and photographs of the suspects – her husband, Corin, Seymour Darling and Kipp Brown. On one of the new ones were grisly photographs of Trish Darling's dismembered body, and on another a fresh association chart for Seymour Darling, along with his face-on and three-quarter-angle profile photographs taken when he was booked into custody last night.

'This is the eighth briefing on Operation Bantam,' the Detective Inspector said. 'Overnight we've had a significant development.' He told the assembled group about the circumstances in which Seymour Darling was found in the bedroom, holding an axe, surrounded by the dismembered remains of his wife, and was arrested at the scene, without a struggle. 'An interview coordinator is currently preparing the interview strategy.'

'I suppose it won't be a piecemeal interview?' Norman Potting said.

'Careful, Norman, you could get poleaxed for a joke that bad,' Glenn Branson said.

'Or you could be for the chop!' DI Dull said, the Direct Entry DI surprising everyone by displaying that he actually had a sense of humour.

Grace smiled. 'OK, we've opened the Christmas crackers and read out all the jokes, shall we now be serious, team?'

Suddenly he heard a rustling, rattling sound that brought back sad memories of Bella Moy eternally rummaging in her box of Maltesers. He glanced round and saw that Velvet Wilde was passing round a large yellow pack of M&M peanut chocolates. Several of the team – some of whom probably hadn't yet had any breakfast – took them gratefully.

He felt a moment of concern as she offered the pack to Norman Potting. The young DC had no way of knowing just how much pain her kind gesture might be causing him.

Potting waved them away, politely.

Then she rolled a few out onto the work surface in front of her, a red, a brown and two green ones, and popped one into her mouth.

He watched Potting carefully. The old detective looked like he was struggling to keep his composure. Grace wondered whether he should have a word with Velvet after the meeting. Then suddenly, to his surprise, Potting leaned across, grabbed the bag, shook several out into the palm of his hand, and gave the bag back to Velvet with a murmured thanks. He popped a green one in his mouth, looking happier. Grace saw him shoot a sly glance at the DC.

Privately, Grace smiled, shaking his head. Did the old stoat have his beady eye on her? He was happy at the thought that Norman was dealing with his loss of Bella, but if he was thinking of making a play for Velvet, he was going to be in for something of a disappointment.

Batchelor went on, reading from his notes. 'What we know about Seymour Darling so far is that he has a criminal history of progressive escalation of violence. He has three previous convictions, the first in 1997 for shoplifting, for which he got a fine and community service order. In 2003 he got two years suspended for demanding money with menaces. Then, significantly, in 2005 he got four years for GBH, when he permanently blinded a woman in one eye in an assault in a pub. He's a regular Mr Nice Guy.'

'He should have chosen a career in politics!' Potting said, popping another M&M in his mouth, and shooting another glance at Velvet to see if she responded, but she was looking up at the white-boards, studying them.

Ignoring the remark, Batchelor continued. 'DS

Exton is currently at the postmortem, which is being carried out by Dr Theobald. I'll be heading over there after this briefing. But I have a feeling establishing the *cause* of death is not going to be an issue in this case.' He glanced down at his notes. 'OK, media strategy. As we are not looking for anyone else in connection with the murder of Mrs Trish Darling, and therefore don't need the assistance of the local media, I'm intending to hold a short press conference later this morning, but with the gruesome bits edited out – I don't want the *Argus* going sensational on us and scaring everyone in the city. I'm proposing to give the bare facts, that a woman was found dead in her home in Hangleton, last night. Her husband is in custody, and he is also under investigation by the police in connection with the murder of another woman, Mrs Lorna Belling, last week. Does anyone have any issues with that?'

DI Donald Dull raised his hand. 'Actually, Guy, I do.'

'Go ahead.' Batchelor raised his arms expansively, his polite smile masking his fury at the hubris of this totally inexperienced parvenu.

'Aren't you making a potentially dangerous assumption here? I believe Detective Superintendent Grace has a very apt expression for assumptions: *Assumptions make an Ass out of U and Me*?'

Glowering at him, Batchelor said, 'And your point is exactly?'

'My point is, Temporary Detective Inspector,' Dull

said, pointedly accentuating the 'Temporary', 'Seymour Darling may have murdered his wife in a fit of rage. Why does that make him a prime suspect in the murder of Lorna Belling? The circumstances are very different.'

Batchelor said nothing for some moments; he was thinking hard how to respond without pissing the man off. 'Not *prime suspect*, Donald, but of course he does remain a suspect.'

Grace looked at the new DI. He was well aware that part of the reasoning behind bringing in Direct Entry officers was precisely what Dull was doing now – bringing fresh thinking. It was easy for policemen with years of experience to become too cynical and just too suspicious to look beyond the basic facts in front of them. Dull had made a good point. Having met Trish Darling himself, he could see what a bitter person she was. They needed to reserve judgement on whether Darling should continue to be linked to Lorna Belling's murder – if it was murder – until after he had been interviewed further.

'I've got a point as well, Guy, about your press conference,' Grace said. 'You need to deal carefully with any potential issue over the fact that Darling was on bail at the time he killed his wife. I suggest we speak after this briefing and involve Media HQ.'

Ray Packham, from the old High Tech Crime Unit, had been brought back to help with training new staff in the Digital Forensics Team. He had been temporarily seconded to the investigation, to report on the contents of all the suspects' seized mobile phones and computers. A quietly methodical man, who looked more like a middle-management executive than a geek, Roy Grace had, over the years he had known him, developed a great respect for his abilities. He raised a hand.

'There is something we've – um – recently been using that might be of value here, with this number of possible suspects,' Packham said. 'Mobile phones are quite chatty things – when the Bluetooth is left switched on – as most people do – they are constantly seeking other Bluetooth connections around them. But what we have only recently realized is that when the Wi-Fi is left on, that also looks to chat with any other Wi-Fi within range – and that leaves digital footprints, as it were, that can be found on certain routers that it passes.'

'What kind of routers, Ray?' Grace asked.

'They're known as "enterprise level" routers – a kind of advanced router, more powerful than the normal domestic one most people have in their homes. Some geeks use them, but they're most common in offices and hotels where they have a network allowing multiple connections. We have a bit of kit – in layman's language – that can suck out the IP address of any device that has tried to connect to the router for up to several previous weeks.'

There was complete silence, except for the sound

of Norman Potting crunching on a chocolate-coated peanut.

'Very interesting, Ray,' Batchelor said. 'What have you found relevant to this enquiry?'

Packham shook his head. 'We haven't started looking yet. But I took a walk around the streets adjacent to and bordering Vallance Mansions and there are several pubs, restaurants and B&Bs, some of which might well have such a router. There are also a few businesses operating in some of the premises. If we did another specific house-to-house in the surrounding area, we might get lucky. Even just one such router might show people who have been recent regular visitors to the area. It is possible one of them might turn out to be this Greg character.'

'Very smart, Ray,' Batchelor said. He shot a glance at Roy Grace, who nodded his approval. 'What would you need to resource this?'

'Just a couple of police officers for credibility – I could start right away.'

Batchelor glanced around, then looked at DC Alexander. 'Jack, I'll delegate this action to you.'

Looking pleased as punch at the responsibility placed on him, the young detective constable said, 'Yes, sir.'

Then Batchelor looked at Arnie Crown, not able to get Potting's nickname for the American detective, NotMuch, out of his mind. 'Arnie, would you like to go with Jack? It'll give you some experience of how we do these house-to-house enquires – if you're OK with that?'

'And we go in unarmed?' the American said.

'Unarmed? No, we always throw a stun grenade through the letterbox first.'

'Are you serious?'

Everyone in the room started to laugh.

CHAPTER 71

Tuesday 26 April

Roy Grace sat with Glenn Branson in the observation room, watching the video screen in front of them. Grace had a mug of coffee and his colleague a bottle of water. Seymour Darling sat in the room with his solicitor. Opposite them were Guy Batchelor and Jon Exton.

For the benefit of the interview process, the two officers introduced themselves. Batchelor gestured in turn to the suspect, then the solicitor. 'Could you please state your names for the recording?'

The man spoke aggressively. 'Seymour Rodney Darling.' Moments later the woman said, stiffly, 'Doris Ishack of Lawson Lewis Blakers, solicitor for Mr Darling.'

Batchelor continued. 'I'm confirming the time as being 10.17 a.m., Tuesday, April 26th.' He looked at the suspect. 'I'd like to remind you, Mr Darling, that you are still under caution.' He repeated the caution to him. 'Is that clear to you?'

Darling nodded. 'Yes.'

'Can you tell us where you were last night?'

'I was at my home.'

'What is the address?'

'I think you know that. 29 Hangleton Rise.'

'Can you give us an account of your actions last night, at 29 Hangleton Rise?'

'Yes. I arrived home from work around 7.30 p.m., and my wife had put the safety chain on the front door, so I couldn't get in. It was only when I threatened to break the door down that the bitch opened it – I was ringing and banging for sodding ages.'

'Is that the normal time you arrive home?' DS Exton asked.

'If you were married to her you'd understand. I needed a couple of pints before I could face her.'

His solicitor tried to interrupt but he brushed her aside. 'She's made my life hell for years. Accusing me all the time of one thing after another.'

'Why had she put the safety chain on?' Batchelor asked.

'To piss me off.'

'Can you tell us why you think she might have done that?' he continued.

'She had it in her head that I was having an affair. Some days I'd come home and she was mental – she'd just fly at me, or throw things at me. Anything. Ashtrays, furniture, a saucepan of hot soup.'

'How did you feel about that?' Batchelor asked.

'She was terminally ill with cancer, I always tried to be understanding.' He glanced at his solicitor then back at the two detectives. 'I don't know how anyone would feel with that hanging over her. She felt anger, you know – *why me?*'

Exton nodded sympathetically.

Batchelor looked down at his notes. 'Mr Darling, when we last interviewed you, on this past Sunday, you told us that she had terminal cancer, with a prognosis of four to six months to live. Is that correct?'

'Yes.'

'The officers who talked to your wife whilst you were in custody asked her about this. She was astonished to hear it and told them she was perfectly healthy. What do you have to say about that?'

Roy Grace shot a glance at Glenn Branson. They saw the fury in Darling's face, as he raised his balled fists in the air. 'She fucking what? She said that?'

Batchelor looked down at his notes again. 'I'll read you out the relevant part of the statement she gave, Mr Darling, in her words: *I am completely healthy. This is a line he spins to all his girlfriends. He has a whole fucking fantasy world inside his head. He'd love it if I was terminally ill, but too bad for him, I'm not.*'

Darling looked, for a moment, crushed and genuinely shocked. 'You're not serious?'

'I'm happy to let you and your solicitor see a copy of the statement she signed. We are also checking her medical history with her GP.'

Darling shook his head. 'What does it matter

any more? One lie after another. Anything she could do to hurt me, she'd find a way and do it. Jesus.' He buried his face in his hands in despair.

Watching Darling, Roy Grace felt a fleeting moment of sadness for the man. Having met Trish Darling, and been shocked by her vitriol, he wondered where the truth actually lay. No one knew what really went on behind any couple's closed doors. Was Darling a monster, or just someone who became one when pushed beyond his limits?

'Could you tell us what happened after you arrived home last night?' Batchelor asked.

Darling was silent for some moments, staring vacantly ahead. Then he said, 'I had had a bit to drink, yes, a couple of pints, and maybe some whisky, too. I was hammering on the door. She let me in and started on at me, right away, that she could smell alcohol on my breath and another woman's perfume. Her eyes were glazed, like they always were when she went off on one.'

'One what?' Exton encouraged.

'One of her fucking moods. Like a veil of mist dropped over her. She was obsessed with the idea I was having an affair.' He raised his arms, looking pathetic. 'Do I look like a bloody womanizer? I'm not exactly Brad Pitt, am I?'

'What happened next?' Batchelor asked.

'I don't remember exactly. She began screaming at me, punching me. I tried to keep my cool. Then she shouted at me about my manhood. Said I'd never satisfied her in years – you know – it was too small – that even on our wedding night she'd faked it. I just lost it. Lost the plot. I don't remember exactly – I punched her. She ran upstairs and locked herself in the bedroom, and was ranting at me through the door. Told me she was screwing someone she'd met who had a twelve-inch dick. That she wanted to have proper sex for the first time in her life before she died. I just couldn't bear it. I tried to get her to open the door, but she wouldn't. So I went out to the garden shed and got the wood axe and hacked the door open. Then I saw her inside. I – I – I—' He broke down into uncontrollable sobs, his head falling forward onto his hands on the table, and just lay there. Crying his heart out.

CHAPTER 72

Tuesday 26 April

Roy Grace sat in the sauna at Wickwoods, cushioned by a towel from the burning hot wooden slats of the bench, thinking hard.

When he'd arrived home earlier this evening, he had hurried upstairs to see Noah, and then Bruno, to find out about his son's first day at his new school, St Christopher's. The boy was once more on his bed, playing a video shooting game online with Erik, and although he politely told Roy his first day had been fine, he clearly did not want to be distracted. Roy had hoped to have a chat with him about his mother's funeral, to see if he wanted to say anything or do a reading, but realized this wasn't a good time, and decided to leave it until the morning, when he would drive him to school. They could talk in the car.

Cleo had persuaded him to take some time out at the country club, in the pool and sauna, before having supper, as it had done his leg so much good last time.

It was good advice. He had done twenty minutes

of lengths in the pool, and now ten in here, and he was determined to stick it out for longer.

He spooned some more water on the brazier and felt the instant burst of searing heat on his face and body. Those grim photographs of Trish Belling were firmly imprinted in his mind. He'd seen so many things that had disturbed him during his career. A drug dealer who had been tortured to death with a branding iron; a once-beautiful fashion model who'd had sulphuric acid sprayed in her face by a disgruntled ex. The capacity for human evil had no boundaries. He had learned, or maybe just become accustomed – or immune – to every kind of horror. But nothing he had ever seen had numbed him to the point where he could accept it.

Evil was evil.

And that quote from Edmund Burke always stayed with him: 'All that is necessary for the triumph of evil is for good men to do nothing.'

But something was still bothering him. Instincts. Always in life he had trusted his own judgement and an alarm bell was ringing. Tiny, muted, like one of those irritating car alarms in a nearby street that keeps sounding every few minutes and you can't quite tune out.

Something.

Not right.

Missing something.

Or was it wishful thinking?

He replayed over and over in his mind the

interview with Seymour Darling today. Thinking about everything Darling had said. And his own experience talking to the man's wife.

He could understand – although not condone, ever – how the man might have lost it with his wife. But the astute observation of Donald Dull stayed with him.

'My point is, Temporary Detective Inspector,' Dull had said to Guy Batchelor, 'Seymour Darling may have murdered his wife in a fit of rage. Why does that make him a prime suspect in the murder of Lorna Belling? The circumstances are very different.'

Grace had not initially been in favour of the recent Direct Entry initiative. It brought into the force a limited number of officers at middle-management level. These new entrants had no experience out on the beat, which was such a huge learning curve for every police officer. But he had to admit that twenty years in the police service would make anyone jaded and automatically suspicious. ABC. *Assume nothing. Believe no one. Check everything.*

It would be all too easy to assume because Darling had chopped his wife into bits that he may have killed Lorna Belling. But he, too, had doubts.

Sure, it would be a fast-track to reassuring the public that a man had been charged with her murder. There had been plenty of circumstantial evidence to support a prosecution of Darling for

Lorna Belling's murder, although that evidence had been reduced with the result back from LGC Forensics confirming that the DNA on the semen was not his. Still, Darling had a motive, he was in the right place, he had a history of violence against people who had upset him – and now he had been caught red-handed after committing murder, and almost certainly would be charged later, after his next interview, when he had had time to compose himself.

It would be a slam-dunk for any prosecuting counsel to go for a conviction for Lorna Belling, if – and it was a big *if* – the police were allowed to link the two crimes. It was a grey area of the law, and it could well turn out that in a trial situation, absurdly in his view, Seymour Darling's murder of his wife would be inadmissible evidence. In that case their evidence would be mostly circumstantial. And from all his experience with juries, it was highly likely they would only convict on the facts before them.

But, in his opinion, it would be a totally unsafe conviction. And when the wrong person was convicted it meant the real killer was still out there, at large. Free to kill again. That was the true danger of a wrong conviction.

He turned his mind to the other suspects. Corin, the husband. Arrogant Kipp Brown. The mysterious Greg. And still not ruling out Lorna Belling having killed herself.

Greg needed to be found and identified urgently.

He would task the Intelligence Cell with a comprehensive social media search.

Then he switched to thinking about the grim task ahead, that of Sandy's funeral, wondering if he had overlooked anything. For Bruno's sake he hoped there would be a decent turnout. The funeral directors had placed an announcement in the *Argus*, and he had circulated the details to all his family, friends and colleagues, and of course to all Sandy's relatives that he knew about; he hoped Sandy's parents had covered the rest. He was really not looking forward to seeing Sandy's parents again. But he'd put on his best face, and he knew that Cleo would, too.

He'd discussed with Cleo what he should wear, and fortunately they'd both favoured the same suit, the black one he kept for special occasions that she liked him wearing, saying it made him look like a character in the movie *Goodfellas*. He had bought it on a whim in New Orleans, from the famous Rubensteins, when he had been attending an International Homicide Investigators' Association conference in the city, and had only been able to afford it because it was in a sale.

Reverend Smale had suggested he give a eulogy, and he knew the wise clergyman was right. But he really didn't know what to say. He'd made a start, but he was struggling. Cleo had advised him to keep it short and personal.

What the hell should he say?

CHAPTER 73

Wednesday 27 April

Once again, as they had done yesterday, Roy Grace and Glenn Branson sat in the observation room, watching the live feed from the interview room. Seymour Darling was still in custody as a result of a superintendent's authorization.

Batchelor and Exton ran through the formal interview procedures with Darling and his solicitor. Darling spoke meekly, like a lost soul, his voice barely a whisper. Very different from the last time he had been in this room.

Batchelor reminded him that he was still under caution and said, 'Do you understand that, Mr Darling?'

'Yes I do.' He shot a baleful glance at Ishack, who gave no reaction, then continued. 'I'm not going to deny killing my wife, who provoked me beyond – beyond – all reasonable endurance. But your accusations against me for killing Lorna Belling are wrong. I didn't kill her, I really didn't. You have to believe me.'

'Why should we believe you?' Batchelor asked. 'You were angry at her because you felt she had screwed you financially over the sale of a motor car and you confronted her. We already know you have a history of violence – particularly against women.'

'I don't need this, I'm in enough shit as it is.'

'Mr Darling,' Batchelor said, 'whatever happens in your own case, you are a witness in our investigation of Lorna Belling's death, and after this interview we have some CCTV footage we'd like you to look at. It may help you to cooperate.'

'I've already told you she had a lover. Isn't he someone you should be looking at? He's the man who killed her.'

'The description Darling gave when he was previously interviewed certainly fits Kipp Brown,' Grace replied, keeping his voice low. The observation room was soundproofed and it would be impossible for anyone in the interview room to hear them even if they were shouting at the top of their voices, but Grace always found himself talking in a hushed tone in here.

'What makes you so certain of that, Mr Darling?' Exton asked, gently.

'I told you before, in an earlier interview, that I'd seen this matt-black Porsche driving around, like it was looking for a parking space, and then a short while later, up in her window, I saw them embracing.'

'The man you told us previously looked like James Bond?' Batchelor asked.

'I said he had James Bond's build. Tall, lean, good posture.'

'Is there anything else you can tell us about this man, Mr Darling?' Batchelor pressed. 'Did you catch sight of him in the car? Getting out of the car?'

Darling shook his head.

'So is there anything else you can think of, beyond what you told us on Sunday, that makes you link the driver of this Porsche to the man you saw with Mrs Belling?' Exton asked.

Darling shrugged. 'Flash personalities and timing. A hunch, right?'

'Did you get any letters or digits of the Porsche's registration plate?' DS Exton asked him.

'I'm afraid not – I'm not a *detective*,' he sneered. 'But there is something else,' Darling said, suddenly raising a pointed finger in the air. Then he gave a smug smile and fell silent.

'Something else?' Batchelor asked. 'Would you like to tell us?'

There was a brief pause as Darling was consulted by his solicitor. They conversed in whispers, which neither Grace nor Branson could hear.

Darling nodded. 'During the time I stood vigil outside that bitch's flat, there was another man who was a visitor to the property. On the afternoon – or evening – you are accusing me of killing her, he visited her twice. And if you want to know the truth, Detective Inspector Batchelor, the way he presented himself, I thought he was one of yours.'

'Mine?'

'A cop.'

CHAPTER 74

Wednesday 27 April

'What a fuckwit!' Guy Batchelor said, sitting in Roy Grace's office.

Grace nodded, reflecting on his thoughts on Darling last night. He was undoubtedly an unstable, dangerous man, a manipulator and a wild card. The kind of criminal who would say anything to get himself out of the shit. And understandably. It went with the territory in that world. Accusations against officers were made all the time by suspects, as pretty much their last line of defence. *Yeah, I was fitted up by the police. Yeah, you know, they look after their own. Yeah . . .*

Historically there was some truth in those accusations, and there had been many instances of retrials, such as with the Birmingham Six, where that had come to light. But he did not believe that to be the case with any of the trusted officers on his team.

'Let's see what Ray Packham comes up with, Guy. We can check out the owners of phones from any IP addresses he gets, and see if any of them fit the description of the man Darling says he saw.'

'Could be a long process, boss. And Darling could be lying.'

Grace nodded. 'We're no longer time-critical. Darling's confessed to his wife's murder and we can now formally charge him. He'll be on remand in prison and won't be going anywhere. That will give us as long as we need to either further charge him with Lorna Belling's murder – or find Greg.'

'What's your hunch, boss?'

'My hunch is that Darling's telling the truth about there being another person in the mix. What's yours?'

'I'm veering between the husband, Darling and Brown,' Batchelor said. 'Darling has shown he has anger management issues and is capable of murder. Could he have been angry enough to kill someone he suspected had ripped him off? I don't know – but we do know what he did to his wife. And that shows a man who has totally lost the plot. With Kipp Brown, you don't get to be rich like that by being Mr Nice Guy. We now have his DNA on semen in the victim's vagina, and we have a possible motive – rejection, or tarnishing his name in the community.' He looked quizzically at Grace. 'So what do you think about him?'

He nodded, saying nothing for some moments. 'It's a good theory, Guy. Our priority is to find our mystery Greg. This seems to be stalling our enquiries.' The spectre of Cassian Pewe hung over his head like the executioner's axe. In the event of any screw-up, there was only one head that would roll.

CHAPTER 75

Thursday 28 April

Funeral weather. Silent rain falling from a pewter sky; the wettest kind, a mist that settles on your hair like dew and permeates every layer of your clothing; the kind that gives England its lush green countryside and inspired the words they would be singing in the church shortly, 'Walk upon England's mountains green'.

The wipers scraped noisily across the windscreen as Roy Grace drove, not helping his jangling nerves. Cleo sat beside him, dressed in black, with a dark silk scarf covering her head, the name *Cornelia James* just visible in one corner. Arriving at Patcham village on the outskirts of Brighton, he turned left beside the former Black Lion pub – now a smart restaurant – which had been his regular watering hole when he'd been based at Sussex House, a five-minute drive away. Nothing stays still in life, he reflected, looking at the building as he headed up the steep, narrow hill, past a row of terraced cottages on his left, and slowed opposite the pretty, ancient church of All Saints.

Parking the Alfa with two wheels on the grass verge, he climbed out, head bowed against the rain, removed an umbrella from the boot then opened the front passenger door for Cleo, ignoring the lone newspaper reporter across the road.

Bruno, in the rear seat, had been silent throughout the journey, holding the small bunch of white lilies, Sandy's favourite flowers, that he was going to place on the coffin when it was lowered into the grave. Cleo had also said very little. All of them were immersed in their own thoughts. Roy couldn't imagine what might be going through his son's mind right now.

He could remember some of how he had felt after losing his first parent, his father, Jack – although he had been more than a decade older than Bruno at the time. It was the sense that the buffer zone between himself and death had gone, that there was no longer a generation standing between him and the great yonder – as well as the realization he was now head of the family, and had to take his father's place looking after his mother. That feeling of there no longer being a generation between him and death intensified even further after his mother died a few years later.

Bruno had dressed smartly, in a suit, white shirt and tie, his fair hair immaculately brushed. As Grace opened the rear door to let him out, Bruno looked up at him darkly. When he spoke, Grace saw a flash of anger in his eyes. 'Papa, why is Cleo coming? She did not know my mother.'

He thought carefully for a moment before responding. 'She did meet your mother, Bruno, when she was in hospital. She's coming out of respect for her and you.'

For an instant the boy's face darkened further, and Roy worried he was about to kick off. But instead Bruno nodded, very seriously, as if this was something he had been brooding over for a long while, unclipped his seat belt and, holding the little bunch of flowers, climbed out.

'Let's leave the flowers in the car,' Roy Grace said. 'We'll take them when we go to your mother's grave later, in the cemetery, OK?'

'OK.' It came out as a whisper.

'You feeling OK about the reading?'

The boy nodded.

Other cars were pulling up and several people were walking up the path to the church but Grace barely noticed anyone other than his sister and her family.

Inside the shelter of the porch, where he folded the umbrella and stuck it in a rack, they were greeted by the rugged, bearded Reverend Ish Smale, who quickly turned his focus onto Bruno, taking his hands and crouching down to his height. 'Hello, young man!' he said. 'It's very brave of you to come and to do the reading, and I'm glad you are.'

'Why is it brave?' Bruno asked, quite coldly. 'She's my mother. What is brave about going to my mother's funeral?'

Grace saw the momentary frown on the wise clergyman's face, before the sympathetic smile reappeared.

'It's brave, Bruno, because not all young people your age would be strong enough to be doing this.'

'I'm ten,' Bruno said, his face deadly serious. 'I'm strong enough.'

'Of course you are!' Reverend Smale smiled. Then, looking over his shoulder, he said, 'Ah, I think they're arriving now.'

Roy and Cleo turned to see the small cortège of black hearse, followed by a solitary black limousine, pull up. Derek and Margot Balkwill. As if this wasn't already a gloomy enough moment, it had just got gloomier still, he thought. It was mildly ironic to see two of the world's meanest people, who wouldn't spend a bean on themselves that they didn't have to, stepping out of this limo. Sandy had made provisions to pay for the funeral – the wake and everything – through her German lawyer, some years back, but with no specific instructions.

If need be he would have stood up to the plate himself, even though legally Sandy had no longer been his wife or his responsibility. But he would not have been able to bear the thought of the shabby apology of a funeral her parents would almost certainly have arranged, if left to them. Whatever he felt today about Sandy, this was much more about Bruno than her. He wanted his son to see his mother buried with dignity and with some show of caring.

Stepping inside the church, an elderly warden handed them order-of-service sheets. Roy led Bruno and Cleo down the aisle, nodding at familiar faces on the way, flashing a brief smile at Glenn Branson, and ushered them into a front-row pew. He took his position at the end with Bruno between them.

Cleo knelt in prayer, while Bruno sat very still. Grace looked around, pleased for his son's sake that there was a reasonable turnout; he had been worried about it being a virtually empty church, but there were a good sixty or seventy people here. Among them he spotted a number of current and former colleagues, as well as a handful of retired police officers. The rest he presumed were friends or relatives of Sandy's. He recognized an elderly couple seated with what looked like their grown-up son and his wife and three small children in the reserved pew over to the left. Sandy's uncle and aunt. They'd always been friendly enough on the few occasions they had met, but Sandy had never been big on family gatherings. He remembered how she used to make him smile by saying, 'Why do you have to like someone just because you're related to them?' Although she was happy to accept a large inheritance from one of her aunts.

Her parents were approaching down the aisle now. Margot, normally drab, had gone to town on her outfit and was looking quite ridiculously melodramatic. She wore a stark, macabre ensemble, entirely in black, with a dramatic veil, but all of it having a slightly moth-eaten feel about it, as if she had bought it in a charity shop – which she probably had. Derek was a broad-shouldered man who had a permanently weak, deflated look about him. He appeared to have dusted off his father's RAF demob suit again – the only suit Roy Grace had ever seen him wear – and spruced it up with a starchily uncomfortable-looking shirt and a wide black tie. To his relief they chose to sit on the pew to his left, with their relatives.

He looked down at the service sheet. On the front was his favourite photograph of Sandy, taken the year after they were married, when they were on holiday in Spetses in Greece. She was standing with her back to the little fishing boats of the port, strands of her blonde hair blowing in the breeze, either side of her freckled face, wearing a sundress and laughing, looking so incredibly happy. It was that image of her that still occasionally came to him in his dreams.

Memories came flooding back to him. Memories of those early days when he had felt so happy, married to the woman he had been certain he would spend the rest of his life with. That beautiful, smart, tempestuous companion and soulmate. So she had seemed back then.

The music started. Simon and Garfunkel's 'The Sound of Silence'.

Reverend Smale walked down the aisle, followed by the four pall-bearers carrying the coffin. It was oak with plain brass handles. Sandy had always hated anything ornate – and clutter – and had decorated their home in an elegant, minimalistic, Zen fashion. He found himself hoping she would have approved of his choice of coffin and furnishings.

Then a reality check caught up with him.

Sandy.

After all these years.

In restless dreams I walked alone.

Sandy was inside that coffin. Her body, damaged, broken and now dead. Inside that box. The nightmare days, weeks, months after she had first vanished; the nightmare years that followed. All the time wondering what had happened to her. Speculating. Knowing from his own experience investigating missing persons that the longer they were absent, the smaller the likelihood of finding them alive. This poor, troubled, lost soul.

Hopefully she was at peace now.

He looked down at his son and saw a solitary tear trickle down his cheek. Tears welled in his own eyes, too. He breathed in the smells of the church, the mustiness, the old wood, the faint, sweet tang of Cleo's perfume.

The song ended. Reverend Smale stood in the pulpit. 'We meet in the name of Jesus Christ, who died and was raised to the glory of God the Father and mercy be with you.' He paused again. 'We have come here today to remember before God our sister, Sandra – *Sandy*; to give thanks for her life; to commend her to God our merciful redeemer and judge; to commit her body to be buried and to comfort one another in our grief.'

Grace could feel Bruno shaking and shot him a sideways glance. The little boy was sobbing; Cleo pressed a handkerchief to his face but he pushed it away. Grace could feel his own self-control slipping away, too, and he needed to keep his composure for the eulogy. He had discussed at length both with Reverend Smale and with Cleo something that would be appropriate for Bruno, and they had settled on a few lines from Michael Rosen's *Sad Book*.

The moment came. Bruno had composed himself. Grace whispered good luck, and watched his son stand up, walk solemnly up to the lectern, and climb up onto the box Smale had placed there for him.

Then he began.

'*Sometimes I'm sad and I don't know why. It's just a cloud that comes along and covers me up. It's not just because my mama's gone. It's just because things now aren't like they were.*' He faltered and then went on, reading the rest of his chosen words slowly and flawlessly.

When he had finished he walked back, stiffly, very upright. It was now Grace's turn. He stood, a bag of nerves, fastening the middle button of his jacket.

'Well done!' he whispered as Bruno sat down again.

As he stepped up to the pulpit the clergyman gave him a reassuring pat on the arm. He climbed the steps, took his short speech from his pocket and laid it down in front of him.

As he glanced up, momentarily taking in the sea of faces, he noticed both the Chief Constable, Lesley Manning, and the Police and Crime Commissioner, Nicola Roigard. It was deeply respectful that they'd made the effort to come.

Then, suddenly, seated alone towards the back of the church, he saw Cassian Pewe, in full dress uniform. He was surprised the ACC had come. Perhaps he did have a heart after all. He took a couple of deep breaths, something he had learned long ago, to calm down before giving any talk. Even so he began reading in a shaky voice, staring rigidly down at the text, not trusting his emotions if he caught anyone's eye.

He allowed himself to look down at the front row of pews, at Cleo and Bruno. His son was staring up at him, staring with that same look he had seen in his eyes a short while earlier before he had got out of the car. Anger at his mother's death? Anger at him for causing it?

By contrast, Cleo was smiling, a sweet, sad smile.

'All of us have to find and take our own paths in life,' he said, his voice stumbling. 'Sandy was a beautiful woman and I was lucky enough to spend so many years of my life with her. She was funny, smart and she had a great interest in so many things, as well as a real talent for interior design, which was her passion. As many of you here today know, she chose some years ago to take her own, different path in life, and had many adventures, some great, some perhaps more challenging for her. Her legacy is our delightful son, Bruno, of whom I'm immensely proud.'

He glanced up and, nearly choking with emotion, looked quickly back down at his script.

'Sandy loved books, and she loved to read me quotes from authors. One of her favourites was a somewhat irreverent line from Kurt Vonnegut. "Listen, we are put on this earth to fart around and don't let anyone tell you any different."'

There was a small ripple of laughter.

'Another, very different and much deeper, was from John Fowles's *The French Lieutenant's Woman*: "Life is not a symbol, is not one riddle and one failure to guess it, is not to inhabit one face alone or to be given up after one losing throw of the dice; but it is to be, however inadequately, emptily, hopelessly into the city's iron heart, endured. And out again, upon the unplumb'd salt, estranging sea."'

He paused and took another deep breath.

'We don't know, none of us, what is around the corner. Life is short, and for some of us far too short. It was far too short for Sandy. But I feel lucky to have spent those years with her, and I was always proud of her. As were her parents, Derek and Margot. I hope this hugely talented and lovely woman is now at peace.'

As he climbed back down the wooden steps from the pulpit, tears were rolling down his face.

CHAPTER 76

Thursday 28 April

All these dead people under these crumbling, weather-beaten gravestones. Their sad little epitaphs. My granddad has this on his tombstone:

Gone but not forgotten.

Well, that's bollocks. Not forgotten by who? They say you only truly die when the last person who knew you dies. After that you are totally forgotten. There's no one left in the world to remember you. Does it matter?

It mattered to Einstein. He was actually a bit pissed off about it. He told a friend that despite all he had to offer mankind, how sad it was that one day he, like everyone else, would just be food for worms.

Yep, Albert, I'm with you on that one.

You're not much more than one step from that when you're banged up on a life sentence in jail. That would happen if I left matters un-checked.

But that's just not an option.

CHAPTER 77

Thursday 28 April

The voice startled him.

'My deepest condolences, Roy.'

He turned. Cassian Pewe was standing right behind him, holding out his hand, rain dripping from the peak of his ceremonial cap, the silver braiding looking, as ever, freshly buffed.

'Thank you, sir,' he replied, stiffly. Then out of courtesy added, 'I appreciate your coming.'

Cleo, beside him, was standing facing the grave, with an arm round Bruno, who was holding his bunch of white lilies.

There was an awkward moment of silence between the two men. 'Yes, well, Roy, we're one big family, the police. We look out for each other, don't we?'

Their eyes met. Grace could hear the man's pitiful screams of terror, the year before last, when he'd hung over a 500-foot drop, held just by his feet entangled in the webbing of Grace's upturned Alfa's seat belt, pleading with Roy to save his life. Which he had done, at great risk to himself. And regretted at times since.

'We do, yes.'

Pewe lowered his voice. 'Just a word, Roy – our friend Mr Tooth. In view of his prognosis I've removed the twenty-four-hour guard on him. It's my job to think about the police budget.' He gave Grace a condescending smile, and moved away, leaving the detective speechless.

Grace was soaked through, despite his raincoat, but he was so incandescent with rage at the ACC he barely noticed, staring around the expanse of graves in this vast cemetery and listening momentarily to the distant hum of traffic along the busy Old Shoreham Road. He watched the last of the mourners, heads bowed, hurrying towards them. He saw Glenn, standing a respectful distance away, alongside Jon Exton. Guy Batchelor, beside him, looked silent and sombre. Respectful.

Derek and Margo Balkwill stood almost pointedly several yards distant from him, staring stonily at the grave, but he could see no real sadness in their faces at all. They had avoided all eye contact with him since arriving at the church. If he never saw them again after today, it would be too soon, Grace thought. But he would have to see them again, they'd made it clear they would be wanting time with their grandson. Poor Bruno, he thought, inflicting those wretched misers on him.

He was surprised and pleased to notice forensic podiatrist Haydn Kelly had come along, down from London. Another person he was happy to see here was Sandy's attorney, Andreas Thomas.

A bulky, genial man in his forties, with long hair and a buzz of stubble, the Munich lawyer was wearing a crumpled grey suit that looked like it had spent the night in a laundry bag, and an equally crumpled cream shirt; the top button was undone, and the knot of his black tie hung a few inches below. Grace was unsure whether he had forgotten to do it up, or whether the shirt did not fit.

Not that it mattered. The lawyer seemed a good guy, and had managed to cut through, or sidestep, a huge amount of bureaucracy that might otherwise have kept Bruno in Germany for many months, making him their equivalent of a Ward of Court.

Roy stepped over to say a quick hello. 'Thank you for coming,' he said.

The German shrugged. 'Of course.'

'I've taken your advice about UK lawyers and I've been recommended by a friend to a local firm in Brighton called Family Law Partners – apparently they specialize in collaborative law. I've spoken on the phone with the owner, Alan Larkin, and Cleo and I have made an appointment with him. I'll let you know how it goes.'

'Good. And please give him my details.'

'Of course.'

Roy rejoined Cleo and Bruno.

The freshly dug grave looked dark and deep. Its sides were lined with bright green Astroturf, which also covered the mound of earth on one side. Two wooden planks were laid across. Reverend Smale stood still, seemingly impervious to the weather, a kindly expression on his avuncular face, waiting for the last mourners, hurrying beneath umbrellas, to reach them.

He wished Pewe would move away and leave them alone at this deeply private moment for himself and for Bruno, instead of hovering behind them. But instead, to his complete surprise, Pewe suddenly said something to the boy in German.

Looking up through his tears, Bruno responded, his voice barely audible. Pewe then spoke again in German, and again the boy responded. As the ACC was about to speak again, the pall-bearers arrived, lowered the coffin at the end of the grave and began to thread tapes through the handles.

There was something rough and ready – almost primitive – about burials, Grace thought. Cremations were slick, almost high-tech in comparison. They could have been hundreds, if not thousands of years back in time right now. Shovels, planks, ropes. A wooden box. A mound of earth.

At this moment, Roy Grace was torn between wondering what Bruno might be feeling, and his own thoughts.

Sandy would have hated this. She would have disliked the Astroturf. She hated anything false or fake. How angry would she be right now?

The angrier she was about the funeral the better, he thought, suddenly, bitterly. Then, instantly, he parked that. This was not the time or place for anger. He was laying her to rest. After long years of having no idea where she was, or if she was even still alive, her body was in that coffin in front of him.

And he could have stopped that from happening.

Could have saved her.

Perhaps.

Possibly. Possibly he could have saved her. That last conversation they'd had in the hospital, the Klinikum München Schwabing, just a few weeks ago, when she had been so full of despair about her injuries and her future. If he had responded differently. If he *could* have responded differently. If he had put his arm round her, hugged her, told her he still loved her, that he would take her back, that they would start their life over again, together?

And destroy everything he now had with Cleo?

That was never going to happen. What he had now was too precious. But in addition, what he had with Cleo was something deeper, more open and honest than he'd ever had with Sandy. She'd been a control freak, and it had taken him all these years to realize that. There was the Sandy he had remembered, through rose-tinted spectacles. Then the reality of the cold, hard woman she could so often be.

And now this reality in front of him. The Rubicon crossed. The point of no return. End of.

Reverend Smale's rich voice cut through his thoughts.

'I am the resurrection and the life, saith the Lord;

he that believeth in me, though he were dead, yet shall he live: and whosoever liveth and believeth in me shall never die.' He paused then continued.

'Friends, welcome here, to these few moments when we come and bring Sandy to her final resting place. We are reminded in the scriptures that we brought nothing into this world, and it is certain we can carry nothing out. The Lord gave and the Lord hath taken away; blessed be the name of the Lord. Let's bow our heads for the first prayer.'

Roy Grace watched the coffin lowering inch by inch. Glanced at his son, holding his flowers. And suddenly he remembered what Marcel Kullen had said to him in Munich. *Your last shirt has no pockets.*

That would have resonated with Sandy. Avaricious people were the kind she had always detested; businessmen who trampled on anyone to get to the top, who would plunder their employees' pension funds to line their own coffers. Whatever her faults, she had an innate sense of decency and fair play. Somewhere inside that troubled mind of hers had been a good and caring person.

What was she wearing inside that plain oak box that was steadily sinking from view, he wondered? A shirt with no pockets?

He put his arm round Bruno's shoulder. For a brief moment he felt him lean towards him, as if seeking comfort and warmth. It was the first time, he realized, his son hadn't shied from his physical contact.

As the pall-bearers stepped back, pulling out the

tapes, Bruno walked forward, holding his bouquet in front of him, his lips moving, as if he was talking to his mother. Roy saw tears running down his face. And felt the tears run down his own cheeks.

This was Sandy.

The woman he had thought, once, all those years back, was the love of his life.

Dead.

Already decomposing.

In a few years she'd be just a skeleton in a leathery shell. Then that shell would rot – be eaten – away. Until there was nothing left but her bones.

Bruno stepped forward again, right up to the edge of the grave, then tossed in his flowers and stood still. Staring down.

Two minutes later he was still standing there, still staring down.

Grace walked over to him, and put his arm round him. Then stared down at the wooden box too, knelt, scooped up a handful of earth and dropped it, listening to the rattle as it struck the lid of the coffin.

Just as earlier he was lost for words, right now he was lost for them again.

He pulled out his handkerchief.

The boy did the same.

After a few moments, Grace felt for Bruno's hand, found it and squeezed it. He felt a faint squeeze back.

They were joined at the edge of the grave by Cleo.

The Reverend Smale continued with the final prayer. 'Forasmuch as it hath pleased almighty God of His great mercy to take unto Himself the soul of our dear sister here departed: we therefore commit her body to the ground, earth to earth, ashes to ashes, dust to dust; in sure and certain hope of the Resurrection to eternal life through our Lord Jesus Christ.'

There was a murmur of 'Amen'.

'Would you like to meet your grandparents in person now?' Grace asked Bruno, nodding at where they stood, still and silent.

'No, I want to stay here with Mama. Just alone with her for a few minutes, please.'

Roy and Cleo stepped back. Cleo turned to Glenn Branson, who was approaching. Roy walked dutifully over to his former in-laws and held out his hand. 'Sad day,' he said.

Neither of them took his hand. Derek looked his usual feeble, slightly lost self. Margot glared at him with utter hatred in her eyes.

'It's very sad,' she said. 'It was a sad day that our daughter ever met you.'

'Hey,' Grace replied. 'I loved her.'

'You loved her?' Margo said, acidly. 'Is that what you really think? If you'd loved her properly, she wouldn't have had to leave you. You were incapable of loving our daughter, you were too obsessed with your career. She told us many times after she'd left you how much happier she was.'

He stood, rooted to the ground, in utter shock.

'You spoke to her after she left me – after she disappeared?'

'Yes, Roy,' she said. 'Regularly.'

'Regularly? You knew where she was – all along – these past years?'

'Oh yes, she contacted us from time to time.' There was grim satisfaction in the woman's voice and her husband gave a smug smile and nodded. Grace could have decked him, happily, at this moment.

'I can't believe it. You knew she was alive and where she was, and yet you put me through living hell for all those years? You didn't even tell me when I let you know about her accident.'

'She didn't want us to tell you, you see, old boy,' Derek said. He spoke, ridiculously, Grace always thought, in the clipped voice of a wartime RAF officer, frequently using some of the lingo. Long retired after redundancy from a small engineering firm, he spent his time making model fighter and bomber aircraft from that era, as if stuck in a make-believe world.

'When she found out she was pregnant, that was the moment she knew she had to find a better life for her and her child,' Margo added.

'You allowed the police to dig up my garden looking for her body, when you knew full well she was alive and safe?'

'You put our daughter through living hell from the day you met her,' Margot said. 'What goes around comes around.' Then she and her husband turned and began walking away.

'Hey!' Grace said, furiously. 'I'm not done talking to you.'

Derek Balkwill turned his head back and, almost jauntily, said, 'We are, old boy.'

CHAPTER 78

Thursday 28 April

Grace was silent in the car as he drove Cleo and Bruno away from the cemetery, thinking back to the different mediums he had consulted in the months and then years after Sandy had vanished. One, he remembered clearly, had said that Sandy was working in the spirit world for a healer, and that she was happy to be back in contact with her mother. A slight problem with that one, Grace had decided at that time, since her mother was still very much alive.

Now it didn't seem that woman was completely off beam, as Sandy had indeed been communicating with her mother. Just not the way the medium had thought.

A small handful of the mediums, one in particular called Ross, whom he had felt was the most credible, had been adamant that Sandy was not in the spirit world. Which meant, he explained to Roy, that she was not dead.

He had been right, he now realized.

Jesus.

That bitch, Margot, had known all along. He felt utterly betrayed.

Half an hour later they arrived at the wake, in the function room of the Elephant and Castle pub in Lewes. Outwardly as he entered he was all polite smiles. Inwardly he was seething with silent fury.

They had known. Had they really? Sandy's father, Derek, had always been a liar. Were they making this up? No. Her mother could not have known the reason she had left him was because she was pregnant, unless Sandy had told her. Told both of them.

It was shortly after midday. Hopefully this wouldn't last too long – an hour perhaps and then he could get to the office. He had several fresh thoughts on Lorna Belling's death and was now itching to get a number of actions implemented, and quickly. Bruno sat with a plate of sandwiches on a chair in a corner, where he was absorbed on his phone. Relieved that, so far at least, Sandy's parents were a no-show, Grace dutifully looked around for some of Sandy's relatives to introduce them to Bruno.

'Nice suit, Roy.'

Grace turned and grinned at Glenn Branson, who pinched some of the fabric between his finger and thumb, rolling it approvingly. A couple of years back, before his first date with Cleo, Glenn had insisted on taking him shopping and getting him a complete makeover, at huge expense. He now considered himself custodian of Roy's appearance.

'It's the suit I bought in New Orleans – quite a while ago.'

'I know. Still looks good on you,' he said, slightly grudgingly. 'What was that place – on Canal Street? Rubensteins?'

'You remember?' Grace asked.

Branson tapped the side of his own head. 'Got it all stored in here. Every designer shop on the planet. I'm a walking encyclopaedia of style.'

'So you don't just keep your brain in your dick, after all?'

'Very funny. Listen, excuse me if I don't stay long – I need to get back.'

'Go as soon as you need to – I'm going to make my escape, too.'

Turning to scan the room again, to see who was here that he needed to speak to, he was surprised to see Pewe had come and curious as to why.

He edged through a knot of people until he was in earshot and heard Pewe and Bruno once more speaking in German. Pewe was looking down kindly at the boy. Was the ACC on a charm offensive? Why?

To his right he saw Cleo talking to Dick and Leslie Pope. He had introduced her to his oldest friends outside the church at the end of the service. He walked over to join them, eager to catch up with them, having not seen them for over two years. But all the time he kept an eye on Pewe and Bruno. They seemed to be chatting happily, quite animated. Perhaps it was a relief for him to be able to speak to someone in German? But why the ACC was giving up quite so much time away from work for this funeral was beyond him. Nicola Roigard and Lesley Manning had both left immediately after the church service, and he'd expected Pewe to have done the same. He had been surprised to see him at the committal – and now at the wake. What was the man after?

Being all kind and caring was not part of Pewe's make-up. Grace suspected he had an ulterior motive, but could not speculate what it might be. A favour of some kind that he was going to ask, he imagined. No doubt he'd find out soon enough.

'All right, chief, bearing up?' Norman Potting said, through a mouthful of sausage roll.

Grace nodded, still watching Pewe. 'Thanks, Norman. I'm pleased to get a chance to talk to you – I keep meaning to ask, what's the latest news on your health?'

Potting had been diagnosed with prostate cancer some months ago, and had asked Grace's advice on a couple of occasions, but hadn't mentioned anything about it for some time.

'I'm having more tests in a few weeks, thanks for asking, chief. But I've been reading quite a bit recently – you know – where they're saying a lot of people are having surgery unnecessarily. That if it's slow-growing you're more likely to die with it than from it. And a big risk of losing your winkie action if you do have the surgery.' He suddenly looked deeply sad.

There was a moment's silence between the two men. 'I hope today didn't bring too many memories back of Bella, for you?'

The Detective Sergeant shook his head, then looked like he was struggling to hold it together. He turned away and walked swiftly across the room, weaving through the small crowd. Out of the corner of his eye Grace saw Guy Batchelor approaching, followed by Jon Exton.

'I'm going to make a move, Roy, if you'll excuse me, need to get back,' Batchelor said.

'Of course, I'll be there as soon as I can.' He glanced at his watch. 'I need to have a talk with you and Glenn – three o'clock in my office?'

'Good with me.'

He shook Guy's big, firm hand and their eyes met. The DI gave him a reassuring smile and said, 'We're going to crack this one soon, boss.'

'We need to.'

Jon Exton approached him, looking gaunt. He smelled rank, as if he had slept in his suit, and looked a little shaky and on edge. Grace wondered if he had an alcohol problem as he could smell a whiff of it on his breath. Fair play, he had provided wine and beer here, but Exton was on duty.

Lowering his voice, he asked, 'Is everything really OK with you, Jon?'

'Oh yes, boss, fine.'

Grace frowned. 'Are you absolutely sure?'

'Well – strictly *entre nous* – I'm just going through a little difficulty with my other half.'

'You and a lot of other police officers – it's a very big club, Jon.'

'Yes, ha ha. I think we will work it out. Things sort of haven't been right since we got back from holiday.' Exton glanced around anxiously. 'Yes, yes, it'll be all right. I'll – I'm going to get back – er – with Guy, if that's all right?'

'See you in a bit – and I mean it, Jon. Anytime you'd like to talk. OK?'

'Appreciate it. I'm getting it sorted, it'll be fine.'

Grace looked around. Pewe was still talking to Bruno. Sandy's parents weren't here. Good. He hadn't been sure what he might say to them if he saw them. He didn't trust himself not to have a blazing row with them and this was not the time or place. But he couldn't help wondering, if they had known Sandy was alive – and presumably her whereabouts since she disappeared over a decade ago – then who else had?

A ridiculous thought came into his head. Pewe? Could he have known?

He dismissed it.

Then he heard a Scottish accent. 'Roy, remember us – cousins of Sandy – we were at your wedding! Bill and Helen Ross, from Aberdeen!'

He turned and saw an elderly but spritely couple.

'Yes, of course, how very nice to see you again,' he said, politely, shaking hands with them. He had pretty much a photographic memory for faces but could not really remember them.

'Such sad circumstances,' Helen said, 'our hearts go out to you.'

He chatted for some minutes with them, aware that the wake was rapidly thinning out. When he next looked around, Pewe had vanished. Cleo said she and Bruno would cadge a lift with Roy's sister, and if he was up for it later, take him for a little drive – he was keen to collect some Pokémon – and it would give her the chance to chat with him.

Grace had been sad in the church, and at the grave, he thought, as he drove away from the pub and headed to the Police HQ. But now he didn't feel sad any more. He felt angry and puzzled. Anger at Sandy's parents, puzzled by Cassian Pewe's behaviour, and wondering.

Were Sandy's parents the only people who had known the truth all this time? Yet Sandy had never been fond of them or close to them. Was it really likely she had been in touch with them, in regular contact, sharing her secret? To spare them the agony of not knowing?

Or had Sandy sent them a suicide note too, that he was not aware of, telling them everything as well? And they were just winding him up, out of spite? But why would they do that?

To score a pathetic little victory?

God, he had thought that in burying Sandy today, he would at last have closure; but instead she had sprung on him not only a son he never knew he had, but also another mystery.

Right now, as he approached the barrier at Malling House, he parked those thoughts, and switched his mind back to the myriad complexities of Operation Bantam. And something that was worrying him about it.

A definite shadow.

As he entered his office that shadow darkened. There was a message awaiting him that instantly made him deeply worried.

CHAPTER 79

Thursday 28 April

Grace stared at the yellow Post-it note stuck, prominently, on his desk. It was written in his secretary's handwriting.

Any request to see a Professional Standards officer was a concern. It might mean a complaint had been made by a member of the public, or by another officer; there were intractable procedures the PS department followed, in some cases requiring an officer's suspension during the enquiry and, fortunately rarely, in some cases his or her dismissal.

That feeling of being back at school and summoned to the headmaster's study, the one he had every time he visited the Chief Constable or one of the ACCs, was with him now. If it was about Corin Belling's death, why was it so urgent?

If Professional Standards just wanted some information from him, on some minor matter, it would have been someone more junior contacting him, not Superintendent Paula Darke. He picked up the phone, wanting to get it over with as quickly as possible. But to his frustration he heard her clear, authoritative voice with its faint North London inflexion, requesting the caller to leave a message.

Shit.

That summons on the little yellow sticky square of paper had totally thrown his concentration. He looked at the separate piles on his desk, and knew, after a whole morning out of the office, there would be a good fifty or more new emails in his inbox awaiting him. He sat and started going through them, quickly, to see if any might hold a clue as to what Darke was going to speak to him about. But moments later his phone rang and he heard the Superintendent's voice.

'Roy, thanks for calling me. I know you've been at your former wife's funeral this morning, but I've got a delicate matter to discuss with you – do you have a moment this afternoon?'

He checked the time on his computer. It was half past two. 'I've got a meeting at 3 p.m., but I could come straight over now, Paula,' he said.

'I think we might need a bit longer than that.' Her tone was neutral, amicable but giving nothing away. 'What about after that?'

Whatever this was, he wanted to find out quickly and not sit in suspense. And he didn't like that it was not going to be a quick meeting – that sounded ominous. 'It's OK, I can put the meeting back and come over now, if you are free?'

'Good,' she said. 'Thank you.'

* * *

For all its power and authority, Professional Standards was, like so much of Sussex Police, squeezed into far too small a space for the number of people in the department. Paula Darke's office was tiny; her tidy desk against the wall, with a view through a large window of a steep grass bank. The only personal object on the desk was a picture of a grinning hunk of a man with a shaven head. Her husband, recently qualified as a detective after years in the Met as a PC. Most of one wall was taken up with a large-scale map of Sussex, sectored up into divisions.

As she swivelled round in her chair to face him, Grace was sitting so close their knees almost touched. The Superintendent had deservedly risen through the ranks, with a reputation for being hardworking, tough but fair. In her early forties, with a strong physique, she was an attractive woman, with classic features framed by short, brown, wavy hair, and dressed, unusually, in uniform – a white shirt with epaulettes bearing her silver crown, a black tie, trousers and shoes.

'Thanks for coming to see me, Roy – I've just returned from a discipline hearing,' she said and smiled. As always, she exuded energy, as if bursting to deal with a challenge. 'Nice suit, by the way!'

'Thank you, what's the fascination with my suit? That's the third compliment I've had today! It's a few years old – I bought it in New Orleans.'

'It's very slimming on you,' she said and added quickly, 'Not that you are exactly overweight!

Lucky you, New Orleans is on my bucket list.' Then her expression became serious and her voice more sombre. 'It's a very delicate matter, I'm afraid, Roy.'

Grace felt his heart sinking. 'What does it involve?' His own voice sounded strange to him, several octaves higher than normal.

'It's about one of your team. DS Exton.'

'DS Exton?'

Instantly the cloud over him lifted. He hoped the relief didn't show in his face. Exton. He had a feeling he knew what she was going to say about him, but he was wrong.

'I think you know, Roy, that at Professional Standards we've been running random checks on all force computers. And now, with phones becoming more like computers, we've started to include those – something not many officers know. I've been tipped off anonymously that DS Exton has recently been accessing escort service sites on his job phone.' She looked at him quizzically for a reaction.

'I'm astonished to hear this. He's one of the most strait-laced officers I know.'

'A dark horse, perhaps?'

'A large number of sites, or just one in particular, Paula?'

'Enough.' She pushed a printout towards him. 'It's all there, the numbers marked.'

'What a bloody idiot. Well, what I can say is I think he has a problem at the moment. I'd actually been planning to speak to him this afternoon.'

'What kind of problem?' In addition to her reputation for being tough, Roy had also seen her caring side before, and was aware he was looking at it now.

'Well, he's been coming to work looking very dishevelled – some days not having shaved or brushed his hair, and he seems withdrawn. He's normally careful with his appearance – as I said, he's very strait-laced and totally dependable. He's got the nickname Agenda Man, because he's so thorough when he gives any instructions to anyone. I'm worried he might be having some kind of a breakdown. Accessing these kinds of sites is totally out of character – and of course quite unacceptable on his police phone.'

'Is he married?'

'He was divorced some years ago – I understand reasonably amicably, from what he told me once, and has a daughter. I believe he's been in a stable relationship with a lady from Australia for some years – a very nice woman called Dawn. He brought her along to an event last year – a Sussex Police Charitable Trust fundraiser. Would you like me to see what I can find out and report back to you?'

She hesitated. 'I had been thinking about someone from this department talking to him.'

'Would you let me speak to him first? He's a good officer – I really believe that.'

She gave him a quizzical look.

'Trust me, I believe in this man.'

'OK, Roy,' she said, hesitantly. 'But we can't let this go on.'

'I'll speak to him as soon as I can this afternoon.'

'I'd be grateful. Any officer behaving erratically is a worry. Perhaps even more so in these days of heightened security.'

'I agree.'

Walking away from her office, he was thinking hard, and extremely concerned. Was there something seriously wrong with his friend and colleague Jon Exton?

CHAPTER 80

Thursday 28 April

Glenn Branson and Guy Batchelor were already heading down the corridor towards his office when Grace entered the building, still reflecting on his meeting with Paula Darke. Gesturing them to sit down at the tiny desk in front of his own that he used as a conference table, he decided not to say anything about Exton at this stage; instead he fetched his notes from his desk and joined them.

'OK, I want to have a word about strategy in advance of this evening's Op Bantam briefing,' he said. 'As I see it we have a number of really good suspects, each of them more than capable of killing Lorna Belling. Her deceased husband, Corin; Seymour Darling; Kipp Brown; and now this mystery lover of Lorna's introduced into the investigation by her friend, known only as Greg. We have a vague description of the person who might be Greg from Seymour Darling, but in my view he's an unreliable witness.'

Both the other detectives nodded.

'Totally,' Batchelor agreed. 'I'm not sure we can trust anything that weasel says. And we're still not able to rule out suicide, especially now we know one of the causes of death was electrocution.'

'Correct. Now, there is one thing we've not considered about Lorna,' Grace said. 'The facts we have so far are that we know she was in an abusive relationship with her husband. She worked from home as a hairdresser. She had a secret apartment, the address where she was found dead. And we know from her sister she was planning to leave her husband and move to Australia, and was in the process of raising cash to do just that – hence the probable reason she was selling her car.' He looked at both men then continued. 'I have a supposition. Think the unthinkable. What if the real reason she had the apartment was not as a bolthole from her husband, but because she had a secret life as an escort of some kind? Could the reason that there was no phone or computer found in her flat be that the offender took them, knowing his details would be on them?'

Glenn Branson nodded. 'Interesting thinking, boss.'

'I think we have just the person to carry out a search of all the escort sites online and advertised in the local media – Spreadsheet Man – Donald Dull. Analysis like that would be right up his alley,' Batchelor said.

'Never a dull day,' Glenn quipped.

'Every day is if your name's *Dull*,' added Batchelor.

Grace barely noticed the comments. He was thinking again. Lorna had told her friend, Kate Harmond, she had a lover, Greg. Wouldn't she have told her the whole name and some details about her lover? Could that have been just a ruse, to distract her from knowing the truth? That she was funding her escape to a new life in Australia through sexual services? He looked down at his notes again. 'Glenn, I want you to pick a small team to look at each of the suspects in depth. Pull together the witness evidence, the forensics, the intel and anything else we have. See if any of them have been accessing escort sites. Grade the suspects – establish who is our most likely one.'

'I'll get straight on it.'

Grace looked at Batchelor. 'Guy, we need a new media strategy targeting the local community. Vallance Mansions is bounded on two sides by residential buildings and Kingsway in front is a very busy thoroughfare. Someone in the apartment block or in the surrounding area may have seen something on the afternoon or night she was killed. And I think we need to update the strategy, and to appoint a house-to-house supervisor to pull in all the PCSOs in the area and get them knocking on doors, and make sure we've not missed any CCTV. You can't walk ten feet in this city without being captured on a camera somewhere. I've said I consider the man an unreliable witness – but *if* Darling is correct and Greg exists and has been a frequent visitor, someone must have seen him, and a CCTV camera must have caught him.'

'Leave it with me, boss.' Batchelor hesitated. 'There is actually something else.' He shot a glance at Branson, then Grace, who both nodded.

'I've been running an ANPR sweep. I created a matrix, with the help of NotMuch – he's had a lot of FBI experience in his previous role in Homeland Security, plotting possible routes for attackers into an area. We used the same basic algorithm to plot vehicles travelling from different parts of the city to Vallance Mansions, to see if we could pick up any non-residents visiting frequently – and something interesting has showed up. I could illustrate it better on my computer, but in short summary,' he said awkwardly, 'DS Exton has been in the vicinity several times, mostly evenings and often all night. Significantly, he was there on the night of Wednesday, April 20th.' He looked at Grace expectantly.

Grace frowned, not liking what he was hearing at all. Exton calling sex workers on his phone. Now known to be in the vicinity on the day Lorna died. There was no one on his team who looked less likely than mild, quiet, serious Exton.

This development was potentially horrendous. Could it possibly be true? What were the implications, and how could he deal with this? It hardly bore thinking about. Surely there must be a simple explanation, otherwise this could be his worst nightmare.

'Where does Exton live, Guy?' he asked.
'Hailsham, boss.'
'And he lives there with his partner, Dawn?'
'As I understand, yes.'
Hailsham was some twenty miles to the east of the city. 'Has anyone said anything to him?' Grace asked.
Batchelor shook his head. 'I've told Glenn but no one else.'
'Do you have any view on this, Glenn?'
'I don't, no. It may be entirely innocent – but he's not his usual self at the moment.'
'He told me he had some issues but didn't go into detail,' Grace replied.
'His relationship's on the rocks, I heard,' Batchelor said.
'I asked him the other day,' Branson said. 'Told him if he wanted to talk about anything, you know, man to man, I'd go and have a beer with him. He nearly bit my head off.'
'He's been like this for a while?'
'Can't say for sure, but that feels about right.'
'Thanks, guys, leave it with me.'
Grace sat still, waiting some moments after the two detectives had left before calling Exton. Thinking. The Detective Sergeant was calling sex workers on his phone. His car repeatedly in the vicinity. His erratic behaviour starting around the time of Lorna Belling's death.
The unthinkable?
He hoped more than anything in the world, right

now, not. Despite all its problems, and the occasional total prick like Cassian Pewe, he loved the police – and particularly his own force, Sussex – with all his heart. There were few things worse than a rogue cop, because internally that damaged the trust that was vital in any team. You looked after each other, watched each other's backs. The day you lost trust in a fellow officer was a slippery slope, because it diminished everyone in your eyes.

Not relishing the task ahead of him, he tapped the speed-dial buttons on his phone for the DS.

CHAPTER 81

Thursday 28 April

Cleo knelt on the living-room floor encouraging Noah, who was sitting on his play mat, to touch the birds and animals on the mobile suspended above him. 'Dog!' she said. 'Duck!'

Noah reached up and suddenly punched an elephant hard. It swung into a pig, making a clacking sound, and he giggled. Humphrey, asleep on his blanket, which he always dragged out of his basket, was making strange squeaking noises and twitching. Having a doggie dream, Cleo thought.

'Humphrey!' she said softly. 'Humphrey, it's OK!'

Suddenly there was a series of crashing sounds above them, like brutal overhead thunder. Noah looked up, startled. Humphrey, instantly awake, began barking loudly.

A metallic clanging sound. Another rumble of thunder.

'Jesus!' Cleo sprinted up the stairs and along to Bruno's room, just as there was another shattering *boom-boom-boom* followed by a cataclysmic clash of cymbals, and pushed open the door.

It was Bruno, with his drum kit assembled, in full flow. He'd already explained them to her yesterday, as she had helped him unpack them, telling her very solemnly in great detail what each was called and its role. There were five black and white drums – a snare drum, a bass drum and three toms; two of them stood flat, three of them were angled towards him and had a black cross taped on them. The brand was stencilled in black on each of the cymbals. *Paiste.*

He was seated on a stool, in a T-shirt, tracksuit bottoms and white socks, wearing headphones, pounding away for all he was worth with the wooden sticks, and working the foot pedals for the bass drum and hi-hat cymbals. He was lost to the world, with a distant smile on his face as he nodded his head, vigorously and in deep concentration. A red and white football lay on the floor near him.

Looking around the room, Cleo saw a ring-bound notebook lying open on his bed. On it were multi-coloured squares. Red, orange, blue, green, yellow. It was headed WEEK 'A', and just below, WEEK 'B'. Divided into periods, blocked days down the left were marked 1–5. She read across some of the classes: Spanish; Science; Maths; Music.

His school timetable. She was pleased and impressed he had already filled it in. Clearly he was meticulous with detail. Something he had inherited from his father, she wondered? Roy had that same methodical mind – something she realized that came with the territory of being a good detective.

He didn't notice her.

She walked across to him, and tapped him gently.

He lifted off his headphones.

'Bruno, you forgot to put the soft pads on! It makes quite a noise downstairs – and you'd wake your brother if he was sleeping.'

Bruno apologized and said he had forgotten and would put them on immediately.

She slipped back out and closed the door, gently – not that he would probably have heard if she had slammed it. She went back downstairs and squatted on the floor with Noah, who now seemed oblivious to the din. Humphrey was looking up at the ceiling and growling.

She stroked the dog's head. 'It's OK, boy!'

Humphrey growled again.

As she played with Noah she was thinking about a book she had read, in translation, as part of her A-level literature studies at school, *The Tin Drum*, by the German writer Günter Grass. From what she could remember, the main character was an autistic boy called Oskar, who could only remember his childhood by getting himself into some kind of a trance by pounding on a toy tin drum.

But Bruno didn't seem like that at all. Maybe right now, up in his room, he was dreaming he was playing in a rock band. Of a future as a rock band drummer? She looked up at the ceiling. He was drumming again without the pads on, obviously ignoring her. Even though he was two floors above her, the sound was reverberating through the house. She was going to have to take this up with Roy.

Noah put a plastic sheep into his mouth. As she pulled it out, he began to cry, then scream, reaching for it back. His screams almost drowned out the sound of the drums. Almost.

Scooping up Noah in her arms, he screamed even louder, scrabbling his hands through the air, reaching out for the sheep again.

Sitting there on the floor, with the stereo din of her son crying and her stepson above her making an increasingly demented sound with the drums, she found herself, very unmaternally, wishing she was back at work right now. She was missing what now seemed the blissful silence of the mortuary.

CHAPTER 82

Thursday 28 April

At a few minutes past 5 p.m. there was a faint knock on Roy Grace's door.

'Come in!' he called out.

Jon Exton entered. The black bags under his eyes seemed to have deepened further, and his stooped posture made him look as if he had shrunk. He smiled nervously. 'Hi, boss.'

Grace gestured him to sit down and stared hard across the table at him. 'Jon, I need to know just what is going on with you. Is there something you want to say to me?'

Exton's hands were shaking as he spoke. 'As I told you earlier, boss, just going through a bit of a bad patch with my beloved.'

'With Dawn?'

'Yes.'

Grace nodded. 'I'm not here to judge you, but I need you to tell me the absolute truth.' Watching his eyes intently, he went on. 'I've been asked to speak to you by Professional Standards – or rather, let me put it another way, I persuaded them to give me the chance to speak to you before they do, OK? So I don't want any bullshit from you.'

'*Professional Standards?* What – what about, boss?'

Looking at him even more intently, Grace asked, 'Jon, have you been using the services of prostitutes?'

The DS's astonishment was real, Grace could see it in his eyes.

'What? Prostitutes? Me?' He sounded incredulous.

'You heard what I just asked you. Have you been using your phone to look for sex?'

'Absolutely not. I – I mean – sex has been the last thing on my mind these past weeks, Roy – boss – honestly. Why are you asking?'

'Because it's not what I've been told.'

'Been told? Been told what? By who?'

Grace pushed the printout that Superintendent Darke had given him across the table. 'These are the records of all calls on your job phone over the past week. Have a look – take your time, have a very careful look through.'

Exton looked over the page. Several phone numbers were ringed in blue ink. Then he looked back up at the Detective Superintendent and shook his head from side to side. 'I don't recognize any of these numbers.'

'Jon,' Grace said calmly. 'These are the phone company records. All these numbers were dialled from your phone. Could anyone else have had access to it?'

'No way.'

'It couldn't have been Dawn?'

Exton ran his eyes back over the page. 'No, these were all made after Dawn and I split up – we haven't seen each other since then.' His voice was cracking and he took some moments to compose himself. 'I haven't called any sex workers, Roy. I nearly called the Samaritans, but I tell you – I just told you – sex is just not – not – on my mind. I just want to be back with Dawn.'

Grace continued staring hard at him. 'I need you to be absolutely truthful with me, Jon. Did you ever meet Lorna Belling?'

'The deceased?'

'Yes, the deceased.'

'*Meet?*'

'Yes.'

'Never.'

'You didn't contact her on a sex worker phone line?'

Exton looked genuinely bewildered. 'Boss, I've never called a sex worker in my life. I – I really haven't.' He hesitated. 'Well, actually, hang on, there was one night when I was a bit drunk – I did make a few calls, but not on my job phone. Not long after Dawn threw me out.'

'OK. Can you explain why you've been in the vicinity of the deceased's flat in Vallance Mansions every night for the past six weeks, Jon? And in particular and most crucially, on the night she was murdered?'

Exton blanched, looking cornered. 'I – I—'

'Yes?'

Exton sat still, with a look of defeat on his face.

'ANPR cameras recorded your BMW in the vicinity of Vallance Mansions on thirty-seven consecutive nights, Jon. The last occasion was the night she died – can you explain that?'

Suddenly, from chalky white, Jon Exton's complexion went to beetroot red. 'I can explain, boss, yes.' He fell silent.

'I'm all ears.'

After some moments the DS, deeply embarrassed and avoiding eye contact, said, 'Dawn threw me out – she said I wasn't committed enough – that I was more in love with my job than with her. I – I tried to explain that's what being a Major Crime detective means, but—' He shrugged his shoulders. 'Shit, you know. You know better than anyone, boss.'

Grace nodded. He did know. Painfully.

'So for the past few weeks I've been sleeping rough in my car. There's a decent-sized free car park behind the King Alfred. I'd been going in there in the morning when they open, and using the facilities.' He shrugged again. 'It's just across the road from Vallance Mansions. But I had to move to a different location a week ago, because of all the police activity.'

Grace nodded. From Exton's eye movements he believed the detective was telling the truth. But equally, Exton knew his eye test and might have been faking it.

'Jon,' he said. 'It's one hell of a coincidence, don't you think?'

'I – I suppose – yes – it looks that way. But I promise you . . .' His voice tailed off.

'Promise me what?'

'That I'm telling you the truth. I'm a detective, Roy, I'm not a murderer, for God's sake!'

Grace was feeling sympathy for the man, who was clearly on the verge of a breakdown. But he couldn't let that influence his treatment of him. 'Have you looked in a mirror today, Jon?'

'Yes – well – yes – I suppose – I must have done.'

'You *must* have done? Your hair's a mess, you haven't shaved – unless you're growing designer stubble – and without being too personal, you need a bath and some deodorant – and some fresh clothes. There's no way you could go out to interview anyone looking how you do.'

'I'm sorry, boss,' he said, looking genuinely contrite. 'I don't want to let you down – and I am, aren't I? That's just what I am doing.'

'Jon, I'm going to have to take your police phone off you and have it forensically tested. I'd also appreciate it if you handed over your personal phone and electronic communications devices voluntarily – will you do that?'

Looking completely startled, Exton handed him his police phone. 'Yes, of course. Please, boss, believe me.'

'Jon, I believe you but the phone records show a different story – and I'm not the ultimate arbiter here. I should have you suspended for what has been found on your job phone; I don't want to do that, but I'm very concerned about your behaviour. You seem under a lot of stress – relationship problems can cause that. If you get too low you reach a point where your judgement goes and you become unable to make good decisions. I want to help you – you're a good detective and I like you, but I can't risk members of my team making mistakes, and you've made a really stupid one. Is there anything else you'd like to say to me? I don't like surprises. The team will support you, but you have to tell me the truth.'

Exton gave him a helpless shrug.

Grace thought hard for some moments. 'Look, would you be willing to see the force doctor, Dr Bell? He's nearby in Ringmer. He might sign you off for a few days. Perhaps send you to the Sussex Police Charitable Trust cottage down in Dorset for some R&R – how would you feel about that?'

'Well – OK – I mean, sure. I'll go and see him, I've nothing to hide.'

'I think it would be inappropriate for you to continue on this investigation, Jon, so I will move you to the trial preparation for Operation Spider, for the time being.'

'I understand, boss, thank you. I appreciate it. I'll go and get my phone and computer.'

As the DS left his office, Ray Packham entered, looking animated. 'Roy,' he said. 'Forgive me barging in – but I may have something for you!'

CHAPTER 83

Thursday 28 April

Ray Packham sat down opposite Grace and placed a tiny blue and black memory card, sealed inside a clear evidence bag, in front of him. Tapping the bag, he said, 'That's from a GoPro camera. I think it might well have images of Lorna Belling's killer.'

With almost every homicide case Grace had ever worked on, there would be hours, days, weeks, months even, of solid plodding graft. Then sometimes out of thin air, and when you were least expecting it, a eureka moment happened, which could lead to everything being unlocked. It might be a phone call out of the blue, an unexpected fingerprint or DNA match, a dog walker stumbling across a body. These were the moments that lifted him out of his seat, punching the air with his fist, that sent adrenaline surging through his veins, that made all the slog that had gone before it suddenly seem worthwhile.

'You do, Ray? Images of her killer?'

'I think so.'

Grace raised a hand, signalling Packham to wait, then picked up his phone and called Batchelor. 'Guy,' he said, 'can you come into my office right away?'

With Batchelor's office only two doors along the corridor, the DI was with them in moments, looking expectant.

'Have a seat, Guy, Ray's got something for us.'

Batchelor glanced down at the evidence bag, then looked at the civilian from Digital Forensics.

'As agreed earlier this week, I've been carrying out enquiries with DC Alexander, NotMuch and the house-to-house team,' Packham said.

'I think you mean Detective *Crown* from the FBI, Ray,' Grace corrected him with a smile.

'Sorry, chief – Arnie Crown – nice man,' Packham said. 'We've worked along the streets bordering Vallance Mansions, checking for occupants of houses, flats, offices and B&Bs who might have enterprise grade routers.' Looking at both detectives, he said, 'I explained previously that these high-level routers might have picked up people walking past in the street, through their phone Wi-Fi trying to communicate with these routers. It's been harder than I thought because a lot of the buildings are divided into flats, and it's taken us two days to cover every property – waiting for people to return from work, or who have been away. Anyhow, I think last night we may have got lucky.' He tapped the plastic bag on the table.

'What is it, Ray?' Grace asked, looking down at it.

'Well, it came from an address in Vallance Street, directly opposite the side entrance to Vallance Mansions. Now it may of course be nothing. But . . .' He tugged a smartphone from his pocket, tapped it and squinted at the display.

Grace waited patiently.

'Flat 4, 38 Vallance Street. A young man by the name of Chris Diplock, who has a website management business, has one of these routers. It logged a mobile phone passing five times between 6 p.m. and 10.30 p.m. on the evening of Wednesday, April 20th.'

'The night Lorna Belling died.'

'Exactly!' Packham had a triumphant smile.

'Do you have the phone number?' Batchelor asked.

He gave it to him and both detectives wrote it down. Then he continued. 'I've checked with the service provider, Vodafone, and it's unfortunately a pay-as-you-go job. But we were able to look back and Mr Diplock's router has picked up a signal from this phone on several occasions, mostly daytime and early evening. I requested a triangulation plot of the phone's movements and – I'm not sure how helpful these might be.' He laid his phone down and turned it so that Grace and Batchelor could see the screen.

Mostly there were random locations in the vicinity of Vallance Mansions and around Brighton and Hove, but one in particular caught Grace's attention. A Lewes location, very close to Malling House, the Police HQ, where they were now.

His thoughts immediately went to Jon Exton. He dialled the Detective Sergeant.

Before he could speak, Exton, panting and sounding out of breath, blurted, 'I'm just on my way, boss, be with you in a tick.'

'What's the number of your private phone?' Grace asked.

Exton gave it to him and Grace wrote it down. It was different from the number Packham had found on the router log.

'Fine.' He hung up and focused back on Packham's report, and the triangulation details. 'Interesting to see this person has been in the vicinity both of Vallance Mansions and the Police HQ.'

'Yes, but I don't think we should read too much into it, boss – they could have been almost anywhere in Lewes,' Batchelor said.

'True, but – if this is another phone involved he's not telling us about, it could be significant.'

Batchelor nodded pensively, then drummed his fingers on the desk surface, looking down intently at the evidence bag.

Grace turned to Packham. 'Ray, could you give us a moment?'

He stood up. 'Sure, boss.'

'Don't go too far, Ray.'

'I'll wait outside.'

After he had closed the door, Grace turned to Batchelor and said, 'I don't know what's going on with Jon, but there are a number of things I'm not happy about. In strict confidence, we are very close to a formal interview, but there's no way I'd want to do that to him – not unless we were a lot more certain, and we're a long way from that.'

The two detectives discussed the new information, and then asked Ray Packham to rejoin them.

'So, Ray,' Batchelor said as he sat back down. 'We have someone walking repeatedly past Lorna Belling's flat on the evening or night she died. But no way of tracing who it was?'

'Well, not quite, Guy,' he replied, and tapped the evidence bag again. 'This man, Chris Diplock, owns a rather flash motor – a BMW M4. He's had it vandalized twice when parked on this street in front of his home – all the body panels keyed, once, and on another occasion the tyres slashed. So he installed a GoPro camera concealed in a dummy headrest he made. He has it set on a time-lapse and runs it continually overnight every night, then checks the footage in the morning. He said that he arrived back from a client at around 7 p.m. on Wednesday, April 20th, and that on the morning of Thursday, April 21st, when he checked the camera footage he noticed someone behaving strangely, and furtively, who walked past his car several times.'

'Did he describe him, Ray?' Batchelor asked.

'Yes, he said it's not a good image – it was raining on and off so the windscreen was blurred. The man was wearing a baseball cap tugged low, and in the darkness he could only see part of the lower half of his face – part of his nose and chin. He said he was tall.'

Exton was tall, Grace thought. So was Kipp Brown. So were a lot of people.

'From the position of the camera,' Packham continued, 'he was able to see the man enter Vallance Mansions' side entrance, and exit some time later. It was a while before he returned. Diplock said the times correlated to when the MAC address of the phone was logged on his router.'

'That's interesting indeed,' Grace said.

Batchelor nodded his concurrence.

Grace picked up the evidence bag. 'Guy, get someone to rush this over to Maria O'Brien at the Forensics Unit at Guildford. They've got video-enhancing capabilities there. Call her or Chris Gargan and alert them this is top priority. Can you do that right away?'

'Yes, boss.'

At that moment there was a knock on the door. Exton entered and handed over his private phone and laptop.

Looking hard at him, Grace asked, 'Jon, is this your only phone?'

'Do you mean apart from my police one, boss?'

'Yes.'

'This is the only one.'

Grace thanked him, then shooting nervous glances at both men, Exton hurried back to the door.

'Jon!' Batchelor said, suddenly.

'Yes, boss?'

'Are you busy at the moment?'

'Well – er – not – nothing that can't wait.'

'Good, I'll come and see you in a moment.'

As Exton left, Grace handed the detective's phone to Packham. 'You might as well take this with you, Ray. Can you clone it and return the original to Jon so he's not stuck without a phone? I need you to do this in strictest confidence and report to no one but me, OK?'

'Yes, right away.' Then he continued. 'Something that may be worth considering, Roy, if we get a good resolution back from Forensics – have you ever worked with the Scotland Yard Super Recognizer team?'

'No, but we're on the same page, Ray – I was thinking about them.'

A few weeks earlier, Grace had attended a seminar on the very new field of Super Recognizers at New Scotland Yard. The DI giving the talk explained that the average human being can recognize 23 per cent of faces that they've seen previously. The average police officer, despite the heightened awareness that comes with the territory, can only manage 24 per cent. But a tiny percentage of the population, now known as Super Recognizers, can achieve up to 90 per cent.

The phenomenon had been discovered during the aftermath of the London Riots, in 2014, when many of the violent rioters and looters had concealed their faces with caps, glasses and scarves. Detectives in London had discovered there were some colleagues who were capable of identifying people, with consistent accuracy, from just one single feature. An earlobe. A nose. A chin.

One of the champion Super Recognizers was a custody officer called Idris, whose abilities had led to over one hundred and fifty arrests to date. Under an initiative set up by the Metropolitan Police Commissioner, Sir Bernard Hogan-Howe, the Super Recognizer team was formed – many of whom were civilians. Some of the unit worked out of Charing Cross police station, but the majority from New Scotland Yard.

'I've got a contact with them, an old friend who used to be a PC in Brighton,' Packham said. 'Jonathan Jackson.'

'I remember him well – good guy. OK, let's wait to see what we get back,' Grace said.

'I'll ping you Jonathan's contact details,' Packham said.

After Batchelor and Packham left, Grace sat thinking again.

Momentarily distracted by an email that had come in about next week's venue for the Thursday-night poker game he tried – and mostly failed – to attend regularly, he was checking his diary when the phone rang.

'Detective Superintendent Grace,' he answered.

'Roy, do you want to tell me just what on earth is going on with DS Exton?' It was Cassian Pewe, sounding his usual friendly self – not. 'I've just had a conversation with Superintendent Darke – why did you not inform me right away about the misuse of his phone?'

'Because, sir, Superintendent Darke asked me to speak to DS Exton as a matter of urgency – to see what I could find out.'

'I trust you've asked PSD to suspend him?'

'Well, actually, sir, I think he's in a pretty bad way, mentally. He's had a relationship breakdown and he's not coping, in my view. I had a talk with him and he's agreed to see the force doctor. He's a highly trusted member of my team and I feel I need to support him, not hang him out to dry – which will just make things worse.'

'Let's hope you're making the right decision, Roy. On your head be it.'

'I understand, sir.'

'Good.'

'Oh – one thing I wanted to ask you, sir,' Grace went on. 'I didn't know you spoke German.'

'What's that got to do with anything?'

'You were talking quite a bit to my son, Bruno, in German.'

'And your point is, Roy?'

'It was very kind of you, sir, to take the time and trouble.'

The ACC made a strange grunting sound and hung up. Grace was curious. Why had Pewe sounded so defensive about speaking German?

But he had bigger issues on his mind right now.

CHAPTER 84

Friday 29 April

SNAFU. It's an old US military expression dating back to the Second World War. Situation Normal, All Fucked Up.

Yep. That's about the size of it.

That's how it would look to the casual observer. Except, I'm not a casual observer; sadly I'm an interested party.

Very interested.

My life might be shit at the moment. It feels like it's all getting out of hand. The hunter and the hunted. But I'll come up with a plan, I always do. I've just got to turn the tables, create that smokescreen. Create that thing we have in the British judiciary. Beyond reasonable doubt.

Innocent?

Beyond reasonable doubt.

Guilty?

Beyond reasonable doubt.

I have the advantage here, I know the truth.

But you know, I was never this way before. I was just an ordinary, decent human being. I never wanted to be a killer. I'm still not even sure I have actually killed, but you are hunting me down like I did.

Just know one thing, Detective Superintendent, and it's this:

I'll do whatever it takes not to be found out and have my life destroyed.

Whatever it takes.

I need help. I really do.

But I'm not sure help would really help.

I'm a mess. It's all a mess. Somehow I've got to pack it all back in the box. Stay one step ahead.

At least I'm in a position to do that.

CHAPTER 85

Friday 29 April

As was his ritual each morning whatever time he arrived at work, Roy Grace checked his emails, Twitter, and had a quick glance through the overnight serials – the log of all reported crimes in the city of Brighton and Hove. Muggings, assaults, fights, break-ins, robberies, RTCs, vehicle thefts, drug arrests, missing persons. He was always curious to see what was going on in his beloved city, although few of these serials ever concerned him directly.

However, there was one particular item today that caught his eye. Made him freeze.

Made him swear out aloud.

An hour later, he sat in on the 8.30 a.m. briefing of Operation Bantam. He could have let Batchelor get on with it, but equally, he had too much riding on this himself, and he felt that Guy needed his steering hand. After all, he was the SIO.

But he was too distracted by the serial he had seen.

The team had now expanded to over twenty

detectives and support staff, but there was one conspicuous absentee in the conference room today: DS Exton. Grace's concerns about this detective he had long trusted were deepening. They were about to deepen further.

His phone rang. It was Chris Gargan from the Forensics Unit, sounding perplexed. 'Sir?' he said.

'Hang on a sec, Chris.'

Grace stepped out of the room into the corridor. 'OK, I'm with you.'

'One of your team, Jon Exton, dropped us over a GoPro memory card last night, with an urgent request to see if we could enhance it.'

'Yes. What have you managed to get?'

'Well, I don't know if someone's made a mistake, but it's blank, sir.'

Grace felt a sharp, sinking sensation. 'Blank? The memory card?'

'Yes, there's nothing on it.'

Gargan had one of those voices that always sounded totally straight, with no hint of disingenuousness. In all his dealings with this CSI, Grace had found that what you saw or heard was what you got.

'There couldn't be any mistake, Chris?' Even as he said the words, he knew they were futile. The Surrey and Sussex Forensics Department in Guildford was one of the most efficiently run units in both forces.

'No, Roy, I'm sorry, not at this end – what we've been given is a blank memory card.'

'Might it have been wiped?'

'Well, yes, either wiped, or it's a new card, never used, which I think is more likely.'

'It couldn't just be a dud?'

'No, we've tested it and it records correctly.'

Grace thanked him and ended the call. Shit. The nightmare he didn't want to believe really did seem to be coming true.

On the serials earlier, the one that had caught his eye was a theft from a motor vehicle. Not something he would ordinarily have paid any attention to, vehicle break-ins happened all the time. Mostly they were random chaotic crimes by drug users desperate to pay for their next fix, grabbing a TomTom or a handbag, or anything of value the owner had left on view.

The thief had gained access the usual way, by smashing one of the rear windows of the BMW, sometime during the night. The car had been ransacked. Among the items taken was the GoPro camera.

The car was parked in Vallance Street.

Its owner's name was Christopher Diplock.

Instead of returning to the briefing, Roy Grace strode back to his office, called Ray Packham and updated him on the blank memory card and the stolen GoPro. 'Ray, is there any way this man, Diplock, could have given you the wrong memory card in error?'

'I doubt it very much, Roy. He doesn't strike me as the kind of person who would make many mistakes.'

'So how might it be blank? Could it have happened by accident – I don't know – such as by being too close to a mobile phone – or some other electronic device?'

'No, Roy, it would need to be something immensely powerful – such as an industrial-scale magnet. Even then there's likely to be some trace – memory cards are extremely hard to erase completely.'

Grace thought for a moment. 'OK. You took the card directly from Diplock and put it in the evidence bag yourself, didn't you, Ray?'

'Yes, I did.'

'Did you see any of the playback yourself?'

'No – Mr Diplock told me what he'd seen and that was enough for me.' Then after a moment he added, 'Are you thinking the theft of the GoPro might be related to this, Roy?'

'It could be someone trying to wipe away the traces, perhaps? Thinking that if they've been recorded on the memory card, then the images would still be on the GoPro?'

'Except the images wouldn't still be on the GoPro, Roy, they would only be on the memory card.'

'Of course,' he said.

But what if that person wasn't thinking straight? he wondered, privately. Someone in Exton's state, clutching at straws, increasingly desperate to conceal any evidence?

CHAPTER 86

Friday 29 April

Moments after ending the call, Grace was wondering why Batchelor had made the decision to send Exton to Guildford. He texted him.

> Guy, come and see me straight after the briefing.

Then he sat, mulling the facts. Could Jon Exton have somehow wiped the memory card – or perhaps, more easily, just substituted it with a blank one? Most detectives routinely carried little plastic evidence bags in their pockets. He would have had plenty of opportunity on the drive from Lewes to Guildford to buy a blank card.

He made a call to the ANPR Unit at John Street, and talked to a duty operator, Jon Pumfrey, asking him for a plot from 5 p.m. last night to midnight of Jon Exton's car.

Pumfrey obtained it while he waited, but it provided no surprise information. Exton had driven from Lewes to the Police HQ in Guildford. Afterwards he had returned to the vicinity of Vallance Mansions, and then much later he had pinged a camera on the A23 near the Withdean Sports Stadium.

Although ANPR cameras could plot the approximate route of vehicles across country, and through many cities, they did not provide blanket, detailed coverage. Exton could have stopped somewhere to shop for a memory card, without this being picked up.

Was it possible that later, in his panicked state, and not thinking clearly, he decided to take the GoPro for belt and braces good measure?

He went and made himself a coffee. Whilst the kettle boiled, his thoughts were boiling too. He just did not, could not, believe that mild Jon Exton was involved in any way.

However, the evidence was mounting all the time against the Detective. Yet he was still reluctant to believe he was a killer. And yet, and yet, and yet . . .

He had to distance himself from how he felt about the man. He'd never arrested – or even seen – a murderer who had I AM A KILLER tattooed on his or her forehead. It was so often the quiet ones. Someone snapping in a pub fight. The quiet, friendly doctor, like Harold Shipman or Edward Crisp. Charming Ted Bundy. Frequently, when a suspected killer was being led away in handcuffs, a television crew would be interviewing his sweet old lady neighbour. She'd be saying what a nice man he was, how he always used to look after her cat when she went away. It was just these types who all too often were the most dangerous.

Returning to his office, he began making notes on a fresh page of his Investigator's Notebook.

According to Exton's police phone records, Grace wrote, DS Exton had been looking at sex-worker sites – despite his vehement denials. He had spent the past few weeks sleeping rough close to Lorna Belling's flat and – pure speculation – might possibly have contacted her through a site on which she advertised herself – if this theory was correct. Could the deceased have threatened him with some form of blackmail, he wondered?

Exton was in the vicinity of her flat on the night she died.

Exton had been entrusted to drive the memory card, with potentially damning evidence, to Guildford. It had arrived blank.

During this past night someone had broken into Christopher Diplock's BMW and taken the GoPro – which Diplock had concealed in a headrest.

Who had done that?

It seemed very coincidental – almost too coincidental – that within hours of Exton delivering a blank memory card from the GoPro to the Forensics team in Guildford, the camera it had come from was stolen.

But if it was Exton, how had he known it was there? How had any thief?

He hesitated, thinking. He and Cleo had a GoPro, and when it was on *record* mode a red light flashed. However well Diplock had concealed it in a headrest, someone might have spotted it.

Especially Exton if he had gone looking for it.

He noted down that all the evidence re Exton was circumstantial. But was it too strong to ignore? Should he arrest him? In addition to his work phone, Digital Forensics was examining his private phone and his laptop. Should he wait to see if there was anything on any of these linking him to Lorna Belling? Then his thoughts were interrupted by another call from Packham.

'Roy, good news. As I thought, this Diplock fellow is no fool. He'd copied the memory card contents to his hard drive before giving it to us.'

Grace felt a massive flood of relief surge through him. 'Brilliant! OK, can you get him to make a copy and take it to Guildford yourself – as quickly as you can – and don't tell anyone, OK? Only report to me.'

'With pleasure! I've just got a new Audi Q3 Quattro TDi, automatic with flappy paddles and 177 BHP! Will be great to give it a run over there.'

'Nice wheels!'

'You're an Alfa man, aren't you?'

'Yep. But Audis are good, too. Always liked them.'

'The only problem is, chief, that Diplock's out with a client in Dorking – he won't be able to get home until mid-afternoon.'

'Can he get back any sooner? Could we get a

traffic car to blue light him home and then back to his client?'

'No, he's installing a new system for them and can't interrupt the process.'

'OK – just ask him to be as quick as he can.'

As he hung up, his thoughts returned to Exton. Why had the errant detective failed to turn up this morning? Moments later a phone call came in, patched through from the Control Room.

It was about Exton.

CHAPTER 87

Friday 29 April

'Detective Superintendent Grace?'

'Yes,' he replied.

'It's PC DuBois here from the Road Policing Unit.'

For an instant Grace thought she was going to refer back to Corin Belling's fatal accident.

'I think we did meet a few years back, sir – at an inquest – a person of interest to you at the time killed on a motorcycle.'

'Sharka, yes?'

'That's right, sir.'

'I do indeed remember you. All well?'

'Very good, thank you, sir. The reason I'm calling is that I'm currently at the scene of a single vehicle RTC near Hailsham. Looks like a BMW failed to negotiate a bend and has rolled a couple of times in a field. The driver is a DS in the Surrey and Sussex Major Crime Team – and the Control Room said he's currently working with you on Operation Bantam. His name's Exton.'

'Shit,' Grace said. 'How is he?'

'He's in the ambulance and the paramedics have just said he's not badly hurt – he's mostly suffering from shock and concussion. They'll know more when they get him X-rayed, but they suspect a couple of broken ribs.'

'Is he conscious?'

'Yes.'

'Has he been breath-tested?'

'Yes, sir, he blew a negative at the scene.'

'Do we know what time this accident occurred, Sharka?'

'It was phoned in by a lorry driver about an hour ago, but it looks like the car could have been there a few hours – its headlights were still on, which indicated it might have been during the night, or very early morning.'

'Any idea of the cause of the accident, or is it too early?' Grace asked.

'It's a fairly tight bend, with adverse camber, sir. It has caught people out before – there are warning signs on the approach. Or he could have fallen asleep at the wheel.'

Hailsham. That was where Exton had been living with his partner, Dawn. Before they'd split up. Was he on his way to see her? Then a more wild thought entered his head: had Exton decided to do a runner? Heading east? To the Eurotunnel, perhaps, less than two hours' drive away?

'There was no one else in the vehicle with him?'

'No, sir, but there's a lot of stuff in the car – and some of it's spewed out all around. A sleeping bag, food, toiletries, clothing tied up in bin bags. We thought it was some kind of homeless person at first, until we found his warrant card. He smells pretty rank, to be honest – the whole car does.'

'Which hospital are they taking him to?' Grace asked.

'Eastbourne. Could you have someone inform his next of kin, sir?'

'Yes, I'll get that done. Now, I want the car and all the contents impounded. I want you to treat it as a crime scene.'

PC DuBois sounded surprised. 'Yes, sir.'

'Presumably you've found nothing of interest or significance so far?'

'Not really, sir, no. As I said, mostly just clothes, toiletries, canned food – oh – and a GoPro camera in the glove box.'

CHAPTER 88

Friday 29 April

Fifteen minutes after he ended the call from PC DuBois, Roy Grace's phone rang again. It was Ray Packham.

'Roy, the serial number on the GoPro in Exton's car – I've just heard back from Christopher Diplock.'

'Yes?'

Packham had a serious, somewhat analytical voice, devoid of emotion. It could often be hard to read a positive or negative into his tone – as it was now. It sounded like it was going to be a negative answer, but then he surprised him.

'The serial number on the GoPro – Diplock has confirmed it's his camera, the one that was stolen from his car during the night.'

Grace thanked him and hung up. *Jon Exton.* The dark horse on his team? This mild-mannered, diligent detective would have been the last person he could have imagined being a killer. Yet the facts were making more and more sense. He'd split up with his partner, Dawn. She needed to be questioned.

Was the reason for their split another woman? Lorna Belling?

Was Exton the secret lover she had told her close friend Kate Harmond about? The man she'd been having an affair with who had told her his name was Greg? Except she had found out, just before she died, that it wasn't his name at all.

He stared down at his handwritten notes and actions. *Jon Exton.*

Every major crime was a puzzle with dozens, hundreds and sometimes thousands of pieces that had to be painstakingly pieced together. As was happening now. But there was something that made him hesitate, stopping him from punching the air in joy.

Was it because he had always liked the Detective Sergeant and was now feeling a measure of sympathy for the man and all that he faced? Misplaced sympathy, he knew. He had no time for officers who discredited the force.

But there was something else here. This puzzle, where at first all the pieces seemed to be fitting into place, felt like a box of flat-pack furniture which had been supplied with one crucial part missing. The bit that would hold the whole assembly together.

Nonetheless, with the evidence now in front of him, he had no alternative but to inform Lesley Manning, the Chief Constable. He picked up the phone and called her secretary. But it went to voicemail. Next he tried Manning's staff officer, a

DI called Tess Duffield. The CC was in a meeting, Duffield told him, and asked if there was a message she could pass on. Grace simply asked if she could call him back, urgently, as soon as convenient.

He had to wait less than fifteen minutes.

'Roy, all OK?' she asked. She was a calm, smart lady and he liked her.

'I'm afraid we have a problem, Lesley,' he said.

'Something we can talk about over the phone, or do you need to come and see me? I've got to leave in five minutes for London – I could meet you after 5 p.m., or is that too late?'

Grace gave her the information over the phone. She listened without interrupting, then was so silent when he had finished, he wondered for a moment if the line had been disconnected. Then she spoke.

'He's in hospital, you said?'

'Yes.'

'Has DS Exton indicated any awareness that he's under suspicion?'

'Not that he's under suspicion – but I've insisted he go to see the force doctor for psychological evaluation. I'm afraid he's in a bad way – very close to a breakdown if not already in the throes of one.'

'Do we know where he was going at the time of the accident?'

'No, I will find out when we interview him – hopefully later today. He was heading towards Hailsham, where his estranged partner, Dawn, lives, maybe to go and see her.'

'Or harm her?' Manning said.

'I think anything is possible in his current state of mind. I did wonder, also, whether he might have been heading towards Eurotunnel.'

'Do you think he's a flight risk?'

'Well, his behaviour is clearly erratic – and he's panicky. I've had a guard put outside his room at the hospital, as a precaution, instructed to not let him leave, but I've not given the reason.'

'But you haven't arrested him yet?'

'No, I'm still waiting for what I think could be one more piece of crucial evidence – which I expect to have later today. And I wanted to speak to you first and inform you. I also want to be completely sure we have the right person. If and when we do arrest him there will inevitably be a massive media circus; it won't look good to arrest one of our own, and it would be even worse if we subsequently released him without charge. I think we need to prepare a media strategy with Comms in advance, to ensure the reputational risk to Sussex Police is minimalized.'

'Roy, I'd like you to brief ACC Pewe, and also update Professional Standards of the latest situation. Then I think we should all have a meeting after I'm back this afternoon. Are you anticipating any developments by then?'

Thinking about the Super Recognizers, he replied, 'There may well be.'

Ending the call, he took a deep breath before dialling Pewe, hoping with luck to get his voicemail, and buy himself some time before talking to him. But he was out of luck.

‘Well, I did tell you yesterday to suspend the man,’ Pewe said with undisguised smugness in his voice.

‘With respect, I don’t see how that would have changed anything, sir,’ Grace retorted, struggling to hold his temper.

‘It appears to me, Roy, that there’s rather a lot of things you don’t see. Perhaps you should consider a trip to those opticians, the ones always advertising on television – what are they called – SpecSavers? You’d better come and see me right now – that is, of course, if you can find your way here.’

CHAPTER 89

Friday 29 April

The ACC sat behind his desk, studiously sharpening a yellow pencil with a tiny silver sharpener, in his elegant office just along the corridor from the Chief Constable. His fair hair was coiffed in neat waves, not a single strand out of place, his shirt was pressed to crisp perfection, the epaulettes bearing his ACC crescent looking, as ever, freshly minted, and his uniform looked like it had been pressed five minutes ago. Mr Immaculate. So perfect in every way, Grace thought, irreverently, that Cassian Pewe's turds probably came out in the shape of smileys.

'Take a seat, Roy,' he said without looking up from his task.

Grace selected one of the two leather chairs in front of the desk.

'I understand DS Exton is being kept in hospital overnight for observation. He has two broken ribs, concussion and a bruised spleen. The doctors, concerned about internal bleeding, will make a decision in the morning about when he could be discharged. Am I correct?'

'Yes, sir.'

Pewe held the pencil up, peered at the tip, then tested it with his finger, before placing it among an assortment in a black pen-holder on his desk. 'Unlike our friend, Mr Tooth, whose condition has not changed, I think there is value to keeping a round-the-clock guard on Exton. Do you have that in hand?'

'I do, sir. I'm arranging for DIs Glenn Branson and Kevin Hall to formally arrest Exton as soon as he is in a fit state, and at that time he will be suspended.'

Pewe stared hard at him. 'All right, can you see your way clear to doing that?' he said, sarcastically.

Holding his anger in, just, Grace replied through clenched teeth, 'Yes, sir.'

'To avoid any embarrassment with his colleagues, and ensure neutral treatment, he needs to be interviewed in a police station outside of Sussex. I've spoken to the former Deputy Chief Constable of Sussex, Olivia Pinkney, who as you know is now Chief Constable of Hampshire, and she has kindly offered us Portsmouth police station.'

'I think that is very sensible,' Grace said. 'And in fact I've already been in touch with Hampshire police. In the interim, before Exton is discharged from hospital, I'm having his fingerprints on the database compared with the lifts taken at the crime scene.'

'And a media strategy?' Pewe asked.

'I've got Comms working on that.'

'Excellent.' He raised his hands in the air. 'You may go. Unless you have anything else for me?'

Grace contemplated pressing him further about his conversations with Bruno in German, yesterday. But decided to hold that for another day.

'Yes, sir,' he said. 'Actually, I do. There is some CCTV footage that has been obtained from a GoPro camera in a car opposite the side entrance to Vallance Mansions. It apparently shows a man, his face partially obscured by a baseball cap, acting suspiciously in the vicinity around the time we believe Lorna Belling died. Maria O'Brien's team are currently enhancing it and I'm intending asking the Super Recognizer team at Scotland Yard to take a look at it.'

'For what reason, Roy?'

Patiently, he explained. 'My hope is a Super Recognizer will be able to positively identify the offender from the facial features visible.'

'And your expectation is that will be DS Exton?'

'If it turns out to be DS Exton, it will strengthen our case against him.'

'Good, you'll keep me posted?'

'Yes, sir.'

Posted, yes. I'd like to stuff you, screaming in pain, through a narrow letterbox, Roy Grace thought.

Momentarily relishing the image, he left the room.

CHAPTER 90

Friday 29 April

As he headed back to his office, his phone rang. It was Kevin Hall.

'Boss,' he said, 'this may be nothing, but I thought you should know. I've just spoken with a Keith Wadey, who's the Assistant Port Engineer of Shoreham Port. He carries out a fortnightly side-scan sonar check of the harbour, looking for obstacles – in particular submerged vehicles – that might damage the propellers or hulls of ships in the harbour. Earlier today he recovered an Apple MacBook Pro laptop from Arlington Basin. It's a recent model, fifteen-inch optical screen, and from its condition he thinks it has only recently been deposited. He reported it, thinking it might be suspicious – perhaps stolen. An alert detective at John Street was aware that we are looking for a laptop and phone that could be missing from Lorna Belling's flat in Vallance Mansions and phoned the Incident Room, and was put through to me.'

'How recently does Wadey think it was dumped, Kevin?'

'Within the past two weeks, he's pretty sure – since his last scan.'

Grace felt a beat of excitement. 'You need to speak to Digital Forensics, Kevin, and see if they can restore any of the data.'

'I'm on it, boss. Ray Packham has collected the laptop from Shoreham. He's going to pack it in rice and believes he'll be able to recover all the data from it as soon as it has dried out – he reckons twenty-four hours will do it. I've also asked Ray for the serial number – I should be able to trace it to the supplier and purchaser from that.'

'Nice work, Kevin,' Grace said. 'Let me know as soon as you have anything.'

'Yes, boss!'

Grace entered his office and sat at his desk, thinking about this. Then he googled MacBook Pro 15-inch screen models. Prices started at around £1,500 for the most basic model. Then he went to eBay and did a search there. Second-hand values were high, from £1,500 upwards.

So, he thought, anyone who had stolen one of these would surely try to sell it – even on a criminal black market it would be worth several hundred pounds, minimum. What possible reason could anyone have for throwing one into the harbour?

Other than to get rid of it. Because?

There was evidence on it?

Possibly. More than possibly?

Could this one be connected to Lorna Belling? He had a feeling that it just might.

Hopefully, he'd find out soon enough.

He opened his address book and looked for the contact details for Jonathan Jackson on the Super Recognizer Team that Ray Packham had sent him yesterday.

It had been a good decade, if not longer, since the detective had left Sussex Police to join the Metropolitan Police – at a time when the Met were recruiting from the provinces, tempting officers with substantially larger pay packets and fewer unsociable work hours.

Grace had been sorry to lose Jackson, who had been a dependable member of his team. He found the number and dialled it. Jackson answered on the second ring.

'Good to hear from you, guv! To what do I owe the pleasure of this call?'

'I'm told you're involved with the Super Recognizer team – is that right?'

'Yes, very much so.'

'If I needed their help, how quickly could that happen?'

'Just as fast as you want, guv. I can put you through to MetCU and they'll allocate a duty Super Recognizer to you.'

'What do they need to work from, Jonathan?'

'Still photographs or video – obviously the better the quality, the more chance we have of making an accurate identification.'

'Would we send it up to you, or do you have someone who could come down and look at it in situ?'

'They'd send someone down to you, preferably.'

'Great. When are you on-call until, Jonathan?'

'Like you, guv. 24/7. Call me anytime you need me.'

Grace thanked him and ended the call.

Jon Exton, now their prime suspect, was in the Eastbourne District General Hospital, under a round-the-clock police guard. As soon as he was well enough to be interviewed he would be arrested and transported to the central police station in Portsmouth.

But. He was still struggling to see Exton as a suspect, despite all he knew and had experienced. There was something about the DS that was just so straight, so honest.

Equally, he knew, from all his experience, it was precisely those qualities that enabled many killers to evade justice for years.

With just a tad of reluctance he made a series of phone calls, to Superintendent Darke at Professional Standards, the Head of Corporate Comms and to the Detective Chief Superintendent, Head of CID, setting up a meeting for late afternoon with Pewe and the Chief Constable to discuss the interview process and media strategy for one of their trusted detectives on his release from hospital.

CHAPTER 91

Friday 29 April

It was nearly 5 p.m. when an apologetic Christopher Diplock arrived home from his client and was finally able to make a copy of the GoPro recording for Packham to take across to Guildford.

The meeting in the Chief Constable's office finished an hour later. With Exton due to be released from hospital in the morning, and both the enhanced GoPro video and, hopefully, data from the laptop recovered from the harbour expected, tomorrow promised to be a big day.

Grace decided to go home early for once, eager to see Noah, and to find out how Bruno was getting on at St Christopher's school – and he hadn't forgotten his promise to teach him firearms techniques. He was also looking forward to having a rare quiet evening with Cleo.

All was fine in the house. Noah had been grizzling earlier, teething, Cleo said, and Bruno had been getting on with his homework. He went up to Bruno's room and chatted to him about how he was getting on at his new school, and if he had made any friends. Then he helped him – with some difficulty – with a couple of maths queries he had. Mathematics had never been Grace's strong point – he'd failed twice before finally struggling through at the third attempt. Failure would have hindered his chances of becoming a police officer.

Bruno thanked him politely, and knuckled back down.

As he left the room he realized he still hadn't fully accepted that this boy really was his son.

Nor, as he lay wide, wide awake at 2 a.m., had he fully accepted what all the evidence pointed to about Jon Exton.

Tossing and turning in bed, plumping his pillow then replumping it as gently as he could, trying not to disturb Cleo, sleep was elusive. He saw the green digits of his clock radio change. 2.03 a.m. 2.17 a.m. 2.38 a.m.

Thinking. Thinking.

Lorna Belling.

Her eyes wide open.

Staring at him from the bathtub.

Find my killer.

Or are you teasing me? Did you kill yourself?

Oh yes, and I wiped that memory card and put the GoPro in Jon's car, from beyond the grave. Sure, to cover my tracks.

The one certainty he had right now was that he could rule out suicide.

At around 4 a.m. he fell into a deep sleep, to be awoken just twenty minutes later by Noah crying.

CHAPTER 92

Saturday 30 April

Just before midday Chris Gargan emailed Roy Grace, telling him they'd done their best with the GoPro images, but they were hampered by the rain on the windscreen. He was sending them over by WeTransfer and they should be with him in minutes.

Grace called Guy Batchelor, updated him and asked him to come to his office and view them with him.

The DS came in a few minutes later, clutching a cup of coffee. He was still smarting after the bollocking he'd been given by Roy for entrusting Exton, clearly in an unreliable state, with a crucial piece of evidence to take to Guildford. He'd already apologized to Roy, telling him he just hadn't thought it through, it was time critical and Exton was available.

'Any updates, Guy?' Grace asked, as he waited for the files to load.

'Exton's on his way to Portsmouth. Glenn Branson and Kevin Hall are accompanying him and will do the interview, as you suggested, boss. He's got a solicitor on the way from Eastbourne.'

'Who's that?' Grace asked.

'Nadine Ashford, from Lawson Lewis Blakers.'

Grace had selected the two trained suspect interviewers carefully. Glenn was good at reading body language – something he'd taught him himself; Hall had a beguiling warmth about him that masked a chip of ice in his heart. Grace had done a number of suspect interviews with him in the past, and no one played the role of good cop better.

The downloads were complete, and Grace opened the first one. 'OK,' he said. 'Let's see what this gives us.'

The image wasn't great, but it was, to Grace's surprise, clearer than Gargan had warned. They could see the residential road, and the flare of the street lights. Orientating himself, he could see that the view through the windscreen of the BMW was north, up Vallance Street, with the seafront directly behind. To the left, across the quiet residential road, was the eastern facade of Vallance Mansions and the side entrance.

After some moments, in a series of staggered, jump-frame time-lapse images, a young female jogger jerked past, the images making her look almost comically fast. Then a male figure emerged from the side door of Vallance Mansions.

The time display showed 9.01 p.m.

Tall, wearing a raincoat, the top half of his face was totally obscured by a plain, long-peaked baseball cap, of the kind favoured by golfers. The features of the lower half of his face were impossible to see clearly. He seemed to be clutching something concealed inside the coat. He was also carrying two bin bags and some flowers.

'What's inside his coat?' Grace said.

'The laptop?' Batchelor replied.

'Could be.'

In the next frame he appeared a yard further on down the pavement. Then another yard. Then he was gone from view.

Grace stopped the video, wound it back to where the man first appeared, then magnified the image. The larger it became, the more blurry it was.

'Exton's height,' Batchelor said.

Grace nodded, uncertainly. 'Exton's height, yes, but not his build – although that could be the quality of the image, distorting through the wet glass.'

'They say television adds pounds to anyone's face – and features,' Batchelor said, staring intently at the screen.

Diplock had done a good editing job; the two detectives observed the time display jump to 10.22 p.m. This time the same man appeared striding up the pavement on the other side of the road now. One hand held an umbrella and he carried a bag in the other. He was visible for three frames, looking carefully around, then went out of shot.

'Hello!' Batchelor said. 'Nice to see you again!'

'Laptop's gone?' Grace suggested.

'Looks like it. He'd have had plenty of time to go to Shoreham Harbour and ditch it.'

'It would have been a round trip of ten minutes in a car.'

'A good half an hour walk each way on foot though,' Batchelor said, thoughtfully.

After another time jump they saw the man again, walking back down the street, on the opposite side of the road, still using what appeared to be a busted umbrella.

'Aha, looks like he's the local Good Samaritan,' Grace said. 'Carrying out everyone's rubbish for them in the middle of the night.'

They looked back at the footage of the man's return to the flat.

When the man reached the side door to Vallance Mansions he stopped, pulled out what both detectives presumed must be a key, opened the door and went in.

'Reminds me of that old Marx Brothers joke,' Grace said.

'Which one, boss?'

'"Hey, Charlie, the garbage man's here!" "Yeah? Go tell him we don't need any today."'

Batchelor smiled wanly.

'So what's our Exton doing at half ten at night carrying a garbage bag into Lorna Belling's apartment building?'

Batchelor stared intently at the screen for some moments. His face looked pale and Grace noticed a faint nervous tic around his jaw. He felt for the man. There was nothing harder than having to arrest and bring evidence against a colleague, particularly one who had been a friend as well.

'Groceries?' he said, finally.

'Not in a bin bag,' Grace said. 'Groceries come in carrier bags, so do cans of booze. Is he planting something, perhaps? Or got some tools in there – is he planning at this stage to chop her up?'

'Of course we don't even know for sure this is Exton, or that this man has any connection to Lorna Belling.'

'Correct, Guy. We need to get him either positively identified, or establish that it's not him.'

'That wouldn't necessarily prove anything either way, would it, boss? What I'm saying is that if this character is Exton, that puts him in Lorna Belling's apartment building, but if it's someone else – a complete stranger – he's not necessarily going to Lorna's flat – he's just behaving very oddly.'

'Very.'

Grace picked up his phone and dialled Jonathan Jackson's number. When he answered, he explained what they had on video, which didn't faze the Met officer, and asked him how soon he could get a member of the Super Recognizer team down to Sussex.

'I should be able to get someone to you within a few hours, Roy. I'll call you back.'

Grace thanked him and ended the call. Then he looked again at the video on the screen. At the man with the bin bag.

His shape looked wrong. Wrong for Exton. Exton was slight – and in recent weeks had become even slighter. This man was quite a different build, quite a bit bulkier. But, on the other hand, the image was pretty crap.

Grace gave Batchelor a quizzical look. 'Spot anything of significance, Guy?'

'No, you?'

'My best guess is he's clearing any evidence. He did a pretty thorough job, as the CSIs weren't able to find anything of real value.'

His colleague nodded, thoughtfully. 'OK, I'll bell you as soon as I have anything more,' Batchelor said.

'I'll go and chase Ray, see what he can find from the laptop.'

Moments after Batchelor left Grace's office, the phone rang. It was Jackson.

'Roy, there's a DS from our Super Recognizer team who's not far from you at the moment. His name's Tim Weatherley. He's familiar with Sussex CID and has been working with one of your colleagues, Superintendent Sloan, on the Crime and Ops team. He's currently at the Surrey Police HQ, working on a development on the multiple homicide of a British family and an unconnected cyclist, at Annecy in France – back in 2012. Apparently there's some new footage come to light.'

'Yes, I remember it,' Grace said. An Iraqi-born British tourist, his wife and his mother-in-law, as well as a French cyclist, had been shot dead in a forest clearing. The family's two young daughters had miraculously survived but had been unable to provide much evidence. It remained one of the darkest unsolved crimes of recent years.

'He could be with you between 4 and 5 p.m. I've given him your number and he'll call you when he has an ETA.'

'Brilliant, thanks JJ.'

'Anytime, Roy. We should have a drink and catch-up sometime.'

'Are you still living in Saltdean?'

'Yep – let me know when's good.'

'I will.'

As he ended the call, Grace wondered, in view of the sensitive nature of their prime suspect, whether he should view the footage with just the Super Recognizer and Guy Batchelor without involving the rest of the team.

But then he had a better idea.

CHAPTER 93

Saturday 30 April

It felt like he was swimming underwater. He could see light above him. The silhouettes of faces. His mind swam, too. He felt all giddy. Nauseous.

Momentarily he broke the surface. Saw a dog at the edge of the pool. A squat, ugly thing. It had different coloured eyes, one bright red, the other grey. It was a mutt. Part Dalmatian and part pug.

It was looking at him balefully. Reproachfully. *Are you abandoning me? Just like my last owner?*

'Yossarian!' he called out. 'Yossarian!'

He cared about it. This ugly mutt that he had found on a Beverly Hills street was the only thing in his life he had ever cared about. It was standing, looking down at him, and hungry.

'Yossarian!' he screamed.

No sound came out of his intubated throat.

The ITU nurse at the Royal Sussex County Hospital ran across to Bed 17 and stared down at the small, shaven-headed man, who was connected to a forest of drip lines and a ventilator. He was thrashing around wildly, his eyes opening and shutting in rapid succession, as if he was fitting.

This patient, who went by the odd, single name of Tooth, was under special watch, and until recently there had been a police guard for him posted on a 24/7 rota outside the unit entrance. She did not know too much about the circumstances that had brought him here, in a persistent vegetative state, a month ago from the Tropical Diseases Unit at Guy's Hospital in London, other than that he had suffered a series of bites and stings from a spider, a scorpion and a saw-scaled viper snake in a reptile house. Because of the police interest in him, she imagined he had been involved in a burglary at a zoo that had gone badly wrong.

She paged the duty doctor, urgently.

Ten minutes later Roy Grace was interrupted from his studies of the Jodie Bentley file by a call. The voice at the other end sounded foreign. 'This is Dr Imran Hassan from the Intensive Care Unit at the Royal Sussex Hospital. We have a note on file to contact you if there is any change in the condition of one of our patients, a gentleman called Mr Tooth.'

This was all he needed right now, Grace thought. 'Yes, thank you, Dr Hassan.'

'He seems to be showing signs of emerging from his coma. He keeps trying to shout. We removed the tube from his throat and immediately he shouted out a name. It sounded like "Yossarian".'

'Yossarian?'

'Yes, but now he seems very distressed about this Yossarian. His eyes remain closed but he screamed that Yossarian needs feeding. Does any of this make any sense to you?'

'It does, yes, Dr Hassan. Yossarian is this man's pet dog – he lives in the Turks and Caicos. Tooth is under suspicion of committing several murders, and the dog is being cared for. He doesn't need to worry.'

But Grace was worried.

'Good, we are regarding this as a positive sign that this patient is improving.'

'To what extent?'

'At this stage very minor. He is still totally incapacitated.'

'Dr Hassan, if at any time you or your colleagues believe that Tooth is capable of standing and walking, I need to know immediately.'

'Yes, this is on his notes, Detective Superintendent.'

Grace thanked him, then immediately sent an email to Pewe, updating him on Tooth's condition. He did not suggest that the scene guard be reinstated at this stage, but instead covered his back by finishing,

> as you know we are dealing with a man of extraordinary reserves and resources. It would be a deep embarrassment to

Sussex Police if he were to disappear. At this time, the staff at the Royal Sussex County Hospital do not believe this is likely. But they know to notify me if the situation changes.

He wasn't expecting a reply. And didn't get one.

CHAPTER 94

Saturday 30 April

Grace liked Tim Weatherley instantly. The detective from the Scotland Yard Super Recognizer Unit arrived in his office shortly before 6 p.m., apologizing effusively for being so late, and looking like he'd already had a long day. He was dressed in a crumpled grey suit, a pink shirt and striped tie at half mast, and had untidy black hair. He reminded Grace of the TV comedian Michael McIntyre.

For some reason he had been expecting an intense, studious geek, but Weatherley, in his late thirties, was warm and open, with a booming voice.

'I've got a message for you from Superintendent Sloan,' he said.

'Oh yes?'

'He said to tell you that you still owe him a beer!'

Grace grinned. 'That's rich coming from him. Short arms, deep pockets.'

Weatherley grinned back.

'Would you like tea? Coffee?' Grace offered.

'No, thanks, I'm fine. It's actually my wedding anniversary and I have to take she-who-must-be-obeyed out to dinner in London – in Battersea – so without wanting to rush anything, the sooner I can get away, the better. How can I help you?'

Grace filled him in on the history and the sensitive nature of the issue. Then he added, 'It has always been my method of operating to include my whole team. We have a briefing scheduled for 6.30 p.m. I'd like you to view the footage before the briefing, and then I'll introduce you to the team so you can educate them on what resources are available. We might have an unknown talent with Super Recognizer abilities on this team. But what I would appreciate is that if you are able to make a positive ID on DS Exton when you initially see the footage, that you don't mention it to the team.'

Weatherley frowned. 'It's your call.' He shot a glance at his watch.

'I'll make sure you're on your way by 7 p.m. You'll be in Battersea by 8.30 p.m latest.'

'Do you have some images of this DS Exton for me to get familiar with?'

Grace showed him a photocopy of Exton's warrant card, and a series of images of him from the internal CCTV at Malling House. Then he took him out into the corridor to the board on the wall where there were photographs, with their names beneath, of all the members of the Major Crime Branch, and pointed out Exton.

As he was standing there his phone rang. It was Ray Packham.

'Roy, some good news. I think you're going to like this.'

'Tell me?'

'It's drying out well – I'm standing here like a twat, with a hairdryer! But in the meantime I've got a result from tracing the serial number. The computer was bought from the Apple store in Churchill Square in Brighton last November 22nd – by Lorna Belling.'

'Bloody hell, that is brilliant, Ray, well done.'

'Thought you'd like that. I'll call you as soon as it's up and running.'

'Brilliant.'

As Weatherley studied the photographs of the team on the board, Guy Batchelor walked along the corridor. 'Boss, just wanted to check the time of this evening's briefing.' Then he hesitated, looking at the visitor.

'Oh, Guy – this is Tim Weatherley, from the Super Recognizer unit.' He turned to Weatherley. 'DI Batchelor is the Deputy SIO on this case, Tim. Feel free to share anything with him.'

The two men shook hands. 'Nice to meet you,' Weatherley said.

'Likewise. Thanks for coming down, we really appreciate it,' Batchelor said. 'I've heard great things about your unit.'

'Feel free to spread the word! Not enough forces know about us yet.' Weatherley smiled warmly.

'Absolutely!' Batchelor said.

'We've a development,' Grace informed him. 'Ray Packham's just called me, he's identified the owner of the Apple MacBook Pro.'

'He has?'

'Lorna Belling.'

'Bloody hell.'

'This could be dynamite for us!' Grace said enthusiastically. 'He hopes to have it up and running tonight.'

'Fantastic,' Batchelor said, but he looked uneasy.

Grace felt uneasy too. The thought of seeing Exton brought down and imprisoned for murder was not something any of them relished, and Batchelor, despite his tough appearance, had a deeply sensitive and caring side that Grace had noticed often in the past.

'As DS Weatherley has to get away by 7 p.m., I thought we'd bring the briefing forward. Could you tell everyone we'll have it in fifteen minutes' time.'

'Yes, boss. I'll get right on it.'

'Good man.'

Grace led Weatherley back into his office, and left him alone to watch the footage, before joining him in the briefing.

CHAPTER 95

Saturday 30 April

At 6.20 p.m., minus Glenn Branson and Kevin Hall, who were down in Portsmouth with Jon Exton, Grace's entire team was assembled in the conference room. He cut to the chase by introducing Tim Weatherley, who had just entered the room, and asking him to give a brief outline of the work of the Scotland Yard Super Recognizer Unit.

When he had finished, the Detective Superintendent said, 'We're now going to view one still from a camera in a fortuitously parked vehicle on Vallance Street, on the night of Wednesday, April 20th – the date that Lorna Belling died. The image is very blurry, partly because it is through a windscreen on a wet night, and partly because of the darkness—'

He was momentarily distracted by a ping from Velvet Wilde's phone. Then he went on.

'If any of you think you know the identity of the person in this image, who may or may not be the offender, let us know immediately. Let's see if any of you have Super Recognizer abilities!' He nodded at Weatherley and he switched on the projector.

All of them turned to look at the blurry image of a figure on the flat screen on the wall, who appeared to be carrying two rubbish bags.

'I recognize him, chief,' Norman Potting said.

'Yes?' Grace encouraged.

'Is it a bird? Is it a plane? No, it's Super Binman!'

There was laughter.

'Thank you, Norman,' Grace retorted, acidly. 'Not terribly helpful.'

'He would be in my neighbourhood, chief. With the bin strikes we've had.'

'Norman!' he cautioned.

'Sorry, chief,' Potting said, blowing on his new designer glasses and wiping them with one of his shirt fronts, exposing his flabby belly.

Grace looked at Weatherley. He seemed pensive.

'Reminds me of *Blackadder*, chief,' Norman Potting suddenly said.

'*Blackadder?*' Grace queried.

'That bit when Rowan Atkinson says, "A blind man, in a dark room, looking for a black cat that isn't there."'

'Your point being, Norman?' EJ Boutwood asked.

'My point is, young lady, that we're being asked to identify *Mr Blurry*, when the only thing we can see clearly is a bin bag. Unless you've got better eyesight than me. Eh?'

Roy Grace looked at Weatherley. The Super

Recognizer had a strange expression. As he caught the Detective Superintendent's eye, he gave him a discreet glance. No one else in the room, other than Guy Batchelor who was looking intently at the man, could have spotted it.

CHAPTER 96

Saturday 30 April

With none of the team having anything useful to offer on the image, Grace ended the meeting, aware that Weatherley needed to get back to London.

He led the Super Recognizer back to his office, followed by Batchelor, and the three of them sat down.

'So, tell us?' Grace said.

Weatherley looked awkward. 'I can tell you it's not DS Exton. I'm afraid the images were not brilliant, as you said. If it's OK with you I'd like to take them back to my office and see how much further we can enhance them.'

'Yes, we can burn them on a disk or email them to you.'

Weatherley glanced at his watch. It was 6.45 p.m. 'Email is fine and I'll work on them first thing in the morning.'

'Thanks, Tim, I really appreciate your help.'

Batchelor stood up. 'Tim, I'll show you back out

to your car. When you get to the gates the barrier will open automatically.'

'Thank you,' he said.

As the two men left his office, Grace sat down at his desk, puzzled. Weatherley had definitely seen something in the footage, but why, he wondered, was he being so reticent?

Five minutes later he got an answer, but not the one he was expecting. A text pinged on his phone that stopped him in his tracks. It was Weatherley's number, he recognized it from earlier.

> Roy, you asked me to be discreet, which is why I said nothing after the meeting. Call me as soon as you are alone in the office.

Grace read it with growing panic. What did he mean by this? Did he mean that it was someone else he had seen here at Police HQ – or, God forbid, one of his team?

He immediately dialled Weatherley's number, but it went straight to voicemail. He left him a message asking him to call him very urgently, and sent him a text as well.

CHAPTER 97

Saturday 30 April

Before joining the Super Recognizer Unit, Tim Weatherley had spent seven years in the Metropolitan Police Road Policing Unit. Like most of his fellow officers during that period, he attended his share of 'fatals' – as collisions resulting in one or more deaths were colloquially known. And he had come to learn which vehicles stood up best in accidents, in terms of protecting their occupants. That was the reason he drove a sturdy Volvo, which he always chose from the police car pool, and insisted that his wife, who ferried their young children to school and back daily, drove them in another large slab of Volvo.

He had discovered his Super Recognizer skills whilst out on patrol, where a big part of the job was observing the occupants of passing cars, checking to see if they were known villains, or not wearing seat belts, or on their mobile phones. His colleagues began to realize, gradually, that he had an almost uncanny ability to spot wanted villains, in almost any light and even in heavy rain. It earned him the nickname Catseyes. A couple of years later, word of his abilities reached Detective Chief Inspector Mick Neville who was recruiting for the Scotland Yard Super Recognizer Unit.

Now, as he followed the snaking ribbon on the TomTom on his dash, taking him away from the Sussex Police HQ, over a couple of junctions and several roundabouts, through a long tunnel, where the pelting rain momentarily stopped, and then onto the A27, he was feeling conflicted and very distracted by the footage he had just viewed.

He was as certain as he could be who the man in the video was, just from the shape of his nose and chin. The implications were immense.

The wipers swished across the screen in front of him, barely keeping up with the rain that was coming down even harder now. He was very distracted by his thoughts, and concentrating so hard on what he could see through the rain and spray of the road ahead that for some minutes he did not look in his mirrors. If he had, he might have noticed a car had followed him out of the Police HQ, and was now a discreet three vehicles behind him in the rapidly falling dusk.

He heard the ping of an incoming text and saw the screen of his phone, in the well behind the gear lever, light up. But, having attended too many accidents caused by people looking at texts whilst driving, he ignored it, despite his curiosity. He would pull over when he saw a layby and check it then, in safety, he decided. Then he yawned.

It had been a long week. He looked forward to a relaxing evening with Michelle. Earlier, whilst he had been waiting to see Superintendent Sloan, he had downloaded the menu of the restaurant they had decided on for their anniversary dinner, and had chosen what he would eat. Scallops with black pudding, followed by aged Black Angus rib-eye. Or possibly the rack of spring lamb.

He was salivating at the thought.

They were going by taxi, and he looked forward to having a few drinks. A glass or two of Prosecco, then a rich red wine – perhaps a Spanish Rioja.

Stopping in a line of traffic at a roundabout, he glanced down at his phone, which was plugged into the hands-free, and hit the speed-dial button.

Moments later, accelerating away from the roundabout, he heard the ringtone, followed by his wife's voice.

'Hi, love, how are you doing?' she asked.

'I'm on my way, baby. Satnav says ETA of 8.23.'

'Brilliant!'

'I love yoooooooooo!'

'Drive safely.'

'I thought I'd drive like one crazy sonofabitch craving his wife.'

'You're crazy!'

'That's why you love me, isn't it?'

Suddenly, approaching a left curve at speed, he heard a massive bang right behind him, that resonated through the car, and simultaneously felt a violent jolt that shook every bone in his body. The steering wheel spun right, windmilling through his hands.

Shit! Shit! What had happened? What had he hit? Had someone hit him?

The car was lurching sideways, the seat moving beneath him.

The steering wheel was spinning the opposite way now.

Then it reversed again.

The Volvo was fishtailing; it slewed sideways, heading towards the crash barrier in the middle of the road, struck it and bounced off.

He fought the wheel and the car fishtailed left this time, then right, then left again, in a massive tank-slapper, hurtling now towards the side of the road, throwing him against the door.

Straight at a hedge.

And suddenly.

Oh shit.

The howling of tyres.

The hedge hurtling towards him.

He was no longer the driver, he was a passenger.

The hedge.

The tyres were biting.

Gripping.

He felt the door against his shoulder again. Shit, shit, shit. They were going over. Rolling. Rumbling. He saw tarmac. Heard drumming. Saw sky. Tarmac. Grass. Sky. Cracks in front of him. Cracked glass. Like spiders' webs. Sky. Tarmac. Grass.

Jesus.

He was going to die.

Metallic rumbling.

Sky.

Rumbling.

Then silence.

Complete silence. Just a ticking sound. He felt dazed. Lay still. Blinked.

I'm alive.

He was hanging from the seat belt.

'Tim? Tim? Tim?'

His wife's voice, faint and panicky. Where was she?

'Tim, what's happening, Tim? Tim? Are you all right, love – Tim?'

Above him. Was he hallucinating?

Then he realized. His mobile phone was lying on the roof lining. He tried to reach it but he was restrained by his seat belt and it was too far away. 'I'm OK!' he shouted, his voice sounding shaky as hell. 'I'm OK, darling. Just a – bit of a—'

Need to get out, he thought, beginning to panic. In case of fire. Although he knew that cars rarely caught fire when they rolled, that was in movies only.

'Darling, I'll call you back in a couple of minutes,' he shouted, fumbling for the seat-belt catch. Then he stopped. *Idiot! Do not release it.*

He'd seen people needlessly paralysed after roll-over accidents because they panicked, unclipped their belts and dropped six inches onto their heads, breaking their necks in the worst place.

He heard the ticking again. A steady tick-tick-tick.

The fuel pump. He reached across and turned the ignition off. Then he raised his right hand and braced himself against the roof of the car. Only when he was confident he was taking his weight did he fumble for the catch with his left hand and pop it. Then, as he gently lowered himself down onto the roof, he heard his wife's voice again. 'Tim? Can you hear me? Tim?'

He saw figures, through the side windows, running towards him.

'Just had a bit of a shunt, darling,' he called out. 'I'm fine, never been better!'

A young man was kneeling down, tugging the driver's door open. A middle-aged woman right behind him stooped down and peered in, with a concerned expression. 'I'm a First Responder from Hassocks,' she said in a commanding voice. 'Are you injured?'

'I – I don't think so.' Something was sticking into his chest, a sharp, painful object like a pointed stick.

'Don't try to move,' she said. 'There's an ambulance on its way.'

He wriggled, checking he could move his toes, legs, fingers. 'I'm fine, I don't need an ambulance – I've got to get to London – my wife – it's our anniversary.'

'Don't even think about it. You are not moving, young man.'

As he tried to move he cried out in pain as the stick jabbed his chest again. Except it wasn't a stick, he recognized this pain, he'd had it before after being kicked in the chest during a rugby game. It was a broken rib sticking into his chest.

He heard a siren, approaching rapidly.

Outside, he heard a gruff male voice, sounding very indignant. 'I saw it! Couldn't believe my eyes. He rammed him, deliberately, he did! You know, it was like in the movies, unbelievable. I nearly went smack into him myself.'

The siren stopped suddenly. He heard footsteps and then a male voice asking, 'Is anyone injured?' and a female voice calling out, 'Are there any witnesses?'

Moments later a Road Policing Unit officer in a yellow fluorescent jacket peered inside. 'Are you all right, sir?' she asked.

'Yes, thank you, I'm fine, I think. May have bust a rib.'

'We'll get you checked over.'

'I'm a police officer,' Weatherley said.

'You are?'

'With the Met.'

'Well, that's a bit of a coincidence!' Sharka DuBois said. 'You're my second copper in two days!'

'I'm very happy for you,' Weatherley replied.

CHAPTER 98

Saturday 30 April

Grace sat quietly in his office, pondering the words of the Super Recognizer's text.

> Roy, you asked me to be discreet, which is why I said nothing after the meeting. Call me as soon as you are alone in the office.

He thought back over Exton's behaviour recently; the coincidence of him being in the vicinity of the dead woman's flat for days before and on the night of her death; the GoPro memory card delivered to the Forensic Unit with nothing on it – presumably wiped clean or replaced with a blank; the GoPro found in his glove box.

But Weatherley said the image of the man leaving the flat was not Exton. So who was it? A different Sussex police officer?

Who?

Hopefully, Weatherley had made a mistake.

The image was terrible, blurred by the rain, how could anyone make a positive ID from that? He appreciated he did not have Super Recognizer skills, but all he could have said, if giving evidence in a court of law, was that the figure in the video entering and leaving the apartment block was of a similar height to DS Exton. Nothing else.

Perhaps when Weatherley examined the footage in the morning, he'd come to the same conclusion, he thought. He went through his team members who were around the same height as Exton. Guy? Jack? Donald? Kevin? Then he was interrupted by his mobile phone ringing. It was Ray Packham, sounding deeply on edge.

'Roy,' he said. 'I'm up at the HTCU offices in Haywards Heath and we've got Lorna Belling's laptop up and running. There's something you need to see on this.'

'Right, what?'

'This is very sensitive, Roy. Very sensitive. I don't want to risk talking about it over the phone.'

'Can you email anything to me?'

'No, too risky. I'll bring it myself. Where are you at the moment?'

'In my office.'

'You need to see this right away, but we need to be private.'

'We can be private in my office.'

'Too risky, Roy.'

'Ray, just what the hell do you have?'

'Believe me, Roy, I have something I do not think you're expecting.'

Grace turned and peered through the window. It was nearly dark outside.

'Ray, what about we meet outside the main gates?'

'No, too close.'

The man was sounding scared, he realized. Shit, what did he have? 'Ray, what about the Tesco Superstore – on the edge of the industrial estate. Meet in the car park there?'

'Good plan.'

'When you enter it, go to the far side and turn left, and drive as far as you can go. Remind me, what car are you in?'

'An Audi Q3, black.'

'I'll be in a plain Mondeo estate, I'll wait for you there.'

'I'll be half an hour – hopefully less. Oh and listen, Roy, don't say a word to anyone, OK?'

Hesitantly, he replied, 'OK.'

Then he ended the call with his mind on fire. What was Packham about to reveal that was too risky to bring in to the Police HQ? Ordinarily he would have spoken to the one person he did totally and utterly trust, Glenn Branson, but he was in Portsmouth right now with Exton. He decided Batchelor, as his deputy, should be notified that they might be about to get a major development. He dialled the number, but it went to voicemail. He left a message asking the DI to call him back very urgently.

Then he texted Cleo to say he did not know when he would be home and would update her in an hour, picked up his car keys and headed outside.

CHAPTER 99

Saturday 30 April

I can't see a damned thing through the windscreen. It's all blurry, like it's covered in rainwater, like that video of the guy walking down the street and in and out of Lorna Belling's apartment building.

I can't see anything and it's only raining very lightly. My eyes won't focus. Nothing will focus. This is the problem with Natural Selection or whatever you want to call it. We've evolved all wrong, we've not kept pace biologically with the way we've evolved sociologically. Go back to our hunter-gatherer days, if you suddenly found yourself face-to-face with a sabre-toothed tiger, your adrenaline would kick in, pumping into your veins to enable you to run like the wind. But if you don't burn that stuff off by running, it makes you all jittery, muzzes your brain, stops your eyes from focusing properly.

We have different kinds of terror now, like being confronted by the VAT inspector, where the response we need is to remain calm, level-headed, highly focused. But still the damned adrenaline kicks in – or in my case, right now, kicks off.

It didn't let me focus.

I got too anxious and blew it.

I should have waited for that damned detective from the Met, the Super Recognizer, to have got onto the M23 motorway, where he'd have been driving eighty, maybe ninety miles per hour, as he was in a hurry. And it would have been fully dark, half an hour, on from now. I was impatient, picked him off in a line of traffic, he was only doing fifty-five, maybe sixty. Did the classic car-chase manoeuvre, tapping him with the front of my car, the heavy part where the engine is, at the lightest point of his, behind the rear wheels. Knocked him sideways, then he rolled, I saw it in my mirror. Nice barrel rolls. But not enough. He might survive.

If I'd hit him at higher speed on the motorway and he'd flipped and barrel-rolled at eighty, that would pretty likely have been goodnight.

Now I don't know where the hell I am. Where to go? He knows. Which means Roy Grace is going to know – if Weatherley lives.

I'm just not thinking straight.

I haven't thought straight since April 20th, since –

Since –

Since Lorna Belling turned out her lights.

Maybe I turned them out.

Or maybe I didn't.

The Super Recognizer knows who turned them out. He saw. He recognized.

This must be what hell feels like.

When everyone you know and love and respect is

about to find out you've done a terrible thing – the worst thing a human being can do – and you're going to lose everything.

This car needs fuel, I'm going to have to stop soon at a petrol station and be careful where I position it so no one spots the damage. I'll have to get out, fill up, then go inside and pay. The guy or the woman I hand the money to will probably smile, and ask if I want a receipt. He – or maybe she – won't know they've just served a murderer – who, if DS Weatherley dies, will be defined as a multiple killer – until they read the papers or watch the news tomorrow, or perhaps the day after. Then they'll be shocked, and one day they'll tell their grandchildren. 'You'll never guess what grandpa/grandma did! I once served a murderer in a petrol station!'

Oh Jesus.

There are blue flashing lights in my mirror.

CHAPTER 100

Saturday 30 April

Eight forty-five on a Saturday night; the car park was thinning out. Grace watched a rotund woman, stuffing her face with a doughnut as she pushed a laden trolley towards her car, parked opposite him. Packham had been almost forty minutes, and had texted to apologize, saying he was in stationary traffic on the A27 because of an accident.

Surprised that Weatherley had still not called him back, Grace was about to dial his number again when he saw a dark-coloured Audi turn left towards him and flash its lights. It was Packham.

Grace slipped out of his car, glancing around carefully, then walked across to the Audi and climbed in the passenger door; the interior had a strong new-car smell.

'Sorry it took so long, Roy,' he said. 'Something on its roof on the other side of the carriageway, and my side was all jammed up with rubberneckers.'

'That's the problem with that stretch of road,'

Grace replied. 'Accidents on it constantly. So, what do you have?'

Packham reached behind him, and pulled a laptop off the rear seat. Then he looked around, cautiously, before raising the lid.

'I've copied Lorna Belling's data onto my laptop.'

'Amazing you've been able to recover it, Ray, and so quickly.'

'The rice cure can work magic, Roy. If you ever drop your phone down the toilet, rice will dry it out.'

Grace grimaced. 'Thanks, I'll remember that.'

Packham tapped the keyboard and the screen came to life. On it was a photograph of a bar on a sandy beach, shaded by the overhang of tropical-looking trees. In the background was calm, turquoise ocean. A couple were seated at the bar, with their arms round each other, staring into each other's eyes. The man was wearing dark glasses and a panama hat at a rakish angle, and the woman a white baseball cap with sunglasses perched on the peak.

Grace gave Packham a quizzical look. 'Why are you showing me this?'

'Take a closer look, Roy – it's Guy Batchelor and his wife, Lena.'

'I can see that. What's their photograph doing on Lorna Belling's computer? I mean – if they knew each other, he'd have told me.'

'I think from what I've found on here, Roy, they did know each other, and he didn't tell you.'

'Meaning?'

But he didn't need the question answering. The uncomfortable truth was dawning on him almost faster than he could process it.

'Shit,' he said, suddenly feeling very shaky. 'I – I don't – I don't believe it. Shit.'

Confirmation came moments later in a phone call from Ops-1.

CHAPTER 101

Saturday 30 April

'Sir, I thought you should know immediately, a vehicle allocated to your Major Crime team has just been involved in a hit and run accident,' Inspector Kim Sherwood said.

'One of our vehicles?' Grace replied, taking a moment to absorb it. 'Hit and run? What vehicle – what exactly's happened, Kim?'

'One of our fleet cars – a Ford Mondeo estate, sir. About forty-five minutes ago on the westbound carriageway of the A27, outside Lewes,' the Ops-1 inspector said.

'What details do you have?'

'An eyewitness in the vehicle behind – a Brighton Streamline taxi driver – told officers at the scene that a silver Ford Mondeo had apparently undertaken him recklessly at high speed, then pulled over into the outside lane in front of him, causing him to brake hard. It then started to overtake a Volvo saloon on the inside lane, when it suddenly swerved – apparently deliberately – into the rear offside. Sounds like a classic tap – the one Traffic often use in a pursuit to stop a vehicle. The Ford knocked it sideways, sending it into a massive slide, then drove off, fast. The Volvo driver lost control, his vehicle struck the central barrier, veered away, then barrel-rolled, finishing upside down. The driver is injured but alive.'

'Jesus,' Grace said. Could it be road rage, he was wondering?

'Fortunately the taxi has a dashboard camera and the driver has the whole incident recorded, with the Ford's registration. He stopped at the scene.'

'What do we know about the Ford – who's logged it out?'

'The car has been assigned to DI Batchelor for the past ten days, for his SIO role on Op Bantam.'

'Guy Batchelor?'

'Yes, sir.'

'*Guy Batchelor?*' he repeated. 'DI Batchelor?'

'That's right.'

'Are you absolutely certain?'

'He has exclusive use of the vehicle at the moment, sir.'

Grace felt physically sick.

The tumblers of a huge lock, opening a door to an unwelcome place, were falling, relentlessly, one after another.

'We don't have any sighting of the driver, it's possible the vehicle might be stolen, sir.'

For a moment, Grace clung to that thought. Or another possibility – he had seen how stressed

Batchelor seemed today. Had he lost his rag over an incident on the road?

But he knew he was clutching at straws, trying to delay the horrific truth.

'Has anyone checked the vehicle log, Kim?'

'It needs someone your end to do that on the paper sign-out. We don't have anything electronic.'

'Yes, yes, of course. I – I'll—'

His mind flashed again to the attempts he had made in the past half-hour to contact Weatherley, and his surprise that he hadn't yet returned his call or text.

'What information do you have on the condition of the driver of the Volvo?'

'He's being attended to by paramedics in an ambulance at the scene. He's conscious and the report I have is that his injuries don't appear to be life-threatening. Coincidentally – he's identified himself as a police officer.'

'A police officer? One of ours?'

'No, he's a DS with Scotland Yard. His name is—'

Grace didn't need to be told the name. He knew it.

'Weatherley, Kim?' he said. 'Detective Sergeant Tim Weatherley?'

He shot Packham a horrified look.

CHAPTER 102

Saturday 30 April

Despite the high speed at which they were travelling along the winding country lane, the two Road Policing Unit officers, cocooned inside the comfortable cabin of the black Audi A6, were calm.

Saturday night. Road deaths in the county of Sussex were at their highest level in years and the Chief Constable had instructed all officers to be extra vigilant, which was why PCs Pip Edwards and Richard Trundle of the Road Policing Unit had taken this unmarked car for their night shift. They were on the prowl for drink-drivers, speeders, people on their mobile phones, those not wearing their seat belts and dangerous drivers in general. Both officers were tired, they were working extra-long hours recently to make up for the reduction in crews. In addition, they had lost more members of their already depleted team to the Firearms Unit, which was recruiting hard – a reflection on escalating concerns about terrorism.

Edwards, a taciturn man, drove, whilst his more

gung-ho long-time work colleague in the passenger seat stared through the windscreen into the darkness ahead. Trundle was hoping for a sighting of the car which had shot across their bows, nearly wiping them out, just a few minutes earlier. It had to be somewhere ahead of them along this road – which was little more than a lane – as there was no junction for several miles. It wouldn't have had the time to turn off somewhere and hide.

The Audi's strobing lights cast an eerie, flickering blue glow along the hedgerows on either side of them. Trundle glanced across at the speedometer, feeling a little out of his comfort zone, despite his faith in his colleague's abilities at the wheel. 80 mph. It was dark now and slightly misty, not the best conditions for a pursuit along country roads, but the idiot in front of them was a massive danger to any road user and needed to be stopped.

The moment of the near collision had been so fleeting – and so sudden – that neither officer had been able to identify for certain the make of the car or get any of its index numbers. It was an estate car, probably a Ford Mondeo, they'd decided. Edwards said he'd put money on it being a kiddy joyrider, high on drugs, either from Crawley or Brighton.

The radio came to life and they heard the bland, emotionless voice of a male Comms operator. 'All vehicles in the A27 and A23 areas, your attention is drawn to the following vehicle which has been involved in a hit and run major RTC on the A27.

Last seen travelling on the westbound carriageway towards Worthing. Vehicle described as a Ford Mondeo estate, colour silver, index Golf Yankee One Four Golf Romeo X-ray. If seen, do not approach the vehicle, but immediately report any sightings back to this office. AD timed at 20.45 hours, Sierra Oscar standing by.'

Trundle pressed his radio's talk button. 'Comms, we've just had a vehicle similar to that driven past us at high speed and we are making after it in an attempt to identify and speak to the driver. We'll come back to you shortly.' He tried, with short stabs of his pen in the lurching car, to write the number down on the back of his hand. Then he called up the registration number to find out where it came from and where it might be headed, and the insurance details to see if had recently changed keeper. To his surprise the information came back that the vehicle was registered to Sussex Police.

'Hotel Tango Two Eight One, can you give me your current position?' the Comms operator replied.

Both officers frowned; there was GPS in all the force's cars as well as on every officer's personal radio, and ordinarily the Comms department always knew exactly where they were, from their positions constantly plotted on the banks of monitors in the Control Room.

'Where are we?' Trundle queried. 'Are we not registering?'

'Our screens are down,' the operator replied. 'Again.'

'OK, we are approximately one mile west of the A23, close to Bolney.'

And suddenly a Mondeo estate was dead ahead, less than a couple of hundred yards in front of them, waiting at the junction with the busy Bolney to Cowfold main road. As they raced towards it, braking hard, Trundle was able to read the licence plate. GY14 GRX.

Yes!

It was moments like this that gave him the biggest bang in the job. Pressing his radio button again, he said, 'Comms, we have visual on Golf Yankee One Four Golf Romeo X-ray.'

Comms replied, 'Go ahead and ascertain who's driving the vehicle, unless it's unsafe to do so.'

Edwards flashed the headlights several times and gave a loud *whup-whup-whup* to let the driver know they were there and that they required him to stay exactly where he was. Trundle unclipped his seat belt and was about to jump out and run forward, when the Ford shot off out into the crossroad, missing being T-boned by an articulated lorry by a fraction of a second. Edwards edged the Audi out into the main road, mindful that in a plain car the front and rear blue flashing lights weren't as visible to vehicles approaching from the side as the roof lights on a marked police car.

'Which way did he go?' he asked.

Traffic was crossing in both directions in front of them and they were in danger of losing him.

'He went right,' Trundle said decisively, pointing

right. He held his breath for a moment as Edwards accelerated hard out into the road, right behind two vehicles travelling at speed, and pressed his talk button.

'Comms, this is Hotel Tango Two Eight One, PC Trundle,' he said.

'Hotel Tango Two Eight One, go ahead,' the reply came back.

'The subject vehicle is now failing to stop. The driver of our vehicle is a green permit holder in a suitable vehicle, may we have permission to pursue?'

Trundle's eyes were glued to the tail lights of the three cars ahead of them. And in particular the one in front that was steadily moving ahead. He knew there weren't many passing opportunities on this road.

'Can you give us an idea of road conditions, Hotel Tango Two Eight One?'

'Misty rain falling, road slippery but visibility still fair at present, traffic level light. At this time my perceived risk is low,' Trundle responded.

'Roger that. Maintain commentary, ongoing dynamic risk assessment and direction of travel, we are making Ops-1 aware.'

'Yes, yes.'

Moments later the voice of Inspector Kim Sherwood came over the radio. 'Hotel Tango Two Eight One, this is Ops-1, permission is granted to continue pursuit.'

'Thank you, ma'am,' Trundle said.

'Our screens are back up and running. We have two divisional cars in your area, and another on its way, and an unmarked heading down from near Gatwick. We are also trying to redirect some more green permit holders to your location.'

Trundle held his breath again as Edwards overtook a car on the approach to a blind brow, waited until they crested it, then raced past the next car. Now they were right behind the Mondeo, 150 yards and closing. Coming up ahead was a long left-hander. The Ford was gaining on a van. Trundle was taking in as much information from all their surroundings as he could, switching his eyes from the road ahead to the speedometer and back. They were currently doing 88 mph.

'Hotel Tango Two Eight One, our speed is eight-eight miles per hour in six-zero limit.' Then as Edwards accelerated harder he said, 'Nine-zero. Now one-zero-zero.'

Then suddenly Trundle froze. The subject vehicle was overtaking on a blind corner – and there was something coming the other way.

CHAPTER 103

Saturday 30 April

There's something big coming the other way, straight towards me. I can see the lights, massive lights, high up. Be good if it's a lorry. Something solid. Please let it be a huge truck or lorry. One of those eighteen-wheelers. The driver high up, so I won't hurt him.

Please.

Please.

Blinding lights. Blaring horn. This is it. This is how the end is. Whiteout. Noise. White lights. Noise. This is how it looks. This is how it feels. One split second. Just one second and then—

There was a small clunk that barely shook the car. That was all. It sounded like a rock thrown against his door. Then the lorry hurtled past and was gone in a blur of tail lights, and turbulence that shook the car.

His wing mirror had gone. Knocked off.

He'd been that close to the lorry. Should have been closer, right across it. Head-on.

Sweat was running down his face, stinging his

eyes. The wipers smeared the screen. The road snaked into the distance.

I can't even kill myself. JESUS!

He pounded the steering wheel in frustration and anger.

I'm running out of fuel and I can't even kill myself. I don't have the guts.

He looked at the needle on the empty mark. At the orange warning light. It had been on empty for a while. He didn't know how much was left in the tank when it showed empty. Not much. There couldn't be much.

He saw the blue lights behind him, in the interior mirror. The police car was moving out, overtaking the line of traffic, gaining on him.

I'm not going to be arrested. Not going to have that humiliation. No way. No. Then he yelled out loud, 'YOU WON'T BLOODY GET ME!'

He was crying. Thinking about his wife. His daughter. What was going to happen when they found out?

Trying to think; to figure something out. But it felt like there was a tornado raging inside his head, ripping all his thoughts off the shelves, off his desk top, out of cupboards, filing cabinets. Flinging them everywhere.

What do I do? Where do I go? Hide? Drive into a tree?

They had plans for him in that car behind him. The car with the blue lights. 'Well, I've got news for you!' he shouted out loud, to himself. 'Whatever you have planned, it isn't going to happen!'

No, no, no. He wasn't going to give them that satisfaction. Wasn't going to let Roy Grace put him behind bars. No way. No one was going to lock him up in the custody suite in Hollingbury and bang that door on him.

He *wouldn't* give them that satisfaction.

And you didn't get bail for murder. They kept you inside.

He wouldn't let them put him on a remand wing in Lewes, or some other prison.

Cops in prison. He knew the stories about what happened to cops in prison. About what other prisoners did to them. Boiling sugared water on their genitals. Urinating in their porridge and soup. Razor blades in apples.

That wasn't going to happen.

The lights of the police car were closing on him.

He drove with one eye locked on the rear-view mirror, thinking, desperately thinking. Their traffic car was faster than his. Any moment now they'd make their move and pull out to overtake him. They'd probably try the same trick he had done. Tap him behind the rear wheel and knock him sideways.

Had to think fast. Fast. Fast.

There was a manoeuvre he remembered from the police driving course he'd done years back, when he was qualifying for his blue lights permit. The instructor was called Roger Pitts. Like the pits at a motor-racing circuit, he'd joked weakly.

Pitts had showed him how to do handbrake turns

at Dunsfold aerodrome. He didn't trust himself to do one now. But there was something else about the handbrake that Pitts had told him: the hand-brake didn't put the rear brake lights on. The car behind wouldn't know you were braking.

There was a narrow lane that he knew was coming up shortly on his right. Coming up in a quarter of a mile or so. He cycled all around this area regularly at weekends.

The police car was right behind him, filling his mirror, blue and white lights flashing, siren wailing, signalling him to stop. Headlights of a vehicle were coming fast in the opposite direction. The police car would wait until it had passed and then make its move.

He gripped the brake handle and waited. Waited. Then as the oncoming vehicle streaked past, he pulled the handbrake on as hard as he could. Instantly the car began snaking, its rear wheels locked up. There was a howl of sirens and the slither of tyres on wet tarmac as the Audi shot past, fishtailing crazily.

Then, only just visible in the headlights, its entrance shrouded with shrubbery, was the lane. Somehow he held on to the car, stopping it from swapping ends, and made the turn. *Yes!* He jammed the accelerator pedal to the floor, anxiously watching his rear-view mirror.

Then the fuel gauge.

The mirror again.

Two shiny pinpricks appeared ahead of him.

Growing bigger. A deer standing in the road, mesmerized by his lights. Shit! He stamped on the brake, slewed round the frozen animal, missing it by inches, and then accelerated hard again.

Where do I go?

Petrol station.

No way.

Got to lose the police. Not going to do that by running out of petrol out here.

Where the hell do I go? Which direction?

He felt as empty as the fuel tank. All his juice gone. Everything gone. It would happen to everyone, eventually. Always had done and always will. All of us run out of life juice. Needle on empty. Dull little amber light showing. Then oblivion.

Or meet our maker.

Trees and shrubs were flashing by: 90 mph – 100 mph – 110 mph. He could swing the wheel to the right or to the left now and plough into them.

But what if it didn't kill him? If he didn't hit a big tree but instead a bunch of saplings? What if he was just injured? Blinded or paralysed?

Then he saw the blue lights again, in his mirror, tiny strobing pinpricks. Doubling in size every second.

Hurtling towards him.

CHAPTER 104

Saturday 30 April

Richard Trundle in the passenger seat of Hotel Tango Two Eight One was maintaining his running commentary to Ops-1, whilst simultaneously carrying out his duties as pursuit commander. In recent months, due to a change of policy, although Ops-1 had the overall responsibility for any chase, and would end it at any time if they felt there was too much danger to the public, it was now up to the officers actually carrying out the pursuit role to decide on the most effective and safest tactics to effect a stop.

A deer darted across the road in front of them, causing Edwards to brake sharply, but Trundle kept a watchful eye on the tail lights ahead. They were gaining on them rapidly.

'Maintaining visual on subject vehicle,' he said. 'Speed one-one-five in six-zero limit.' As he spoke he was thinking hard, glancing intermittently at the area map he had brought up on the screen showing their current position and the road options around them.

He knew roughly the positions of the three division cars close by and he was trying to work out his chances of containing the Mondeo and forcing it to a halt at a roadblock if viable. A stop-stick would be another option, but he didn't have enough details on the locations of any of the other cars as yet. If he could coordinate them, and the subject vehicle was on a wide-enough road, they could try to use the safest method of all, TPAC – containing the vehicle by boxing it in with one or more other vehicles.

'Subject vehicle turning left, left left,' he announced, as Edwards braked hard and continued following. 'South on the A281, passing Ginger Fox pub.'

There was a roundabout a mile ahead. A left turn would take the Mondeo down towards the A23 with then a choice of routes north towards London or south towards Brighton. If another car was close enough, perhaps they could take control of that road, he contemplated, but he only had seconds to make that decision. If the Mondeo continued straight over the roundabout it would enter a narrow, winding three-mile-long road over the Devil's Dyke leading towards the outskirts of Brighton, with only two turn-off options. They should be able to get a Brighton car to position itself at the far end and, with luck, another one at the other end near Small Dole.

He gave Ops-1 the two requests. The Mondeo

was approaching the roundabout, and they were now again less than a hundred yards behind it.

'What about the paraffin parrot?' Edwards said.

'I think we can get him without the helicopter,' Trundle replied, watching the car entering the small roundabout. Into his radio he said, 'Subject vehicle going off at not one – not two – not three – Oh shit! Off at four! Back the way we've just come from!'

The one exit he had not anticipated, effectively a U-turn.

Trundle gripped the grab handle as Edwards kept the Audi in a controlled power slide round the roundabout, and accelerated out of it.

'You could be on *Top Gear* with that one, Pip,' Trundle said.

Edwards grinned.

'Nooooooo!' Trundle yelled. 'Stop, get back, you idiot!'

An articulated lorry was pulling out of the entrance to a garden centre, a short distance ahead. The car they were chasing shot past it but, seemingly blind to their blue lights and deaf to their siren, the lorry continued pulling out, turning right, completely blocking their path.

All Trundle and Edwards could do was sit tight.

'Comms, we have momentarily lost visual contact – due to a lorry turning across us.'

Finally, as the lorry completed its turn, there was enough of a gap to get by it. Edwards started to pull out then immediately braked and pulled in again, as a Range Rover came past from the opposite direction. Then Edwards pulled out again and the road was clear.

Too clear.

Just a long black ribbon with dark woodland on either side.

The subject vehicle was no longer in sight.

CHAPTER 105

Saturday 30 April

Need to get to the city.

I've just got to get there. Got to, got to, GOT TO.

Out here in the countryside, if he ran out of fuel they'd find the car quickly, he knew. Then they'd put up the helicopter with its heat-source night vision and they'd pick him out. He'd be better off in the city, invisible there, plenty of hiding places, and it would make it harder for a dog handler to find him.

He just had to get there.

Ten miles.

There has to be ten miles more in the tank.

He looked in his mirror.

Just darkness.

He was hurtling up towards a three-way junction that he knew well. The Ginger Fox restaurant, where he'd sometimes come with Lena for Sunday lunch, was on the right. A sharp right in front of it would be the fastest way to the city from here. It would take him to the A23. But that's where they'd be expecting him.

Turning off the main road – more or less straight on into another lane – would take him back out into the countryside. Where he did not want to be.

Had to carry on along the main road. That was his best option. Nothing showed in his mirror, to his relief. They still weren't in sight.

He drove too fast round the sharp left-hand bend, feeling the car twitching and sliding on the wet, greasy road, then a right-hander was coming up. He braked hard and turned sharp left just on the apex, down a narrow road he'd cycled along many times in the past, Clappers Lane. It would take him on a back route into Brighton that hopefully they wouldn't be expecting him to go for. Via Shoreham, to the west of the city.

If his fuel lasted.

If they didn't find him again.

He looked at the fuel gauge. There was always a couple of gallons in the tank when it showed empty. There had to be. He gripped the wheel, looked in the mirror, the road ahead, the mirror, the road ahead.

I don't know what I'm doing.

Just got to keep going. Keep going. All the time I'm going I'm alive.

When I stop, I'm dead.

CHAPTER 106

Saturday 30 April

'Shit!' PC Trundle said. 'Shit, shit, shit, shit, shit!'

They had stopped, momentarily, outside the Ginger Fox, staring at the road signs – although they knew this area like the back of their hands.

Trundle was trying to guess which way the car had gone. Which road would he have taken, he wondered? And every second that they wasted here meant the Mondeo was getting further and further away.

'A23?' Pip Edwards suggested. 'That's where I'd head.'

'If that's where he wanted to get to, he'd have hit it sooner.' Trundle shook his head. 'He's been keeping to the back roads and obviously has local knowledge.'

'Right, so let's think for a moment,' Edwards said. 'Where's he actually going?'

'I've no idea.'

'You've nicked a car, the police are on to you. You need to ditch it – but preferably somewhere else you can nick another car to shake them off.'

'A pub car park?'

Edwards shrugged. 'If he had the presence of mind, maybe. Not sure I'd think that if I was in a red-mist panic, I'd just keep driving, in the hope of getting away – as he has done. Perhaps losing us in a town. Crawley? Haywards Heath? Burgess Hill? Brighton? Could be any of those. So, straight on or one of the rights?'

The two officers stared ahead.

'I don't think he's turned off – I think he's carried on towards Henfield,' said Trundle.

'Do we toss a coin?'

Trundle pressed his radio button. 'Ops-1, we have lost Golf Yankee One Four Golf Romeo X-ray. He could have gone one of three ways. We are terminating the pursuit.' He gave the road numbers.

'OK, Hotel Tango Two Eight One, stand down and stay where you are. We'll see if he's spotted on any of those routes. You're in a good position if he doubles back, so stay put.'

'Stay put,' he repeated, flatly, sensing from the tone of Kim Sherwood's voice that she felt they'd fucked up. 'Yes, yes.'

Moments later Inspector Sherwood's voice came through the radio again, sounding much more animated. 'Subject vehicle has just been sighted! Single male occupant.'

CHAPTER 107

Saturday 30 April

Roy Grace had returned to his office and, patched into Ops-1 on his radio, was following the pursuit. Ray Packham, at the spare desk in front of him, was going through the contents from Lorna Belling's laptop.

Grace had spoken to both the duty Gold and Silver Commanders about the POLACC – police accident – with the possibility of a case of potential murder committed by a member of his team, and he had also alerted Professional Standards.

Batchelor's Ford Mondeo had been put on the ANPR hot list, and police vehicles heading towards the area to attempt to contain and stop the car had been ordered to minimalize their use of blue lights and sirens, where safe, in order to avoid alerting him.

'Some very angry emails to Lorna Belling from Seymour Darling, Roy,' Packham said, suddenly.

'Yes?'

'Get this one, from Darling: *Oh right, Mrs Belling. If you call screwing someone behind your husband's back "honest", then I'm a banana. SD.*'

Grace smiled distantly, his focus entirely on his thoughts about Batchelor. He was distracted by a voice on the Ops-1 patch. 'Charlie Romeo Zero Five. We have visual on subject vehicle entering the Shoreham flyover roundabout. Off at three. Now heading towards Shoreham.'

Then he heard Sherwood direct local division cars down to the coast road.

A male voice, presumably in the pursuit car, was calling out the speed. 'Seven-zero in three-zero limit. Eight-zero in three-zero limit.'

Grace knew that stretch of road well. It was two-lane, residential, cars parked on both sides, only just room for two vehicles to pass each other in opposite directions. A 30 mph limit, and Batchelor was hurtling down it at eighty.

The officer's voice suddenly shouted out, 'Jesus, near miss, he's driving like a lunatic, he's passed an oncoming vehicle on the wrong side, driving along the pavement!'

'Charlie Romeo Zero Five,' Ops-1 said. 'It's too dangerous. Discontinue the pursuit. Maintain your course, but discontinue the pursuit.'

'Yes, yes. We have pulled over and switched off our lights.'

'Ops-1,' Grace said, 'is the helicopter available?'

'I've already checked, Roy, it's attending a serious injury RTC in Kent at the moment. Won't be available for an hour, on their best estimate.'

'What about the drone?'

Brighton Police used a drone to supplement

their network of CCTV cameras around the city.

'I've just alerted the duty Gold Commander and requested it. But we have CAA flight restriction issues – it can only overfly the coastline, not the city itself.'

'Can you get it directed towards Shoreham?'

'Yes, it's being dispatched now.'

'Bloody hell!' Packham exclaimed.

'What, Ray?'

'He's making a pretty explicit threat to her in this one.'

Then Kim Sherwood spoke again. 'Subject vehicle has just pinged an ANPR camera on Albion Street, heading east.'

Into Brighton, Grace thought.

'I have another divisional car that's sighted him. He's gone the wrong side of an island and run a red light.'

Just what was going on with Batchelor, Grace wondered? This was so utterly out of character – complete madness – if indeed it was him driving, and they still did not have confirmation of that. It was still possible someone had stolen the car, or kidnapped the DI. He just could not believe this was Batchelor. No way. This was not the gentle giant, Guy Batchelor, that he knew.

And it sounded like it was going to end badly.

He stood up, pulled on his jacket and grabbed his car keys. 'Ops-1, I'm on my way into Brighton, will keep my radio live.'

'He's now passing Hove Lagoon, travelling on the wrong side of the Kingsway dual carriageway. Two oncoming vehicles have been forced off the road and crashed.'

Shit.

Leaving Packham in mid-sentence trying to tell him something, Grace raced out of his office.

CHAPTER 108

Saturday 30 April

He just wanted to get home. To explain to Lena. But that wasn't an option, he knew. He had to hide, lie low, lie doggo. Let it all calm down.

Lights were coming at him. Headlights straight at him. Street lights above him. He heard a siren wailing.

This is not me.

This is not happening.

In a minute I will wake up. All will be fine. I'll be in bed, at home.

My nice luxurious bed.

A glass of wine and a cigarette. We'll be laughing.

Oh yes!

We'll just be laughing.

Why did I ever get involved with Lorna in the first place? I was having a good life with Lena. Why? Why? Why?

He leaned forward and switched on the Mondeo's blue lights and siren, wondering why he hadn't thought to utilize them sooner.

He swerved past a taxi, then undertook a car in front of it. A speed camera flashed at him.

Great, send me a ticket, do. I'm on a shout!

His speedometer read 70.

He was passing the King Alfred. Memories – Vallance Mansions directly across the road, to his left, where this nightmare had begun.

Moments later Hove Lawns were on his right. The darkness of the English Channel beyond. Brighton. His city. The place he worked to keep safe. Now he was a fugitive. It was all a mistake.

They'll realize.

Oh, you are so smart, Roy Grace. I thought you were my friend. You've got to understand we can all make a mistake. Any of our lives can turn on a sixpence. Or whatever the damned smallest coin is now.

Headlights in his mirror.

Red traffic lights ahead.

Suddenly the engine spluttered.

No, no, no!

It picked up. A car was crossing the road ahead of him. He swerved right, around the front of it, ignored its angry horn.

Then spluttered again.

Don't do this. Not yet. Please, not yet. I need a plan.

Plan B. Plan C. Plan D.

Keep moving.

Plan E.

Find a hiding place.

Plan F.

His radio crackled. All the radio chatter had been

white noise up until now, but suddenly he heard a familiar voice. Except he didn't sound the warm, friendly way he usually did. He was all cold, formal. Like the stranger he really was, and always had been.

'Guy? This is Roy. Are you OK?'

The engine picked up. The car spurted forward, then slowed again. Then spurted.

He looked at the fuel gauge.

Flashing blue lights. Two police officers at the roadside signalling him, frantically.

He felt a rumble beneath him as if he had gone over a cattle grid. Heard four explosions, like gun shots, and the car veered, crazily left, then right.

He gripped the wheel, kept the accelerator floored. The car was snaking along the road, bumping along, the back end trying to come round and overtake the front. He fought the wheel, spinning it right, left, right. There was a loud flapping, slapping noise.

Bastards.

He'd driven over a stinger. All four tyres gone. Now he was driving on the rims.

The engine spluttered again and then picked up once more. 50 mph. He hurtled over another red light. The Metropole Hotel was coming up on his left. Followed by The Grand.

To his right, the latest addition to the Brighton landscape. The i360. The 162-metre-high observation tower. The world's tallest moving observation tower, or something like that. It had a huge glass doughnut-like thing, an observation room, that rose up towards the top. A lot of people hated it. He thought it was cool.

It looked really cool right now.

Jump off the top of it? That would teach Roy Grace a lesson about—

About something.

You have to realize, Roy, that people make mistakes. OK? Didn't you ever make a mistake?

Traffic was backed up in front of him.

There was a street coming up, to the left, just past The Grand.

Shit. A police car was parked across the entrance.

His engine died.

He pressed the accelerator, several times.

The car was coasting. Bumping along on the rims.

Shit, shit, shit, shit.

He unclipped his belt, opened the door and rolled out onto the road – and hit the hard, wet surface with far more force than he had anticipated. He was flung over, rolling, rolling, rolling. Heard a massive bang. Then as he came to a halt and lay winded, he caught a glance of his Mondeo slewed at an angle, and another car, just ahead of it, almost sideways across the road, its rear end stoved in. The Mondeo's blue lights were still flashing.

He hauled himself to his feet, and fell over, as if the gyroscope inside his body hadn't stopped spinning yet. He got up again and staggered across the road, dodging a car then a bus, and reached the pavement on the promenade side. Saw the bright lights of Brighton's Palace Pier over to his left. A cyclist clattered past, furiously ringing his bell. He turned and looked behind him. A police officer was sprinting towards him.

He turned right and ran.

Ran.

Seized with panic.

The tower of the i360 was right ahead of him. Rising to the heavens, disappearing into the mist. Ahead was a wall of glass with the BRITISH AIRWAYS i360 logo above it.

Two people, a young man and woman in British Airways uniforms, stood at the ticket gate. He ran between them, pushing them both out of the way, yelling, 'Police!'

He found himself on smart decking. A few groups of people were standing around, under umbrellas. The massive tubular structure rose up in front of him. The huge, illuminated glass pod, like a spaceship, was slowly descending with its load of passengers.

He looked over his shoulder. A police officer was talking to the two uniformed BA staff at the gate.

A round glass fence ringed off the space where the doughnut was about to arrive. Suddenly, a door opened at the bottom of the tower and a workman in a yellow hard hat came out.

Batchelor vaulted the glass fence and fell with an agonizing, jarring thump on the ground fifteen feet below. His left leg hurt but he ignored it, ran stumbling past the workman, ignoring his shouts.

'Police!' he yelled back at the man, and ran in through the door.

It felt like he had entered a vertical tunnel.

There was a metal ladder directly in front of him, with cables clipped to the core of the tubular structure on either side. He began to climb up.

'Oi!' a voice shouted. 'Oi! What do you think you're doing?'

'Police!' he shouted back. 'Police!'

He carried on climbing.

Climbing.

Looking down. Another man in a hard hat was at the bottom, looking up at him.

He climbed on. Shit. He was already starting to feel exhausted. Looked up, and the ladder continued, way up into the shadows and out of sight.

He climbed on, then finally came to a small gridded platform, with railings around it. He stepped onto it, leaned back against the railings, and gulped down hot, oily-smelling air.

What am I doing here?

He looked down again. It must be a good hundred feet. He could just step off the platform and fall. It was high enough.

Then he saw someone run in. A man with fair hair, in a dark suit, looking up at him.

Shit. Shit. Shit.

'Guy! Guy! What the hell are you doing?' Roy Grace called up at him.

The Detective Superintendent began to scale the ladder like a creature possessed.

Batchelor started climbing again.

'Guy!' Grace shouted. 'Guy, stop! For Christ's sake stop!

CHAPTER 109

Saturday 30 April

Ignoring him, Batchelor climbed on. His arms were so tired he could barely grip each rung above him. But he kept going. Driven by grim determination. Desperation. He just had to keep climbing. Higher. Higher.

'Guy!'

The voice was a distant echo below him, but getting louder with every shout.

'Guy!'

With every rung he climbed, Roy Grace seemed to climb two. He was gaining on him. Rung by rung.

'Guy. We need to talk.'

In front of his face, Batchelor saw a sign. It read 50 METRES.

He was less than halfway up.

'Screw you, Roy! Leave me alone!' he yelled.

He climbed higher.

His chest was tight. His heart was hammering. His grip was getting weaker. Weaker.

Roy Grace was less than twenty feet below him

now. Still scaling the ladder like a sodding rat up a drainpipe.

There was another platform just above him. And a door, with a handle on it.

Using the last of his strength, he reached the platform and hauled himself onto it. Grace, below him, was still climbing strongly. Batchelor lashed out with his shiny boot, a warning. 'Don't try it, Roy. I'll kick you off, I promise you, I will!'

Grace stopped. 'Guy, come on, whatever it is, we can sort it out. OK?'

'No fucking way.'

Finding some strength from somewhere inside him, Batchelor threw himself at the ladder and climbed on. On.

Past the **100 METRES** sign.

On.

He looked down.

Roy Grace had stopped, some distance below him, for breath; he was having to grip the ladder tightly, his hands dangerously slippery with perspiration.

'How did you do in the "beep" test, eh, Roy?' he chided. 'Not so well?'

He climbed on.

'Guy! Guy, what's wrong with you?'

Grace's strength was sapping as he climbed on up, also passing the **100 METRES** sign. He did not dare look down. All his life he had been bad with heights. He just kept staring at the rungs in front of his face. Trying to convince himself that he was only a few feet above the ground. His hands were running out of feeling, out of grip. But he had to keep going. His chest was pounding, his breath rasping and he was feeling giddy.

Batchelor's feet were just inches above him now. He could have reached up and grabbed one of them. But he had no strength for a struggle. He just had to keep clinging on. Keep climbing. He had no idea what was going to happen, all he knew was to keep going.

Now above him he saw the **150 METRES** sign. Batchelor was standing, stooped, gasping, on the platform beside it. A torch beam shot up around him, but he ignored it.

'Guy!' he grunted. 'Guy, just tell me?'

'Tell you what?'

'What the hell's happening?'

'Leave me alone. Just leave, Roy, it's too late for me.'

Batchelor began climbing again.

Grace reached the platform and stepped onto it, gripping the rails, gulping down air. He saw his colleague's boots disappearing above him. Saw the flickering torch beam from below him, and made the mistake of glancing down.

Into the void.

He swayed, vertigo drawing him down.

Shit.

'Guy!' he yelled. 'Guy!'

Jesus.

He felt scared now. Out of his depth. But he had

to keep going. Had to reach him, had to find out just what was going on inside this man's mind.

Then suddenly he saw Batchelor, some rungs above him, push open a flap – an inspection hatch – and haul himself up and out, through it.

'Guy!' he yelled. 'Guy, no, no!'

Frantically he scrambled up more rungs until he was level with the flap. A strong blast of cooling wet wind blew on his face. He was grateful for it. Guy Batchelor, sodden, was standing on some form of platform, outside, misty darkness beyond him, the wind flapping his coat.

'Stay where you are, Roy,' he said, his voice threatening. 'I mean it.'

'Guy, for God's sake, man, let's talk.'

'You want to talk? Talk!'

Grace was gripping the rung for all he was worth. He was remembering some health and safety advice he'd been given on a training day. Always keep three limbs on a ladder at any time. Right now he had all four. 'Let me onto the platform with you, Guy, we can talk. I can't hang on here, I'm sodding exhausted.'

'Stay where you are, I'm going to have a fag. A last cigarette. Did you know, some execution chambers don't let you have that any more? In this ridiculous world they actually have *no smoking* execution chambers. What do you think about that?'

'I'll join you, I'll have a cigarette too.'

'Bad for your health, Roy.' Batchelor raised a leg, as if about to kick him.

'It'll be worse for my health if I fall off this bloody ladder,' he panted.

'You didn't have to come up here.'

'Guy, you're my friend! Just tell me, what's happened to you?'

'I'm finished, Roy. You're wasting your time – don't forget I'm a trained suicide negotiator too. I know all the tricks. They're not going to work on me.'

Grace heard a click, then smelled cigarette smoke.

'You're not my friend, Roy, you're no one's friend. You're a copper, you'd nick your best friend if it helped you get a result.'

'Guy, listen to me.'

'I'm finished.'

Then Grace heard the voice of Ops-1. 'Roy, we have the drone approaching the i360 tower, but visibility is bad. What assistance do you need?'

His arms were aching. He didn't know how much longer he could hold on for. Using all his strength, he wrapped first his right arm then his left around the ladder and pulled himself tightly into it. That eased some of the strain and he felt slightly more secure. 'I'm OK,' he replied. 'No assistance at this moment.'

'There's nothing worse than a corrupt officer, is there, Roy? One who lets the team down?'

Grace could hear him sobbing.

'Guy, come on, let's talk, tell me what is going on. Talk to me, be honest with me, and I'll tell you what I can do for you.'

‘I didn’t mean to kill her. We just had an argument and it all got out of hand. She hit her head, I panicked. You know the rest. I thought I might get away with it – I nearly did. But he recognized me, that Weatherley, I could see it in his face. That’s why he didn’t want to say anything in front of me. I saw it, Roy. He knew it was me.’

‘If you didn’t mean to kill her, you need to tell your story. A decent barrister might be able to argue self-defence, or whatever. OK, you’ll lose your job, but this doesn’t sound like murder. Maybe manslaughter? You know the evidence, Guy. If you think you can convince a jury to believe you panicked and it was an accident, or worst case, manslaughter, you’ll get a sentence, yes, but maybe not a long one.’

‘How’m I going to explain running the Met guy – the Super Recognizer – off the road, Roy? You and I both know I’m going down for a long time. I’ll lose my family, my career. I’ve just two choices, I give myself up to you or I jump.’

‘Think of your family, Guy. Let’s talk.’

‘What’s there to talk about?’ Batchelor suddenly sounded calm. ‘I’ve betrayed you and I’ve betrayed Sussex Police by trying to cover it up. By attempting to set up a friend and colleague – Jon Exton. I did it pretty well, didn’t I? Well enough so you arrested him. I just tried to kill a cop. I’ve betrayed everything I signed up for.’

‘Look, it’s bad, I’m not going to deny it, Guy. But come down, the Federation will help you.

You'll get a fair trial. You'll go to jail, but there's life beyond, try to think about that for a moment. You have a lovely wife, a daughter, you have so much to live for. You're still a young man. Come down and tell us the truth about everything that's happened.'

'No way, that's not going to happen!'

'Let me come on the platform with you – I bloody need a cigarette!'

'There aren't any ashtrays. This is a no-smoking tower. I would hate to be an accomplice to you committing a crime, too.'

Suddenly, Batchelor moved out of sight.

'Guy!' Grace yelled. 'Guy!'

Silence.

'GUY!'

Frantically, finding strength from somewhere inside him, he scrambled up the last few rungs and, petrified of looking down, pulled himself through the hatch, onto the narrow, gridded platform.

There was no sign of Batchelor.

'Guy!' he yelled, running round the entire circumference of the tower.

He was gone.

He stood in numb silence. Stared at a smouldering cigarette butt. Then he heard the voice of Kim Sherwood through his radio.

'Roy, the drone is on site now. What is your position?'

For some moments he did not know what to

reply. He felt gutted. He'd had Batchelor in his grasp and had let him go.

'Man down,' he said finally, flatly.

'Man down?' she queried.

He hauled himself inside, onto the ladder, and began the long, long descent.

CHAPTER 110

Saturday 30 April

Fifteen minutes later, completely and utterly spent, Grace stepped gratefully down from the last rung, back onto terra firma. There were three police officers as well as two men in yellow hard hats all looking at him.

He wasn't often lost for words, but he was now. He felt close to collapsing from exhaustion. He staggered forward and stumbled. A sturdy man in a hard hat grabbed him, supporting him.

'All right, mate?'

'Where is he?' Grace gasped.

'Where's who?'

It wasn't going to be a pretty sight, he knew that much. That sort of vertical drop. He'd seen what that did to people. They exploded. Limbs came off, their innards burst out through their stomachs. He was feeling sick at the thought.

The thought that his friend, and colleague, was lying out there in the darkness. His body broken.

'Is he still up there, sir?' a uniformed officer whom he did not recognize asked him.

'Is who still up there?' he replied, puzzled.

'DI Batchelor, sir,' the PC said, looking equally puzzled.

'He jumped,' Grace replied. 'He's not still up there.' His voice was choked. 'I'm sorry but – but – he jumped.'

He turned away, suddenly feeling deeply emotional and close to tears. He should have scrambled up those last few rungs and grabbed him. Held on to him. Knocked him out.

'No one's jumped, sir,' another voice said.

'He jumped! I saw him! Didn't you see him? Didn't anyone find him yet?'

A siren was wailing in the distance, approaching.

Ops-1's voice came through the radio. 'Roy, can you give me an update?'

'Give me a couple of minutes, Kim,' he said. Then he looked at the group standing around him. 'He must be somewhere close,' he said, then ran for the door and outside. Right above him was the illuminated glass observation car.

The first officer he had spoken to followed him. 'Sir, we have ten officers around the base of the tower – they would have seen anyone falling.'

Grace heard an electronic whirring sound above him. He looked up and saw a drone hovering, a red light blinking beneath it.

He called Ops-1 back. 'Kim, have the drone do a search around the base of the tower for a body.'

'Golf 99 at Brighton, Inspector Anakin is controlling it, sir. He's already carried out a search and there is no sighting of a body.'

'Kim, he jumped, for God's sake! The man jumped! He was on a platform outside, right in front of me, then he vanished. Tell him to look again.'

The drone rose into the air and was swallowed by the mist in seconds. Grace looked around at everyone, bewildered. 'He's not sodding Superman,' he said. 'He didn't fly off into the night, he jumped, I'm telling you.'

The siren was approaching now. Arriving at the scene.

Then he heard Kim Sherwood again. 'Roy, Golf 99 has found him. The drone is filming him now.'

'Finally.'

'He's entangled in some kind of netting near the top of the tower.'

'What?'

One of the maintenance men in a hard hat said, 'That's the safety net put up for the inspection and maintenance team.'

Grace could scarcely believe what he was hearing. 'Safety net?'

'We put it up for night-time cleaning.'

'Is he alive? Kim?'

'He's moving, Roy – apparently with difficulty. I can patch a live feed through to your phone.'

He turned to the hard hat. 'How do we get him down?'

'With difficulty. Not something we've yet had to do.' The man turned to his fellow hard hat, who nodded his concurrence.

'We're going to need a helicopter,' he said. 'Could be a problem with the visibility.'

Grace called Batchelor's phone.

After some moments, to his amazement, the detective answered, sounded in a lot of pain.

'Guy?' He looked up, but all he could see was misty darkness.

'Can't you just leave me alone?'

'If I didn't care for you, I probably would. Just sit tight, we're calling up the coastguard to helicopter you down.'

'I don't need a fucking helicopter.'

'OK, so what do you need?'

'How strong is this bloody netting?'

'Strong enough to hold an elephant.'

'That would be nice – an elephant ride. Just what I need right now.'

'Just sit tight, we'll get you down.'

'I'm not going anywhere, Roy. Jesus, I'm a failure. Couldn't even fucking kill myself.'

'One day you'll be grateful you didn't.'

'Yeah? You come and find me on that day and tell me about it.'

'I will, Guy,' he promised.

'You'll be able to recognize me. I'll be the man in the prison visiting room with the scars and bruises and his teeth knocked out.'

'I've been told prisons are better at protecting police officers these days.'

He heard a hollow laugh.

CHAPTER 111

Sunday 1 May

Nine eggs! Roy Grace stood in the hen coop in his cottage garden at a few minutes before 6 a.m., every muscle in his body aching. Last night's rain had morphed into a stunning dawn. The air felt pleasantly warm. A red sun was rising and a mist lay across all the fields around the cottage. Humphrey sat patiently outside the hen run door.

Each morning he took a bowl of sweetcorn, kale, bread, grapes, blueberries, mealworms and ground oyster shells as well as other scraps, mostly of fruit that was on the cusp of going rotten, and scattered it around the run. There were two hen houses that their little brood used, and normally they produced anything up to six eggs. But today was a record!

Perhaps a good omen, he thought, placing them in the empty food bowl and taking them into the kitchen. Then he went back outside and took Humphrey for a brisk, thirty-minute jog across the fields. Thinking all the time about Guy Batchelor.

How had this hard-working, seemingly happily

married detective gone so wrong? How did such a decent man as Guy turn into a monster?

Could it happen to any of us?

To me?

How much – or how little – did it take?

After the helicopter had brought Batchelor down, he'd accompanied him in the ambulance to the Royal Sussex County Hospital to be checked out. No bones were broken but he had a few bruises. Despite his discomfort, he wanted to be interviewed straight away.

Grace formally arrested him and took him to Worthing Custody Suite, where Batchelor wasn't known. During the interview, in the presence of his solicitor and under caution, he'd opened up, as if all his guard had dropped, telling Grace about his affair with Lorna Belling. And then how she had turned on him when she discovered the truth.

He suspected the detective had left some details out. But it was clear Guy had acted in panic, his one thought in the aftermath of the row, ending up with Lorna dead, was to save his skin, regardless of the consequences to anyone else. He told Roy how he had tried to resuscitate Lorna after their fight, but had failed. And although he accepted his responsibility, he hadn't been sure whether it was the head injury or the electrocution which had actually killed her.

A part of him did actually feel sorry for Batchelor, as a human being. But equally, he hated the idea of a rogue cop. The Sussex police force, to which he had dedicated his life, depended totally on trust. Officers who let the force down deserved all they got. And Guy Batchelor faced years of hell in prison.

Maybe they would meet again one day, when they were old men, and look back at what had been – and what might have been. All of us, he was so deeply aware, had the potential for both good and evil. Just how thin was that line between the two?

As he ran across a field, Humphrey came running towards him with a live pheasant in his mouth.

'Drop!' he yelled, aghast. 'Humphrey, drop, drop, drop!'

Humphrey stood a few yards from him, defiant. The pheasant was flapping.

It was breeding time now for them.

'Drop!' he yelled.

Humphrey finally yielded the bird.

Grace ran over to it and picked it up. It gave him a look, out of one barely focusing eye, then it died as he held it.

'Bad boy!' he yelled. 'Bad, bad boy!'

The dog gave him a quizzical look, and then ran off, disappearing into the tall green crop.

Roy Grace stood, holding the dead bird, feeling very upset for it. He laid it down under the hedgerow at the side of the field. 'I'm sorry,' he said to it.

Then he continued on his run. But when he arrived back home, with Humphrey at his side, he was still feeling bad about the pheasant.

Upstairs in their bedroom, Cleo would still be asleep. Along the corridor, Noah would be asleep too. And up on the next floor, Bruno also.

Entering the kitchen, Humphrey nudged him, signalling he wanted his end-of-run treat. A chew stick.

'You're not having one, you've been a bad boy!'

Then he relented, and pulled a yellow one out of the pack, made him sit, then handed it to him.

The dog wolfed it down, greedily, in seconds.

Roy Grace went upstairs and showered with the water as hot as he could bear, helping to soothe his aching muscles. His whole body was sore from last night. Throughout his mostly sleepless night he'd thought constantly of Guy Batchelor.

What a mess.

He had not yet seen the video evidence against his colleague, ramming Weatherley's car, but it sounded damning. The Super Recognizer had two broken ribs and severe bruising; the outcome could have been a lot worse. He was being kept in hospital for a few days, under observation. Batchelor could be facing an attempted murder charge – on top of any charge he would be facing over Lorna Belling's death. Hopefully more would become clear after his computer and phone were examined, and maybe more would be revealed by the search of his home, which was already under way. Grace felt for Guy's wife and their daughter.

A life ruined.

Jon Exton had been freed last night. Hopefully

no mud would stick, and Roy Grace would do his best to make sure it didn't. He would meet him at the office later this morning.

If Guy had somehow managed to get away with it, would he have let Exton go to trial on the evidence he had planted? Be convicted? Desperation was a dangerous spiral.

He dressed in a work suit, then ate a quick breakfast of cereal and fruit in the kitchen, with the television turned on, to see if there was anything about last night on the news. Then he stared wistfully at the empty glass tank on the end of the work surface, where until recently his companion of eleven years, his goldfish, Marlon, had lived. Neither he nor Cleo had had the heart to get rid of the tank, and they had talked, vaguely, about getting a replacement, maybe a selection of tropical fish. Cleo thought the boys might like them.

He went upstairs and she was still asleep. He kissed her on the cheek and she stirred, then winced suddenly.

'Darling, what is it?'

'My back,' she said sleepily. 'Must have slept awkwardly.'

'That reminds me, I forgot to ask, how did it go with that new chair – weren't you seeing someone about one?'

'Really nice guy – he said he knows you!'

'Oh?'

'Played rugby against the police team once.'

'What's his name?'
'Ian – erm – someone. Erm – Fletcher-Price – owns a company called Posture something – Posturite.'
Grace thought for a moment. 'Rings a faint bell.'
He kissed her again. 'Got to dash.'
'Busy day?'
'Yep, I've got a lot to do. Looks like it's going to be a beautiful day.'
'Try and come home early, darling. Maybe we could sit out in the garden – have a barbecue later? And don't forget we're going to the concert tonight.'
'Yes, where is it again?'
'The Hope and Ruin – Queens Road. I've got Kaitlynn booked.'
'I promise I'll do what I can.'
She took his hand and held it. 'I know you always do what you can. Try doing something you can't for once!'
'And what's that?'
'Time with us, your family. Me.' She turned her head and looked at the clock radio, then back at him. 'White rabbits, white rabbits!' she said suddenly.
'What?'
'It's the first of the month!'
'You're right, it is.'
'I always say it first thing, if I remember. This is the first time I've remembered in ages! Done it ever since I was a child – it's meant to bring good luck.'
'The first of May.'

She ran a finger provocatively down his stomach, over his belt and down his flies and smiled very knowingly at him. 'The first of May. Hmmmn. Know that saying? *Hooray, hooray, the first of May – outdoor bonking starts today*. I think you should come home just as soon as you can, don't you?'

He kissed her on the lips, and she put her arms round his neck. 'I think it's a good plan, don't you? Bruno's going to spend the day with Stan Tingley and I don't think Noah's going to bother us too much. We have the house to ourselves until this evening. I think it would be a shame to waste it.'

'I like your thinking,' he said.

She stroked the front of his trousers again, feeling him harden. 'Mmmmm, Detective Superintendent, I think you're liking it quite a lot.'

CHAPTER 112

Sunday 1 May

At midday the conference room at the CID HQ was alive with shock and gossip as Grace informed his team of the developments. No police officer liked to hear of a colleague who had gone rogue.

Neil Fisher from the Media team had joined the briefing, to discuss the media strategy, as well as newly promoted Inspector Fiona Ashcroft from Professional Standards.

'If anyone has doubts,' Grace said, 'then I'm afraid what Ray Packham has to say will, unfortunately, allay them.' He signalled to the Digital Forensics expert to tell them his latest findings.

Packham yawned, looking exhausted. 'Apologies,' he said. 'I've not yet been to bed. The search team recovered a pay-as-you-go mobile phone and a personal laptop from Guy's home in the early hours of this morning, and I've been going through them. I've only had time, you'll understand, for a cursory look, but I'm afraid what I've discovered already shows some damning evidence.' He paused and took a sip from a mug of coffee.

'The first thing is that there are a number of emails, under a Hotmail account in the name of "Greg Wilson", to Lorna Belling – which tally with those on her laptop recovered from Shoreham Harbour. These go back approximately eighteen months.'

'Greg Wilson?' Norman Potting queried.

'A false name, Norman,' Packham replied.

'Greg was the name of her lover she confided to her close friend, Kate Harmond, who you interviewed, Norman,' Grace interjected.

The Detective Sergeant nodded.

'Secondly,' Packham continued, 'the weekend following Lorna Belling's death, his website history shows he looked at a number of sex sites. I've not had the time yet to check on them all, but the ones I've done so far tally exactly with the calls made on DS Exton's work phone to sex workers.' He looked at the team, and shrugged. 'In my opinion that is too much to be a coincidence.'

'He sneakily got hold of DS Exton's phone somehow, and made these calls?' Donald Dull said.

'That's the way it looks,' Grace said.

'What a devious bastard,' Dull retorted.

There was a long silence.

'Is there any other explanation, boss?' Kevin Hall asked.

'I'm all ears if you have one, Kevin,' Grace replied.

Hall shook his head.

'There's something else the search team recovered from Guy's home,' Grace added, his tone grim. 'Lorna Belling's appointments diary for her hairdressing clients. It was still in an evidence bag, concealed under a case of wine in his garage.'

'Stupid sod.' Potting shook his head. 'What a stupid sod.'

There was a long silence, finally broken by Jack Alexander.

'Where's DS Exton now, sir?' he asked.

'I saw him an hour ago. I'm happy to say that Dawn picked him up from here and has taken him home. Hopefully that is at least one good outcome from this sodding, sad mess.'

'What will happen to Batchelor?' Arnie Crown asked.

'Not much!' Potting quipped and turned to Velvet Wilde for approval.

But neither she nor any of the team was in any mood for laughter. Grace glared at the old sweat. Fond though he was of Norman Potting, there were times when he thought this dinosaur should be in a museum, not on his major enquiry team. But equally, he knew, there were other times when the man could be invaluable. As he had proved on this operation. 'In answer to your question, Arnie,' Grace said, 'he will be taken to a police station outside of Sussex and Surrey – probably Hampshire again, for further questioning under caution. Following that he'll be remanded in custody pending trial.'

'What a stupid, bloody idiot,' Potting murmured again, shaking his head as if bewildered by Batchelor's actions.

Grace then read out Dr Frazer Theobald's findings, which the pathologist had now produced in a formal report. It gave the cause of death as firstly a head injury causing a brain haemorrhage, and secondly, electrocution. He told his team that the head injury was a fatal blow from which Lorna Belling would have died, but the hairdryer dropping in the bath had actually caused her heart to stop. Batchelor had of course been responsible for both events and the Crown Prosecution Service were looking at a charge of manslaughter in regard to Lorna, and attempted murder in respect of the police officer, Tim Weatherley.

Forty minutes later, after delegating evidence and paperwork duties, Grace thanked his team and told them to take the rest of the day off. They would meet again the following evening, at 6 p.m.

Then he went home. Despite being desperately upset about Guy, he looked forward to some time at home. May Day. A fine, sunny afternoon.

And he was on a promise . . .

CHAPTER 113

Sunday 1 May

Jason Tingley dropped Bruno home shortly after 5 p.m. Roy Grace had the barbecue well alight, and cooked them all a supper of corn on the cob, chicken wings, sausages, burgers and baked potatoes, and Bruno came back for seconds.

He was pleased to see his appetite, taking it as a positive that he was feeling settled and as reasonably OK as a boy who had recently lost his mother could be. After eating, Bruno went up to his room, saying he was going to be playing another online game with Erik. Before he did so he reminded Grace of his promise to teach him shooting tactics. He told Bruno he had not forgotten.

Roy cooked some extra food for Kaitlynn, who arrived an hour later to babysit, then he and Cleo headed into Brighton for the concert.

He had temporarily parked the shadow of Guy Batchelor in another compartment and was feeling relaxed and happy. He was looking forward to his night out with Cleo and seeing the rock band again – they had been to see them at this same venue a year ago on the recommendation of friends, when they had played their first gig in Brighton, and both of them had really liked their music.

When they walked into the Hope and Ruin pub, near the bottom of Queens Road, there was a sign up saying that the concert was delayed, and would start in approximately one hour. Grace stood with Cleo just inside the entrance for some moments, glancing around the packed room, clocking every face. He couldn't help it, he did it every time he entered a restaurant or a bar, like many coppers. He never wanted to find he had spent an hour in a room where there was a wanted villain he had missed, nor to enter a place that was about to kick off.

He bought a glass of Chardonnay for Cleo and a pint of Guinness for himself and they found a small, free table at the back of the packed downstairs bar. One chair was against the wall, the other facing it.

'Which would you like, darling?' he asked.

She took the one facing the wall. 'I think you're going to want the *policeman's chair*, aren't you?'

She was right, she knew him too well. He grinned, setting their glasses down and squeezing behind the table. He was never comfortable sitting with his back to a crowded room.

He raised his glass and chinked against hers. 'Cheers, darling.'

'Cheers. Quite a treat to have you for a whole

afternoon and evening as well!' She looked genuinely happy. 'You haven't told me how it was, climbing up that ladder. I don't know how you did it.'

He shrugged.

'Weren't you scared? You hate heights.'

He sipped his beer. 'You know, it's a funny thing, I've talked to many colleagues over the years. At some point in their career, almost every police officer is going to be in a situation where his or her life is in danger. Your training just kicks in and you don't think about it at the time. It's only afterwards, when it's over. That's when you think, *Shit, what the hell did I do that for?* But you know what you did it for. You did it because that's what you signed up to do.'

'At *some point* in their career?'

'Uh-huh.'

'You've been in danger more than once, my love. Every time you leave home I worry about you, wondering what your day will bring.'

'Both of us do a tough job. You are dealing with dead bodies all day long. Some of them pretty gruesome. But you cope.'

'There's a big difference, Roy. I respect the dead, but they don't pose any threat to me. You are dealing with dangerous people all the time. Even one of your most trusted colleagues turns out to be dangerous. You've got two children now, dependent on you. I know I'm never going to change you, and I wouldn't ever want to. I understand you're a decent man doing your best. I just don't ever want you to be a dead hero. You know what would be my worst nightmare?'

'No.'

'You arriving in the mortuary for a postmortem.'

He tapped his chest. 'Probably mine too.'

'I'll drink to that.'

He raised his glass.

CHAPTER 114

Sunday 1 May

Kaitlynn settled down in front of the television, with a small tub of pistachio ice cream Cleo had left her, and began channel surfing. An hour later, watching an old episode of *Californication* – one of her favourites – she heard Noah crying on the monitor. Then his cries turned to screams.

She paused the television and hurried upstairs, but the screams died down, almost as suddenly as they had started. Entering Noah's bedroom, she was surprised to see Bruno in there, cradling his little half-brother in his arms. He turned and gave Kaitlynn a smile.

'He's OK! I think he was having a bad dream, perhaps. Do babies have bad dreams?'

'I don't remember,' she said with a grin. 'I was too young.'

He gave her a quizzical look, as if trying to work that one out. Then he said, looking very serious, 'I think I was also too young to remember. But he is OK now.' Looking down with a loving smile, he said, 'You're OK, Noah, aren't you? Yes, yes you are!'

Noah giggled.

'Want me to take him?' she asked.

Bruno raised a finger to his lips. 'I will put him back in his cot. Let's see. Maybe he goes to sleep again.'

She stood and watched as Bruno laid him tenderly down, and pulled his knitted blanket over him. Noah put his thumb in his mouth and closed his eyes.

'Magic!' she said.

'I don't think so,' Bruno replied. 'But he's fine now, he's OK.'

They both walked to the door. 'You seem to have an amazingly calming effect on him, Bruno,' Kaitlynn said quietly.

'Maybe. Perhaps.' He turned the dial, dimming the light in the room low. Then they both went out.

A few minutes later, as Noah slept, a spider with a two-inch span crept slowly up the inside of the cot. It had a brown, shiny abdomen, and a white marking that looked a little like a skull. There had recently been an invasion of them due to the milder climate. It was a Noble False Widow, the most poisonous spider in the UK.

But fortunately for Noah, its bite is seldom fatal. And it would only bite if attacked.

Noah slept on, oblivious to the creature.

CHAPTER 115

Sunday 1 May

Grace and Cleo stood in the rammed upstairs room. Against the backdrop of a huge Jack Daniel's sign, the musicians were playing a crowd-pleaser. The whole room swayed to the rhythm of the song, 'Furr'.

Roy had his arm round Cleo. They both sang along to the lyrics.

'When suddenly a girl, with skin the colour of a pearl,

Wandered aimlessly, but she didn't seem to see,

She was listenin' for the angels, just like me.'

He kissed her on the cheek and she squeezed him back hard.

These were the moments, he thought. Listening to great music, with the person you loved, surrounded by happy people all enjoying the same thing, the same feeling.

The moments when you forgot about all the evil that was out there in this city and in the world beyond.

He was thinking about an interview he had read

with Neil Armstrong, the first man to walk on the moon. The astronaut had said that looking down at Earth, just an incredibly beautiful sight, it was almost impossible to imagine or understand all the evil deeds that happened on that planet. Why couldn't everyone just enjoy it?

Then he felt his phone vibrating in his pocket.

Still with an arm round Cleo, he pulled it out and peered at the display. There was a text message from Glenn Branson, whom he had this morning appointed his deputy SIO.

> Call me as soon as you can, Roy, it's urgent.

Tempted to ignore it, he jammed the phone back in his pocket. Then, moments later, he felt it vibrating again. This time it was ringing. He pulled it out again, signalled an apology to Cleo and squeezed through the crowd to the back of the room, putting the phone to his ear.

'Roy Grace,' he answered.

But the sound of the music was too loud to hear anything.

'Hold on a sec!' he said.

He hurried downstairs, through the bar and out onto the street. 'Sorry about that!'

'Where are you?'

It was Glenn.

'At a concert.'

'Shit, old-timer, at your age?'

'Sod off! This had better be good.'
'Roy, this is important. I've just had a call from Panicking Anakin at John Street nick. He's—'
Branson's next words were drowned out by a police car on blues and twos ripping up the road past him. He had to wait until the siren had faded before responding.
'Sorry, mate, lost you after Panicking Anakin!'
'Happens at your age. Hearing goes first, then everything else.'
'Yeah yeah. Listen, I'm missing a very good concert so this had better be worth it. What's happened?'
'Anakin's had a call from the hospital.'
'Sussex County?' Grace felt a stab of panic. Had Guy Batchelor killed himself?
'Our friend Tooth. He's vanished. Done a runner.'
'What?'
'He was improving, apparently, so because of a shortage of beds in Intensive Care they moved him yesterday into the High Dependency ward. A nurse went to give him his medication a couple of hours or so ago, and he wasn't there.'
Despite the seriousness of the situation, Roy Grace found himself grinning. He couldn't help it. He was remembering that at Sandy's funeral, ACC Pewe had delighted in telling him he had ordered the guard on Tooth to be removed.
'Have they searched the hospital, Glenn?'
'Three response units have attended. They've searched it top to bottom. Just like the times he's

disappeared on us before, he seems to have done it again. You all right, Roy? You don't sound very worried.'

'Worried? Me? I'm having a night off.'

'Yeah? Well I think you'd better cancel that.'

'No way, life's too short. You sort it out. Go find him. Don't forget the all-ports warning.'

'You can't be serious.'

'Listen, mate, trust me, I'm serious.'

He ended the call and hurried back upstairs to join Cleo.

'Everything OK?' she asked.

Blitzen Trapper were playing 'Not Your Lover'.

He stood listening to the song.

Thinking and smiling. He should not be thinking like this, but he could not help it.

He was smiling about the phone call he would make in a few minutes, after the song had ended, to ACC Cassian Pewe.

Yes!

There is a God!